Old Tom
MAN OF
MYSTERY

Leigh HOBBS

LITTLE HARE

Angela Throgmorton was exhausted.
The time had come to make a few changes.

Old Tom had been a beautiful baby.
But now he was big enough to help with the housework.

So Angela made a list of things for him to do.

She knew, of course, that it might not be easy to get Old Tom to help.

However, Angela wasn't one to give up.
"Where would you like to start?" she asked nicely.

All of a sudden, Old Tom felt sick.

Angela gave him a kiss and put him to bed.
"Now be a good boy, lie still, and you'll soon get well," she said.
Old Tom had other ideas.

Angela had to dust and wipe and brush and sweep all by herself.

Meanwhile, Old Tom was busy, too.
He had changed into…the Man of Mystery!

Later, in the kitchen, Angela was baking.

But her cooking was interrupted
when she saw fresh fur on her clean floor.

Then Angela heard a noise in the next room.
And saw cake crumbs on the carpet!
"Where could *they* have come from?" she wondered.

Angela paid a surprise visit to Old Tom, with a card and some flowers.

"I do hope you'll be better soon," she said.
"And then you can help around the house."

Angela had worked hard all day. She was tired, and went to bed early —
only to be woken by mysterious footsteps.

Angela decided to investigate.
She followed the footsteps through the house,

and out the window.

The Man of Mystery ran off into the night,

and so did Angela Throgmorton.

She watched as the Man of Mystery called on the neighbours.

"He reminds me of someone," thought Angela.

Then the Man of Mystery stopped for a late-night snack.
Angela moved in for a closer look.

She noticed that the Man of Mystery seemed interested
in a window full of dusters, brushes and brooms.

And when he paused at a restaurant,
Angela thought his manners looked strangely familiar.

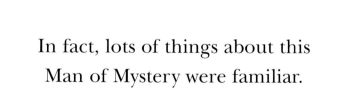

In fact, lots of things about this
Man of Mystery were familiar.

Who could it be?

Angela thought she knew.

She hurried home to look in someone's room.

And as she suspected, no one was there.

Angela was waiting when Old Tom came home late.

"So! Too sick to help!" snapped Angela Throgmorton.
The Man of Mystery knew he'd been naughty.
He was sent straight to bed.

Angela couldn't stay cross for long, though.
In the morning, she made a hearty breakfast for Old Tom — he'd be
needing his strength. After all, there was still a long, long list of things for
the Man of Mystery to do around the house.

For Ann Haddon (Jess)
and Ali Lavau

Little Hare Books
4/21 Mary Street, Surry Hills
NSW 2010 AUSTRALIA
www.littleharebooks.com

Copyright © Leigh Hobbs 2003

First published 2003
First published in paperback 2004
Reprinted in paperback 2005

A CIP catalogue record for this book is available from the British Library.
ISBN 1 877003 31 X hardcover
ISBN 1 877003 53 0 paperback

Designed by ANTART
Produced by Phoenix Offset
Printed in China

2 4 5 3

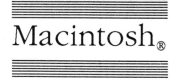 Macintosh® Technical Introduction
to the Macintosh Family

▲▼
Addison-Wesley Publishing Company, Inc.
Reading, Massachusetts   Menlo Park, California   New York   Don Mills,
Ontario Wokingham, England Amsterdam Bonn Sydney Singapore
Tokyo Madrid   San Juan

Contents

Figures and tables

Preface

With the introduction of the second generation of Apple® Macintosh® computers, the Macintosh SE and the Macintosh II, Apple has broadened the definition of the Macintosh system with two open machines. These machines add significant new capabilities to the Macintosh family, at the same time fitting well within the flexible Macintosh software architecture. This book describes that software architecture, as well as the hardware architectures of the various Macintosh machines.

About this book

Technical Introduction to the Macintosh Family introduces the hardware and software design of the Macintosh family of computers and serves as a starting point to the Macintosh technical documentation. The discussion is primarily oriented toward the Macintosh Plus, Macintosh SE, and Macintosh II computers, but it also touches on earlier versions of the Macintosh where these differ from the Macintosh Plus. The information in this book can provide a starting point for programmers, particularly those who are new to the Macintosh. This book can also serve as a stand-alone handbook for technically minded users and system administrators.

Note that this book will not tell you how to write a Macintosh application. That task is undertaken by a second short volume, *Programmer's Introduction to the Macintosh Family.*

In describing the architecture of the Macintosh system, this book follows an "outside–in" plan, beginning with the parts of the system seen by the user and proceeding to the lower-level details of the Operating System and the hardware:

☐ Chapters 1 and 2 introduce the basic pieces of the system hardware and software.

☐ Chapter 3 describes the graphical, window-based interface that the Macintosh presents to the user, beginning with a discussion of how mouse and keyboard actions are interpreted. Chapter 4 expands upon the discussion of this interface by describing **resources,** specially formatted chunks of data that are used to store user interface elements such as menus, windows, and icons.

☐ Chapters 5 through 8 describe other elements of the Macintosh software—graphics, the Macintosh Finder and system software, the Macintosh's use of memory, and files. Chapter 9 finishes the discussion of the Macintosh software by describing the low-level stuff of the Macintosh Operating System: the managers and device drivers that talk directly to the computer's hardware.

☐ Chapter 10 describes the hardware itself, contrasting the Macintosh Plus, the Macintosh SE, and the Macintosh II.

☐ Chapter 11 concludes the book by outlining the **A/UX®** operating system, Apple's implementation of the AT&T UNIX® Operating System for the Macintosh II.

This book surveys only the surface of the Macintosh hardware and software. If this book were presented interactively, as a piece of Macintosh software, it would represent no more than the Macintosh desktop, where each item could be double-clicked to reveal many deeper levels of information. You can find these deeper levels of information in the other volumes of the *Inside Macintosh Library.*

About the Macintosh technical documentation

Apple Computer has produced several books that explain the hardware and software of the Macintosh family of computers. There are *Inside Macintosh* Volumes 1 through 5, books about single aspects of the Macintosh, introductory books, and Macintosh-related books.

The original Macintosh documentation consisted solely of the noble tome *Inside Macintosh,* a three-volume compendium covering the whole of the Macintosh Toolbox and Operating System for the original 64K Macintosh ROM, together with user interface guidelines and hardware information. With the introduction of the Macintosh Plus (128K ROM), Volume 4 of *Inside Macintosh* was released. A fifth volume has now been added, covering the Macintosh SE and Macintosh II computers (both containing 256K of ROM). Volumes 4 and 5 are **delta guides;** that is, they explain only what is different about the new machines. Taken all together, the five volumes of *Inside Macintosh* provide a comprehensive reference for the Macintosh family of computers.

With the growth of the Macintosh family, some of the material in *Inside Macintosh* is starting to appear in single-subject books. Each of those books provides complete information about its subject, including information that may appear in one or more volumes of *Inside Macintosh.*

For people who are new to the Macintosh world, Apple has created two introductory books, *Technical Introduction to the Macintosh Family* and *Programmer's Introduction to the Macintosh Family.* These books provide explanations and guidelines for using the features described in *Inside Macintosh.*

In addition to the books about the Macintosh itself, there are books on related subjects, including books about the user interface and Apple's floating-point numerics, and the reference books for the Macintosh Programmer's Workshop.

Table P-1 gives a brief description of each of the books in the Macintosh technical documentation. The books are described in more detail in Appendix B, together with a more extensive bibliography.

Figure P-1 is a roadmap to the Macintosh technical documentation. Starting with this book, *Technical Introduction to the Macintosh Family,* the paths in the roadmap show the relationships among books. For example, it's logical to read *Programmer's Introduction to the Macintosh Family* before you start on *Inside Macintosh.*

Table P-1
Macintosh technical documentation

Original *Inside Macintosh* :

Inside Macintosh, Volumes 1–3   Complete reference to the Macintosh Toolbox and Operating System for the original 64K ROM

Inside Macintosh, Volume 4   Delta guide to the Macintosh Plus (128K ROM)

Inside Macintosh, Volume 5   Delta guide to the Macintosh SE and Macintosh II (256K ROM versions)

Introductory books:
Technical Introduction to the Macintosh Family   Introduction to the Macintosh software and hardware for all Macintosh computers: the original Macintosh, Macintosh Plus, Macintosh SE, and Macintosh II

Programmer's Introduction to the Macintosh Family   Introduction to programming the Macintosh system for programmers who are new to it

Single-subject books:
Macintosh Family Hardware Reference   Reference to the Macintosh hardware for all Macintosh computers, excluding the Macintosh XL

Designing Cards and Drivers for Macintosh II and Macintosh SE   Hardware and device driver reference to the expansion capabilities of the Macintosh II and the Macintosh SE

Related books:
Human Interface Guidelines: The Apple Desktop Interface   Detailed guidelines for developers implementing the Macintosh user interface

Apple Numerics Manual   Description of the Standard Apple Numerics Environment (SANE®), an IEEE-standard floating-point environment supported by all Apple computers

Macintosh Programmer's Workshop 2.0 Reference   Description of the Macintosh Programmer's Workshop (MPW), Apple's software development environment for all Macintosh computers

These books are described in more detail in Appendix B, together with a more extensive bibliography.

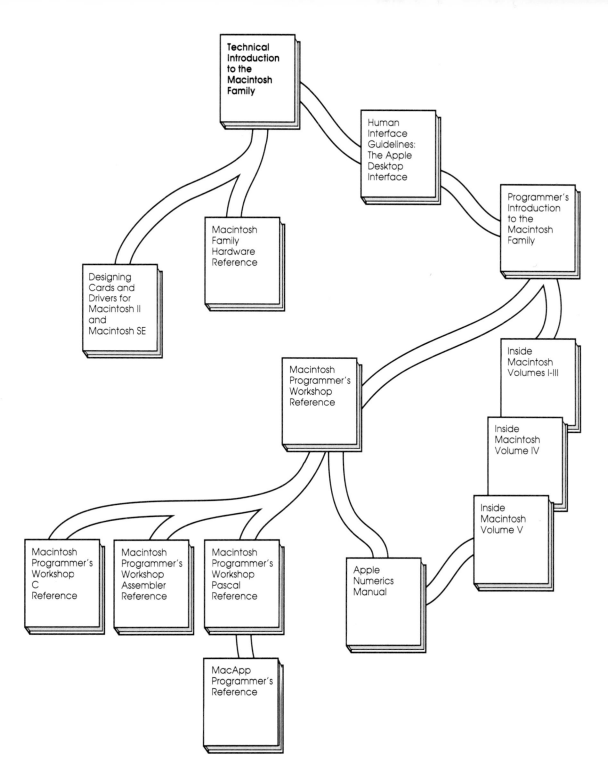

Figure P-1
Roadmap to the Macintosh technical documentation

Some conventions

This book discusses several generations of Macintosh computers, describing their similarities and differences. On the software side, the architecture of the various machines is quite similar. On the hardware side, the differences multiply, but there are still broad family resemblances. The Macintosh Plus in particular is much like the original Macintosh, but faster and more powerful. The following terminological conventions have therefore been adopted:

□ Unless otherwise indicated, the discussion refers to *all Macintosh computers*. The term *Macintosh* is used generically to refer to the entire product line.

□ Unless otherwise indicated, information relating to the Macintosh Plus also holds true for the original 128K Macintosh, the Macintosh 512K, and the 512K enhanced (512K e).

❖ *Note:* The Macintosh XL differs in many respects from the other Macintosh computers and is not described in this book. The Macintosh XL is based on the Lisa hardware, with RAM-based software that emulates the operation of the Macintosh 64K ROM.

Numerous special terms are introduced throughout this book. Those terms appear in **boldface** type and are defined in the glossary at the end of the book.

Programming the Macintosh

Programming the Macintosh can be quite unlike programming other computers. This book touches on some of the ways the Macintosh is different, but without going into detail about how you would program those features.

In order to program the Macintosh, you'll need the original five volumes of *Inside Macintosh*. You'll also need a Macintosh development system such as the Macintosh Programmer's Workshop (MPW), Apple's own Macintosh development system. The MPW system includes Pascal and C compilers and a 68000/68020/68030 assembler, together with Pascal, C, and assembly-language interfaces to the Macintosh Toolbox and Operating System. MPW also includes a programmable shell/editor and numerous utilities, such as a linker, resource editor, and resource compiler. Many other language compilers and interpreters are also available, from COBOL to SmallTalk, and including almost everything in between. Apple also provides an expandable application, MacApp®, which automatically implements most of the standard features of the Macintosh user interface.

There are also ways you can easily write programs on the Macintosh short of producing a full-fledged application. Macintosh Pascal, for instance, is an application that provides a complete environment so that you can write simple Pascal programs that execute within Macintosh windows.

For valuable information about how to approach the process of programming the Macintosh, refer to the *Programmer's Introduction to the Macintosh Family*. For additional information and support, you can contact the Apple Programmer's and Developer's Association (APDA™) and Apple's certified developer program. See Appendix B for addresses and telephone numbers.

Chapter 1

The Macintosh Family

This chapter introduces the various Macintosh computers and outlines their similarities and differences. It explains both what is involved in software compatiblity and which peripherals are compatible with which computers. The chapter ends with a point-by-point comparison of the hardware features of the Macintosh Plus, Macintosh SE, and Macintosh II.

This chapter provides only the broadest overview of the Macintosh computers. Detailed information about the hardware features of each of the Macintosh machines can be found in Chapter 10.

The evolving Macintosh

The Macintosh computer was introduced in January 1984. The original Macintosh was built around a Motorola MC68000 microprocessor, with 128K of **RAM** and 64K of **ROM** containing a programmer's toolbox: hundreds of routines providing powerful graphics support, user-interface features, and much more.

Seen from the level of the hardware, the various Macintosh machines present many important differences, but from the level of software, the Macintosh systems show one continuous evolution. In fact, many new software features that are not tied to hardware have been "back-fitted" onto the older machines by including them in updated versions of the Macintosh **System file.** (The System file is discussed further in Chapter 2.) This means that properly written applications can run on any version of the Macintosh.

From its inception up through the Macintosh Plus, the Macintosh went through the following revisions:

□ original Macintosh (Macintosh 128K), with 128K of RAM and 64K of ROM (version $69)

□ Macintosh 512K (same as the original Macintosh, but with 512K of RAM)

□ Macintosh 512K enhanced, which includes a new 800K disk drive with the new 128K Macintosh Plus ROM, containing a hierarchical file system and other new features

□ Macintosh Plus, which includes an 800K disk drive, a new 128K ROM (version $75), 1 megabyte (1 MB) of RAM, and new I/O ports, as explained in the following section

Collectively, these Macintosh models are known as the **classic Macintosh.** The Macintosh Plus embodies a number of new software and hardware features, but can still be thought of as a bigger, faster version of the original Macintosh. In fact, any of the first three machines listed above can easily be upgraded to a Macintosh Plus.

❖ *Note:* Throughout the rest of this manual, the **classic Macintosh** is described from the standpoint of the Macintosh Plus. In the few instances in which there are important differences in the software or hardware between the earlier machines and the Macintosh Plus, the fact is pointed out explicitly.

Macintosh Plus

The Macintosh Plus, introduced in January 1986, is a much enhanced version of the original Macintosh, containing many new routines in a larger 128K ROM, more RAM, more disk storage, and several other new features. Figure 1-1 shows the Macintosh Plus, which is almost identical in appearance to the original Macintosh.

Figure 1-1
The Macintosh Plus computer

The features of the Macintosh Plus (not found in the Macintosh 128K and 512K) are

- 128K ROM (version $75; this ROM is also on the Macintosh 512K enhanced)
- 1 MB of RAM, expandable to 2 MB, 2.5 MB, or 4 MB
- an 800K internal disk drive (also on Macintosh 512K enhanced)
- a **Small Computer System Interface (SCSI)** port for high-speed parallel communications with peripheral devices such as hard disks
- two Mini-8 connectors for serial ports, replacing the two 9-pin D-type connectors found on the Macintosh 128K, 512K, and 512K enhanced
- a keyboard with built-in cursor keys and numeric keypad

Macintosh SE

The Macintosh SE is the first Macintosh computer to provide for internal expansion via an internal expansion slot. Although the Macintosh SE is superficially similar to the Macintosh Plus, most of its components are new. A new ROM (now 256K) supports all of the old Macintosh features, and much more besides. Figure 1-2 shows the external appearance of the Macintosh SE.

Figure 1-2
The Macintosh SE computer

The new features of the Macintosh SE are

- 256K Macintosh SE ROM (version $76) containing new Operating System and Toolbox software

- Optional internal 20 MB SCSI hard disk, or optional second 800K internal floppy disk drive

- Much faster hard disk access, doubling the maximum transfer rate over the Macintosh Plus

- 25 percent greater speed when accessing RAM

- One expansion slot, providing for an internal custom expansion card to communicate with the MC68000 bus. A removable accessory access port in the rear housing allows access to custom I/O connectors on an expansion card

☐ Increased capacity power supply to provide power for an internal hard disk and expansion card

☐ Fan to provide cooling for internal disk and expansion card

☐ **Apple Desktop Bus™ (ADB)** for connecting the keyboard, mouse, and optional input devices

Like the classic Macintosh, the Macintosh SE is based on the Motorola MC68000 microprocessor, and is fully compatible with almost all existing Macintosh software.

Macintosh II

The Macintosh II, shown in Figure 1-3, is a big, open-architecture Macintosh, the most powerful computer in the Macintosh family. It offers hardware flexibility while retaining compatibility with most existing Macintosh software. The Macintosh II is more powerful than any previous Macintosh, with a fast 16-megahertz (16 MHz), 32-bit MC68020 microprocessor that can directly address up to 4 gigabytes (4 GB, or 4096 MB), teamed with an MC68881 floating-point coprocessor for numerics support.

The most important new features of the Macintosh II are

☐ 256K Macintosh II ROM (version $78), a superset of the Macintosh SE ROM that adds full color support

☐ MC68020 full 32-bit microprocessor

☐ MC68881 floating-point coprocessor for high-speed, precise numerics support

☐ Optional MC68851 Paged Memory Management Unit to support multitasking operating systems

☐ Optional internal SCSI hard disk, as well as an optional second 800K internal disk drive

☐ Six NuBus™ expansion slots (described below)

☐ Apple Desktop Bus (ADB), as on the Macintosh SE

The most significant innovation on the Macintosh II is the addition of six **NuBus slots** for expansion cards. The Macintosh II has no built-in video; instead, one or more of the slots can be used for a video card. A variety of video cards and monitors provides a range of video options, including high-resolution color and gray-scale capabilities. (Macintosh II video capabilities are explained in Chapter 5.)

Figure 1-3
The Macintosh II computer

The Macintosh II is, in fact, a desktop computer with near-minicomputer capabilities. In its native mode, the Macintosh II runs the Macintosh Operating System, but it can also run the UNIX Operating System, which provides full multitasking, multiuser support. Under the UNIX system, multiple terminals can be attached to the Macintosh II. (Apple's implementation of UNIX, A/UX, is outlined in Chapter 11.)

The many new hardware features of the Macintosh II are detailed in Chapter 10.

International versions

Except for different keyboards, the hardware of the base Macintosh machines is identical for all international versions of the machine: the only real difference is in software.

No particular language is built into the Macintosh ROM; rather, localized versions of the Macintosh System file contain the appropriate information for each language. For example, the Japanese version of the Macintosh System file includes complete support for kanji and kana characters, as well as for Roman characters. The versions of the Macintosh sold in Japan do include additional ROM, but the ROM only contains fonts that would otherwise be stored on a disk. (For more information, see the section "Using Non-Roman Writing Systems" in Chapter 5.) With a minimum of resource editing, which is easily done by a nonprogrammer, properly written applications can function equally well in any language. Chapter 4 gives more details about resources.

On the Macintosh Plus, there are two versions of the power supply, for 110 and 220 volts. On the Macintosh II and Macintosh SE, a universal power supply can function at either voltage.

Software compatibility

The Macintosh system software is organized so that programs are insulated from the actual hardware of the computer. That is, rather than directly accessing the hardware, a program calls the Macintosh Toolbox and Operating System, which in turn perform the necessary hardware operations. Programmers can also read from a set of **global variables,** stored in low memory, and use them in place of direct hardware addresses. By taking advantage of these techniques, an application program can be fully compatible with all of the Macintosh machines.

Figure 1-4 is a simplified diagram of the relationship between the Macintosh hardware and software. At the highest level is the user who directly manipulates the execution of the application program that runs on the machine. The application, in turn, interacts directly with lower levels of software—the built-in Toolbox and Operating System. The Toolbox provides the standard Macintosh user interface. Operating System routines directly manipulate the registers and input/output devices that constitute the computer's hardware. (For further discussion of the Toolbox and Operating System, refer to Chapter 2.)

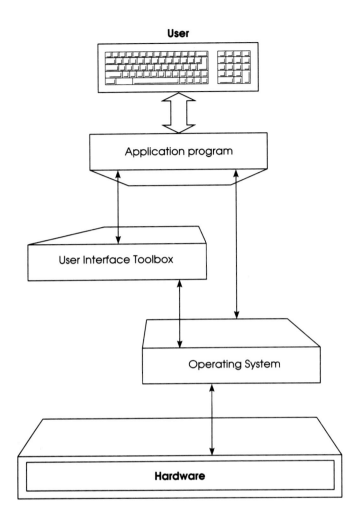

Figure 1-4
Relationship between Macintosh hardware and software

Most Macintosh software will run on any of the Macintosh computers; Apple has gone to great lengths, testing hundreds of programs, to ensure that this is the case. Of course, programs that don't follow the guidelines given throughout *Inside Macintosh* will need to be reworked to run on newer computers such as the Macintosh II. These include programs that directly access the hardware, instead of using low-memory global variables or system calls. Software that follows the *Inside Macintosh* guidelines is likely to work on the Macintosh SE and Macintosh II, while benefitting from the increased speed and memory.

Hardware compatibility

The Macintosh Plus, Macintosh SE, and Macintosh II all support the standard Apple peripherals, including

☐ Apple LaserWriter® and LaserWriter Plus® laser printers

☐ Apple ImageWriter® and ImageWriter II® dot-matrix printers

☐ the Apple Personal Modem

☐ SCSI hard disks: the Apple Hard Disk 20SC, Hard Disk 40SC, and Hard Disk 80SC (20, 40, and 80 megabytes). (SCSI disks are not supported by the original Macintosh, which has no SCSI port.)

☐ the Apple Tape Backup 40SC SCSI tape backup unit

☐ the AppleTalk® network (and AppleShare® file server)

The Macintosh Plus and Macintosh SE also include an external disk drive port, supporting the Macintosh external disk drives (the Apple external 400K and 800K floppy disk drives, and the Apple Hard Disk 20).

Important

The Macintosh II *does not* support the Apple external floppy disk drives or the Apple Hard Disk 20. (It has two internal floppy disk connectors but no external floppy disk connector.)

For quick reference, Table 1-1 lists the features of the Macintosh Plus, Macintosh SE, and Macintosh II computers. Many new hardware features are merely mentioned in this table. The reader who is interested an a detailed explanation of the hardware differences between the machines is invited to look ahead to Chapter 10, "The Macintosh Family Hardware."

Table 1-1
Macintosh family hardware comparison

Feature	Macintosh Plus	Macintosh SE	Macintosh II
Processor	MC68000 CPU	MC68000 CPU	MC68020 CPU
Addressing	24/32 bit	24/32 bit	True 32 bit (24-bit mode for software compatibility)
Clock frequency	7.8336 MHz	7.8336 MHz	15.6672 MHz

(continued)

Table 1-1 (continued)
Macintosh family hardware comparison

Feature	Macintosh Plus	Macintosh SE	Macintosh II
Coprocessor	None	None built-in	Built-in MC68881 floating-point coprocessor
Hardware memory management	None	None	Built-in 24/32-bit hardware unit for address translation; optional MC68851 Paged Memory Management Unit (PMMU)
Internal floppy disk	800K internal	800K internal with optional second 800K internal drive	800K internal with optional second 800K internal drive
External floppy disk	Optional 400K external drive; optional 800K external drive	Optional 400K external drive; optional 800K external drive	No built-in support
High-speed peripherals	SCSI port (not available on pre-Macintosh Plus machines)	SCSI port	SCSI port
Hard disk	Optional Hard Disk 20 (external); optional SCSI hard disk (external)	Optional Hard Disk 20 (external); optional SCSI hard disk (internal/external)	Optional SCSI hard disk (internal/external)

Table 1-1 (continued)
Macintosh family hardware comparison

Feature	Macintosh Plus	Macintosh SE	Macintosh II
Serial ports	Two Mini-8 built-in serial ports (DB-9 connnectors were used on pre-Macintosh Plus machines)	Two Mini-8 built-in serial ports (slightly enhanced over the Macintosh Plus serial ports)	Two Mini-8 built-in serial ports (same as Macintosh SE)
Slot expansion	No slots	SE-bus (68000-bus) expansion connector	Six slots with NuBus architecture
Sound	Macintosh sound chip four-voice	Macintosh sound chip four-voice	Custom Apple Sound Chip (ASC) four-voice
RAM	1 MB expandable to 4 MB RAM	1 MB expandable to 4 MB RAM	1 MB expandable to 128 MB RAM (when available) on motherboard; expandable to 2 GB in NuBus slots
ROM	128K ROM (optional 256K)	256K ROM	256K ROM (optional 512K on motherboard)
Keyboard	Macintosh Plus keyboard with built-in numeric keypad (compatible with original Macintosh keyboard/keypad)	Apple Keyboard or Apple Extended Keyboard, via Apple Desktop Bus (allows additional input devices, such as a graphics tablet)	Apple Keyboard or Apple Extended Keyboard, via Apple Desktop Bus (same as Macintosh SE)

(continued)

Table 1-1 (continued)
Macintosh family hardware comparison

Feature	Macintosh Plus	Macintosh SE	Macintosh II
Mouse	Macintosh mouse (same as Lisa mouse)	Apple Desktop Bus mouse	Apple Desktop Bus mouse
Video display	Built-in monitor: 9 inch, 512 X 342 pixel, black-and-white	Built-in monitor: 9 inch, 512 X 342 pixel, black-and-white	External monitor: video circuitry is on a NuBus expansion card

The full specifications for each computer are given in Appendix A.

Chapter 2

Introduction to the Macintosh Software

This chapter introduces the software that makes the Macintosh work—the Macintosh ROM and RAM-based system software—and briefly describes how this software relates to your application software. The chapter begins by introducing the contents of the ROM—the User Interface Toolbox and the Operating System—and then describes how ROM calls work. It then discusses the RAM-based system software, including the Finder and System file, and concludes with a discussion of event-driven programs; that is, how standard application programs operate in the Macintosh environment.

The Macintosh software has been designed to allow a program to run on any Macintosh, and this chapter describes information that is common to all Macintosh computers. The Toolbox, Operating System, and system software are discussed at greater length in the chapters that follow.

Overview of the Macintosh ROM

Above all else, it's the Macintosh ROM that makes the Macintosh unique. The Macintosh ROM contains over 700 routines for performing operating system and user interface functions. These routines can be broken down into two general categories: the Macintosh Operating System and the User Interface Toolbox. The **Operating System** is at the lowest level; it takes care of basic tasks such as input and output, memory management, and interrupt handling. The **User Interface Toolbox** is a level above the Operating System; it enables programs to implement the standard Macintosh user interface. The Macintosh user interface consists of the pull-down menus, windows, dialog boxes, and standard control mechanisms that allow all Macintosh software to have the same look and feel.

From the point of view of the user, the Toolbox provides a standard, intuitive way of doing things across applications:

□ Instead of remembering and typing commands, you use a mouse to select commands from **menus.** Parameters to commands are specified by using **dialog boxes.**

□ Instead of remembering and typing filenames, you select **icons,** or select names from a **Standard File** dialog box.

□ High-resolution bit-mapped graphics unify the presentation of text and graphics so that bit-mapped images can be copied and pasted between different types of applications. Macintosh graphics also make possible the window environment which displays multiple open files on the screen.

All Macintosh applications rely on the Toolbox to provide their user interface. For managing files and disks, a system application called the Macintosh **Finder**™ presents a graphical model of a desktop where you use the mouse to select and drag graphic objects, rather than having to type commands in response to a traditional command-line prompt.

From the point of view of the programmer, the Macintosh system can be compared to a minicomputer or mainframe system in the size and complexity of its built-in libraries. ROM routines are provided for implementing the entire Macintosh user interface. Another novel feature is the use of **resources,** which provide templates for the standard Toolbox objects, such as menus and windows, and separate these objects from the application's code. The Macintosh also provides sophisticated memory management, which allows large programs to run with relatively little memory while enabling programs to automatically take advantage of machines with more memory.

In addition to the distinction between the Toolbox and the Operating System, the routines available to Macintosh programmers are further divided according to function into a set of software **managers,** as shown in Figure 2-1. Each manager is a set of routines and data structures needed for the performance of a related set of tasks. For example, the Window Manager provides routines for drawing and manipulating windows on the screen.

Almost all of the Toolbox and Operating System routines are contained in the Macintosh ROM. However, newer versions of routines may frequently be based in RAM until the next ROM revision, as explained in the next section. From the standpoint of the program, this difference is not important: the program calls the routine in exactly the same way, wherever the routine's code may actually be.

Versions of the Macintosh ROM

As we indicated in Chapter 1, the Macintosh ROM has gone through two significant revisions since it was first introduced. The original 64K ROM contains more than 500 routines (together with another hundred or so RAM-based routines in the Macintosh **System file**).

The 128K Macintosh Plus ROM incorporated many of the RAM-based routines into the ROM and added major new functions, such as a new **File Manager** that supports a hierarchical file system. The 128K ROM is also provided on the Macintosh 512K enhanced.

The Macintosh SE and Macintosh II both include 256K of ROM, although the ROMs for the two machines are not identical. As Figure 2-1 indicates, many functions are new to these ROM versions. In addition, several packages and software managers that were previously based in RAM (that is, located in the System file) have been built into the 256K ROMs of the Macintosh SE and Macintosh II. Note that the Macintosh II ROM includes software for color and slot support that is lacking on the Macintosh SE (70K to 80K of the Macintosh SE ROM is not utilized).

In between major ROM revisions, new routines and corrected versions of old routines are provided by revising the System file. Because they work so closely together, the System file and Finder are usually revised in tandem. From the standpoint of a program that calls a ROM routine, there is no functional difference between a routine in ROM and a routine in the System file. The system's dispatch mechanism for determining which routine to call is explained later in this chapter under "The Trap Mechanism."

In Figure 2-1, an asterisk (*) indicates that the software is new in the 256K (Macintosh II/Macintosh SE) ROMs. Two asterisks (**) indicate that the software is found only in the Macintosh II ROM.

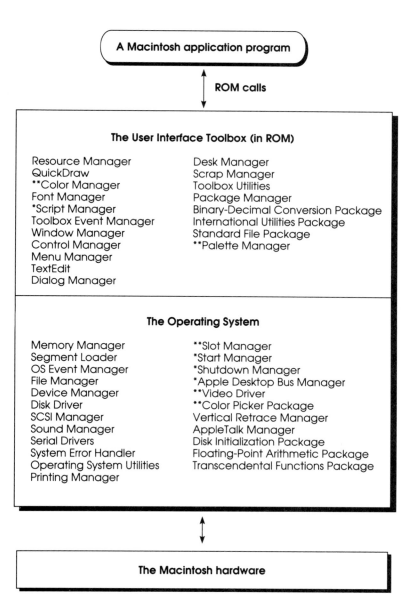

Figure 2-1
Components of the Toolbox and the Operating System

The Toolbox calls the Operating System to do low-level operations; the Operating System may also call the Toolbox. Applications call both the Toolbox and the Operating System directly.

The Toolbox

The User Interface Toolbox gives programmers hundreds of routines that provide the means for creating applications that conform to the standard Macintosh user interface. By offering a common set of routines that every application calls, the Toolbox ensures familiarity and consistency for the user. For the programmer, the Toolbox can reduce both the application's code size and development time. At the same time, it allows plenty of flexibility: if necessary, an application can use its own code instead of a Toolbox routine, and can define its own types of windows, menus, and so on.

Figure 2-2 shows the various parts of the Toolbox in a very rough approximation of their relationship. There are many more interconnections between these parts than can be shown diagrammatically. The higher-level segments call those at the lower levels, but the reverse may also be true.

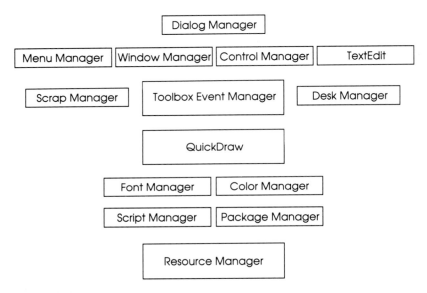

Figure 2-2
Parts of the Toolbox

A brief description of the most important parts of the Toolbox is given below. For more details about each aspect of the Toolbox, see Chapter 3, "The User Interface Toolbox."

Event Manager	Reports **events** to an application. An application decides what to do from moment to moment by examining input from the user in the form of mouse and keyboard actions. It learns of such actions by repeatedly calling the Toolbox Event Manager, which in turn calls another, lower-level Event Manager in the Operating System.
Resource Manager	Locates and delivers the **resources** needed by a program. Resources are chunks of static data, such as menus, cursors, window templates, and much more; even the application's code segments are stored as resources. The other parts of the Toolbox listed below also rely on the Resource Manager. Resources are discussed at greater length in Chapter 4.
QuickDraw	Performs all screen display operations on the Macintosh, including graphics and text. Applications call QuickDraw to draw inside a window, or just to set up constructs like rectangles that are needed for other Toolbox calls. Other parts of the Toolbox also call QuickDraw. QuickDraw's underlying concepts, like those of the Resource Manager, are key to the Macintosh system. All versions of QuickDraw support a limited version of color for optional color output devices. The Macintosh II ROM includes a new Color QuickDraw, for greatly enhanced color support.
Color Manager	Supplies color-selection support for Color QuickDraw and provides a consistent way to produce color displays on the Macintosh II. The Color Manager supports a variety of color formats and representations, allowing programs to make full use of the color capabilities available on different video cards and devices. (Macintosh II only)
Palette Manager	Supports the use of a collection of colors when you draw objects with Color QuickDraw. The Palette Manager provides routines to manage shared color resources, to provide exact colors for imaging, or to initiate color table animation. (Macintosh II only)
Font Manager	Supports the drawing of text by QuickDraw. Before drawing text, QuickDraw calls the Font Manager, which does the background work necessary to make a variety of character fonts available in various sizes and styles.
Script Manager	Enables applications to function correctly with non-Roman writing systems (or **scripts**) such as Japanese and Arabic, as well as with Roman-based writing systems such as English.

Window Manager	Manages windows on the Macintosh screen. All information presented by a standard Macintosh application appears in windows. Window Manager routines create windows, move them, resize them, and close them. The Window Manager also keeps track of overlapping windows, so that you can manipulate windows without concern for how they overlap, and tells the Toolbox Event Manager when a window must be redrawn.
Control Manager	Creates **controls,** such as buttons, check boxes, and scroll bars. When the Window Manager informs a program that the user clicked the mouse button inside a window containing controls, the Control Manager can find out which control the mouse button was clicked in, if any.
Menu Manager	Sets up and manages menus in the menu bar. When the user selects a menu item or types a keyboard equivalent for a menu command, the Menu Manager finds out which command was selected.
TextEdit	Accepts and displays text typed by the user and provides the standard editing capabilities, including cutting and pasting text via the Clipboard. Also handles basic formatting functions such as word wraparound and justification.
Scrap Manager	Supports the use of the Clipboard for cutting and pasting text or graphics between programs.
Dialog Manager	Creates and presents dialog and alert boxes, and returns the user's responses to the application. When an application needs more information from the user about a command, it presents a dialog box. In case of errors or potential mishaps, the application uses Dialog Manager calls to alert the user with a box containing a message or with sound from the Macintosh's speaker.
Desk Manager	Supports **desk accessories,** which are small programs that can be run from within an application. The user opens desk accessories through the Apple menu. When the Event Manager learns that the user has pressed the mouse button in a desk accessory window, it passes that information on to the accessory by calling the Desk Manager.
Package Manager	Supports the use of special pieces of system software called **packages.** For example, the List Manager is stored as a package. (Packages were originally based in RAM, but a number of packages have been built into the 128K and 256K versions of the ROM.)

Standard File Package	Presents the standard user interface for locating and specifying a document file. The Standard File Package is called by every application whose File menu includes the standard Open, Save, and Save As commands. (The actual file operations are performed by the Operating System's File Manager.)
List Manager	Supports the use of one-dimensional and two-dimensional lists by applications.

A number of miscellaneous functions are also available. These include operations such as fixed-point arithmetic, string manipulation, and logical operations on bits. The routines that perform these functions are collectively known as the **Toolbox Utilities.**

Two of the Macintosh packages can be seen as extensions to the Toolbox Utilities: the **Binary-Decimal Conversion Package** converts integers to decimal strings and vice versa, and the **International Utilities Package** helps to make applications independent of country-specific information, such as the formats for numbers, currency, dates, and times.

The Operating System

The Macintosh Operating System provides the low-level support that applications need in order to use the Macintosh hardware. Just as the Toolbox provides a program's interface to the user, the Operating System provides its interface to the computer.

The most important parts of the Operating System are briefly described below.

Memory Manager	Dynamically allocates and releases memory for the use of applications and other parts of the Operating System. Most of the memory that programs use is in an area called the **heap;** the code of the program itself occupies space in the heap. Memory space in the heap must be obtained through the Memory Manager.
Segment Loader	Loads pieces of an application's code into memory to be executed. An application can be loaded all at once, or it may be divided into dynamically loaded **code segments** to economize on the use of memory. The Segment Loader also serves as a bridge between the Finder and the application, letting the application know whether it has to open or print a document when it starts up.
OS Event Manager	Reports low-level, hardware-related events, such as mouse-button presses and keystrokes. The Toolbox Event Manager then passes these events to the application.

File Manager	Provides the routines for file I/O.
Device Manager	Provides the routines for device I/O.
Device Drivers	Performs the task of making the various types of devices present the same type of interface to the application. The Operating System includes several built-in drivers:

□ The **Disk Driver** controls data storage and retrieval on 3.5-inch floppy disks and the Apple Hard Disk 20.

□ The **Sound Driver** controls sound and music generation in the Macintosh Plus.

□ The **Serial Driver** reads and writes asynchronous data through the two serial ports, providing communication between applications and serial peripheral devices, such as a modem or printer.

The preceding drivers are all in ROM. Several other drivers are RAM-based:

□ The **Printer Driver** in RAM enables applications to print information on different kinds of printers via the same interface (called the Printing Manager).

□ On the Macintosh II, a **Video Driver** enables a particular video device to communicate with the rest of the system.

More RAM drivers can be added independently or built on the existing drivers (by calling the routines in those drivers). For example, the Printer Driver was built on the Serial Driver, and a music driver could be built on the Sound Driver.

Sound Manager	Supports sound and music generation on the Macintosh II. (Macintosh II only)
SCSI Manager	Supports the Small Computer System Interface (SCSI) for hard disks and other high-speed peripheral devices.
AppleTalk Manager	Provides an interface to a set of AppleTalk drivers that enable programs to send and receive information over an AppleTalk network.
Slot Manager	Enables programs to communicate with expansion cards in NuBus slots. (Macintosh II only)
ADB Manager	Supports the Apple Desktop Bus, which is used for connecting low-speed input devices, including the mouse and keyboard, to the Macintosh SE and Macintosh II. (Macintosh SE and Macintosh II)

Vertical Retrace Manager	The built-in video circuitry generates a **vertical retrace interrupt** 60 times a second. An application can schedule routines to be executed at regular intervals based on this system "heartbeat." The Vertical Retrace Manager handles the scheduling and execution of tasks during the vertical retrace interval. (On the Macintosh II, the vertical retrace interrupt is emulated for compatibility with previous machines.)
Time Manager	Provides a hardware-independent means of timing program operations.
System Error Handler	Assumes control if a system error occurs. The System Error Handler displays a "bomb" box containing an error message and provides a mechanism for the user to restart the system or attempt to resume execution of the application.
Start Manager	Orchestrates all of the activities related to system testing and startup.
Shutdown Manager	Provides the ability to restart the Macintosh or turn it off.
Packages	Three Macintosh packages perform low-level operations:

□ The **Disk Initialization Package,** which the Standard File Package calls to initialize and name disks

□ The **Floating-Point Arithmetic Package,** which supports extended-precision arithmetic according to Standard 754 of the Institute of Electrical and Electronics Engineers (IEEE)

□ The **Transcendental Functions Package,** which contains trigonometric, logarithmic, exponential, and financial functions, as well as a random number generator

(These two numerics packages support the Standard Apple Numeric Environment [SANE™].)

The **Operating System Utilities** provide several assorted functions. These include utilities for miscellaneous operations, such as getting the date and time, setting user preferences (for example, the speaker volume), and doing simple string comparison.

The following section describes how Operating System and Toolbox calls are actually dispatched when an application is running.

The trap mechanism

The Toolbox and Operating System reside mainly in ROM. However, to allow
flexibility for future development, application code must be kept free of any specific
ROM addresses. For this reason, all references to Toolbox and Operating System
routines are made indirectly through the **trap dispatcher,** which looks up the
addresses of the routines in the **trap dispatch table** in RAM. The trap dispatch
mechanism allows the routines themselves to be moved to different locations in
ROM, or be replaced altogether by RAM-based routines, without disturbing the
operation of programs that depend on them. Figure 2-3 shows the flow of control
when an application calls a Toolbox or Operating System routine.

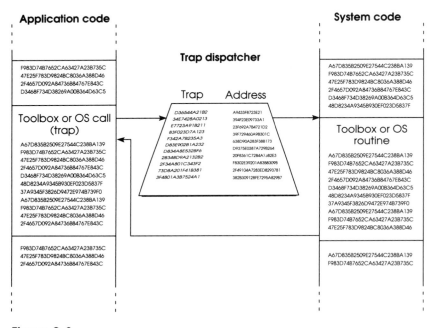

Figure 2-3
The trap mechanism

Information about the locations of the various Toolbox and Operating System
routines is encoded in compressed form in the ROM itself. When the system starts
up, this encoded information is expanded to form the trap dispatch table. Because
the trap dispatch table resides in RAM, individual entries in the table can be **patched**
to point to addresses other than the original ROM address. This allows changes to be
made in the ROM code: at startup time, the system can load corrected versions of
individual routines from the System file into RAM, and then patch the trap dispatch
table to point to them. This means that the ROM can be fixed, in effect, with a new
System file. This mechanism also allows an application to replace specific Toolbox
and Operating System routines with its own custom versions.

The trap mechanism is directly supported by the Macintosh computer's MC68000 (or MC68020) microprocessor. A **trap** is a kind of microprocessor exception that arises directly from the execution of a machine-language instruction. Calls to the Toolbox and Operating System are implemented by means of the 68000's 1010 emulator trap. In the 68000 instruction set, instruction words that begin with binary 1010 (hexadecimal $A—so-called **A-line instructions**) don't correspond to any valid machine-language instruction and are known as **unimplemented instructions.** These unimplemented instructions can be used to augment the processor's native instruction set with additional operations that are emulated in software instead of being executed directly by the hardware. That is, calls to the Macintosh Toolbox and Operating System look like machine-language instructions, but actually cause the execution of software routines. On a Macintosh, A-line instructions provide access to the Toolbox and Operating System routines.

When a program attempts to execute such an instruction, it causes a trap to the trap dispatcher. The trap dispatcher examines the bit pattern of the trap word to determine what operation it stands for, looks up the address of the corresponding routine in the trap dispatch table, and jumps to the routine. A trap word always begins with the hexadecimal digit $A; the rest of the word identifies the routine your program is calling, along with some additional information pertaining to the call.

Interface and library files

In order to write Macintosh programs, most software developers need high-level language access to the routines available in the Toolbox and Operating System. This is made possible by a set of **interface files** (or **include files**) provided as part of a development system, like the Macintosh Programmer's Workshop (MPW). Interface files define the variables, constants, data structures, and routine names that are used in programming with the Toolbox and Operating System.

Programmers may also need to link their applications with particular **library files,** which contain executable code for performing certain run-time functions. Note that the Macintosh ROM can also be thought of as a library of routines. Library files simply contain system code that was not included in the ROM or in the System file, either because it is rarely used, or because it is specific to a single programming language.

For more information about programming with the Toolbox and Operating System, see the *Programmer's Introduction to the Macintosh Family* and the documentation for Macintosh Programmer's Workshop (MPW) or another development system. The rest of this chapter discusses the various kinds of Macintosh programs.

Types of Macintosh programs

There are two standard kinds of Macintosh application programs:

☐ **Applications** are stand-alone programs, such as MacPaint™ or the Finder, that take control of the machine when they are launched. All of the familiar Macintosh programs—word processors, graphics programs, and so on—are implemented as applications.

☐ **Desk accessories,** such as the **Chooser** or Key Caps, are mini-applications, implemented as device drivers, that can be run from within an application. Desk accessories may perform quite sophisticated functions but are limited in size.

Two other types of programs are also worth mentioning. Device drivers were introduced in the section "The Operating System." Device drivers other than desk accessories perform functions such as driving a printer or the video display. Although they are invisible to the user, they provide the application's interface to a peripheral device. Some standard device drivers are built into the Macintosh ROM or provided in the System Folder; others may be supplied by third-party developers. **MPW tools** are utility programs that execute only within the MPW environment. These tools provide only a limited user interface and perform useful utility functions for programmers and system developers.

Macintosh system software

In addition to the ROM-based software, the Macintosh also depends upon certain disk-based software. This **system software**, contained in the System Folder on the startup disk, consists of the following:

☐ The **System file,** which contains resources available to all applications, including fonts and desk accessories. The System file also contains parts of the Toolbox and Operating System. Newer versions of the System file contain features from newer versions of the ROM, enabling these features to be used on machines with older ROMs.

☐ The **Finder,** the application that maintains the Macintosh desktop. The Finder provides the user interface for traditional operating system functions, such as managing files and disks and starting other applications.

☐ **Printer drivers** (also called **printing resources**), which provide the interface to particular printers, such as the LaserWriter or ImageWriter.

☐ The **Clipboard file,** which holds data that is cut and pasted between applications.

This system software is universal: the same files are used for all Macintosh computers, no matter what version of the ROM the computer may contain.

Additional RAM-based software allows you to have several applications in memory at the same time. **Switcher™**, a Macintosh application, allows you to instantly switch from one application to another. **MultiFinder™**, a special Finder option available with Finder version 6.0, goes a step further by allowing multiple applications to be open simultaneously on the Macintosh desktop.

The contents of the System file are described in "The System Resource File" in Chapter 4. The Finder and the rest of the Macintosh system software are discussed at greater length in Chapter 6.

Event-driven programming

Just as all well-written Macintosh programs look similar to the user, they also have the same internal structure. However, when compared to conventional applications software, Macintosh applications are built upon a very different structure: instead of being program-driven, Macintosh programs are **event-driven,** which is to say, user-driven. This means that the Macintosh user guides the interaction with the program rather than vice versa. Where conventional programs will simply solicit user input through a fixed series of prompts, Macintosh programs must be able to respond to a wide range of **events.** (Events include keyboard events, mouse-button events, and network events.) This kind of programming obviously requires considerably more design work, but it results in a user interface that is both more flexible and more efficient, allowing a style of interaction that is less mechanistic and more creative.

Figure 2-4 illustrates some of the most common types of events.

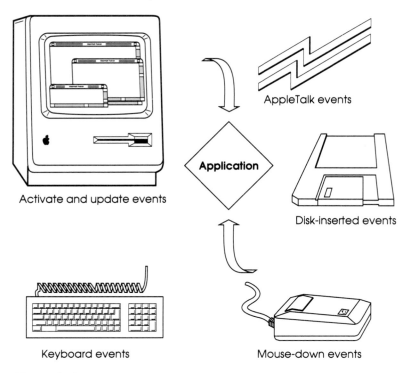

Activate and update events

AppleTalk events

Application

Disk-inserted events

Keyboard events

Mouse-down events

Figure 2-4
Some common event types

At first glance, the situation of the application surrounded by potential events may remind you of a kung-fu fighter surrounded by members of the rival kung-fu school. But where the fighter is aided only by the ancient kung-fu movie convention that opponents shall attack one at a time, the application has material assistance in the form of the Macintosh Event Manager, which enforces the one-at-a-time rule. (There are actually two Event Managers: one in the Operating System and one in the Toolbox.) The Operating System Event Manager performs its task by placing the events in an event queue, where the program can respond to them more or less at its leisure.

This process is shown in Figure 2-5. As the figure shows, the Toolbox Event Manager passes events on to the program, along with higher-level, software-generated events added at the Toolbox level. Note that programs ordinarily deal only with the Toolbox Event Manager and rarely call the Operating System Event Manager directly.

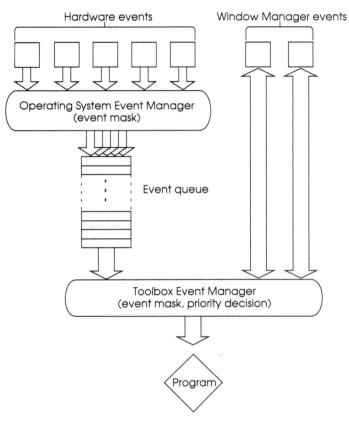

Hardware events   Window Manager events

Operating System Event Manager
(event mask)

Event queue

Toolbox Event Manager
(event mask, priority decision)

Program

Figure 2-5
The Event Managers

Toolbox events and the Toolbox Event Manager are discussed further in the next chapter.

Structure of an event-driven program

Macintosh programs are built around a **main event loop:** the program simply goes through a cycle, waiting for events and then responding to them appropriately. Figure 2-6 illustrates the typical program flow for a Macintosh program. The content of each program is unique, but this sort of a structure underlies all Macintosh applications.

```
make standard initialization calls
put up window
### begin main event loop ###
wait for events
    key-down event?
        Command key down?
            yes: do a command
            no:  accept typing from user
    mouse-down event?
        where is the mouse?
            in one of my windows?
                is it the front window?
                    no:  bring it to the front
                    yes: user is selecting something
            in a desk accessory window?
                pass event to the Desk Manager
            in the menu bar?
                call Menu Manager, then do command
            in the window's title bar?
                call Window Manager to drag the window
            in the window's size box?
                call Window Manager to resize the window
            in a control (button, scroll bar...)
                call Control Manager to find out which control
                then act on that control
    activate event? (a new window is being activated)
        enable some menu items, disable others, etc.
    update event? (part of a window needs to be redrawn)
        redraw the window
repeat until the user chooses "Quit" from the File menu
```

Figure 2-6
Event-driven programming: typical program flow

At the beginning of a program, various parts of system software must be initialized
and pending events are flushed from the event queue. Additional initialization
needed by the program follows. This includes setting up the menus and the menu bar
and creating the application's document window (by reading its description from the
resource file and displaying it on the screen).

The heart of the program is the main event loop, which repeatedly calls the Toolbox
Event Manager to get events and then responds to them. The most common event is
a press of the mouse button (called a **mouse-down event**). Depending on where
the mouse button was pressed, as reported by the Window Manager, the program
may execute a command, move the document window, or make the window active.

Events are generated not only as a direct result of user actions, but indirectly as a side effect of those actions. For example, when a window changes from active to inactive or vice versa, the Window Manager tells the Toolbox Event Manager to report it to the application. A similar process happens when all or part of a window needs to be updated (that is, redrawn).

The main event loop terminates when the user takes some action to leave the program, as in the example shown in Figure 2-6, when the Quit command is chosen.

That's it. Of course, the program structure becomes more complicated as the application becomes more complex, but each program will be based on the structure illustrated here.

For a more detailed description of event-driven programming, refer to the *Programmer's Introduction to the Macintosh Family*.

As you may by now have surmised, the Macintosh is a software-intensive machine: relatively more processing takes place in software than is the case on previous types of computers. This allows for a very flexible system architecture, enabling high-performance application software to run on machines with differing hardware. As we indicated at the outset of this chapter, the next seven chapters go into detail about the various parts of the Macintosh software, beginning again with the Toolbox.

Chapter 3

The User Interface Toolbox

This chapter discusses the main parts of the Macintosh User Interface Toolbox, the set of routines that enables applications to present the unified Macintosh interface. The chapter begins with a discussion of the principles of the Macintosh user interface. It then discusses the Toolbox Event Manager, which is the part of the Toolbox that relates user actions to the other elements of the Toolbox. Following that is a discussion of each of those elements: menus, windows, controls, and dialogs.

Some aspects of the Toolbox are not discussed in this chapter. Menus, windows, controls, and dialogs are all stored as **resources** in resource files. More information about resources can be found in the next chapter. This chapter also doesn't discuss QuickDraw or the Font Manager, which provide the graphical basis for the Macintosh Toolbox; that discussion is deferred to Chapter 5.

Overview: the desktop interface

One of the great strengths of the Macintosh is a carefully considered user interface, which can be used by all programs. The Macintosh interface is based on the metaphor of a working surface, the **desktop,** where documents are presented within **windows.** Actions are performed by moving objects on the screen, selecting commmands from **menus,** or by manipulating **controls,** such as check boxes and scroll bars. Some of these user-interface elements are illustrated in Figure 3-1.

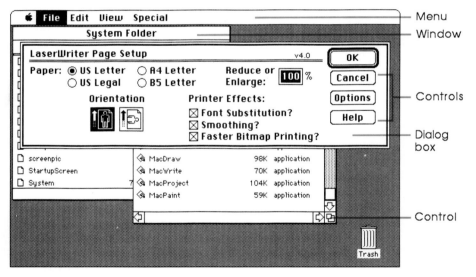

Figure 3-1
Elements of the Macintosh user interface

Close attention to the many ways that people use computers has resulted in a set of specific ergonomic principles that should be studied by all Macintosh programmers. These guidelines, published in *Human Interface Guidelines: The Apple Desktop Interface,* describe the shared interface ideas of Macintosh applications, so that developers of new applications can gain leverage from the time spent developing and testing existing applications.

User interface guidelines

The Macintosh is designed to appeal to the broadest possible audience of nonprogrammers, including people who have previously feared and distrusted computers. To achieve this goal, Macintosh applications should be easy to learn and to use. Applications should build on skills that people already have, not force them to learn new ones. The user should feel in control of the computer, not the other way around. These goals are achieved in applications that embody three cardinal interface virtues: responsiveness, permissiveness, and consistency.

□ *Responsiveness* means that the user's actions tend to have direct results. The user should be able to accomplish things spontaneously and intuitively, rather than by having to work out some long series of commands. For example, with pull-down menus, the user can choose the desired command directly and instantaneously.

□ *Permissiveness* means that the application tends to allow the user to do anything reasonable. The user, not the system, decides what to do next. It also means that the user should be able to undo any changes made to a document.

□ *Consistency* is the third and most important principle. Because Macintosh users usually divide their time among several applications, they would be confused and irritated if they had to learn a completely new interface for each application.

Consistency is easier to achieve on the Macintosh than on most other computers, because the routines used to implement the user interface are supplied in the Macintosh User Interface Toolbox. Because Macintosh programs don't rely on the more-or-less arbitrary conventions that conventional programs make do with, learning time is reduced to a small fraction of that required with other systems.

Each of these principles is elaborated into a specific set of recommendations in *Human Interface Guidelines: The Apple Desktop Interface.*

What's in the Toolbox

The various Toolbox managers were introduced in Chapter 2. Each manager consists of a set of data structures together with a set of associated routines.

It's important to understand the primacy of these data structures in the organization of the Toolbox; in fact, most ROM routines operate on data structures. For example, a window is represented in a window record, which applications manipulate indirectly via high-level Window Manager calls. Toolbox objects such as windows are referred to via **pointers** or **handles;** objects that are referred to by handles can be relocated in memory, as described in Chapter 7. A Toolbox object can also be stored on a disk as a resource, as described in Chapter 4. A Toolbox object is created by another resource called its **definition procedure,** as described later in this chapter.

However, before discussing the particular elements of the desktop interface, it will be helpful to return to the subject of events, and the **Toolbox Event Manager,** which links user actions with the various elements of the user interface.

Managing Toolbox events

The Toolbox Event Manager is the application's link to its user. Whenever the user presses the mouse button, types on the keyboard, or inserts a disk in a disk drive, the application is notified by means of an **event.** A typical Macintosh application program is **event-driven:** it decides what to do from moment to moment by asking the Event Manager for events and responding to them one-by-one in whatever way is appropriate. Event-driven programs have a main loop that repeatedly calls a Toolbox Event Manager routine (named GetNextEvent) to retrieve the next available event, and then takes whatever action is appropriate for each type of event.

Although the Event Manager's main purpose is to monitor the user's actions and pass them on to the application in an orderly way, it also serves as a mechanism for sending signals to other parts of the Toolbox. For instance, the Window Manager uses events to coordinate the ordering and display of windows as the user activates and deactivates them and moves them around on the screen.

The Toolbox Event Manager calls the Operating System Event Manager and serves as an interface between it and the application. (The Operating System's Event Manager detects low-level, hardware-related events: mouse, keyboard, disk-inserted, device driver, and network events. In this section, all references to the Event Manager should be understood to refer to the Toolbox Event Manager.)

Most events waiting to be processed are kept in an **event queue,** where they're **posted,** or stored, by the Operating System (OS) Event Manager. The Toolbox Event Manager retrieves events from this queue and also reports other events that aren't kept in the queue, such as those related to windows. Events are collected from a variety of sources and reported at the application's demand, one at a time. Events aren't necessarily reported in the order they occurred; some have a higher priority than others.

Other Event Manager functions include

☐ directly reading the current state of the keyboard and mouse button

☐ monitoring the location of the mouse

☐ finding out how much time has elapsed since the system last started up

The Event Manager dispatches system events to the appropriate part of the system, including sending desk accessory events to desk accessories.

The Event Manager also provides a **journaling mechanism.** By using this mechanism, a program can decouple the Event Manager from the user and feed it events from some other source. Such a source might be a file that has been used to record all the events that occurred during some portion of a user's session with the Macintosh. These events can then be played back to the Event Manager by a special device driver. This journaling capability is especially useful for recording macros and for the development of on-line demonstrations or tutorials.

Types of events

Events are of various types. Some events are handled by the system before the application ever sees them; others are left for the application to handle in its own way. An application can use an **event mask** to restrict some Event Manager routines to handle only certain event types, in effect disabling the other types.

The most important types of events record actions by the user:

■ **Mouse-down** and **mouse-up events** occur when the user presses or releases the mouse button.

■ **Key-down** and **key-up events** occur when the user presses or releases a key on the keyboard or keypad. **Auto-key events** are generated when the user holds down a repeating key. Together, these event types are called **keyboard events.**

■ **Disk-inserted events** occur when the user inserts a disk into a disk drive or takes any other action that requires a volume to be mounted. For example, a hard disk that contains several volumes may also post a disk-inserted event.

Mere movements of the mouse are *not* reported as events. If necessary, an application can keep track of them by periodically asking the Event Manager for the current location of the mouse.

The following event types are generated by the Window Manager to coordinate the display of windows on the screen:

■ **Activate events** are generated whenever an inactive window becomes active or an active window becomes inactive. They generally occur in pairs (that is, one window is deactivated and another is activated).

■ **Update events** occur when a window's contents need to be drawn or redrawn, usually as a result of the user's opening, closing, activating, or moving a window.

Another event type, **device driver events,** may be generated by device drivers in certain situations. For example, a driver might be set up to report an event when its transmission of data is interrupted.

A **network event** may be generated by the AppleTalk Manager, which is described in Chapter 9.

One final type of event is the **null event,** which is what the Event Manager returns if it has nothing else to report. In addition, an application may define as many as four event types of its own and use them for any purpose.

The Event Manager also handles two other types of events internally, without the knowledge of the application:

□ Alarm clock events. If the alarm is set and the current time is the alarm time, the alarm goes off—that is, a beep is generated, followed by blinking the Apple symbol in the menu bar. The user can set the alarm with the Alarm Clock desk accessory.

□ Command-Shift-number key combinations. (The standard keys are 1 and 2 for ejecting the disk in the internal or external drive, and 3 and 4 for writing a snapshot of the screen to a MacPaint document or to the printer.)

❖ *Note:* On the Macintosh SE and Macintosh II keyboards, the Command key symbol (⌘) has been replaced by two symbols, the outline Apple symbol (⌃) and the Command symbol, for compatibility with all Apple computers. The owner's guides now refer to the key as the **Apple key,** but its functionality is identical to the Command key on the classic Macintosh keyboard. For consistency with the technical documentation, this guide will continue to refer to the key as the Command key. More information about keyboard events is given later in this chapter.

❖ *Note:* Advanced programmers can implement their own code to be executed in response to Command-Shift-number combinations (except for Command-Shift-1 and 2, which can't be changed). The code corresponding to a particular number is stored in a resource whose type is 'FKEY' and whose ID is the number itself. The **system resource file** contains code for the numbers 3 and 4.

Every event is represented internally by an **event record** containing all pertinent information about that event. The event record includes the following information:

□ the type of event

□ the time the event was posted (in ticks since system startup)

□ the location of the mouse at the time the event was posted

□ the state of the mouse button and modifier keys at the time the event was posted

□ any additional information required for a particular type of event, such as which key the user pressed or which window is being activated

System events

Before reporting an event to the application, the Event Manager first calls the **Desk Manager** to see whether the system wants to intercept and respond to the event. The Desk Manager intercepts the following events:

☐ activate and update events directed to a desk accessory

☐ mouse-up and keyboard events, if the currently active window belongs to a desk accessory

In each case, the event is intercepted by the Desk Manager only if the particular desk accessory can handle that type of event.

The Desk Manager also intercepts all disk-inserted events and attempts to mount the volume on the disk by calling the File Manager. All other events (including all mouse-down events, regardless of which window is active) are left for the application to handle.

❖ *Note:* When running under the MultiFinder, update events cause the MultiFinder to switch in an application whenever an update event occurs for one of the application's windows. See "Versions of the Finder" in Chapter 6.

Priority of events

The event queue is a first-in, first-out (FIFO) list; that is, events are normally retrieved from the queue in the order they were originally posted. However, the way that various types of events are generated and detected causes some events to have higher priority than others. Furthermore, when a program asks the Event Manager for an event, it can specify particular types of events, causing some events to be passed over in favor of others that were actually posted later.

The Event Manager always returns the highest-priority event available of the types requested by the application. The priority ranking is as follows:

1. *Activate events.* The Event Manager always returns a window activate event if one is available.

2. *Mouse events, key-down, key-up, disk-inserted, network, device driver,* and *application-defined events.* Within this large category, events are retrieved from the event queue in the order that they were posted.

3. *Auto-key events.* If no event is available in categories 1 and 2, the Event Manager reports an auto-key event, if the appropriate conditions hold. (These conditions are described in the next section, "Keyboard Events.")

4. *Update events.* If no higher-priority event is available, the Event Manager checks for windows whose contents need to be drawn. If two or more windows need to be updated, an update event will be returned for the frontmost window.

5. *Null events.* Finally, if no other event is available, the Event Manager returns a null event.

The event queue normally has a capacity of 20 events. If the queue becomes full, the OS Event Manager will begin discarding old events to make room for new ones as they are posted. The events discarded are always the oldest ones in the queue. (However, activate events and update events are not kept in the event queue, and events will be discarded only in an unusually busy environment.)

❖ *Note:* The capacity of the event queue is determined by the **system startup information** stored on a volume. Utilities such as Fedit Plus allow you to modify a volume's system startup blocks. (Fedit Plus is available from the Apple Programmer's and Developer's Association [APDA]; see Appendix B for the address.)

Some Event Manager routines can be restricted to operating only on specific types of events. To specify which event types a particular Event Manager call applies to, a program supplies an event mask. For instance, a program can specifically ask for the next keyboard event instead of just requesting the next available event.

Keyboard events

The character keys on the Macintosh keyboard and numeric keypad generate key-down and key-up events when pressed and released. **Character keys** include all keys except Shift, Caps Lock, Command, and Option, which are called **modifier keys.** Modifier keys are treated specially, as we'll describe in a moment, and they generate no keyboard events of their own.

When the user presses, holds down, or releases a character key, the character generated by that key is identified internally with a **character code.** Character codes are given in the extended version of the American Standard Code for Information Interchange (ASCII) used by the Macintosh. A table showing the hexadecimal character codes for the standard Macintosh character set appears in Figure 3-2. The first digit of a character's hexadecimal value is shown at the top of the table, the second down the left side. For example, character code $47 stands for "G", which appears in the table at the intersection of column 4 and row 7.

The printing characters (codes $20 through $D8) shown in Figure 3-2 can be generated with the Option or Shift and Option keys, as described in the computer's owner's guide.

Figure 3-2
Macintosh character set

Second digit \ First digit	0	1	2	3	4	5	6	7	8	9	A	B	C	D	E	F
0	NUL	DLE	space	0	@	P	`	p	Ä	ê	†	∞	¿	–		
1	SCH	DC1	!	1	A	Q	a	q	Å	ë	°	±	¡	—		
2	STX	DC2	"	2	B	R	b	r	Ç	í	¢	≤	¬	"		
3	ETX	DC3	#	3	C	S	c	s	É	ì	£	≥	√	"		
4	EOT	DC4	$	4	D	T	d	t	Ñ	î	§	¥	ƒ	`		
5	ENQ	NAK	%	5	E	U	e	u	Ö	ï	•	µ	≈	'		
6	ACK	SYN	&	6	F	V	f	v	Ü	ñ	¶	∂	Δ	÷		
7	BEL	ETB	'	7	G	W	g	w	á	ó	ß	Σ	«	◊		
8	BS	CAN	(	8	H	X	h	x	à	ò	®	Π	»	ÿ		
9	HT	EM	)	9	I	Y	i	y	â	ô	©	π	…			
A	LF	SUB	*	:	J	Z	j	z	ä	ö	™	∫	⎯			
B	VT	ESC	+	;	K	[	k	{	ã	õ	´	º	À			
C	FF	FS	,	<	L	\	l	|	å	ú	¨	º	Ã			
D	CR	GS	-	=	M	]	m	}	ç	ù	≠	Ω	Õ			
E	SO	RS	.	>	N	^	n	~	é	û	Æ	œ	Œ			
F	SI	US	/	?	O	_	o	DEL	è	ü	Ø	ø	œ			

⎯ stands for a nonbreaking space, the same width as a digit.
The shaded characters cannot normally be generated from
the Macintosh keyboard or keypad.

Nonprinting or **control characters** ($00 through $1F, as well as $7F) are identified in Figure 3-2 by their traditional ASCII abbreviations; the shaded ones have no special meaning on the Macintosh and cannot normally be generated from the Macintosh Plus keyboard. (They are available on the Apple Desktop Bus keyboards used with the Macintosh SE and Macintosh II; see "ADB Keyboards" in Chapter 10 for details.) The control characters that can be generated from the keyboard are as follows:

Code	Abbreviation	Key
$03	ETX	Enter key (keyboard or keypad)
$08	BS	Backspace key
$09	HT	Tab key
$0D	CR	Return key
$1B	ESC	Clear key (Esc key on ADB keyboards)
$1C	FS	Left Arrow key
$1D	GS	Right Arrow key
$1E	RS	Up Arrow key
$1F	US	Down Arrow key

How character codes are processed

The association between characters and keys on the keyboard and keypad is defined by a **keyboard mapping procedure,** a routine that is usually stored as a resource in the system resource file. The particular character that's generated by a character key, then, depends on three things:

□ the character key being pressed

□ which, if any, of the modifier keys were held down when the character key was pressed

□ the keyboard mapping procedure currently in effect

The modifier keys don't generate keyboard events themselves; rather, they modify the meaning of the character keys by changing the character codes that those keys generate. For example, under the standard U.S. keyboard configuration, the C key generates any of the following, depending on which modifier keys are held down:

Key(s) pressed	Character generated
C by itself	Lowercase c
C with Shift down	Capital C
C with Option down	Lowercase c with a cedilla(ç)
C with Option and Shift down	Capital C with a cedilla (Ç)

The state of each of the modifier keys is also reported individually in a field of the event record, where the application can examine it directly. (Although the Caps Lock key is reported independently of the Shift key, it has the same effects.)

❖ *Note:* As described in the owner's guide, some accented characters are generated by pressing Option along with another key for the accent, and then typing the character to be accented. In these cases, a single key-down event occurs for the accented character; there's no event corresponding to the typing of the accent, which is known as a **dead key.**

Under the standard keyboard configuration, only the Shift, Caps Lock, and Option keys actually modify the character code generated by a character key on the keyboard; the Command key has no effect on the character code generated. Similarly, character codes for the keypad are affected only by the Shift key.

For keyboard events, the event message contains the ASCII character code generated by the key or combination of keys that was pressed or released. The event message also contains a **key code** that represents the character key that was pressed or released. This value is always the same for any given character key, regardless of the modifier keys pressed along with it.

❖ *Note:* In some cases the key codes for the U.S. and international keyboards are quite different; for example, the codes for space and Enter are reversed.

Two system resources are responsible for mapping keys to ASCII codes: a 'KMAP' resource maps the physical positions of the keys to key codes, and a 'KCHR' resource maps key codes to ASCII codes.

Auto-key events

In addition to key-down and key-up events, **auto-key events** are posted whenever all of the following conditions apply:

☐ Auto-key events haven't been disabled.

☐ No higher-priority event is available.

☐ The user is currently holding down a character key.

☐ The appropriate time interval has elapsed since the last key-down or auto-key event.

Two different time intervals are associated with auto-key events. If the user holds down a character key, the initial auto-key event is generated after a certain time (called the **auto-key threshold**) has elapsed. The default threshold is 16 **ticks,** with each tick equalling one-sixtieth of a second. Subsequent auto-key events are then generated each time a certain repeat interval (determined by the **auto-key rate**) has elapsed. The default auto-key rate is once every four ticks. The user can change these two settings with the Control Panel desk accessory by adjusting the keyboard touch and the rate of repeating keys.

Menus

Menus allow users to examine all choices available to them at any time without being forced to choose one of them, and without having to remember command words or special keys. The Toolbox's **Menu Manager** supports the use of menus. This section describes both what the Menu Manager does and how menus are commonly implemented on the Macintosh.

As shown in Figure 3-3, the **menu bar** always appears at the top of the Macintosh screen; nothing but the cursor ever appears in front of it. The menu titles in it are always in the system font and the system font size (normally Chicago 12 in Roman-based writing systems).

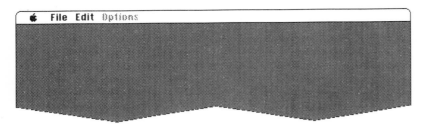

Figure 3-3
The menu bar

Menus and resources

The general appearance and behavior of a menu is determined by a routine called its **menu definition procedure,** which is stored as a resource in a resource file. The standard menu definition procedure is part of the system resource file. It lists the menu items vertically, and each item may have an icon, a check mark or other symbol, a keyboard equivalent, a particular character style, or a dimmed appearance, as described in the next section. On the Macintosh II, the menu definition procedure has been extended by a new resource that provides support for color, pop-up, and hierarchical menus.

Resource files are also used to store the contents of menus. This practice allows the menus to be edited or translated to another language without affecting the application's source code. (For more information about resources, see Chapter 4.)

The following section describes how menus behave, as defined by the standard menu definition procedure. Note that this standard behavior can be modified by programs that provide their own custom menu definition procedures. For example, a program may create menus with extra graphics or a nonlinear text arrangement. Custom menus still respond to the standard Menu Manager calls.

How menus work

When the Macintosh user positions the cursor in the menu bar and presses the mouse button over a menu title, the application calls the Menu Manager, which highlights that title (by inverting it) and pulls down the menu below it. The menu is displayed as long as the mouse button is held down. Dragging the mouse through the menu causes each of its **menu items** (commands) to be highlighted in turn.

If the mouse button is released over an item, that item is chosen: the item blinks briefly to confirm the choice, and the menu disappears. When the user chooses an item, the Menu Manager tells the application which item was chosen, and the application performs the corresponding action. When the application completes the action, it removes the highlighting from the menu title, indicating to the user that the operation is complete.

If the user moves the cursor out of the menu with the mouse button held down, the menu remains visible, though no menu items are highlighted. If the mouse button is released outside the menu, the menu just disappears and the application takes no action. The user can always look at a menu without causing any changes in the document or on the screen.

A menu may be temporarily **disabled,** so that none of its items can be chosen. A disabled menu can still be pulled down so that the menu items can be viewed, but its title and all the items in it are dimmed.

A menu item may be the text of a command, or just a line dividing groups of choices (see Figure 3-4). An ellipsis (...) following the text of an item indicates that selecting the item will bring up a dialog box requesting further information before the command is executed. The keyboard equivalents to the right of each menu item will be discussed in a moment.

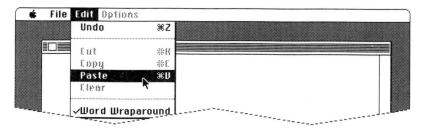

Figure 3-4
A standard menu

Hierarchical menus are also available in the Macintosh SE and Macintosh II ROMs. (Like other new software features, hierarchical menus have also been back-fitted to the Macintosh Plus via version 4.1 of the System file.) Figure 3-5 shows a hierarchical menu.

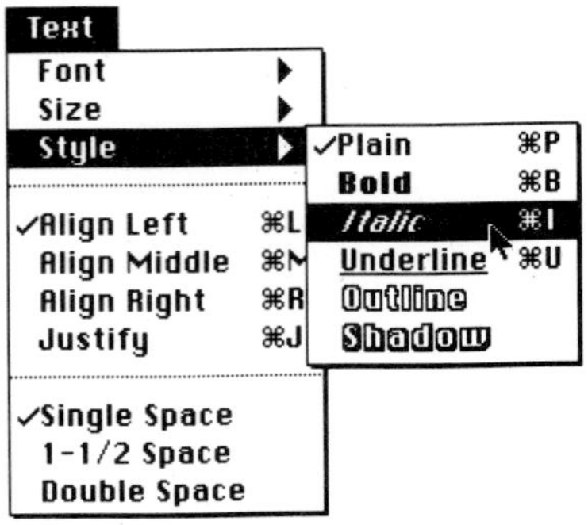

Figure 3-5
A hierarchical menu before and after a submenu appears

Although five levels of hierarchical menus are available using the new Menu Manager routines, one level or hierarchy should suffice for most needs.

When there are too many items to fit on the screen, a menu becomes scrollable. When this happens, a scrolling arrow appears in place of the last item to show that there are more items below (see Figure 3-6). If the cursor is moved into this scrolling arrow, the menu scrolls. As soon as the menu scrolls, a scrolling arrow appears in place of the top item to show that there are now more items above.

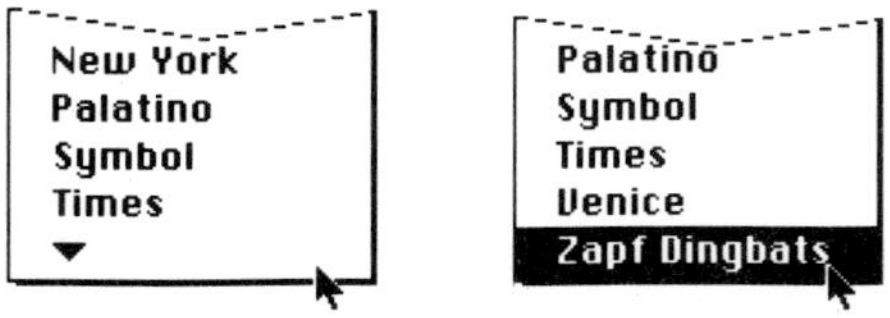

Figure 3-6
Scrolling menu indicator

The text of a menu item always appears in the system font and the system font size. Each item can have a few visual variations from the standard appearance:

- ☐ An icon to the left of the item's text, to provide visual clues to the item's function.
- ☐ A check mark or other character to the left of the item's text, to indicate whether a software setting indicated by the item is selected or not.
- ☐ The Command key (propeller) symbol along with another character, both placed to the right of the item's text to show that the item can be invoked from the keyboard (that is, it has a **keyboard equivalent**). Pressing the indicated key while holding down the Command key invokes the item just as if it had been chosen from the menu.

□ A character style such as bold, italic, or underline.

□ A dimmed appearance to indicate that the item is disabled and can't be chosen. (The Cut, Copy, and Clear commands in Figure 3-4 are disabled.)

The first menu in an application should be the standard Apple menu, which contains the names of all available desk accessories. When the user chooses a desk accessory from the menu, the title of a menu belonging to the desk accessory may appear in the menu bar for as long as the desk accessory is active, or the entire menu bar may be replaced by menus belonging to the desk accessory.

The 256K ROMs (and System file 4.1) also support another new feature: pop-up menus. A pop-up menu isn't in the menu bar; it appears somewhere else on the screen (usually in a dialog box) when the user presses in a particular place. A pop-up menu may also have submenus. Pop-up menus are typically used for lists of items, for example, a list of fonts.

Keyboard equivalents for commands

A program can set up a keyboard equivalent for any of its menu commands, so that the menu item can be invoked by holding down the Command key and pressing another character key. (Recall that the Command key is referred to as the Apple key in some of the user documentation.) The character specified for a keyboard equivalent will usually be a letter; the user can type the letter in either uppercase or lowercase.

A program can also specify characters other than letters for keyboard equivalents. However, the Shift key will be ignored when the equivalent is typed. For example, Command-+ is read as Command-=.

❖ *Note:* Command-Shift-number combinations are *not* keyboard equivalents. They're detected and handled by the Toolbox Event Manager and are never returned to the program. (This is how disk ejection with Command-Shift-1 or Command-Shift-2 is implemented.)

The standard keyboard equivalents Command-Z, Command-X, Command-C, and Command-V should always be used for the editing commands Undo, Cut, Copy, and Paste, or editing won't work correctly in desk accessories, which share these menu items with the application.

Windows

A **window** is an object on the desktop that presents information, such as a document or a message. Windows can be any size, shape, or color and there can be one or many of them, depending on the application. The Toolbox's **Window Manager** is a set of data structures and routines that programs use for dealing with windows on the Macintosh screen. This section will briefly explain how the Window Manager helps applications manage windows as well as some conventions of window implementation on the Macintosh.

With the Window Manager, an application can easily create standard types of windows as well as define its own types of windows. Some windows are created indirectly by other parts of the Toolbox. For example, the **Dialog Manager** uses a window to display an alert box.

Windows and resources

Some standard types of windows are predefined. One of these is the **document window,** as illustrated in Figure 3-7. Every document window has a title bar containing a title in the system font and system font size. A document window may also have a close box, a size box, or scroll bars. (Scroll bars are **controls** and are supported by the Control Manager.)

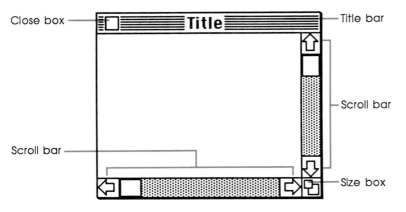

Figure 3-7
An active document window

The general appearance and behavior of a window is determined by a routine called its **window definition function,** which is stored as a resource in a resource file, and accessed through the Resource Manager. The system resource file includes window definition functions for the standard document window and other standard types of windows. Nonstandard window types can also be defined.

To create a window, the Window Manager needs to know information such as the resource ID of the window definition, the window title (if any), its location, and its plane. The needed information is usually stored in a single resource called a **window template.** Window templates make it easy for programs to create a number of windows of the same type. What's more, they allow the isolation of specific window descriptions. Translation of window titles to another language, for example, then requires only a simple change to the resource file. (For more information about resources and resource files, see Chapter 4.)

❖ *Note:* Color windows are supported in the Macintosh II ROM, in a fashion fully compatible with previous versions of the Window Manager.

How windows work

The document window shown in Figure 3-7 is the **active** (frontmost) window, the one that will be acted on when the user types, gives commands, or whatever. Its title bar is **highlighted**—displayed in a distinctive way—so that the window will stand out from other, inactive windows that may be on the screen. Since a close box, size box, zoom box, and scroll bars can affect only the active window, these elements don't appear in an inactive window (see Figure 3-8).

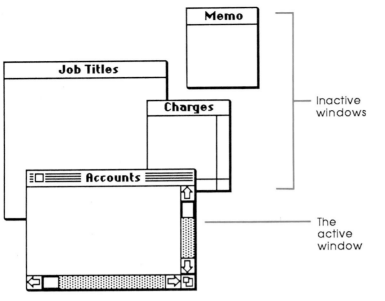

Figure 3-8
Overlapping document windows

An important function of the Window Manager is to keep track of overlapping windows. This allows programs to draw in any window without running over onto other windows in front of it, to move windows on the screen, to change their plane (their front-to-back ordering), or to change their size, all without concern for how the various windows overlap. The Window Manager keeps track of any newly exposed areas and provides a mechanism to ensure that they're properly redrawn.

A number of Window Manager routines change the state of a window from inactive to active or vice versa. For each such change, the Window Manager generates an **activate event.** The Toolbox Event Manager, in turn, passes the event on to the application. Activate events have the highest priority of any type of event.

Usually when one window becomes active, another becomes inactive, so that activate events are commonly generated in pairs. When this happens, the Window Manager generates first the event for the window becoming inactive, and then the event for the window becoming active.

A window can never be moved completely off the screen: by convention, it can't be moved such that the visible area of the title bar is less than four pixels square. (If multiple screens are connected to the computer, the window can be moved from one screen to another.)

Window regions

When the user clicks the mouse button, the Window Manager indicates which part of which window it was clicked in. Clicking anywhere in an inactive window makes it the active window. The Window Manager brings the window to the front and highlights its title bar.

It's easy for applications to use windows; to the application, a window is a QuickDraw **graphics port** that it can draw into with QuickDraw routines. (For more information, see the discussion of graphics ports in Chapter 5.)

There is, however, more to a window than just the graphics port that the application draws in. In a standard document window, for example, the title bar and outline of the window are drawn by the Window Manager, not by the application. The part of a window that the Window Manager draws is called the **window frame,** since it usually surrounds the rest of the window.

Every window has the following two regions:

☐ The **content region** is the area that the application draws in. This is where an application presents information and where the size box and scroll bars of a document window are located.

☐ The **structure region** is the entire window (the content region plus the window frame).

A window may additionally have any of the regions listed below:

☐ A **go-away region** (close box) within the window frame. Clicking in this region of the active window closes the window.

☐ A **drag region** within the window frame. Dragging in this region moves the window and makes it the active window (if it isn't already), unless the Command key was held down.

☐ A **grow region** (size box). Dragging in this region of the active window changes the size of the window.

☐ A **zoom region** within the window frame. Clicking in this region zooms the window so that it fills the entire screen.

Figure 3-9 illustrates the various regions of a standard document window and its window frame.

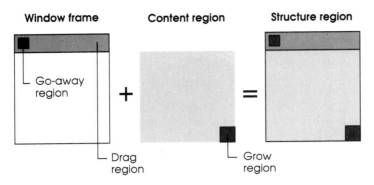

Figure 3-9
Document window regions and frame

Another important window region is the **update region.** The Window Manager keeps track of all areas of the content region that have to be redrawn and accumulates them into the update region. For example, if you bring to the front a window that was overlapped by another window, the Window Manager adds the newly exposed area of the front window's content region to its update region.

How a window is drawn

A two-step process usually takes place when a window is drawn or redrawn:

1. The window definition procedure draws the window frame.

2. The application draws the window's contents.

To perform the first step, the Window Manager calls the window definition function. It manipulates regions of the Window Manager port (that is, the entire desktop) as necessary before calling the window definition function, in order to ensure that only what should and must be drawn is actually drawn on the screen. (See Figure 5-6, "GrafPort Regions," in Chapter 5 for an illustration.)

To perform the second step, the Window Manager generates an **update event** to get the application to draw the window's contents; this event is passed to the application by the Toolbox Event Manager. The Event Manager periodically checks to see if there's any window whose update region is not empty; if it finds one, it reports to the application that an update event has occurred. The application is then responsible for updating the window.

Controls

Controls are objects on the Macintosh screen, such as buttons, check boxes, and scroll bars, which the user manipulates with the mouse. Controls can cause instant action with visible results, or they can change software settings to modify a future action. Except for scroll bars, most controls appear only in dialog or alert boxes.

The **Control Manager** is the part of the Toolbox that deals with controls. Applications create, read, and manipulate controls by calling Control Manager routines. The Control Manager carries out the actual operations.

Controls may be of various types, each with its own characteristic appearance on the screen and responses to the mouse (see Figure 3-10).

❖ *Note:* The Macintosh II ROM version of the Control Manager has been extended to support color controls. This version of the Control Manager is fully compatible with previous versions.

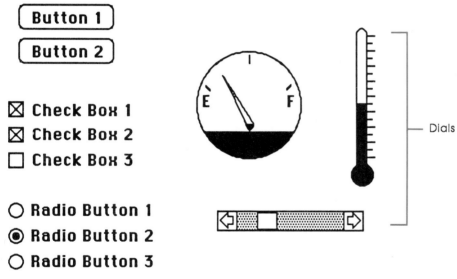

Figure 3-10
Some sample controls

Controls and resources

The relationship between controls and resources is analogous to the relationship between windows and resources: just as there are window definition functions and window templates, there are **control definition functions** and **control templates.**

Each type of control has a control definition function that determines how controls of that type look and behave. The system resource file includes definition functions for the standard control types (buttons, check boxes, radio buttons, and scroll bars). Nonstandard control types require their own control definition functions.

How controls work

Certain standard types of controls are predefined. An application can also define its own custom control types. Among the standard control types are the following:

□ **Buttons** cause an action when clicked or pressed with the mouse. They appear on the screen as rounded-corner rectangles with a title centered inside.

□ **Check boxes** retain and display a setting, which is either checked (on) or unchecked (off); clicking with the mouse reverses the setting. Check boxes are frequently used to control or modify some future action, instead of causing an immediate action of their own.

□ **Radio buttons** also retain and display an on-or-off setting, and are used to offer a choice among several alternatives. They're organized into groups, with the provision that only one button in the group can be on at a time, like the buttons on a car radio.

Another important category of controls is **dials,** which display a value, magnitude, or position in a pseudoanalog form, such as the position of a sliding switch or the angle of a needle on a gauge. (The setting may be displayed digitally as well.) The user may be able to change a dial's setting by dragging its indicator with the mouse, or the dial may simply display a value not under the user's direct control, such as the amount of free space remaining on a disk.

One type of dial is predefined: the standard Macintosh scroll bars. An application can define other dials of any shape or complexity.

Every control belongs to a particular window: the control appears within the window's content region, and it acts on that window.

Buttons and check boxes are normally used in dialog or alert windows only. Such windows are created with the Dialog Manager, and the Dialog Manager takes care of drawing the controls and letting the program know whether the user clicked one of them.

A control may be active or inactive. Active controls respond to the user's mouse actions; inactive controls don't. When an active control is clicked or pressed, it's usually highlighted (see Figure 3-11). Standard button controls are inverted, but some control types may use other forms of highlighting, such as making the outline heavier.

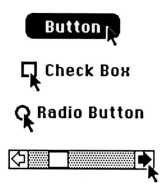

Figure 3-11
Highlighted active controls

A control is made inactive when it has no meaning or effect in the current context. An inactive control remains visible, but it is highlighted in some special way, depending on its control type (see Figure 3-12). For example, the title of an inactive button, check box, or radio button is **dimmed** (drawn in gray rather than black).

Figure 3-12
Inactive controls

Dialogs and alerts

Dialogs are a mechanism for displaying information or program settings and soliciting user input. As shown in Figure 3-13, a dialog box typically resembles a paper form on which the user checks boxes and fills in blanks.

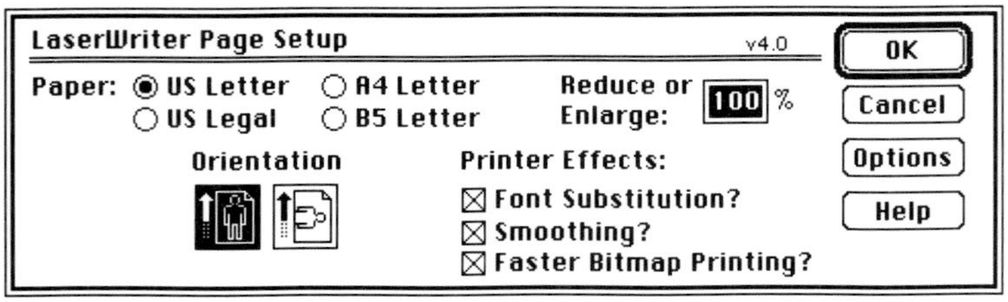

Figure 3-13
A typical dialog box

Alerts are a subset of dialogs, used to report errors or give warnings. The **Dialog Manager** allows programs to implement dialog boxes and alerts.

A dialog box may contain any or all of the following:

□ informative text

□ rectangles in which text may be entered (initially blank or containing default text that can be edited)

□ controls of any kind, as defined in the preceding section

□ graphics (icons or QuickDraw pictures)

□ anything else as defined by the application

The user provides the necessary information in the dialog box by entering text or manipulating controls. There's usually a control button labeled *OK* to tell the application to accept the information provided and perform the command, as well as a control button labeled *Cancel* to cancel the command. There may be more than one button that will perform the command, each in a different way.

A dialog may have a **default button,** outlined in bold, which is the preferred (safest) button to use in the current situation. Pressing the Return key or the Enter key has the same effect as clicking the outlined button (or the OK button, if no button is outlined).

Most dialog boxes can be categorized as modal dialog boxes; that is, they require the user to respond before doing anything else. This type is called *modal* because it puts the user in the state or "mode" of being able to work only inside the dialog box. Clicking outside the dialog box only causes a beep from the Macintosh's speaker. A modal dialog box usually has the same general appearance as the dialog box shown earlier in Figure 3-13.

Other dialog boxes do not require the user to respond before performing another action; these are called **modeless** dialog boxes. A modeless dialog box looks like a document window. It can be moved, made inactive and active again, or closed like any document window. The user can, for example, work in document windows on the desktop before clicking a button in the dialog box, and modeless dialog boxes can be set up to respond to the standard editing commands in the Edit menu.

Dialog boxes may in fact require no response at all. For example, while an application is performing a time-consuming process, it can display a dialog box that contains only a message telling what it's doing; then, when the process is complete, it can simply remove the dialog box.

A dialog box appears in a dialog window, which a program can manipulate just like any other window with Window Manager or QuickDraw routines.

Dialogs and resources

The Dialog Manager gets most of the descriptive information about the dialogs and alerts from resources in a resource file. As necessary, the Dialog Manager calls the Resource Manager to read what it needs from the resource file into memory.

To create a dialog, the Dialog Manager needs the same information about the dialog window as the Window Manager needs when it creates a new window. The Dialog Manager also needs to know what items the dialog box contains. The required information can be stored as a resource in a resource file. This type of resource, which is called a **dialog template,** is analogous to a window template. The Dialog Manager calls the Resource Manager to read the dialog template from the resource file. It then incorporates the information in the template into a dialog data structure in memory, called a **dialog record,** analogous to a window record. Like window templates, dialog templates isolate descriptive information from your application code for ease of modification or translation to other languages.

The information about all the **items** (text, controls, or graphics) in a dialog or alert box is stored in an **item list** in a resource file. As illustrated in Figure 3-14, the dialog template includes the resource ID of the item list. The item list in turn contains the resource IDs of any icons or QuickDraw pictures in the dialog box, and possibly the resource IDs of control templates for controls in the box. After calling the Resource Manager to read a dialog or alert template into memory, the Dialog Manager calls the Resource Manager again to read in the item list. It then makes a copy of the item list and uses that copy. Finally, the Dialog Manager calls the Resource Manager to read in any individual items as necessary.

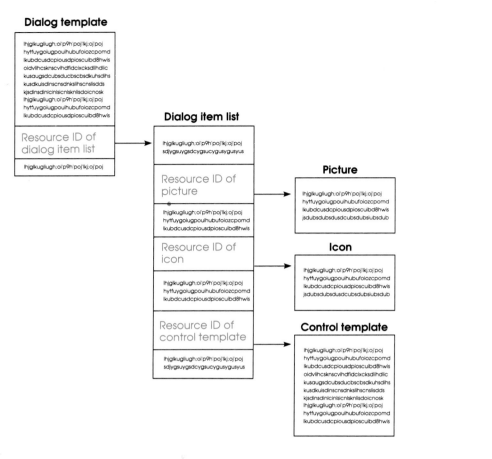

Figure 3-14
Dialogs and associated resources

An item list contains an entry for each item, giving the item's type (control, text, or whatever), a pointer or handle to the item, and a rectangle that determines the location of the item within the dialog box.

The text of an editable item may initially be either default text or empty. Text entry and editing is handled in the conventional way, as in TextEdit; in fact, the Dialog Manager calls TextEdit to handle it. (TextEdit is discussed in the next section.) The user can press the Tab key to advance to the next editable text item in the item list, wrapping around to the first if there aren't any more.

Alerts

The **alert** mechanism provides applications with a means of reporting errors or giving warnings (Figure 3-15). An **alert box** is a type of a modal dialog box, but it appears only when something has gone wrong or must be brought to the user's attention. Every alert has four stages. Different actions may take place at different stages.

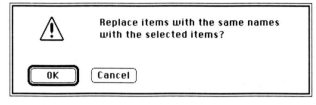

Figure 3-15
A typical alert box

There are three standard kinds of alerts—Stop, Note, and Caution—each indicated by a particular icon in the top-left corner of the alert box. Figure 3-15 illustrates a Caution alert. The icons identifying Stop and Note alerts are similar. (In earlier versions of the System file, these were represented by a question mark, exclamation point, and asterisk, respectively.) Other alerts can have anything in the the top-left corner, including blank space.

The alert mechanism also provides sound from the Macintosh's speaker. The alert sounds are determined by a sound procedure that emits one of up to four tones or sequences of tones. The volume of each beep depends on the current speaker volume setting, which the user can adjust with the Control Panel desk accessory. If the user has set the speaker volume to zero, the menu bar will blink once in place of each beep.

When the Dialog Manager detects a click outside an alert box or a modal dialog box, it doesn't perform any actions beyond emitting the sound associated with stage 1 of the alert. (For consistency with *Human Interface Guidelines: The Apple Desktop Interface,* this sound should be a single beep.)

Text editing

TextEdit is a set of built-in Toolbox routines and data types that make it simple for programs to provide basic text editing and formatting capabilities. These capabilities include

☐ inserting new text

☐ deleting characters that are backspaced over

☐ translating mouse activity into text selection

☐ automatic scrolling of text within a window

☐ deleting selected text and possibly inserting it elsewhere, or copying text without deleting it

☐ automatic movement of the insertion point with the keyboard arrow keys (with the System file version 3.0 or later)

The TextEdit routines follow *Human Interface Guidelines: The Apple Desktop Interface;* using them ensures that an application will present a consistent user interface. The Dialog Manager also uses TextEdit for text editing in dialog boxes. TextEdit fully supports the Script Manager, providing complete international support for any writing system.

❖ *Note:* Because of the special needs of word processing programs, they generally do not use TextEdit.

TextEdit supports these standard features:

☐ Using more than one font, color, or stylistic variation in a single block of text (this feature is new with the 256K ROMs and System file 4.1).

☐ Selecting text by clicking and dragging with the mouse, double-clicking to select words. To TextEdit, a **word** is any series of printing characters, excluding spaces (ASCII code $20) but including nonbreaking spaces (ASCII code $CA).

☐ Extending or shortening the selection by Shift-clicking.

☐ Inverse highlighting of the current text selection or display of a blinking vertical bar at the insertion point.

☐ **Word wraparound,** which prevents a word from being split between lines when text is drawn.

☐ Cutting (or copying) and pasting within an application via the Clipboard. TextEd puts text you cut or copy into the **desk scrap.** (Earlier versions of TextEdit used a separate TextEdit scrap. See the section "Cutting and Pasting" in this chapter for discussion of scraps.)

Although TextEdit is useful for most standard text-editing operations, there are some additional features that it doesn't support. TextEdit does *not* support

☐ fully justified text (text aligned with both the left and right margins)

☐ intelligent cut and paste (adjusting spaces between words during cutting and pasting)

☐ tabs

TextEdit does provide software hooks for implementing features such as automatic scrolling or a more precise definition of a word for purposes of selection by double-clicking.

Lists

The Toolbox's **List Manager** is a package that creates, displays, and manipulates lists. The List Manager contains routines for storing and updating elements of data within a list and for displaying the list in a rectangle within a window. It handles all selection and scrolling of **list elements** within that list. Because a list element is simply a group of consecutive bytes of data, it can be used to store anything: a name, the bits of an icon, or the resource ID of an icon. There's no specific restriction on the size of a list element, but the total size of a list cannot exceed 32K.

In its simplest form, the List Manager can be used to display a text-only list of names. With some additional effort, it can be used to display an array of images and text—for example, in a spreadsheet application.

Warning

The List Manager Package is found only in System 3.0 and later versions of the System file.

The List Manager Package is automatically read into memory from the system resource file when one of its routines is called; it occupies a total of about 5K bytes.

As shown in Figure 3-16, a list is drawn in a rectangle within a window. The rectangle can take up the entire area of the window's content region (except for the space needed by scroll bars, if any), or it can occupy only a small portion of the content region.

A Sample				
Cell 0,0	Cell 1,0	Cell 2,0	Cell 3,0	Cell 4,0
Cell 0,1	Cell 1,1	Cell 2,1	Cell 3,1	Cell 4,1
Cell 0,2	**Cell 1,2**	Cell 2,2	Cell 3,2	Cell 4,2
Cell 0,3	Cell 1,3	Cell 2,3	Cell 3,3	Cell 4,3
Cell 0,4	Cell 1,4	Cell 2,4	Cell 3,4	Cell 4,4
Cell 0,5	Cell 1,5	Cell 2,5	Cell 3,5	Cell 4,5
Cell 0,6	Cell 1,6	Cell 2,6	Cell 3,6	Cell 4,6
Cell 0,7	Cell 1,7	Cell 2,7	Cell 3,7	Cell 4,7
Cell 0,8	Cell 1,8	Cell 2,8	Cell 3,8	Cell 4,8
Cell 0,9	Cell 1,9	Cell 2,9	Cell 3,9	Cell 4,9
Cell 0,10	Cell 1,10	Cell 2,10	Cell 3,10	Cell 4,10
Cell 0,11	Cell 1,11	Cell 2,11	Cell 3,11	Cell 4,11
Cell 0,12	Cell 1,12	Cell 2,12	Cell 3,12	Cell 4,12
Cell 0,13	Cell 1,13	Cell 2,13	Cell 3,13	Cell 4,13
Cell 0,14	Cell 1,14	Cell 2,14	Cell 3,14	Cell 4,14
Cell 0,15	Cell 1,15	Cell 2,15	Cell 3,15	Cell 4,15
Cell 0,16	Cell 1,16	Cell 2,16	Cell 3,16	Cell 4,16

Figure 3-16
A sample list

List elements are displayed in **cells,** which provide the basic structure of a list. While list elements (the actual data) may vary in length, the cells in which they're displayed are the same size for any given list.

As with the parts of the Toolbox we've already discussed, the appearance and behavior of a list is determined by a routine called its **list definition procedure,** which is stored as a resource in a resource file. The system resource file includes a list definition procedure for a standard text-only list. A program can also define a custom list definition procedure.

Like TextEdit, the List Manager makes it easy for applications to implement the techniques described in *Human Interface Guidelines: The Apple Desktop Interface.* The default algorithm used by the List Manager for user selection of cells implements these techniques as follows:

1. If neither the Shift nor the Command key is held down, a click selects a cell, causing all current selections to be deselected. While the mouse button is held down and the mouse is moved around, only the cell under the cursor is selected.

2. If the Shift key is held down, as long as the mouse button is down, the List Manager expands and shrinks a selected rectangle defined by the mouse location and the anchor. When the mouse is first pressed, the List Manager calculates the smallest rectangle that encloses all selected cells. If the click is above or to the left of this rectangle (or on the top-left corner), the bottom-right corner of the rectangle becomes the anchor; otherwise, the top-left corner becomes the anchor.

3. If the Command key is held down, as long as the mouse button is also held down, all cells the mouse passes over are either selected or deselected. Like MacPaint FatBits, if the initial cell was off, cells are turned on; otherwise they're turned off.

An application programmer can also choose to change the way selections work by implementing a custom list definition procedure.

Cutting and pasting

The **desk scrap** is the vehicle for transferring data between two programs; it can also be used for transferring data that's cut and pasted within a program. The **Scrap Manager** is a set of Toolbox routines and data types that supports cutting and pasting among applications and desk accessories through the use of the desk scrap.

From the user's point of view, all data that's cut or copied resides in the Clipboard, whether the data is stored in the desk scrap or in a private scrap provided by the application. The Cut command deletes data from a document and places it in the Clipboard; the Copy command copies data into the Clipboard without deleting it from the document. The next Paste command—whether applied to the same document or another, in the same application or another—inserts the contents of the Clipboard at a specified place. Applications may also provide a Clipboard window for displaying the current contents of the scrap.

The desk scrap is usually stored in memory, but it can be stored on the disk (in the **Clipboard file,** or **scrap file**) if there's not enough room for it in memory. The desk scrap may remain on the disk throughout the use of the application, but it must be read back into memory when the application terminates, because the user may then remove that disk and insert another.

Note also that the desk scrap is written on the system startup volume—the volume that contains the currently open System file—rather than the default volume, as it was in the original 64K ROM version of the Scrap Manager. With hierarchical volumes, the Clipboard file is placed in the folder containing the currently open System file.

❖ *Note:* The Scrap Manager was designed to transfer small amounts of data; attempts to transfer very large amounts of data may fail due to lack of memory. (The desk scrap can never be larger than half that amount of memory allocated for the stack and the application heap.) Applications may use a private scrap to transfer large amounts of data.

The nature of the data to be transferred varies according to the application. For example, in a text processor, the data is text; in a graphics application, it's a picture. The amount of information that is retained about the data being transferred also varies. Between two text applications, text can be cut and pasted without any loss of information; however, if the user of a graphics application cuts a picture consisting of text and then pastes it into a word processor document, the text in the picture may not be editable in the word processor, or it may be editable but not look exactly the same as in the graphics application. The Scrap Manager allows for a variety of data types and provides a mechanism so that applications can control how much information is retained when data is transferred.

Types of desk scrap data

From the user's point of view, there can be only one thing in the Clipboard at a time. However, applications may store more than one version of the same information in the scrap, each representing the same Clipboard contents in a different form. For example, text cut by a word processor may be stored in the desk scrap both as text and as a QuickDraw picture.

Desk scrap data types, like resource types, are a sequence of four characters. Two standard types of data are defined:

☐ 'TEXT': a series of ASCII characters.

☐ 'PICT': a QuickDraw picture, which is a saved sequence of drawing commands that can be played back with a QuickDraw command and that may include picture comments. (QuickDraw pictures are discussed in Chapter 5.)

Applications must write at least one of these standard types of data to the desk scrap and must be able to read *both* types.

An application reading the desk scrap will look for its preferred data type. If its preferred type isn't there, or if it's there but was written by an application with a different preferred type, the receiving application may or may not be able to convert the data to the type it needs. If not, some information may be lost in the transfer process. For example, a graphics application can easily convert text to a picture, but the reverse isn't true.

Figure 3-17 illustrates this situation: a picture consisting of text is cut from a graphics application, and then pasted into a word processor document.

If the graphics application—like application A in Figure 3-17—writes only its preferred data type (a picture) to the desk scrap, then the text in the picture will not be editable in the word processor because it will be seen as just a series of drawing commands and not as a sequence of characters. (MacDraw® is an example of an application that does this.) On the other hand, if the graphics application takes the trouble to recognize *which* characters have been drawn in the picture, and writes them out to the desk scrap both as a picture and as text—like application B in Figure 3-17—the word processor will be able to treat them as editable text. In this case, however, any part of the picture that isn't text will be lost.

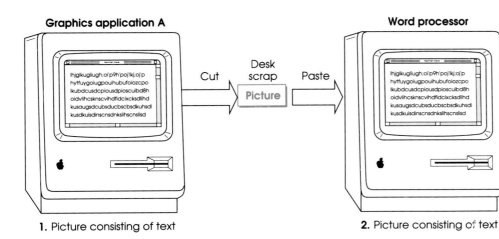

Graphics application A

Word processor

Cut → Desk scrap → Paste

Picture

1. Picture consisting of text

2. Picture consisting of text

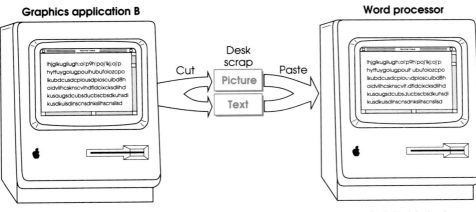

Graphics application B

Word processor

Cut → Desk scrap → Paste

Picture

Text

1. Picture consisting of text

2. Editable text

Figure 3-17
Inter-application cutting and pasting

In addition to the two standard data types, the desk scrap may also contain application-specific types of data. If several applications are to support the transfer of a private type of data, each one will write and read that type, but they still must write at least one of the standard types and be able to read both standard types.

Private scraps

Instead of using the desk scrap for storing data that is cut and pasted within an application, some programs may set up a private scrap for this purpose. In applications that use the standard 'TEXT' or 'PICT' data types, it's simpler to use the desk scrap, but if an application defines its own private type of data, or if it's likely that very large amounts of data will be cut and pasted, using a private scrap may result in faster cutting and pasting within the application. (The application must, however, be able to convert data between the format of its private scrap and the format of the desk scrap.)

As the preceding discussion makes clear, graphics are a key element of the representation of data by the Macintosh. You may also have read between the lines and seen that text display is only a special form of graphics. On the Macintosh, all text and graphics—including the desktop, menus, and windows—are drawn by a set of graphics procedures called QuickDraw. QuickDraw's handling of text is in turn supported by the Toolbox's Font Manager and Script Manager. All of these Toolbox managers are discussed in Chapter 5. But before going on to the subject of graphics, we'll return to a topic we've already touched upon many times: **resources,** upon which the rest of the Toolbox is built.

Chapter 4

Resources

This chapter outlines the structure of a Macintosh file and introduces **resources,** one of the keys to the design of the Macintosh software. It discusses the functions of the **Resource Manager,** the part of the Toolbox responsible for keeping track of and accessing resources, and briefly lists the various standard resources that you'll find in Macintosh applications. This chapter also describes the system resource file, which contains resources shared by different parts of the system, and concludes by introducing some of the tools that you can use to edit resources.

The information in this chapter applies equally to all Macintosh machines.

Structure of a Macintosh file

A Macintosh **volume** is a piece of storage medium, normally a disk; information on a volume is divided into files. A **file** is a named, ordered sequence of bytes. There are two parts or **forks** to a Macintosh file: the **data fork** and the **resource fork** (Figure 4-1).

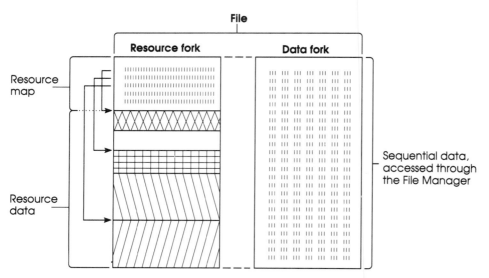

Figure 4-1
Structure of a Macintosh file

Resources are specially formatted chunks of data stored in the resource fork of a Macintosh file and accessed via the Resource Manager. Typical resources are pieces of static text, static graphics, or static code. For an application file, for instance, the resource fork normally contains the resources used by the application, such as menus, fonts, and icons, and also the application code itself. The data fork can contain anything an application wants to store there (often nothing).

Either fork of a file may be empty.

Because it's functionally like a file in many ways, the resource fork is often referred to simply as a **resource file.** As Figure 4-1 shows, the resource fork itself is internally divided into the **resource map** and the **resource data.** The resource map is the index that the Resource Manager uses to locate individual resources in the file; the resource data is the actual contents of the resources themselves.

The information in the data fork of a file is separately accessed via the File Manager, which is discussed in Chapter 8.

Overview of resources

Resources form the foundation of every Macintosh application; in fact, a Macintosh program *is* a collection of resources. Objects such as menus, fonts, and icons are stored as resources; an application's code is also stored as resources. The term *resource* can be taken literally: a resource may be anything that is of use to a program or to the system. A resource can be almost any chunk of data; in fact, that's all that the various types of resources have in common. An icon, for example, resides in a resource file as a 32-by-32 bit image, and a font as a large bit image containing the characters of the font. In some cases the resource consists of descriptive information, such as, for a menu, the menu title, the text of each command in the menu, and so on.

The resources used by the application are created, stored, and changed separately from the application's code for flexibility and ease of maintenance. This separation is the great advantage of the resource file scheme. Menus, for example, are stored separately from code so that they can be edited or translated without the code having to be recompiled. Resources also allow different programs to get standard data, such as the I-beam pointer for inserting text, from a shared system resource file. Resources also facilitate responsive memory management because a program is made up of lots of little pieces rather than a few large blocks.

Resources are grouped logically by function into **resource types,** which are identified by four-character names. For example, menus are stored as resources of type 'MENU'. Within a resource type, individual resources are identified by the **resource ID** number. Resource types and IDs are described in greater detail later in this chapter.

An application's resource file

Each application is stored in a resource file, which contains the resources specific to that application, including the application code, as shown in Figure 4-2. The code may be divided into different segments, each of which is a resource. This allows various parts of the program to be dynamically loaded and unloaded (as described in Chapter 7).

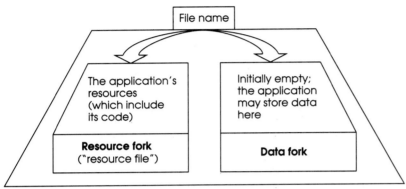

Figure 4-2
An application file

As we've mentioned, the resource approach enables easy editing of resources without affecting the way the resource functions in the program. For example, menus and dialogs can be easily translated into a foreign language. (In non-Macintosh environments, translating an application would involve substantial changes to the application's actual code and recompilation, a slow and laborious process.) Properly written applications store all localization-sensitive data (and operations) as resources. For example, menu items, text strings, and so on are all stored as resources.

❖ *Note:* Because an application may be shared on a file server, default settings should stay with individual document files rather than with the application.

Resource editing is introduced later in this chapter.

Other types of resource files

Resource files aren't limited to applications; anything stored in a file can have its own resources.

The **system resource file** (the file named *System,* located in the System Folder) contains standard resources shared by all applications. These common resources are called **system resources.** (Shared resources are usually stored in the system resource file, but other resource files may also contain shared resources.) As shown in Figure 4-3, the system resource file has the same structure as an application file.

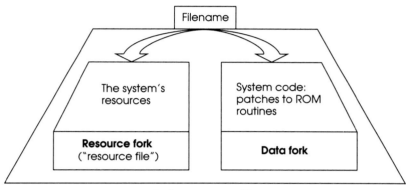

System resource file

Figure 4-3
Structure of the system resource file

For more information about what's in the system resource file, see the section "The System Resource File" later in this chapter.

Figure 4-4 shows the structure of a document file; the resource fork contains the document's resources and the data fork contains the data that comprise the document. Special resources needed by a document may also be included in the document's resource file. For instance, an unusual font used in only one document can be included in the resource file for that document rather than in the system resource file.

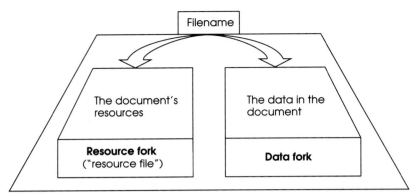

Figure 4-4
Structure of a document file

How resources are accessed

The Resource Manager keeps track of resources in resource files and provides routines so that applications and other parts of the Toolbox can access them. The Resource Manager knows nothing about the formats of the individual types of resources. To the Resource Manager, all resources are just sequences of bytes; the contents of the resource are meaningful only to the software that uses the resource.

It's also important to note that applications often access resources indirectly through other parts of the Toolbox, such as the Menu Manager and the Font Manager, which in turn call the Resource Manager to do low-level resource operations.

Given a resource specification, the Resource Manager will read the resource into memory and return a **handle** to it. (A handle is a pointer to a relocatable block in memory; see Chapter 7 for details.) In effect, resources provide a form of virtual memory on the Macintosh: from the standpoint of the program that is requesting the resource, it is unimportant whether the resource is in memory or on the disk. The Resource Manager handles all the details of delivering the resource to the calling program.

As we indicated earlier, a resource file consists primarily of a **resource map** and **resource data.** The resource map is an index to the resource data; it contains an entry for each resource that provides the location of its resource data. Each entry in the map gives the offset of the resource data in the file and contains a handle to the data if it's in memory. The resource data consists of the resources themselves (for example, the bit image for an icon or the title and commands for a menu).

Resource data is normally read into memory when needed, though a program can specify that it be read in as soon as the resource file is opened. When read in, resource data is stored in a relocatable block in the heap (see "How Heap Space is Allocated" in Chapter 7). The entries in the resource map that identify and locate the resources in a resource file are known as **resource references.** Every resource reference includes the type, ID number, and optional name of the resource.

Every resource reference also contains certain **resource attributes** that determine how the resource should be dealt with. Table 4-1 lists these attributes and explains what they mean.

Table 4-1
Resource attributes

Resource attribute	Meaning
System heap	Indicates that the resource will be loaded into the system heap. This attribute should not be set for an application's resources.
Purgeable	Indicates whether a resource may be purged by the Memory Manager.
Locked	Indicates whether a resource may be moved by the Memory Manager. Since a locked resource is neither relocatable nor purgeable, the Locked attribute overrides the Purgeable attribute.
Protected	If the Protected attribute is set, the application can't use Resource Manager routines to change the ID number or name of the resource, modify its contents, or remove the resource from the resource file.
Preload	Tells the Resource Manager to read this resource into memory immediately after opening the resource file.
Changed	Tells the Resource Manager whether this resource has been changed. (This attribute is set by the Resource Manager; a program should never set it directly.)

Resources are designated in the resource map as being either **purgeable** or unpurgeable; if purgeable, they may be removed from the heap when space is required by the Memory Manager, as explained in Chapter 7. Larger resources are usually designated as purgeable.

The system resource file is opened at system startup. When you start up an application, its resource file is also opened. In fact, a large number of resource files may be open at one time. The Resource Manager normally searches the files in the reverse of the order that they were opened, beginning with the most recently opened resource file. When the Resource Manager is called upon to get a certain resource, it therefore looks first in the application's resource file and then, if the search isn't successful, in the system resource file, as shown in in Figure 4-5. (Although for simplicity we say that the Resource Manager searches resource files, it actually searches the resource maps that were read into memory, and not the resource files on the disk.)

Understanding this search order makes it easy to share resources among applications and also to override a system resource with a custom resource. A program can redirect the search to start at any file.

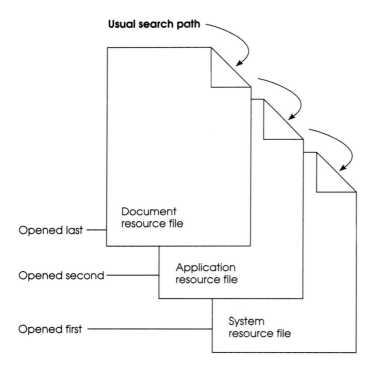

Figure 4-5
Resource file searching

Resource types

The resource type is a sequence of any four characters, printing or nonprinting. To give you an idea of the many ways resources may be used, Table 4-2 lists most of the standard Macintosh resource types. (By convention, resource types are shown enclosed in single quotation marks; the quotation marks are not part of the name.)

Table 4-2
Some standard resource types

Resource type	Meaning
'ALRT'	Alert template
'BNDL'	Bundle (associates files and their icons for the Finder)
'CDEF'	Control definition function
'CNTL'	Control template
'CODE'	Application code segment
'CURS'	Cursor
'DITL'	Item list in a dialog or alert
'DLOG'	Dialog template
'DRVR'	Desk accessory or other device driver
'DSAT'	System error alert table
'FKEY'	Command-Shift-number routine
'FOND'	Font familiy
'FONT'	Font
'FREF'	File reference
'FRSV'	IDs of fonts reserved for system use
'FWID'	Font widths
'ICN#'	Icon list
'ICON'	Icon
'INIT'	Initialization resource
'INTL'	International resource
'MBAR'	Menu bar
'MDEF'	Menu definition procedure
'MENU'	Menu
'NFNT'	Font
'PACK'	Package (RAM-based system software)
'PAT '	QuickDraw pattern (the space is part of the name)
'PAT#'	Pattern list
'PDEF'	Printing code

(continued)

Table 4-2 (continued)
Some standard resource types

Resource type	Meaning
'PICT'	Picture
'PREC'	Print record
'SERD'	RAM Serial Driver
'STR '	String (the space is part of the name)
'STR#'	String list
'WDEF'	Window definition function
'WIND'	Window template

Macintosh II resource types:

'actb'	Alert color table
'dctb'	Dialog color table
'wctb'	Window color table
'cctb'	Control color table
'mctb'	Menu color information table
'mbdf'	Menu bar definition procedure (also in System 4.1)
'crsr'	Color cursor
'pllt'	Color palette resource
'ppat'	Pixel pattern
'cicn'	Color icon
'clut'	Color lookup table
'scrn'	Screen configuration

❖ *Note:* Uppercase and lowercase letters are distinguished in resource types. For example, 'Menu' will not be recognized as the resource type for menus. By convention, new resource types defined by Apple are given lowercase names.

Notice that some of the resources listed above are **templates.** As we explained in the previous chapter, Toolbox objects such as menus and windows are associated with resources that describe their contents (templates) and how they are built (definition procedures). A template is a list of the parameters used to build a Toolbox object; it is not the object itself. For example, a window template contains information specifying the size and location of the window, its title, whether it's visible, and so on. After the Window Manager has used this information to build the window in memory, the template isn't needed again until the next window using that template is created.

Every resource has an ID number, or **resource ID.** The resource ID should be unique within each resource type, but resources of different types may have the same ID.

While most access to resources is read-only, certain applications may want to modify resources.

The system resource file

The **System file,** also known as the system resource file, contains standard resources that are shared by all applications and by the Macintosh Toolbox and Operating System. The System file can be modified by the user with the Installer and Font/DA Mover programs.

Warning

You should not add resources to, or delete resources from, the system resource file directly. Use only the Installer or Font/DA Mover to do so.

Some of the resources in the system resource file, such as the Floating-Point Arithmetic Package and the Chicago 12 font, are also contained in the 128K or 256K ROM. They're duplicated in the system resource file for compatibility with machines that are not equipped with the newer ROMs. For instance, System file version 4.1 and later includes many new features of the 256K ROM that are also compatible with the Macintosh Plus. Other resources, such as fonts, are put in the system resource file because they are too large to be put in ROM.

Table 4-3 shows some of the contents of the system resource file.

Table 4-3
System resources (as of System 4.1)

Resource	Description and owned resources
Standard Macintosh packages and the resources they use:	
'PACK' 0	List Manager Package and standard list definition procedure ('LDEF' 0)
'PACK' 2	Disk Initialization Package and code (resource type 'FMTR') used in formatting disks
'PACK' 3	Standard File Package and resources used to create its alerts and dialogs (resource types 'ALRT', 'DITL', and 'DLOG')
'PACK' 4	Floating-Point Arithmetic Package
'PACK' 5	Transcendental Functions Package
'PACK' 6	International Utilities Package
'PACK' 7	Binary-Decimal Conversion Package
'PACK' 12	Color Picker Package

(continued)

Table 4-3 (continued)
System resources (as of System 4.1)

Resource	Description and owned resources

**Device drivers (Including desk accessories)
and the resources they use:**

'DRVR' 2	.PRINT driver that communicates between the Printing Manager and the printer
'DRVR's 9 and 10	.MPP and .ATP drivers used by AppleTalk
'DRVR' 12	Calculator desk accessory
'DRVR' 13	Alarm Clock desk accessory
'DRVR' 14	Key Caps desk accessory
'DRVR' 15	Control Panel desk accessory and the dialogs, item lists, list definition procedures, and other resources used in displaying its various options
'DRVR' 16	Chooser desk accessory and the dialogs, item lists, list definition procedures, and other resources that it uses (or owns)

Other general resources:

'WDEF', 'MDEF', etc.	Standard definition procedures for creating windows, menus, controls, lists, and so on
'FONT' and 'FOND'	System fonts and font families
'ICON'	System icons
'PTCH'	Code for patching ROM routines (described below)
'INIT'	Initialization resources (described below) used during system startup
'FKEY's 3 and 4	Screen utility resources, which create a MacPaint snapshot of the screen when Command-Shift-3 is pressed and print a screen dump when Command-Shift-4 is pressed
'mcky' and 'MMAP'	Mouse tracking resources, which provide parameters for various mouse tracking setups
'ADBS', 'KMAP', and 'KCHR'	ADB keyboard mapping resources, which implement keyboard mapping in conjunction with the Apple Desktop Bus on the Macintosh SE and Macintosh II. There is a different 'KCHR' resource for each language. Note that 'INIT' resources 1 and 2, which used to handle key translation, now point to the 'ADBS'-'KCHR' system instead.

Patches

For each version of the Macintosh ROM, there are two patch resources (type 'PTCH') that provide updates for ROM routines. At startup, the machine's ROM is checked and the appropriate 'PTCH' resources are installed in the system heap. The 'PTCH' resources are

'PTCH' 0   All ROMS
'PTCH' 105   Original 64K ROM (version $69)
'PTCH' 117   Macintosh Plus ROM (128K ROM, version $75)
'PTCH' 630   Macintosh SE ROM (256K ROM, version $76)
'PTCH' 375   Macintosh II ROM (256K ROM, version $78)

Initialization resources

As indicated in Table 4-2, the system resource file contains **initialization resources** (resource type 'INIT') used during system startup. During startup, 'INIT' resources are loaded into the system heap immediately after patch resources.

Applications should not normally add resources to the system resource file. A mechanism has been provided so that applications can supply code to be executed during system startup by placing the code in a separate file with a file type of 'INIT' or 'RDEV'. A special initialization resource in the System file searches the System Folder of the system startup volume for files of type 'INIT' or 'RDEV'. When it finds such a file, it opens the file, gets all resources in that file of type 'INIT', and executes them.

Resource editing tools

Resources can be put in a resource file with the aid of a resource editor or compiler, or with whatever other tools are provided by a particular development system. You can change the content of a resource or its ID number, name, or other attributes—everything except its type. To modify a resource, you change the resource data or resource map in memory. The change becomes permanent only when you save the file to a disk.

A number of resource editing tools are available from Apple:

☐ ResEdit, an interactive resource editor. ResEdit is very useful for exploring the contents of resource files. Note that ResEdit allows you to change any resource at all, which can have dangerous consequences.

☐ REdit, another interactive editor. Although less comprehensive than ResEdit, REdit is safer and better suited to international localization.

☐ Rez and DeRez, a textually oriented resource compiler and decompiler that run under the Macintosh Programmer's Workshop (MPW).

Various font editors are also available from third parties.

Warning

Changing certain resources in a file can cause unpredictable and disastrous results. Never change the resources in your only copy of a file; always edit a backup copy.

Figure 4-6 illustrates the ResEdit resource editor.

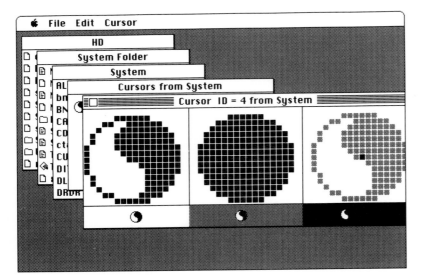

Figure 4-6
Cursor editor from ResEdit

For more information about creating, editing, and decompiling resources, programmers can refer to *Macintosh Programmer's Workshop 2.0 Reference*.

Chapter 5

Macintosh Graphics

Everything on the Macintosh, including text, is presented graphically: there is no separate text mode as there was in earlier types of computers. High-resolution bit-mapped graphics makes possible the graphical user interface of the Macintosh. It also means that characters can be presented in any size or style and are not even limited to alphabetic characters. For instance, a Macintosh program can display Chinese characters almost as easily as it can display English text. The unification of text and graphics also makes it possible to transport text and graphics across applications via the Macintosh Clipboard.

This chapter introduces the graphics capabilities of the Macintosh computers, including color, the use of fonts, non-Roman writing systems (or **scripts**) such as Chinese or Arabic, and printing.

Video principles

The Macintosh uses a high-resolution **bit-mapped** display. That is, in monochrome mode, each bit in a certain part of the computer's memory is displayed as a dot on the screen. With a monochrome display, bits whose value is 0 are displayed as white dots (background), and bits whose value is 1 are displayed as black. The electron beam in the picture tube turns on and off as it scans to create the screen image, turning on or off individual dots on the screen. (In color or gray-scale, the situation is more complex, because more than one bit is required to represent a single color pixel on the screen, as discussed later in the "Color" section of this chapter.)

Because the video display is continually being refreshed (that is, generated over and over), the data being used to generate the display must be available all the time. This means that the computer must have memory set aside for storing the screen data. This area in memory is called the **screen buffer;** it occupies 22K on the Macintosh Plus and the Macintosh SE. A program draws by writing to the screen buffer. On the Macintosh, however, this is not done directly, but through a powerful set of graphics procedures called **QuickDraw.**

The operation of the video hardware is discussed in the "Video" section of Chapter 10.

QuickDraw graphics

The speed and responsiveness of the Macintosh graphical interface are due mainly to the speed of the QuickDraw graphics package, a set of data structures and routines in the Macintosh ROM. As shown in Figure 5-1, the rest of the Toolbox and Operating System rely on QuickDraw for graphical operations. QuickDraw's mathematical model—a global coordinate system that associates points and rectangles with physical pixels on the screen—underlies the entire Macintosh user interface. For instance, mouse-down commands are defined in terms of QuickDraw coordinates within a particular rectangle. In short, everything that happens on the screen is processed through QuickDraw.

QuickDraw not only supports the Macintosh video display, but also provides the means for writing to output devices such as printers. On the Macintosh II, an extended version of QuickDraw, **Color QuickDraw,** provides general support for a wide range of color devices, even allowing a program to draw to multiple display devices at one time. (Color QuickDraw is described at the end of this section.)

The rest of this section is a broad-brushed sketch of QuickDraw's salient features, which are portrayed in grainy detail in the Chapter 6, Volume I, of *Inside Macintosh*.

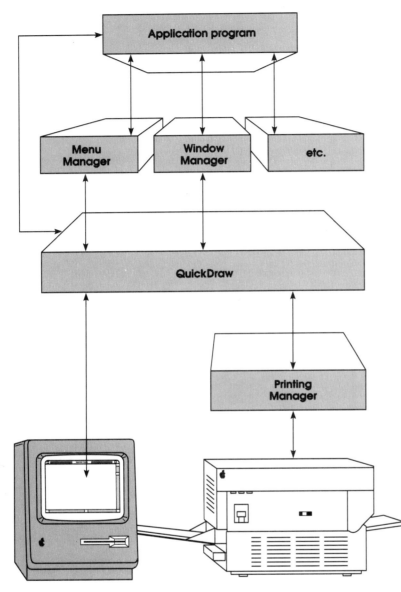

Figure 5-1
Relationship of QuickDraw to other parts of the Toolbox

QuickDraw allows Macintosh programmers to perform complicated graphical operations quickly and easily. Graphical operations include fast interactive graphics, complex yet speedy text displays, and animation. QuickDraw can draw many types of graphic objects, including

☐ text characters in a number of proportionally spaced fonts, with variations that include boldfacing, italicizing, underlining, and outlining of characters

☐ straight lines of any length, width, and pattern

☐ a variety of shapes, including rectangles, rounded-corner rectangles, circles and ovals, and polygons, all either outlined and hollow or filled in with a pattern

☐ arcs of ovals, or wedge-shaped sections filled in with a pattern

☐ any other arbitrary shape or collection of shapes

☐ a picture composed of any combination of the above, drawn with just a single procedure call

Some of these graphic objects are illustrated in Figure 5-2.

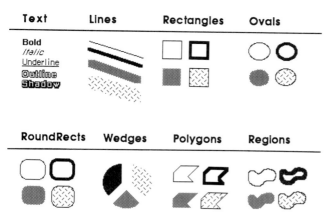

Figure 5-2
Examples of shapes drawn by QuickDraw

QuickDraw can perform the following graphic operations on rectangles, rounded-corner rectangles, ovals, arcs/wedges, regions, and polygons:

☐ *frame*, to outline the shape using the current pen pattern and size

☐ *paint*, to fill the shape using the current pen pattern

☐ *erase*, to erase the shape (actually paints the shape using the current background pattern)

☐ *invert*, to invert the pixels in the shape (that is, black pixels are changed to white and vice versa; in color a pixel is changed to the color defined as its inverse, such as from red to green)

☐ *fill*, to fill the shape with a specified pattern

QuickDraw also has some features that you won't find in many other graphics packages, including:

- **Graphics ports.** An application can define many distinct **ports** on the screen. Each port has its own complete drawing environment—that is, its own coordinate system, drawing location, character set, location on the screen, and so on. Each window, for instance, is a separate graphics port. You can easily switch from one drawing port to another.

- **Clipping.** QuickDraw provides full and complete **clipping** to arbitrary areas, so that drawing will occur only where you want. Each graphics port includes a clipping region which limits where graphics will be drawn. Programmers don't have to worry about accidentally drawing over something else on the screen, or drawing off the screen and trashing memory.

- **Off-screen drawing.** Anything you can draw on the screen, you can also draw into an off-screen buffer. This makes it possible to prepare an image for an output device without disturbing the screen or to prepare a picture and move it onto the screen very quickly.

- **Regions.** Unlike most graphics packages that can manipulate only simple geometric structures, QuickDraw can gather an arbitrary set of points into a structure called a **region** and perform complex yet rapid manipulations and calculations on such structures. A program defines a region by calling routines that draw lines and shapes (and even other regions). A region can consist of one area or many disjoint areas and can even have holes in the middle (see Figure 5-3). A region can be expanded or shrunk, and given any two regions, QuickDraw can find their union, intersection, difference, and **exclusive-OR.** It can also determine whether a given point intersects a region, and so on.

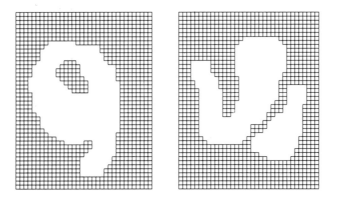

Regions

Figure 5-3
Regions

- **Pictures and polygons.** QuickDraw can also save a sequence of drawing commands and play them back later with a single procedure call. There are two such mechanisms: one for drawing any picture to scale in a specified destination rectangle, and another for drawing polygons.

QuickDraw pictures

QuickDraw pictures are used to record and play back complex drawing sequences. A **picture** in QuickDraw is a transcript of calls to routines that draw something—anything—in a bit image. Pictures make it easy for one program to draw something defined by another program, without knowing the details about what's being drawn.

For each picture, the program must specify a rectangle, called the **picture frame,** that surrounds the picture. When a program later calls the procedure to play back the saved picture, it supplies a destination rectangle. QuickDraw then scales the picture so that its frame is completely aligned with the destination rectangle. Thus, the picture may be expanded or shrunk to fit its destination rectangle. For example, if the picture is a circle inside a square picture frame and the destination rectangle is not square, the picture will be drawn as an oval.

QuickDraw also allows a programmer to intersperse **picture comments** with the definition of a picture. These comments, which are ignored by QuickDraw, can be used to provide additional information about the picture when it's played back. This is especially valuable when pictures are transmitted from one application to another. Programmers can also use picture comments to send commands to the PostScript processor contained in the ROM of the Apple LaserWriter. (**PostScript** is a page description language used to drive the LaserWriter; for details, see the "Printing" section later in this chapter.)

The mathematical model

This section discusses the mathematical foundation of QuickDraw. It introduces some simple data types—the point and the rectangle—that are fundamental to QuickDraw operations.

All information about location or movement is given to QuickDraw in terms of coordinates on a plane. The **coordinate plane** is a two-dimensional grid, 65535 by 65535 in extent, as illustrated in Figure 5-4.

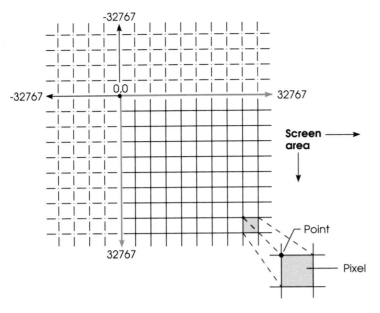

Figure 5-4
The coordinate plane

There are 4,294,836,224 unique **points** on the coordinate plane. Each point is at the intersection of a horizontal grid line and a vertical grid line. As the grid lines are infinitely thin, so a point is infinitely small. Of course, there are many more points on this grid than there are dots on the Macintosh screen. As a programmer using QuickDraw, you associate small parts of the grid with areas on the screen.

Figure 5-4 also shows the relationship between points, grid lines, and **pixels,** the physical dots on the screen. Note that pixels lie between points, not on them. Pixels correspond to bits in memory, as described in the next section.

The coordinate origin (0,0) is in the middle of the grid. Horizontal coordinates increase as you move right from the origin, and vertical coordinates increase as you move down. This is the way both a TV screen and a page of Greco-Roman text are scanned: from the top left to the bottom right. For this reason, the lower-right quadrant of the coordinate plane is ordinarily the quadrant associated with the screen.

Recall that points, rectangles, and regions are all mathematical models rather than actual graphic elements. That is, they're data types that QuickDraw uses for drawing, but they don't actually appear on the screen. Other entities that do have a direct graphic interpretation are the bit image, bit map, pattern, and cursor. The next section describes some of these graphic entities and relates them to the mathematical constructs mentioned above.

Pixels and bits

In the standard monochrome mode, each pixel on the screen represents one bit in a bit image. Extra bits per pixel allow gray scale, smoothing, and color displays.

❖ *Note:* In monochrome mode, *bit* and *pixel* are synonymous if the bit image is the screen (or to be precise, the active screen buffer). This discussion often refers to pixels on the screen where the discussion could apply equally to bits in an off-screen bit image.

Bit images

A **bit image** is a collection of bits in memory that represent a two-dimensional space, as follows. Take a collection of 16-bit words in memory and lay them end to end so that the lowest-numbered word is on the left and the highest-numbered word is on the far right. Then take this array of bits and divide it, on word boundaries, into a number of equal-sized rows. Stack these rows vertically so that the first row is on the top and the last row is on the bottom. The result is a matrix like the one shown in Figure 5-5—rows and columns of bits, with each row containing the same number of bytes. The offset from a byte in one row to the corresponding byte in the next row of the bit image is called the **row width** of that image.

The screen itself is one large visible bit image. On the Macintosh Plus and Macintosh SE, the screen is a 512-by-342 bit image, with a row width of 64 bytes. These 21,888 bytes of memory are displayed as a matrix of 175,104 pixels on the screen, each bit corresponding to a single pixel. If a bit's value is 0, its pixel is white; if the bit's value is 1, the pixel is black.

On the Macintosh II, graphics may be represented by a simple monochrome bit image or by a **pixel image** that conveys additional information for each bit, either color or gray scale. (QuickDraw color models and multiplane bit images are discussed in the "Color" section later in this chapter.)

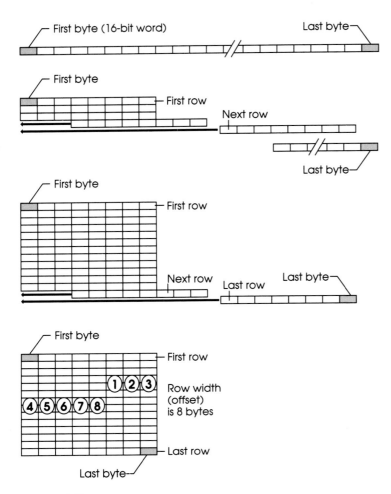

Figure 5-5
A bit image

❖ *Note:* To allow for any version of the Macintosh, programs should never use explicit numbers for screen dimensions. Rather, they should refer to a QuickDraw global variable named screenBits, which gives the correct screen dimensions, whatever version of the Macintosh is being used. Properly written programs will thus work correctly no matter what the screen size.

On the Macintosh, each pixel on the screen is square, and there are 72 pixels per inch in each direction. (The measurement on the screen may not be exactly 72 pixels per inch, but that's the value QuickDraw uses when calculating the size of printed output.)

Although the term *bit map* is generally used in the same sense as bit image, in QuickDraw, **bit map** refers to a QuickDraw data structure that defines a physical bit image in terms of the coordinate plane. A QuickDraw bit map has three parts: a pointer to a bit image, the row width of that image, and a boundary rectangle that gives the bit map both its dimensions and a coordinate system. There can be several bit maps pointing to a single bit image (such as the screen), each imposing a different coordinate system on it. For instance, the dimensions of each graphics port are defined by a bit map, as explained in the next section. (In Color QuickDraw, bit maps have been extended to **pixel maps,** which include a pixel depth—a number of bits per pixel—for representing colors or shades of gray.)

The drawing environment: graphics ports

All graphic operations are performed in **graphics ports.** A graphics port is a complete drawing environment that defines where and how graphic operations will take place. Graphics ports are the structures upon which a program builds windows, which are fundamental to the Macintosh user interface with its overlapping windows. In an application that uses multiple windows, each window is a separate graphics port.

Many graphics ports may be open at once—each one has its own local coordinate system, fill pattern, background pattern, graphics pen, character font, and bit map in which drawing takes place. Programs can instantly switch from one port to another. Besides being used for windows on the screen, graphics ports are used for printing and for off-screen drawing. A graphics port is specified in a QuickDraw data structure of type **grafPort.** A special printing grafPort is used for drawing to a printer.

What a graphics port contains

This section describes some of the information that's included in a grafPort. (In program terms, each of these individual items is a field in a data structure of type grafPort.)

Device information: Each grafPort contains device-specific information that is used by the Font Manager to achieve the best possible results when drawing text in the port. In other words, there may be physical differences in the same font for different output devices in order to ensure the highest-quality printing on the device being used.

Dimensions: The dimensions of a graphics port are defined by a bit map, boundary rectangle, port rectangle, visible region (the area not covered by another window), and clipping region (typically the window's content region minus the scroll bars). Figure 5-6 illustrates a typical case.

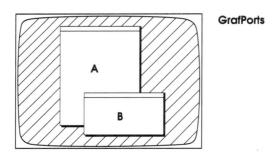

GrafPorts

Boundary rectangle of bit map
for grafPort A

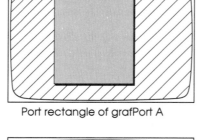

Port rectangle of grafPort A

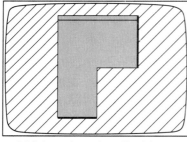

Visible region of grafPort A

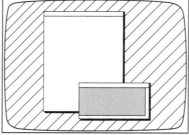

Clipping region of grafPort B

Figure 5-6
GrafPort regions

Pattern: Each port has a background pattern and a fill pattern, as described in the next section.

Graphics pen: Each grafPort has a graphics pen, which is used for drawing lines, shapes, and text. The pen has four characteristics: a location, a size (height and width), a drawing pattern, and a drawing mode. The first three of these elements are illustrated by Figure 5-7.

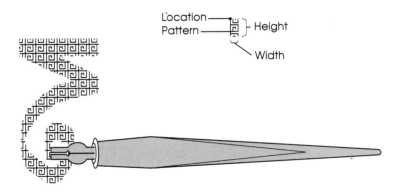

Figure 5-7
A graphics pen

The pen location is the point that defines the top-left corner of the pen; the pen hangs below and to the right of this point. The pen pattern is like the ink in the pen. This pattern, like all other patterns drawn in the grafPort, is always aligned with the port's coordinate system, so that adjacent areas of the same pattern will blend into one continuous pattern.

The pen mode determines how the pen pattern is to affect what's already in the bit image when lines or shapes are drawn. When the pen draws, QuickDraw first determines what bits in the bit image will be affected and finds their corresponding bits in the pattern. It then does a bit-by-bit comparison based on the pen mode, which specifies one of eight Boolean operations to perform. The resulting bit is stored into its proper place in the bit image.

Text characteristics: Each grafPort contains several fields that determine how text will be drawn: the font number, style, and size of characters and how they will be placed in the bit image. QuickDraw can draw characters as quickly and easily as it draws lines and shapes, and in many prepared fonts. **Font** means the complete set of characters of one typeface. The characters may be drawn in any size and **character style** (that is, with stylistic variations such as boldfacing, italics, and underlining). Figure 5-8 shows two characters drawn by QuickDraw and some terms associated with drawing text.

Figure 5-8
QuickDraw characters and some terms associated with drawing text

Text is drawn with the **baseline** positioned at the current pen location.

A font is defined by a collection of images that make up the individual characters of the font. The characters can be of unequal widths, and they're not restricted to their cells: the lower curl of a lowercase *j*, for example, can stretch back under the previous character (typographers call this **kerning**). A font can consist of up to 255 distinct characters, yet not all characters need to be defined in a single font. In addition, each font contains a **missing symbol** to be drawn in case of a request to draw a character that's missing from the font. (For more information about fonts, see the "Fonts" section later in this chapter.)

Color: All grafPorts, both old and new (Color QuickDraw), include information specifying a foreground color and a background color. (This relatively limited color model has been supplanted on the Macintosh II by a new color graphics port, described in the next section.)

GrafPorts also include a number of other miscellaneous fields, described in detail in *Inside Macintosh,* Volumes 1–3.

Color graphics ports

Color QuickDraw on the Macintosh II provides powerful color support via a new data structure called a **color graphics port.** Drawing in a color graphics port works the same way as in a conventional grafPort. All the original QuickDraw commands work in color grafPorts, and the new Color QuickDraw commands work in the original grafPorts. However, the power of the new data structures can only be fully exercised in a color grafPort.

Color ports are generally created indirectly, by opening a color window with the new Window Manager routines. (The earlier Window Manager routines open a regular grafPort by default.) A color grafPort may also be opened when certain resources are used. For instance, when a dialog box uses a 'dctb' (dialog color table) resource, a color grafPort will be opened for that dialog.

The new color grafPort structure is the same size as the old-style grafPort and most of its fields are unchanged. A detailed discussion can be found in the "Color QuickDraw" chapter of *Inside Macintosh*, Volume 5. The Macintosh II color architecture is treated at greater length in the "Color" section later in this chapter.

Some graphic entities: patterns, cursors, and icons

This section describes some of the graphical images used by all applications: patterns, cursors, and icons.

Patterns and cursors are usually stored in a resource file and read in when needed. Each cursor is usually stored as a resource of type 'CURS'. Standard cursors and patterns are available through the global variables provided by QuickDraw or as system resources stored in the system resource file. (QuickDraw itself operates independently of the Resource Manager, so it doesn't contain routines for accessing graphics-related resources.)

Besides patterns and cursors, two other graphic entities that may be stored in resource files are an **icon,** a 32-by-32 bit image that is used to graphically represent an object, concept, or message, and a QuickDraw **picture,** discussed earlier in this chapter.

The idea of a pattern was already introduced in the discussion of a grafPort's graphics pen. A **pattern** is a 64-bit image, organized as an 8-by-8-bit square, that is used to define a repeating design (such as stripes or plaid) or a tone (such as gray). Patterns can be used to draw lines and shapes or to fill areas on the screen.

When a pattern is drawn, it's aligned so that adjacent areas of the same pattern in the same graphics port will blend with it into a single continuous pattern. QuickDraw provides predefined patterns in global variables; any other 64-bit variable or constant can also be used as a pattern.

A **cursor** is a small image that appears on the screen and is controlled by the mouse. It appears only on the screen, never in an off-screen bit image.

❖ *Note:* Macintosh user manuals call this image a *pointer,* since it points to a location on the screen. To avoid confusion with other meanings of pointer in the technical documentation, we use the alternate term *cursor.*

A cursor is defined as a 256-bit image, organized as a 16-by-16-bit square. Figure 5-9 illustrates four cursors.

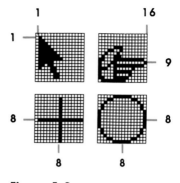

Figure 5-9
Cursors

As defined in a program, a cursor has three elements: a data field that contains the image itself, a mask field that contains information about the screen appearance of each bit of the cursor, and a **hot spot** point that determines the point in the cursor that corresponds with the mouse location.

The appearance of each bit of the 16-by-16-bit square is determined by the corresponding bits in the data and mask and, if the mask bit is 0, by the pixel under the cursor.

The cursor's hot spot aligns a point (*not* a bit) in the image with the mouse location. Whenever you move the mouse, the low-level interrupt-driven mouse routines move the cursor so that its hot spot is aligned with the new mouse location.

QuickDraw supplies a predefined cursor in the global variable named Arrow; this is the standard arrow cursor illustrated in Figure 5-9.

Color

In the Macintosh II hardware, color graphics are supported by slot-based graphics cards of varying capabilities and resolutions. This wide variety is supported in software by an extended version of QuickDraw, called **Color QuickDraw,** together with several other software entities collectively known as the **Color Toolbox.**

As mentioned in Chapter 3, the Window Manager, Menu Manager, Dialog Manager, and Control Manager in the Macintosh II ROM have also been extended to support color.

The Color Toolbox

Color QuickDraw passes its requests for colors to the **Color Manager** software. The Color Manager, in turn, accesses any necessary information on the video card, including a **color lookup table** for translating QuickDraw's color specifications into hardware terms. This process is, for the most part, transparent to the user or application designer. Figure 5-10 portrays the various components involved in producing a color picture on a display device.

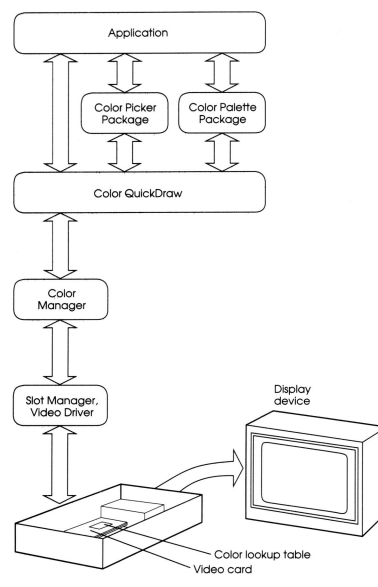

Figure 5-10
Macintosh II Color Toolbox

Color QuickDraw

The main difference between the original QuickDraw and the new Macintosh II ROM version of QuickDraw is enhanced color and gray-scale support. (Limited color support was already present in the original version of QuickDraw.)

Color QuickDraw, like the original version of QuickDraw, exists to provide an environment for drawing to bit maps. Although enhanced color capabilities add a level of complexity to QuickDraw, most QuickDraw functions remain essentially unchanged.

Features that are new to Color QuickDraw include

- a color lookup-table mechanism via the Color Manager (discussed in the next section)
- support for high-resolution and very-high-resolution color
- new data structures such as color pixel maps (a multiple-bit-per-pixel bit map) and color graphics ports
- new QuickDraw calls provided to support color graphics ports
- use of **RGB** (red-green-blue) color space for internal representation (as explained in the next section)
- multiple-color drawing modes, such as replace with transparency, additive, subtractive, maximum and minimum, and average
- support of color output devices such as printers and plotters; gray-scale conversion for the LaserWriter

These features are discussed more fully in the following section.

The Macintosh II provides two models for representing color. The simplest graphics model, used by the original QuickDraw software, represents each pixel on the screen as a single bit in memory. As a single bit can have two values, 0 or 1, a pixel mapped to a single bit can have two values: off or on (white or black on the Macintosh screen). To produce color graphics, more bits per pixel are required. If 2 bits are available per pixel, 2^2 colors can be displayed; with 4 bits per pixel, 2^4 or 16 colors can be displayed; and 8 bits per pixel allow 2^8 or 256 colors. Color QuickDraw is designed to support as many as 48 bits of color information per pixel, providing a theoretical total of 2^{48} colors.

On the Macintosh II, these bits are stored in RAM on a video card rather than in the main memory of the computer. Thus the quality of the graphics depends on the capabilties of the video card. Each pixel will usually have 4 or 8 bits of color data per pixel (that is, 16 or 256 colors), depending on the video card. A color lookup-table mechanism is provided (by the Color Manager) to allow absolute RGB colors to be mapped to the 4- or 8-bit colors actually supported in hardware.

Color principles

The primary colors used in computer graphics—red, blue, and green—are called the **additive primaries.** On a video screen, three kinds of phosphors produce light of the primary colors that add together to produce the desired color.

For color video, a separate signal is generated for each of the primary colors. This approach is called **RGB** (red, green, blue). If the signal for each color has just two states (off and on), the display will have eight possible colors, as follows:

Red	Green	Blue	Result
—	—	—	Black
On	—	—	Red
—	On	—	Green
—	—	On	Blue
On	On	—	Yellow
On	—	On	Magenta
—	On	On	Cyan
On	On	On	White

Such a display requires three bits of memory for each dot on the screen, three times as much as a black-and-white display. Additional bits per pixel make possible more colors; for example, 6 bits per pixel (2 per color) gives 4 possible intensities for each color, for a total of 64 possible colors. To allow for flexibility, the screen buffer on the Macintosh II has been moved onto the video card. On the standard Macintosh II video card, up to eight bits per pixel are provided, allowing for 256 colors.

In Color QuickDraw, colors are represented in terms of **RGB space.** These components can be visualized as a three-dimensional Cartesian space, as shown in Figure 5-11.

Three 16-bit integers may be used to describe a single pixel. The additive RGB color is the sum of the three components. A color is displayed as black if all three components have a value equal to 0, and white if all the components have the maximum value of 65535. Values between these two extremes can be combined to yield all the possible colors for a given device. The Color Picker package allows the user to experiment with the possible color combinations. (This package can also be incorporated into individual applications.)

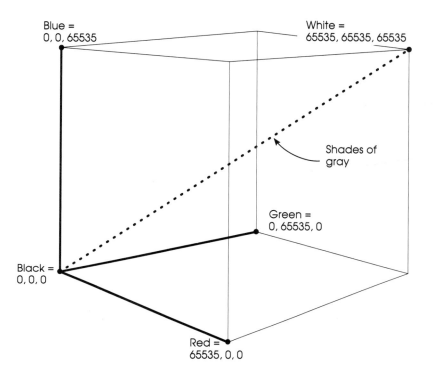

Figure 5-11
RGB space

As we've mentioned, Color QuickDraw supports the definition of as many as 2^{48} colors. The actual colors used for a given application will be a subset of the possible colors. When used with the Macintosh II video card, Color QuickDraw can be used to display up to 256 colors or shades of gray on the screen at once.

Color QuickDraw stores RGB components in a color lookup table, supported by the Color Manager. QuickDraw specifies an **RGB value** (or *absolute* color value) in RGB space. This color is independent of the display device being used. The color table maps this value to a **pixel value** (or *concrete* color value), a representation of the absolute color in terms of the current display device.

The Color Manager performs a color-table lookup by building a table of all possible RGB values. For each position in the table, it selects the closest match available on the current display device. Each drawing routine converts the source and destination pixels to their RGB components, performs an operation or comparison on the components to provide a new RGB value for the destination, and then assigns the destination a pixel value closest to the calculated RGB value.

Fonts

On the Macintosh, text is displayed as graphics. That is, QuickDraw graphics routines actually draw the text on the screen, as described in the previous section. The Macintosh **Font Manager** supports the use of various character fonts by QuickDraw; whenever QuickDraw needs to do anything with text, it requests information from the Font Manager about the characters. The Font Manager performs any necessary calculations and returns the information to QuickDraw, which then draws the characters. The Font Manager may also need to communicate with the device driver of the device on which the characters are being drawn or printed. These interactions are sketched out in Figure 5-12.

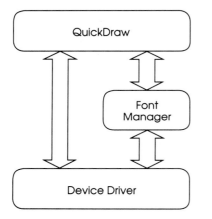

Figure 5-12
Communication between the Font Manager and QuickDraw

A **font** means the complete set of characters of one typeface. Every font has a name (such as *Helvetica*); the font name is what identifies a font in an application's Font menu. Fonts are identified internally by a **font number.**

The size of the characters, called the **font size,** is given in **points.** Here this term doesn't have the same meaning as the "point" that's an intersection of lines on the QuickDraw coordinate plane, but instead it is a typographical term that stands for approximately 1/72 of an inch. The font size measures the distance between the ascent line of one line of text and the ascent line of the next line of single-spaced text (see Figure 5-13). Theoretically, the size may range from 1 point to 127 points. However, the practical font size limit for a full font is about 40 points.

❖ *Note:* The actual font size on a particular output device may be slightly different from what it would be in normal typography. Also be aware that two fonts with the same font size may not actually be the same size on the screen. The font size is more useful for distinguishing different sizes within the same font; this is true even in typography.

Figure 5-13
Font size

The **leading** is the amount of blank space to draw between lines of single-spaced text—that is, the distance between the descent line of one line of text and the ascent line of the next line of text.

Fonts and resources

Fonts are stored as resources in resource files; the Font Manager calls the Resource Manager to read a font into memory. Fonts known to the system are stored in the system resource file (by using the **Font/DA Mover**). Customized fonts may also be included in an application's resource file or even in the resource file for a document. (For a description of resources and resource files, refer to Chapter 4.)

Every size of a font is stored as a separate resource, and any number of sizes of a single font may be stored in a resource file. The resource type for a font is 'FONT' or 'NFNT'.

Font resources contain a separate bit image for every character in the font. For this reason, fonts occupy a large amount of storage: a 12-point font typically occupies about 3K bytes, and a 24-point font, about 10K bytes. Fonts for use on a high-resolution output device such as the LaserWriter can take up four times as much space as that (up to 32K bytes). Fonts are normally purgeable, which means they may be removed from the heap when space is required by the Memory Manager.

In the 64K ROM version of the Font Manager, a font ('FONT' resource) usually doesn't include stylistic variations, such as bold and italic. That is, fonts are defined in the plain style and stylistic variations are applied to them by QuickDraw. For example, the italic style simply slants the plain characters.

In the 128K version of the Macintosh ROM, the definition of a font was broadened to include stylistic variations. That is, a separate font ('NFNT' resource) can be defined for certain stylistic variations of a particular typeface, such as Helvetica or Times. The set of available fonts for a given typeface is known as a **font family.** Font families allow a greater number of fonts than was possible with the 64K ROM version of the Font Manager. They also provide some new features: **fractional character widths** (character widths expressed as fixed-point numbers rather than simple integers), and the option of disabling **font scaling** for improved speed and legibility. (Font scaling is the derivation of a particular font size from a font of another size.)

A font family allows QuickDraw to use an actual font instead of modifying a plain font, thereby improving speed and readability. For example, suppose the user selects a phrase in 12-point Times Roman and chooses the italic style from a menu. QuickDraw asks the Font Manager for an italic Times, and, assuming the proper font resources are available, the Font Manager returns a 12-point Times Italic font. QuickDraw can then draw the phrase from an actual italic font rather than having to slant the plain font. (QuickDraw will still perform the standard stylistic variations if they're not available as actual fonts.)

Intrinsic fonts are fonts whose characteristics are entirely defined in a 'FONT' or 'NFNT' font resource. The plain-style font of any family is an intrinsic font. Other styles may or may not be intrinsic. An intrinsic font can be used by QuickDraw or the LaserWriter without modification. **Derived fonts** are fonts whose characteristics are partially determined by modifying an intrinsic font. A derived font might be one whose characters are scaled from an intrinsic font to achieve a desired size or slanted to achieve an italic style.

As we've stated, information about fonts is stored as resources of type 'FONT' or 'NFNT'. The information about a font family is stored as a resource of type 'FOND'. The 'FOND' resource includes the resource IDs of all the fonts in the family.

❖ *64K ROM note:* The 64K ROM can only handle 'FONT' resources; it ignores resources of type 'NFNT' and 'FOND'.

When QuickDraw requests a font, the Font Manager first looks for a 'FOND' resource matching the ID of the requested font or font family. If it finds one, it searches the family record's **font association table** for an 'NFNT' or 'FONT' resource matching the requested style and size. If it can match the size but not the style, it returns a font that matches as many properties as possible, giving priority first to italic, then to bold. Quickdraw must then add any additional stylistic variations that are needed.

If the Font Manager can't find a 'FOND' resource, it looks for a 'FONT' resource with the requested font number and size. (It doesn't look for a 'NFNT' resource since these occur only in conjunction with 'FOND' resources.)

If the Font Manager cannot find a font for a particular style, the Font Manager and QuickDraw derive a font, as in the 64K ROM version.

❖ *64K ROM note:* In the 64K ROM version of the Font Manager, font numbers are limited to the range 0 to 255. Therefore, only font families with family numbers in this range are recognized by the 64K ROM version of the Font Manager. All fonts with family numbers from 0 through 255 are stored as resources of type 'FONT', so that the 64K ROM's version of the Font Manager can recognize them.

An application can also use the 'NFNT' resource type to mask all but plain fonts from appearing in a font menu. In this way, the system resource file can contain Times, Times Italic, Times Bold, and Times Bold Italic, yet only Times will appear on the Font menu. (The user would choose the Times Italic font by choosing Italic from the Style menu.)

All new fonts have a corresponding 'FOND' resource. A minimal 'FOND' resource can be made for a font by using the Font/DA Mover (version 3.0 or later) to copy the font into a different file that has no font with the same name; the Font/DA Mover will automatically create an appropriate 'FOND' resource. For details, see the Font Manager chapter of Volume 4 of *Inside Macintosh*.

Warning

When a 'FOND' is present, the Font Manager uses it exclusively to determine which fonts are available. Fonts should be added to or deleted from the System file only with a tool like the Font/DA Mover, which correctly updates the 'FOND' as well as the 'FONT' resource.

Font names and numbers

Fonts can be accessed by number as well as name. (A list of font numbers is given in the Font Manager chapters of *Inside Macintosh,* Volumes 1–3, and the *Macintosh Family Toolbox Reference.*) When the Font/DA Mover moves a font or font family into a file in which there's already a font (or font family) with that number (but with a different name), the new font (or font family) is automatically renumbered.

The **system font** (font 0) is so called because it's the font used by the system (for drawing menu titles and commands in menus, for example). The name of the system font is Chicago. The size of text drawn by the system in this font is fixed at 12 points. (Of course, the system font is different when another writing system is used; for example, with the Japanese Interface System, the system font is Kyoto 18.)

The **application font** (font 1) is the font an application will use unless you specify otherwise. Unlike the system font, the application font isn't a separate font but a reference to another font—Geneva, by default. (The application font number is determined by a value that you can set in **parameter RAM;** see "The Control Panel" section of Chapter 6.)

Characters in a font

A font can consist of up to 255 distinct characters. Every character in a font need not be defined. (The standard printing characters on the Macintosh and their ASCII codes are shown in Figure 3-2 in the "Keyboard Events" section of Chapter 3.)

❖ *Note:* Codes $00 through $1F and code $7F are normally nonprinting characters (see the "Keyboard Events" section of Chapter 3 for details).

In addition to its maximum of 255 characters, every font contains a **missing symbol** (□) that's drawn in case of a request to draw a character that's missing from the font.

Font scaling

If a font is needed in a size that's not available as a resource, the Font Manager takes the font in an available size and scales it to the requested size.

The information QuickDraw passes to the Font Manager includes the font size and the scaling factors QuickDraw wants to use. If the requested size isn't available, the Font Manager looks for a font that's twice the size or half the size, and scales that size. If there's no font that's twice or half the size, it looks for any other size and scales it. If the font isn't available in any size at all, the Font Manager uses the application font instead, scaling the font to the size requested. If the application font isn't available, the Font Manager uses the system font as a last resort, scaling it to the size requested.

Figure 5-14 shows the effects of font scaling. Scaling looks best when the scaled size is an even multiple of an available size.

Chicago -- 12 point scaled to 10 point
Chicago -- 12 point scaled to 11 point
Chicago -- 12 point
Chicago -- 12 point scaled to 13 point
Chicago -- 12 point scaled to 14 point
Chicago -- 12 point scaled to 15 point
Chicago -- 12 point scaled to 16 point
Chicago -- 12 point scaled to 17 point
Chicago -- 12 point scaled to 18 point

Figure 5-14
Effects of font scaling

Font scaling can also be disabled by a program (disabled for display on the screen, that is, not on the printer). If the Font Manager can't find a font of the requested size and font scaling is disabled, the Font Manager uses a smaller font closest to the requested size but uses the widths for the *requested* size. Thus, QuickDraw draws the smaller font with the spacing of the larger, requested font. This is generally preferable to font scaling since it's faster and more readable. Also, it accurately mirrors the word spacing and line breaks that the document will have when printed, especially if fractional character widths are used.

Fractional character widths

The use of fractional character widths allows more accurate character placement on high-resolution output devices such as the LaserWriter. Although QuickDraw cannot actually draw a letter 3.5 pixels wide, for instance, the Font Manager can store the locations of characters more accurately than any particular screen can display.

Given exact widths for characters, words, and lines, the LaserWriter can print faster and give better spacing. A price must be paid, however; since screen characters are made up of whole pixels, spacing between characters and words will be uneven as the fractional parts are rounded off. The extent of the distortion depends on the font size relative to the screen resolution.

For further discussion of printer fonts on the LaserWriter, see the section "LaserWriter Fonts" at the end of this chapter.

Format of a font

Each character in a font is defined by bits arranged in rows and columns. This bit arrangement, which is called a **character image,** is the image inside each of the character rectangles, as shown in Figure 5-15.

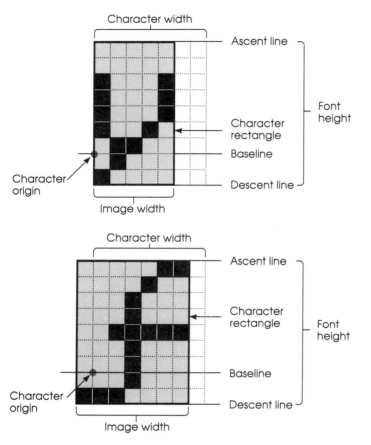

Figure 5-15
Character Images

The **baseline** is a horizontal line coincident with the bottom of each character, excluding descenders. The **character origin** is a point on the baseline used as a reference location for drawing the character. Conceptually, the character origin is the point where the graphics pen starts drawing.

The **character rectangle** is a rectangle enclosing the character image; its sides are defined by the **image width** and the **font height:**

☐ The *image width* is the width of the character image, which varies among characters in the font. It may or may not include space on either side of the character.

☐ The *font height* is the distance from the ascent line to the descent line. The font height is the same for all characters in the font.

The image width is different from the **character width,** which is the distance to move the pen from this character's origin to the next character's origin while drawing. The character width may be 0, in which case the following character will be superimposed onto it (useful for accents, underscores, and so on). Characters whose image width is 0, such as a space, can have a nonzero character width. Characters in a **proportional font** have character widths proportional to their image width, whereas characters in a **fixed-width** font all have the same character width.

Characters can **kern;** that is, they can overlap adjacent characters. The *y* character in Figure 5-15 doesn't kern, but the *f* character kerns left.

Every font has a bit image that contains a complete sequence of all its character images (see Figure 5-16). The number of rows in the bit image is equivalent to the font height. The character images in the font are stored in the bit image as though the characters were laid out horizontally (in ASCII order, by convention) along a common baseline.

Figure 5-16
Partial bit image for a font

Using non-Roman writing systems

Roman writing systems, or **scripts,** are writing systems whose alphabets have evolved from Latin. Non-Roman writing systems, such as Japanese, Chinese, and Arabic, have quite different characteristics. For example, Roman scripts generally have less than 256 characters, whereas the Japanese language utilizes more than 40,000. Characters of Roman scripts are relatively independent of each other, but Arabic characters change form depending on surrounding characters.

The **Script Manager** is a set of extensions to the Macintosh Toolbox and Operating System that enables applications to function correctly with non-Roman writing systems, such as Japanese, Chinese, Korean, Arabic, Hebrew, and Indian scripts, as well as with Roman (or Latin-based) alphabets, such as English, French, and German. The Script Manager provides standard, easy-to-use tools for the sophisticated manipulation of ordinary text and makes it easy to translate an application into another writing system. The Script Manager is built into the ROMs of the Macintosh SE and Macintosh II; it is back-fitted to previous Macintosh models via the system resource file. Script Manager capabilities make the Macintosh the first truly international machine.

Most applications do not need to call the Script Manager routines directly, since they can handle text by means of TextEdit, which functions correctly with the Script Manager. Applications that need to call the Script Manager routines are those that directly manipulate text, such as word processors or programs that parse text.

❖ *Note:* The process of adapting an application to different languages, called **localization,** is made easier if certain principles are kept in mind when the application is written. General guidelines for writing applications that are easy to localize are presented in *Human Interface Guidelines: The Apple Desktop Interface.*

For example, Figure 5-17 shows how the Key Caps desk accessory looks with Arabic script. (This desk accessory is the same for all systems; it automatically displays keyboard characters in the current script system.)

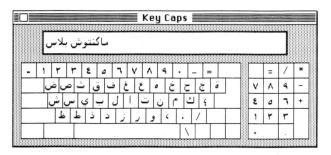

Figure 5-17
Key Caps b'l'arabiyya

The Script Manager is the low-level software that enables Macintosh applications to work with such different scripts. In order for an application to use a particular script, a **script interface system** to support that script must also be present. All the currently available script interface systems are written by Apple. The Macintosh normally uses the Roman script, so the Roman Interface System (RIS) is always present.

At this writing, script interface systems are also available for Japanese, Chinese, Arabic, and Hebrew. The Japanese Interface System (also called KanjiTalk) is based in ROM in machines sold in Japan (otherwise, it is based in RAM). The Kanji ROMs differ from the Macintosh Plus ROMs only in that the Japanese font is built in.

The Script Manager uses established International Standards Organization (ISO) conventions for the representation of Arabic and Hebrew characters.

A script interface system typically provides the following:

☐ fonts for the target language

☐ keyboard mapping tables

☐ special routines to perform character input, conversion, sorting, and text manipulation

☐ a desk accessory utility for system maintenance and control

The Script Manager calls a script interface system to perform specific procedure calls for a given script. Figure 5-18 shows how a typical Script Manager call is passed from an application through the Script Manager to a script interface system and back.

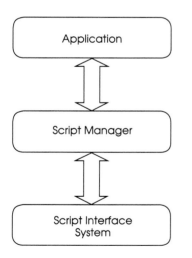

Figure 5-18
How a typical Script Manager call is processed

In many cases the versatility provided by script interface systems allows applications to be localized for non-Roman languages with no change at all to their program code (assuming they were written to permit localization to Roman script). Up to 64 different script interface systems can be installed at one time on the Macintosh, allowing an application to switch back and forth between different scripts. When more than one script interface system is installed, an icon symbolizing the script in use appears at the right side of the menu bar.

The Script Manager provides the functions needed to extend the Macintosh's text manipulation capabilities beyond any implicit assumptions that would limit it to Roman scripts. Some of the limitations that have been overcome are

- **Character set size.** Large character sets, such as Japanese, require two-byte codes for computer storage in place of the one-byte codes that are sufficient for Roman scripts. Script Manager routines permit applications to run without knowing whether one- or two-byte codes are being used.

- **Writing direction.** The Script Manager provides the capability to write from right to left, as required by Arabic, Hebrew, and other languages, and to mix right-to-left and left-to-right directions within lines and blocks of text.

- **Context dependence.** Context dependence means that characters may be modified by the values of preceding and following characters in the input stream. In Arabic, for example, many characters change their form depending on other characters they are next to. Context analysis is usually handled by the appropriate script interface system under the control of the Script Manager.

- **Word demarcation.** Words in Roman scripts are generally delimited by spaces and punctuation marks. In contrast, Japanese scripts may have no word delimiters, so the Script Manager provides a more sophisticated method of finding word boundaries. TextEdit calls may be intercepted by the Script Manager, which calls the appropriate script interface system routines to perform selection, highlighting, dragging, and word wrapping correctly for the current script.

- **Text justification.** Justification (spreading text out to fill a given line width) is usually performed in Roman text by increasing the size of the interword spaces. Arabic, however, inserts extension bar characters between joined characters and widens blank characters to fill any remaining gap. The Script Manager provides routines that take these alternate justification methods into account when drawing, measuring, or selecting text.

For more information about the Script Manager, see Chapter 15 of *Inside Macintosh,* Volume V. The individual script interface systems such as Kanji or Arabic are being distributed through APDA (see Appendix B).

Printing

Because text and graphics are completely integrated, printing from the Macintosh must address many of the same problems presented by writing to the screen. In fact, the same high-level QuickDraw calls are used in both printing and in video display.

The **Printing Manager** is a set of routines and data types that allow a program to use standard QuickDraw routines to print text or graphics on a printer. The Printing Manager calls the Printer Driver, a device driver in RAM.

❖ *Note:* Prior to the 256K ROM, the Printing Manager wasn't in the Macintosh ROM. To access the Printing Manager routines, programmers had to link their applications with a library object file or files provided with a Macintosh development system.

The Printing Manager is designed so that applications don't need to know what kind of printer is connected to the Macintosh; applications call the same printing routines, regardless of the printer. This printer independence is possible because the actual printing code, which is different for different printers, is contained in a separate **printer resource file** on the user's disk. The printer resource file contains a device driver, called the **Printer Driver,** that communicates between the Printing Manager and the printer. When the user chooses a printer, the printer's device driver becomes the active Printer Driver.

The user installs a new printer by making sure the proper printer driver file is present in the System Folder, and by then selecting the printer with the Chooser desk accessory, which gives the Printing Manager a new printer resource file. This process is transparent to applications, and it absolves the application of the need to make assumptions about the printer type.

Figure 5-19 shows the flow of control for printing on the Macintosh.

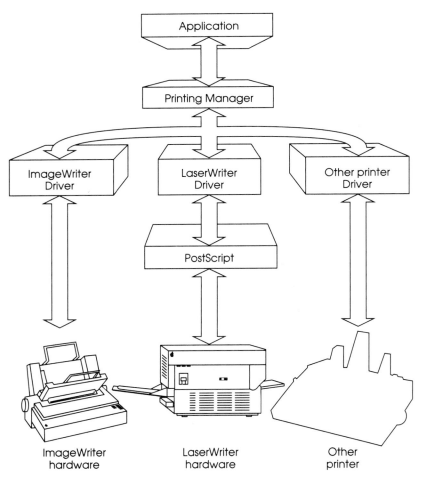

Figure 5-19
Printing overview

The image to be printed is defined in a data structure called a **printing grafPort,** a QuickDraw grafPort with additional fields that customize it for printing. The application prints text and graphics by drawing into the printing port with QuickDraw, just as if it were drawing on the screen. The Printing Manager installs its own versions of QuickDraw's low-level drawing routines in the printing grafPort; higher-level QuickDraw calls drive the printer instead of drawing on the screen.

On the Apple ImageWriter dot-matrix printer, QuickDraw calls are translated directly into a bit image. On the LaserWriter, QuickDraw calls are translated into the PostScript page description language, as described in a following section, "QuickDraw and PostScript."

The Macintosh user prints a document by choosing the Print command from the application's File menu; a dialog then requests information such as the print quality and number of copies. The Page Setup command in the File menu lets the user specify formatting information, such as the page size, that rarely needs to be changed and is saved with the document. The Printing Manager provides applications with two standard dialogs for obtaining page setup and print information. Figure 5-20 shows the standard Print dialog for the LaserWriter.

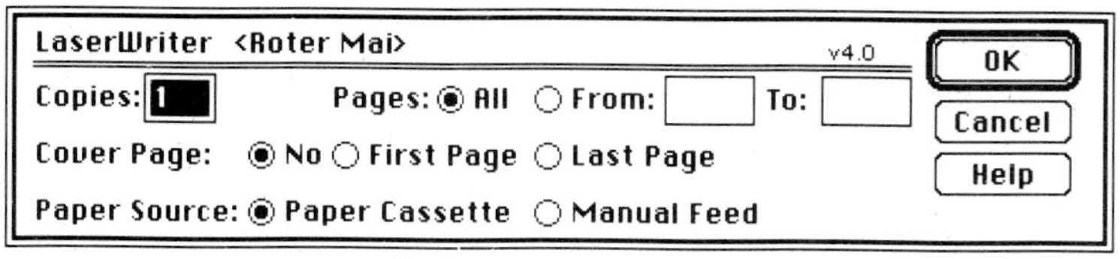

```
┌─────────────────────────────────────────────────────────┐
│ LaserWriter  <Roter Mai>                 v4.0   ┌──────────┐ │
│                                                 │    OK    │ │
│ Copies:[1]        Pages:◉ All  ○ From:[ ] To:[ ]└──────────┘ │
│                                                 ┌──────────┐ │
│ Cover Page:   ◉ No ○ First Page ○ Last Page     │  Cancel  │ │
│                                                 ├──────────┤ │
│ Paper Source:◉ Paper Cassette  ○ Manual Feed    │   Help   │ │
│                                                 └──────────┘ │
└─────────────────────────────────────────────────────────┘
```

Figure 5-20
Example Print dialog

❖ *Note:* Whenever an application saves a document, it may write an appropriate print record in the document's resource file. This lets the document remember its own printing parameters for use the next time it's printed.

The user can also print directly from the Finder by selecting one or more documents and choosing Print from the Finder's File menu. The Print dialog is then applied to all of the documents selected, as discussed in a following section, "Printing from the Finder."

Methods of printing

There are two basic methods of printing documents: immediate printing and deferred printing. **Immediate printing** (sometimes called **draft printing**) means that the document will be printed immediately. **Deferred printing** means that printing may be deferred: the Printing Manager writes out a representation of the document's printed image to a disk file. This information is later converted into a bit image and printed.

These two methods are implemented in different ways for different printers. In immediate printing, QuickDraw calls are converted directly into command codes the printer understands, which are then immediately used to drive the printer.

□ On the ImageWriter, immediate printing is used for printing quick, low-quality drafts of text documents that are printed straight down the page from top to bottom and left to right. On the ImageWriter, deferred printing is used for standard or high-quality printing, which requires more memory.

□ On the LaserWriter, immediate printing is the only method used, and it produces high-quality output. (This typically uses 15K of memory for data and printing code.)

Deferred printing is a two-stage process. First, the Printing Manager **spools** your document; that is, writes out a representation of your document's printed image to a disk file or to memory. This information is then converted into a bit image and printed. Spooling and printing are done in separate stages because of memory considerations. Spooling a document takes only about 3K of memory, but may require large portions of the application's code and data in memory; printing the spooled document typically requires from 20K to 40K for the printing code, buffers, and fonts, but most of the application's code and data are no longer needed. (This use of the term *spooling* should not be confused with spooling to a print server connected over AppleTalk, such as Apple's LaserShare™ spooler.)

❖ *Note:* Spool files can be identified by their file type ('PFIL') and creator ('PSYS'). The internal format of spool files is private to the Printing Manager and may vary from one printer to another. This means that spool files destined for one printer can't be printed on another. In spool files for the ImageWriter, for instance, each page is stored as a QuickDraw picture.

Normally an application's printing code is a separate program segment that is loaded into memory during printing and unloaded when printing is finished (see "The Segment Loader" section of Chapter 7).

Printing from the Finder

The Macintosh user can choose to print from the Finder as well as from within an application. To print a document from the Finder, the user selects the document's icon and chooses the Print command from the File menu. You can select more than one document (by Shift-clicking or dragging) or even a document and an application—for instance, when printing a 'TEXT' file using an application other than its creator.

When the Print command is chosen, the Finder starts up the application and passes information to it indicating that the document is to be printed rather than opened (this is the **Finder information** discussed in Chapter 6). The application must verify that it can print the document before proceeding. It should then call the Print dialog. If the user selected more than one document, the same Print dialog can be applied to all of the documents.

QuickDraw and PostScript

PostScript is an industry-standard page description language used to drive the LaserWriter and LaserWriter Plus. When printing to the LaserWriter, QuickDraw calls are translated into PostScript by the LaserWriter driver. Figure 5-21 shows the relationship between the Macintosh printing software and the LaserWriter.

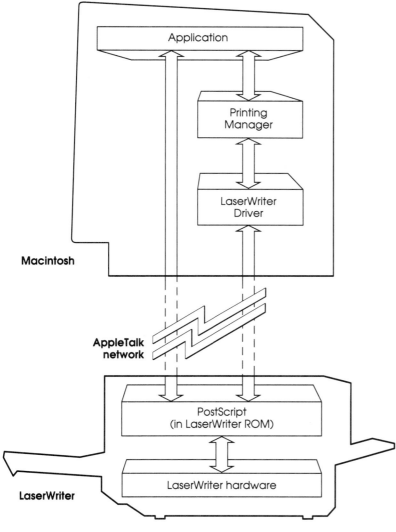

Figure 5-21
Printing on the LaserWriter

PostScript offers many capabilities not present in QuickDraw; it's possible to send PostScript commands directly to the LaserWriter, as explained in the *LaserWriter Reference* manual.

LaserWriter fonts

The resolution of the Macintosh Plus screen is about 72 dots per inch. In contrast, the LaserWriter can print 300 dots per inch. Fonts designed to be displayed on the Macintosh screen are known as **screen fonts;** fonts designed for printing on the LaserWriter are known as **printer fonts.**

Screen fonts are the ordinary Macintosh fonts we've already described; they're defined as bit maps, where a bit image of each character in the font is stored in memory. When the user types a character, each pixel of the character is drawn on the screen as specified by the corresponding bit in memory. The bit-mapped approach works well for a screen display, but storing a bit image for a single font requires about 30K. Enabling the user to freely specify different sizes of characters requires either a bit image for each size or a mechanism for enlarging and reducing bit images. (As indicated earlier in this chapter, both methods are used by the Macintosh.)

LaserWriter printer fonts are not defined as bit images. The image of a character is instead defined as a series of Bézier curves, or B-splines. These curves are stored as mathematical constructs that form the outline of the character. The LaserWriter printer draws this outline and then simply fills it.

This type of character definition has several advantages:

☐ Drawing the image of the character takes much less time than constructing the image from a bit map.

☐ The sizes of the curves are easily reduced or enlarged, producing a clear image of the character, regardless of its size.

☐ Because one definition specifies all sizes of a character, less memory is required to store many sizes of a font.

☐ The definition is device-independent and can be reproduced on any PostScript printer or phototypesetter. The resolution of the output device determines the quality of the printed image.

The LaserWriter has a number of built-in printer font families in its ROM, including several intrinsic bold and italic fonts. In addition, the LaserWriter Plus can use fonts that are downloaded to it. Fonts can be temporarily downloaded either on a per-document basis or permanently downloaded until the printer's power is turned off. The user can have as many downloadable fonts on the printer as the LaserWriter Plus's virtual memory allows. Depending on the size of the downloadable font files, the limit is usually between two and five.

At the beginning of every document, the LaserWriter Printer Driver asks the LaserWriter to list all the fonts it has. The driver stores this information in a temporary font cache. Whenever the driver encounters a new font in a document, it checks this cache. If the desired font is in the cache, the driver switches the printer to that font. If it is not, the driver searches the disk(s) on-line for a font file to download to the printer. If it finds an appropriate printer font, it downloads it to the printer and enters the font name in the cache.

If the driver does not find a printer font, it gets a bit-mapped version of the font and downloads that to the printer. At this point, the differences between screen and printer fonts become painfully obvious. If the user selects a character in a size that is not defined in the screen font's bit map, QuickDraw attempts to resize the character by scaling the font, as discussed earlier in this chapter. This may result in distorted characters, with rough curves and jagged edges. This image is sent to the LaserWriter, which accurately reproduces the bit map on the printed page. Figure 5-22 shows the difference in quality between a true printer font and a bit-map font. As in the case of printer fonts, the font name is entered in the temporary font cache.

36-pt printer font
36-pt scaled bit map

Figure 5-22
Effects of font scaling on the LaserWriter

For more information about printing with the LaserWriter, see the *LaserWriter Reference* manual.

This chapter completes the discussion of the Macintosh User Interface Toolbox and its foundations in resources and graphics. The next chapter describes another aspect of the Macintosh user interface: the RAM-based system software that provides the user's interface to some of the functions of the Operating System.

Chapter 6

System Software

This chapter discusses the RAM-based system software that enables the Macintosh to operate. It begins by describing the contents of the Macintosh System Folder and explaining how the Macintosh may switch between multiple system folders. It then describes the operation of the Finder, the application that is responsible for maintaining the Macintosh desktop and for launching other applications. The chapter concludes by discussing some other applications and desk accessories that perform system utility functions on the Macintosh. The System file, which contains system resources shared by all applications, is discussed separately in Chapter 4, "Resources."

❖ *Note:* The term **system software** is often used in a general sense to include the Toolbox and Operating System—that is, all of the software that makes the Macintosh work. Here the term is used in a more restrictive sense to refer only to the RAM-based software contained in the System Folder.

The System Folder

In order for the Macintosh to start up, it needs certain RAM-based software in addition to the built-in Toolbox and Operating System. This software is located in the **System Folder** on the user's startup disk. (A startup disk, or bootable disk, may be any disk that contains a system folder.)

In particular, the Macintosh requires a startup application for it to run; ordinarily, this application is the Finder. The Macintosh also needs the system resource file (named System) described in Chapter 4. The System file and the Finder are revised much more frequently than the ROM, and the System file contains newer versions of many of the ROM routines (through the patch mechanism, discussed earlier).

It's important to note that the Macintosh System Folder is *universal:* the same System file and Finder are used for all Macintosh computers.

Contents of the System Folder

The System Folder is actually defined as the folder (that is, the directory) containing both a System file and a Finder file. This folder need not be named *System Folder* since the Macintosh uses the first such folder that it encounters—that is, it uses the first folder that contains a System file and a Finder. In searching for such a folder, the Macintosh looks for a startup disk, first in the internal drive, and then in an external hard disk or floppy drive. A setting stored in battery-powered parameter RAM tells the Macintosh which disk is the preferred startup disk. You can change this setting with the Control Panel desk accessory.

The files in the System Folder include the following:

- System file
- Finder file
- Printing resources, including LaserWriter, LaserPrep, ImageWriter, and AppleTalk ImageWriter files
- Files used by desk accessories: Scrapbook File and Note Pad File
- Clipboard File for cutting and pasting across applications
- Control Panel device files: Keyboard, Mouse, and additional files on the Macintosh II (see "The Control Panel" section of this chapter)

The System file and printer files were discussed in previous chapters. The Finder is discussed later in this chapter in the section "The Finder."

Switch-launching: which System Folder is active?

Because more than one version of the system folder may be on-line at one time, it's important to understand how the Macintosh decides which system folder is active. If you launch an application from a disk containing a system folder on a floppy-disk-only system, the Macintosh will normally switch system folders. You can prevent this **switch-launching** by holding down the Option key when you start the application.

Switch-launching is done to optimize the system for users who are running the Macintosh from floppy disks so that the system won't continue asking you to reinsert the original disk. However, switching system folders is generally undesirable if you are running from a hard disk. Version 5.0 and later versions of the Finder *will not* switch launch from a hard disk unless you hold down the Option key.

You may occasionally want to switch system folders in order to use a System file configured with particular fonts or desk accessories or to use a script interface system such as Apple's Kanji Interface System. You can also force the system to switch system folders by holding down the Option and Command keys and double-clicking on the Finder icon in the system folder that you wish to make active.

The Finder

The Finder is the Macintosh application that maintains the desktop and provides the user interface to Operating System functions such as moving, copying, and deleting files, and launching other applications. Figure 6-1 shows the standard Finder screen, the familiar Macintosh desktop.

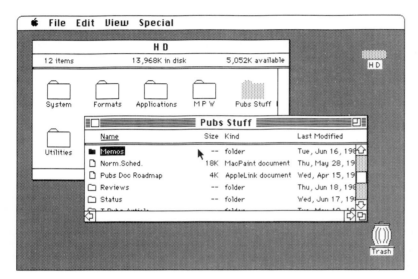

Figure 6-1
The Finder screen

The Finder maintains the graphical desktop and manages files by calling on QuickDraw and the Macintosh File Manager, described in Chapter 8. In order to launch other applications, the Finder must also know which applications are associated with which document files. It does this by maintaining information in an invisible file called the **Desktop file,** described later in this chapter.

As mentioned earlier, the Finder is *not* the Macintosh Operating System; it's only an application. When you launch another application, the standard version of the Finder is no longer present; when you quit from another application, the Finder is relaunched. Ordinarily, the Finder is designated as the **startup application,** that is, the application that takes control when the system is first started up. The user can change the boot-blocks entry that designates the startup application via the Finder's Set Startup menu item. The Finder is also normally designated as the **shell application,** that is, the application that takes control when you quit from another application. (This setting is stored in the *shell* entry of a volume's boot blocks; see "Data Organization on Volumes" in Chapter 8.)

❖ *64K ROM note:* In the original 64K ROM (that is, prior to the hierarchical file system), the user's perceived desktop hierarchy of folders and files is essentially an illusion maintained by the Finder. In the 128K and 256K ROM versions of the File Manager, this hierarchy is recorded in the file directory itself, relieving the Finder of the task of maintaining this information.

Unlike the standard Finder, the MultiFinder option, described below, does remain present while you are running other applications.

Versions of the Finder

The Finder has been revised many times, generally in tandem with the System file. The Finder supports an option called **MiniFinder,** which uses less memory and therefore may be useful on smaller machines. Finder version 6.0 and later support an option called **MultiFinder,** which represents a major step toward the full integration of the variety of Macintosh applications.

MultiFinder

MultiFinder is a virtual multitasking system available as an option in version 6.0 and later versions of the Finder. Like the Switcher (discussed later in this chapter), MultiFinder allows you to have multiple applications open at once, limited only by the computer's available memory. Unlike the case with the Switcher, applications run under MultiFinder can all share the same screen. As shown in Figure 6-2, MultiFinder provides continual access to the Finder, presenting applications within Finder windows. Clicking in an application's window opens that application.

Figure 6-2
The MultiFinder screen

Great care has been taken to introduce the MultiFinder functionality without disturbing the Macintosh programming model. However, as with the Switcher, certain programming techniques will place an application beyond the pale of MultiFinder compatibility. In particular, applications that make assumptions about the size and location of the system and application heaps in memory will not work, because MultiFinder reallocates memory. (See Chapter 7 for more information about memory management.)

Launching an application

From the Finder, the Macintosh user launches an application by selecting and opening the application's resource file itself or by opening a document file that the application created. By selecting the Print command rather than the Open command, it's possible to specify that a file should only be printed. It's also possible to select more than one file to be opened or printed from the Finder; this can be done by Shift-clicking or dragging.

When the Finder starts up an application, it passes along a list of the documents that the user has selected to be printed or opened; this information is called the **Finder information.** It's then up to the application to access the Finder information and open or print the documents selected by the user.

If no documents are listed in the Finder information, the application normally starts up with an empty untitled document on the desktop. If one or more documents are to be opened, the application should open each document (up to its maximum number of documents). If a document can be printed and Print was selected instead of Open, the application should display the standard Print dialog box, print each document, and quit.

Every application is identified to the Finder by a unique resource type called its **signature;** every file also contains two fields called the **file type** and the **creator** field. Signatures and file types identify the relationship between files and the applications that created them; they work together to enable the user to open or print a document from the Finder. A document file's creator field is normally set to the signature of the application that created it. When the user asks the Finder to open or print a file, the Finder starts up the application whose signature is the file's creator and passes the file type to the application along with other identifying information, such as the filename. (Signatures and file types will be explained in more detail in the next section.)

Finder-related resources

This section describes some of the resources that the Finder uses to keep track of the relationships between applications, files, and the Macintosh desktop.

To establish the proper interface with the Finder, every application's resource file must identify the application and provide version information. Most applications also include resources that provide information about icons and files related to the application. A document file must provide information identifying its type and the application that created it.

An application's resource file contains a special resource called the **version data** of the application. The resource type of the version data is actually the application's signature: a unique four-character code identifying the application. The version data itself is typically a string that gives the name, version number, and creation date of the application, but it can in fact be any data at all.

When an application creates a file, it sets two fields in the file's Finder Information: the creator and file type fields. Normally the application sets the creator field to its own signature, so that the Finder will know which application to launch when the file is opened. (The creator '????' is used to indicate files that aren't to be opened or printed from the Finder, as may be the case for certain data files used by applications.) The application sets the file type to a four-character code that identifies the type of file. For example, MPW sets its document files to type 'TEXT' and creator 'MPS '. (Signatures and custom file types must be registered with Macintosh Technical Support to ensure uniqueness.)

For each application that it finds, the Finder copies the application's version data into a resource file named **Desktop.** The Desktop file is where the Finder looks to find out about the application to be opened; this file is described in the section "The Desktop File" later in this chapter.

❖ *Note:* Additional, related resources may be copied into the Desktop file; see the section "Files and Icons" for more information.

File types

An application may create its own special types of files. When the user chooses Open from an application's File menu, the application will display (via the Standard File Package) the names of all files of a specified type or types, regardless of which application created the files. By using a unique file type for its own files, an application can ensure that only the names of those files will be displayed for opening. Some applications will also display all files of a general type, such as 'TEXT' (ASCII files) or 'PICT' (QuickDraw pictures).

The file type for an application itself is always 'APPL'.

Files that consist only of text—a stream of extended ASCII characters, with Return characters at the ends of paragraphs or lines—should be given the standard file type 'TEXT'. This is the type that editors such as MacWrite® or the MPW editor give to text-only files they create. Most applications will accept text-only files, regardless of the file creator. The file's creator field still differentiates various 'TEXT' files so that the proper application will be called to open or print the file when the user requests this from the Finder.

Files and icons

For each application, the Finder needs to know the icon to display on the desktop, if this icon is different from the Finder's default icon for applications (shown in Figure 6-3). If the application creates its own files, the Finder also needs to know the icon to display for each type of file the application creates, if this icon is different from the Finder's default icon for documents.

The Finder learns this information from resources called **file references** ('FREF' resources) in the application's resource file. Each file reference contains two things: a file type, such as we've just discussed, and an ID number that identifies the icon to be displayed for that type of file.

Replication  **Document**

Figure 6-3
The Finder's default Icons

The ID number in a file reference corresponds not to a single icon but to an **icon list** in the application's resource file. As shown in Figure 6-4, the icon list consists of two icons: the actual icon to be displayed on the desktop, and a mask usually consisting of that icon's outline filled with black. (The relationship between a graphic object and its mask is touched on in Chapter 5.)

Icon   **Mask**

Figure 6-4
Icon and mask

A **bundle** (resource type 'BNDL') in the application's resource file binds together all the Finder-related resources. It specifies the application's signature—that is, its version data—together with the resource IDs of the icon lists, and the resource IDs for the file references themselves.

When the Finder first encounters an application, it normally copies the application's version data, bundle, icon lists, and file references from the application's resource file into the invisible Desktop file mentioned earlier. If there are any resource ID conflicts between the icon lists and file references in the application's resource file and those in the Desktop file, the Finder will change those resource IDs in Desktop. The Finder does this same resource copying and ID conflict resolution when you transfer an application to another volume.

The Desktop file

Most of the information used by the Finder is kept in a resource file named Desktop. (To ensure that it won't be tampered with, the Finder doesn't display this file on the Macintosh desktop.)

With nonhierarchical volumes, the Finder enumerates the entire volume; this means that it locates a particular application by scanning through all the file objects in memory. With hierarchical volumes, the Finder searches only open folders, so there's no guarantee that it will see the application. For this reason, the Finder also maintains an **application list** in the Desktop file so that applications can be launched from their documents. For each application in the list, an entry is maintained that includes the name and signature of the application, as well as the directory ID of the folder containing it.

Whenever an application is moved or renamed, its old entry in the application list is removed, and a new entry is added to the top of the list. The list is rebuilt when the Finder rebuilds the desktop; this makes the process of rebuilding the desktop much slower since the entire volume must be scanned.

❖ *Note:* The user can control this search order in the sense that the most recently moved or added applications will be at the top of the list and will be matched first.

The Desktop file ordinarily retains information for every application that has ever been on a disk. On a hard disk, this may result in some congestion over time, slowing down the process of launching an application. You can rebuild a volume's Desktop file by holding down the Command and Option keys when the disk is first mounted.

Note, however, that rebuilding the desktop will remove all Finder Get Info comments. In addition, on 400K nonhierarchical volumes your folders will also be renamed. This results because on 400K nonhierarchical volumes the Desktop file stores some file and folder information in resources known as **file objects** (resources of type 'FOBJ'). On hierarchical volumes, the only file data remaining in the Desktop file are the Get Info comments created via the Finder's Get Info dialog; all the other information about files and folders is maintained by the File Manager. (On nonhierarchical volumes, folders do not represent directories as they do on hierarchical volumes.) For more details about the file system, see the section "Overview of Files and Volumes" in Chapter 8.

System desk accessories

A pair of desk accessories in the system resource file, the **Control Panel** and the **Chooser,** work together so that the user can access peripheral devices such as printers and file servers. The Control Panel is also where the user sets a number of preferences that are stored in the battery-powered **parameter RAM.** On the Macintosh II, the **Color Picker** desk accessory allows the user to select colors for the display.

The Control Panel

The Control Panel desk accessory, pictured in Figure 6-5, controls a variety of software and hardware settings.

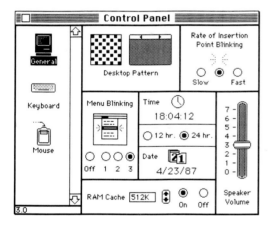

Figure 6-5
The Control Panel window

As of version 4.1 of the System file, a new, extensible Control Panel has been added. As shown in Figure 6-5, a scrollable list of icons appears in the left quarter of the window. Selecting an icon brings up a display of the controls for that icon on the right side of the panel.

Each controllable item is controlled by a Control Panel device resource, called a 'cdev'. Each 'cdev' resource is contained in a separate resource file in the System Folder. The following 'cdev' files are supplied by Apple; they're listed in order of appearance:

General	All Macintosh computers
Color Card	Macintosh II only
Keyboard	All Macintosh computers
Monitors	Macintosh II only
Mouse	All Macintosh computers
Sound	Macintosh II only
Startup Device	Macintosh SE and Macintosh II

When the Control Panel is first brought up, it scans the System Folder for resource files of type 'cdev'. Upon finding a 'cdev' file, it takes the file's icon and name and adds it to the scrollable icon list.

Parameter RAM settings

Various user settings need to be preserved when the Macintosh is off so that they will still be present at the next system startup. This information is kept in parameter RAM, located in the computer's **clock chip,** which is discussed in Chapter 10. The clock chip is powered by a battery when the system is off, thereby preserving all the settings stored in it. You can change most of the values in parameter RAM by using the Control Panel desk accessory.

The date and time setting is also maintained by the clock chip. It's stored as the number of seconds since "antiquity"—midnight January 1, 1904—and is updated every second. (You can set the date and time with the Alarm Clock desk accessory as well as with the Control Panel.)

The default values contained in the parameter RAM are shown in Table 6-1.

Table 6-1
Parameter RAM settings

Parameter	Default value and meaning
Information used by the AppleTalk Manager	
Node ID hint for modem port	0
Node ID hint for printer port	0
Information indicating which device or devices may use each of the serial ports	0 (both ports)
Modem port configuration	9600 baud, 8 data bits, 2 stop bits, no parity*
Printer port configuration	Same as for modem port

(continued)

Table 6-1 (continued)
Parameter RAM settings

Parameter	Default value and meaning
Printer connection: indicates whether the printer (if any) is connected to the printer port (0) or the modem port (1)	0 (printer port)
Alarm setting (in seconds since midnight, January 1, 1904)	0 (midnight, January 1, 1904)
Application font number minus 1	2 (Geneva)[†]
Auto-key threshold: the length of time the key must be held down before it begins to repeat	6 (24 ticks, or sixtieths of a second)
Auto-key rate: the rate of the repeat when a character key is held down	3 (6 ticks)
Speaker volume: ranges from silent (0) to loud (7)	3 (medium)[‡]
Double-click time: the greatest interval between a mouse-up and mouse-down event that would qualify two mouse clicks as a double-click	8 (32 ticks)
Caret-blink time: the interval between blinks of the caret that marks the insertion point in text	8 (32 ticks)
Mouse scaling (described in "The Mouse" section in Chapter 10)	1 (on)
Preferred system startup disk: indicates whether the preferred startup disk is in the internal (0) or the external (1) drive	0 (internal drive)[§]
Menu blink: a value from 0 to 3 designating how many times a menu item will blink when it's chosen	3

[*] These terms are explained in the "Serial Communication" section of Chapter 9.
[†] See the Font Manager chapter of *Inside Macintosh*, Volumes 1–3, for a list of font numbers.
[‡] The speaker volume can also be changed by the Sound Driver, without affecting the setting in parameter RAM, so it's possible for the actual volume to be different from the Control Panel setting.
[§] If there's any problem using the disk in the specified drive, the other drive will be used.

Note that the AppleTalk information that was formerly set by the Control Panel is now set by the Chooser, described in the next section.

The Chooser

The Chooser is a desk accessory that provides a standard interface so that devices can solicit and accept choices from the user. It allows new device drivers to prompt the user for choices such as which serial port to use, which AppleTalk zone to communicate with, and which LaserWriter to use. The Chooser window is pictured in Figure 6-6.

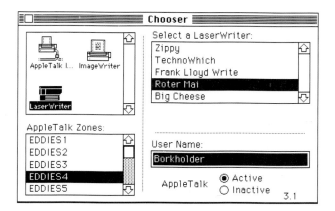

Figure 6-6
The Chooser window

Under the Chooser, each device is represented by a **device resource file** in the System Folder on the user's system startup disk. (This is an extension of the concept of printer resource files, described in Chapter 4.) The Chooser accepts three types of device resource files to identify different kinds of devices:

File type	Device type
'PRES'	Serial printer (including the LaserWriter and ImageWriter)
'PRER'	Nonserial printer
'RDEV'	Other devices

In addition to any actual driver code, each device resource file of type 'PRER' or 'RDEV' contains a set of resources that tells the Chooser how to handle the device. These resources include a device package (resource type 'PACK') that contains the driver code.

Each device type should have a distinctive icon, since this may be the only way that devices are identified in the Chooser's screen display.

Device resource files of type 'PRES' (serial printers) contain only the driver code, without any additional resources. The configuration of such devices is implemented entirely by the Chooser.

The Chooser relies heavily on the List Manager for creating, displaying, and manipulating possible user selections.

Operation of the Chooser

When the user selects the Chooser from the desk accessory menu, the Chooser first searches the System Folder of the startup disk for device resource files (resource files of type 'PRER', 'PRES', or 'RDEV'). For each one that it finds, it opens the file, fetches the device's icon, displays it in the Chooser's window, and closes the file. If the device is an AppleTalk device and AppleTalk is not connected, the Chooser grays the device's icon.

When the user selects a device icon that is not grayed, the Chooser reopens the corresponding device resource file. It then does the following:

□ If the device is type 'PRER' or 'PRES', it sets the current printer type to that device.

□ It labels the device's list box with the string in the resource 'STR ' with an ID of −4091.

□ If the device is a local printer, the Chooser fills its list box with the two icons for the printer port and modem port serial drivers. Later it will record the user's choice (in low memory and parameter RAM).

□ If the device is an AppleTalk device, the Chooser initiates a routine that interrogates the current AppleTalk zone for all devices of the type specified. As responses arrive, the Chooser updates the list box.

□ Whenever the user selects or deselects a device, the Chooser will call the device package with the appropriate message.

When the Chooser is deactivated, it updates the device resource file and flushes the system startup volume.

When the user chooses a different device type icon or closes the Chooser, the Chooser calls the device with the terminate message. After this check, the Chooser closes the device resource file if the device is not the current printer and flushes the system startup volume.

The Color Picker

On the Macintosh II, the Color Picker desk accessory allows applications to present a standard user interface for selecting colors. Once the user chooses a color, the Color Picker returns it to the application, leaving the graphics device in its original state. The application can then do what it likes with the color selection, with as much or as little attention to the available graphics hardware as it deems appropriate. On most hardware, such as Apple's color graphics card, the Color Picker takes advantage of the hardware, displaying the exact color by borrowing a color table entry. (For more information about the color table, see the section "Color" in Chapter 5.)

Figure 6-7 shows the Color Picker window.

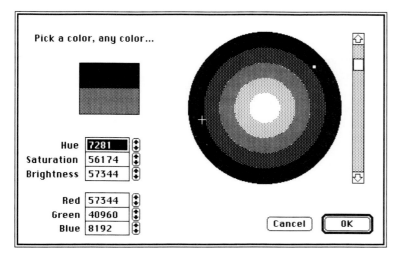

Figure 6-7
Color Picker dialog box

The Color Picker dialog allows the user to pick a color from the entire range that the
hardware can produce. The color wheel allows users to select a given hue and
saturation simultaneously. The center of the wheel is zero saturation (no hue mixed
in); the outer boundary is maximum saturation (pure hues). The scroll bar controls
the brightness of the wheel. The range of the values is 0 to 65535; larger values are
clipped to the maximum after the user exits the field.

The Switcher

Like the new MultiFinder, the Switcher is a program that allows multiple applications
to reside in memory at the same time. The Switcher assumes some of the functions
normally performed by the Finder and Segment Loader (described in the next
chapter), supervising the selection and launching of applications. By thus
interposing itself between applications and the Operating System, the Switcher allows
a number of applications to coexist in memory without the applications being aware
of the difference.

The user launches the Switcher like an application; the Switcher changes the allocation of memory and then launches other applications selected by the user. Figure 6-8 shows the Switcher screen.

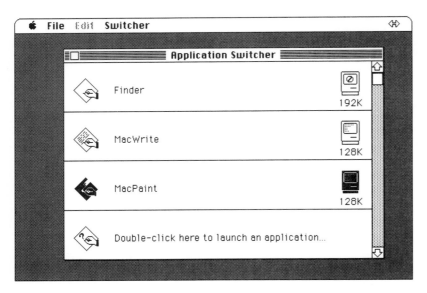

Figure 6-8
Switcher screen

To applications that run under it, the Switcher appears in the guise of a desk accessory. Each application that runs under the Switcher runs normally, as if it were in complete control of the machine, because the Switcher intercepts certain calls to the Operating System so that it can control the allocation of memory to each program.

At installation time, as pictured in Figure 6-8, the Switcher lets you allocate memory space for each application. The Switcher partitions the total Macintosh application space into separate blocks for each application. It gives each application its own small world, creating a separate stack and heap for each. Figure 6-9 shows a memory map of the application space when four applications are running under the Switcher. (The stack and the heap are discussed in the next chapter. You may want to refer to Figure 6-9 again after reading that discussion.)

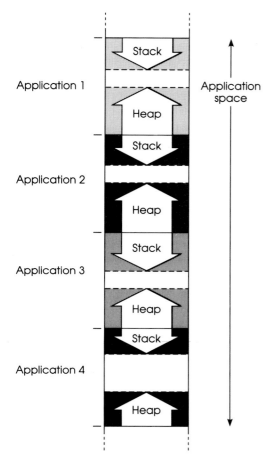

Figure 6-9
Switcher's use of memory

Note that to an individual application, running under the Switcher may be like running on a Macintosh with 128K of RAM, and this can affect performance. (A special 'SIZE' resource allows applications to set their own preferred and minimum memory sizes.) The Switcher works, as it were, with mirrors, and unpredictable things will happen if an application doesn't do things (especially memory management) in the expected way. The wise user will recognize this and save changes more frequently when running under the Switcher than otherwise.

In the last four chapters, we've seen a broad outline of the higher-level parts of the Macintosh system. The next two chapters delve into some important lower-level topics: how the Macintosh Operating System dynamically manages the computer's built-in volatile memory and how it manages disk storage.

Chapter 7

Macintosh Memory

Built-in memory in the Macintosh consists of RAM and ROM. As described in Chapter 2, the Macintosh ROM contains the Macintosh Toolbox and Operating System. Certain devices within the computer also have their own RAM and ROM.

This chapter discusses the organization and management of memory on the Macintosh. On the various Macintosh machines, the amount of RAM memory can range from 128K on the original Macintosh to a theoretical limit of 2 gigabytes on the Macintosh II. The Macintosh **Memory Manager** enables a program to run with any size of memory by dynamically loading pieces of a program into and out of memory and moving them within memory as needed.

Memory organization

RAM is the working memory of the system. Up to 4 megabytes (4 MB) of RAM can be installed on the Macintosh Plus and the Macintosh SE; the standard configuration is 1 MB. As of this writing, up to 8 MB can be accommodated on the Macintosh II main circuit board (the theoretical limit is 128 MB, as higher-density RAMs become available), and more than 2 gigabytes (2 GB) on expansion cards. For information about adding more memory to your machine, see Chapter 10 and the *Macintosh Family Hardware Reference.*

Each time you turn on the computer, the system software does a memory test and determines how much RAM is present in the machine.

The organization of the Macintosh RAM is shown in Figure 7-1.

❖ *Note:* The Macintosh SE memory map is identical to the memory map pictured in Figure 7-1, except that the alternate sound buffer has been eliminated. On the Macintosh II, the sound buffer and screen buffers have been eliminated altogether, as explained below.

High memory

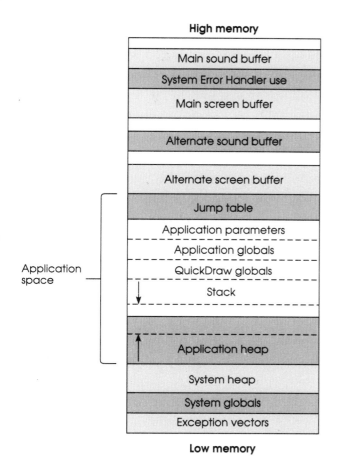

Figure 7-1
Macintosh Plus RAM allocation

The first 256 bytes of RAM (starting from low memory) are used by the MC68000 microprocessor as **exception vectors;** these are the addresses of the routines that gain control whenever an exception such as an interrupt or a trap occurs. (The Macintosh Operating System and Toolbox routines are implemented as 68000 exceptions; interrupts and traps are explained in Chapter 2.)

The next 2K bytes are used for the system global variables, immediately followed by the **system heap,** which contains resources used by the system.

The **application space** is memory available for dynamic allocation by applications. Most of the application space is shared between the **stack** and the **application heap**, with the heap growing forward from the bottom of the space and the stack growing backward from the top. (The stack and the heap are explained in the next section of this chapter.) The remainder of the application space is occupied by QuickDraw's global variables, the application's global variables, and the application's **jump table.** (The jump table is discussed in "The Segment Loader" section of this chapter.)

On the Macintosh Plus and Macintosh SE, the following hardware devices also share the use of RAM with the 68000:

□ The video display, which reads the bit image to be displayed on the Macintosh screen from one of two **screen buffers.** (Note that the alternate screen buffer is only present if it's being used; normally, the application space begins below the main screen buffer.)

□ The sound generator, which reads its information from a **sound buffer.**

□ The disk speed controller for 400K floppy disk drives, which shares its data space with the sound buffer.

The sound buffer is near the top end of the Macintosh RAM. The area between the main screen and sound buffers is used by the **System Error Handler.** Some special applications may also use the alternate screen buffer on the Macintosh Plus and Macintosh SE and the alternate sound buffer on the Macintosh Plus. For more information about these devices, see the discussion of hardware in Chapter 10.

On the Macintosh II, things are done differently (see Figure 7-2). The video interface is through NuBus to a video card, and the video screen buffers do not appear in system RAM. Instead, they are located on a card in the NuBus slot address space, as explained in the "Address Space" section of Chapter 10. Macintosh II sound is also not mapped into RAM: the sound buffer is on the custom Apple Sound Chip rather than in main memory.

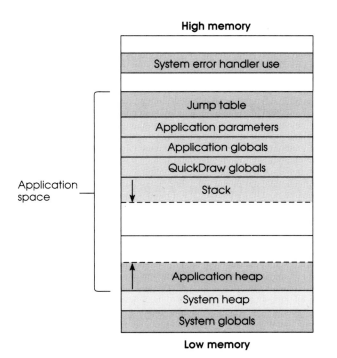

High memory

System error handler use

Jump table
Application parameters
Application globals
QuickDraw globals
Stack

Application heap
System heap
System globals

Low memory

Application space

Figure 7-2
Macintosh II RAM Allocation

Memory addresses and screen size differ on the various Macintoshes. The Macintosh software has been designed to allow a program to run without modification on any Macintosh. To maintain software compatibility across the Macintosh line and to allow for future changes to the hardware, software developers should always use the Toolbox and Operating System routines. For referencing hardware, a set of low-memory global variables is available; by using these variables, a program never needs to use absolute addresses, which would tie it down to a particular machine. (Complete guidelines for software development can be found in the five volumes of *Inside Macintosh.*

When programmers need to use addresses in their code, they specify them as relative offsets from the appropriate global variables. For instance, a global variable named ScrnBase always points to the beginning of the screen buffer in memory, no matter how much memory is installed in the Macintosh—indeed, without the program having to know whether the screen buffer is even in main memory at all. (On the Macintosh II, the RAM for the screen buffer is located on a separate video card.) Of course, writing directly to the screen buffer in this fashion would only be necessary if a program were bypassing QuickDraw for its graphic operations.

Macintosh memory management

Memory management is the allocation and deallocation of objects in memory. These objects may be a program's code, data, or other resources needed by the program or system. Macintosh memory management means that only what is being used needs to be in memory, making it possible for large programs to run on machines with limited memory. (Even on a Macintosh Plus or larger machine, programs may be running in only 128K of memory—for instance, when they are running under the Switcher or with a RAM cache.)

Memory management is one of the most powerful features of the Macintosh system, but it can also be one of the most difficult to program.

The stack and the heap

A running program can dynamically allocate and release memory in two places: the stack or the heap. The **stack** is an area of memory that can grow or shrink at one end while the other end remains fixed, as shown in Figure 7-3. This means that space on the stack is always allocated and released in last-in, first-out (LIFO) order: the last item allocated is always the first to be released. Thus, the allocated area of the stack is always contiguous. Space is released only at the top of the stack, never in the middle, so there can never be any unallocated holes in the stack.

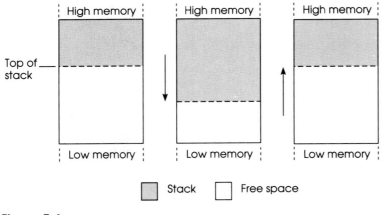

Figure 7-3
The stack

By convention, the stack grows from high toward low memory addresses. The end of the stack that grows and shrinks is usually referred to as the *top* of the stack, even though it's actually at the lower memory address.

When programs in high-level languages declare static variables, such as with the Pascal VAR declaration, those variables are allocated on the stack. The stack is also used by ROM routines for temporary storage.

The LIFO nature of the stack makes it especially convenient for memory allocation connected with the activation and deactivation of routines (procedures and functions). Each time a routine is called, space is allocated for a **stack frame.** The stack frame holds the routine's parameters, local variables, and return address. After the routine is done executing, the stack frame is released, restoring the stack to the state it was in when the routine was called.

In Pascal, for example, all stack management is automatically done by the compiler. When a program calls a routine, the compiler generates code to reserve space for a function result (if necessary), places the parameter values and return address on the stack, and jumps to the routine. The routine can then allocate space on the stack for its own local variables. Before returning, the routine releases the stack space occupied by its local variables, return address, and parameters. If the routine is a Pascal function, it leaves its result on the stack for the calling program. In C, the caller is responsible for cleaning up the stack. For an explanation of the parameter-passing conventions in C and Pascal, see the *Macintosh Programmer's Workshop C 2.0 Reference* and *Macintosh Programmer's Workshop Pascal 2.0 Reference* manuals.

The other method of dynamic memory allocation is from the **heap.** A program's code and resources are all loaded into the heap. System resources are also placed in the heap. The **Memory Manager** is a set of Operating System routines that control the dynamic allocation of memory space in the heap. Using the Memory Manager, a program can maintain one or more independent areas of heap memory (called **heap zones**) and use them to allocate blocks of memory of any desired size. Other parts of the Toolbox also rely on the Memory Manager to allocate space for their own data structures. Heap space is allocated and released only at the program's explicit request, through calls to the Memory Manager.

The Memory Manager always maintains at least two heap zones: a **system heap zone** that's used by the Operating System and an **application heap zone** used by the Toolbox and the application program.

The application heap and the stack share the same area in memory, growing toward each other from opposite ends (see Figure 7-4). Naturally it would be disastrous for either to grow so far that it collides with the other. To help prevent such collisions, the Memory Manager enforces a limit on how far the application heap can grow toward the stack.

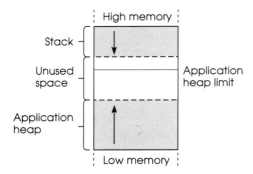

Figure 7-4
The stack and the heap

The application heap limit marks the boundary between the space available for the application heap zone and the space reserved exclusively for the stack. At the start of each application program, the limit is initialized to allow 8K bytes for the stack (16K on a Macintosh II). Notice that the limit applies only to expansion of the *heap;* it has no effect on how far the *stack* can expand. Athough the heap can never expand beyond the limit into space reserved for the stack, there's nothing to prevent the stack from crossing the limit.

Regardless of the setting of the application heap limit, however, the application heap zone is never allowed to grow to closer than within 1K of the current end of the stack. This gives a little extra protection in case the stack is approaching the boundary or has crossed over onto the heap's side, and it allows some safety margin for the stack to expand even further.

To help detect collisions between the stack and the heap, a routine called the *stack sniffer* is run 60 times a second, during the Macintosh's vertical retrace interval. (See "Timing of System Operations" in Chapter 9.) This routine compares the current ends of the stack and the heap and invokes the System Error Handler in case of a collision. In this case, the System Error Handler puts up the bomb box. Although this may not be the happiest result, it's far better than allowing a program to continue with the possibility of permanently corrupting files.

Note that the stack sniffer can't prevent collisions; it can only detect them after the fact. A lot of computation can take place in a sixtieth of a second; in fact, the stack can easily expand into the heap, overwrite it, and then shrink back again before the next activation of the stack sniffer, escaping detection completely. In rare cases, the error may not be detected until a call is made to the trashed section of memory, at which time the computer may appear to bomb "out of a clear blue sky."

How heap space is allocated

The initial size of the system heap zone is determined by the system startup information stored on a volume. Objects in the system heap remain allocated even when one application terminates and another starts up.

A program's code typically resides in the application zone, in space allocated for it by the Segment Loader (introduced in the next section). Similarly, the Resource Manager requests space in the application zone to hold resources it has read into memory from a resource file. Toolbox routines that create new entities such as windows and menus also call the Memory Manager to allocate the space they need in the application zone.

The application heap zone is automatically reinitialized at the start of each new application program, and the previous contents are lost.

Space within a heap zone is divided into contiguous pieces called **blocks.** The blocks in a zone fill it completely: every byte in the zone is part of exactly one block, which may be either **allocated** (reserved for use) or **free** (available for allocation). A block can be of any size, limited only by the size of the heap zone itself.

The Memory Manager does all the necessary housekeeping to keep track of the blocks as they're allocated and released. Unlike stack space, which is always allocated and released in strict last-in, first-out (LIFO) order, blocks in the heap can be allocated and released in any order, according to a program's needs. So instead of growing and shrinking in an orderly way like the stack, the heap tends to become fragmented into a patchwork of allocated and free blocks, as shown in the first part of Figure 7-5.

An allocated block may be **relocatable** or **nonrelocatable.** If all blocks in the heap were nonrelocatable, there would be no way to prevent the heap's free space from becoming fragmented. Because the Memory Manager needs to be able to move blocks around in order to compact the heap, it also uses relocatable blocks.

Relocatable blocks can be moved around within the heap zone to create space for other blocks; nonrelocatable blocks can never be moved. These are permanent properties of a block. If relocatable, a block may be **locked** or **unlocked;** locking a relocatable block prevents it from being moved. If unlocked, a block may be **purgeable** or **unpurgeable.** Making a block purgeable allows the Memory Manager to remove it from the heap zone, if necessary, to make room for another block. A newly allocated relocatable block is initially unlocked and unpurgeable. These attributes can be set and changed as necessary.

The Memory Manager allocates space for relocatable blocks according to a "first fit" strategy: as soon as it finds a free block big enough, it allocates the requested number of bytes from that block.

When the heap becomes fragmented, it may be impossible to satisfy an application's request to allocate a new block of a certain size, even though there's enough free space available, because the space is broken up into blocks smaller than the requested size. If a single free block can't be found that's big enough, the Memory Manager will try to create the needed space by **compacting** the heap: that is, by moving allocated blocks together in order to collect the free space into a single larger block (see Figure 7-5). Only relocatable, unlocked blocks are moved. The compaction continues until either a free block of at least the requested size has been created or the entire heap zone has been compacted.

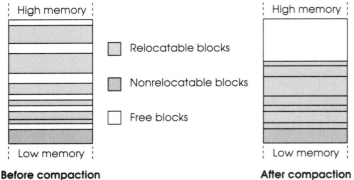

**Before compaction
(fragmented heap)**

After compaction

Figure 7-5
Heap fragmentation and heap compaction

Nonrelocatable blocks (and relocatable ones that are temporarily locked) interfere with the compaction process by forming immovable islands in the heap. This can prevent free blocks from being collected together and lead to fragmentation of the available free space, as shown in the first part of Figure 7-5. To minimize this problem, the Memory Manager tries to keep all the nonrelocatable blocks together at the bottom of the heap zone. When a program allocates a nonrelocatable block, the Memory Manager will try to make room for the new block near the bottom of the heap zone, by moving other blocks upward, by expanding the zone, or by purging blocks from the zone.

If the Memory Manager can't satisfy an allocation request after compacting the entire heap zone, it next tries expanding the zone by the requested number of bytes (rounded up to the nearest 1K bytes).

Next the Memory Manager tries to free space by **purging** blocks from the zone. Only relocatable blocks can be purged, and then only if they're explicitly marked as unlocked and purgeable. Purging a block removes it from its heap zone and frees the space it occupies.

Finally, if all else fails, the Memory Manager calls the **grow-zone function,** if any, for the current heap zone. This is an optional routine that an application can provide to take any last-ditch measures to try to "grow" the zone by freeing some space in it. The grow-zone function can try to create additional free space by purging blocks that were previously marked unpurgeable, unlocking previously locked blocks, and so on. The Memory Manager will call the grow-zone function repeatedly, compacting the heap again after each call, until either it finds the space it's looking for or the grow-zone function has exhausted all possibilities. In the latter case, the Memory Manager will finally give up and report that it's unable to satisfy the allocation request. The application should handle the error and display an error message to the user.

Pointers and handles

Programs refer to relocatable and nonrelocatable blocks in different ways: nonrelocatable blocks by **pointers,** relocatable blocks by **handles** (a pointer to a pointer). When the Memory Manager allocates a new block, it returns a pointer or handle to the contents of the block (not to the block's header) depending on whether the block is nonrelocatable (Figure 7-6) or relocatable (Figure 7-7).

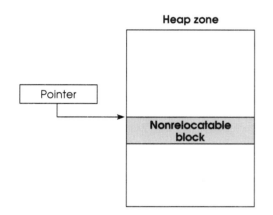

Figure 7-6
A pointer to a nonrelocatable block

A pointer to a nonrelocatable block never changes, since the block itself can't move. A pointer to a relocatable block can change, however, since the block can move. For this reason, the Memory Manager maintains a single nonrelocatable **master pointer** to each relocatable block. The master pointer is created at the same time as the block and is set to point to it. When you allocate a relocatable block, the Memory Manager returns a pointer to the master pointer, called a **handle** to the block (see Figure 7-7). If the Memory Manager moves the block later, it only has to update the master pointer to point to the block's new location.

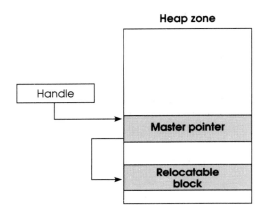

Figure 7-7
A handle to a relocatable block

❖ *Note:* Relocatable blocks are moved only by the Memory Manager, and only at well-defined, predictable times. (For more information, see the Memory Manager chapter of *Inside Macintosh,* Volumes 1–3.)

The Segment Loader

The **Segment Loader** is the part of the Operating System that makes it possible to divide an application's code into several parts, or **segments,** and have only some of them in memory at a time. The Finder starts up an application by calling a Segment Loader routine that loads in the **main segment** (the one containing the main program). Other segments are loaded in automatically when they're needed. An application can call the Segment Loader to have these segments removed from memory when they're no longer needed.

The Segment Loader enables programs to be larger than 32K bytes, the maximum size of a single segment. Also, any code that isn't executed often, such as code for printing, needn't occupy memory when it isn't being used, but can instead be placed in a separate segment that's loaded when needed.

This mechanism may remind you of the resources of an application, which the Resource Manager reads into memory when necessary. An application's segments are in fact stored as resources; their resource type is 'CODE'. A loaded segment has been read into memory by the Resource Manager and locked so that it's neither relocatable nor purgeable. When a segment is unloaded, it's made relocatable and purgeable. However, it's not actually purged until the memory space is needed, as described earlier.

The Segment Loader also provides the routines that programs use to access Finder information about documents that the user has selected to be opened or printed.

In Macintosh programs, entry points to code are not hard-coded into the program. Because segments may be loaded into different locations in memory, dispatching is done via a **jump table** in the system heap.

The loading and unloading of segments is implemented through the application's jump table. The jump table contains one entry for every externally referenced routine in every segment. (An externally referenced routine is a routine called by code in another segment.) If the segment is loaded, the jump-table entry contains code that jumps to the routine. If the segment isn't loaded, the entry contains code that loads the segment.

When a program is constructed, the jump table is created by a utility program called a **linker.**

When an application starts up, its jump table is read in from segment 0, which is the 'CODE' resource with an ID of 0. The Segment Loader then executes the first entry in the jump table, which loads the main segment ('CODE' resource 1) and starts the application.

As we've seen, the Memory Manager dynamically allocates heap memory in cooperation with the Segment Loader, the Resource Manager, and the other parts of the Toolbox that maintain objects in memory. As explained in Chapter 4, resources, such as program segments, are permanently stored in resource files on a disk. Operations on closed files are performed by the Macintosh File Manager, which also contains routines for accessing the information in the data fork of a Macintosh file. The next chapter provides an overview of the Macintosh file system.

Chapter 8

Files and Volumes

This chapter describes file input and output on the Macintosh, normally controlled by the Macintosh **File Manager.** The File Manager controls the exchange of information between a Macintosh application and files on block devices such as disk drives. (Block devices are discussed in the "Devices and Device Drivers" section of Chapter 9.)

The File Manager contains routines used to manipulate volumes and to create and delete entire files. The File Manager also contains routines for reading from and writing to the **data fork** of a Macintosh file. (**Resources,** stored in the resource fork of a file, are accessed differently, through the Resource Manager described in Chapter 4.) This chapter begins by describing volumes and the files contained on them. In addition, the chapter describes some software packages—the Standard File Package and the Disk Initialization Package—which perform other functions with files and volumes.

Overview of files and volumes

A Macintosh **volume** is a piece of storage medium, such as a disk, formatted to contain files. A volume can be an entire disk or only part of a disk. A 3.5-inch Macintosh disk is one volume. Larger storage devices, such as hard disks and file servers, can contain one or many volumes.

As described in Chapter 4, Macintosh files consist of two parts: a resource fork and a data fork. The resource fork consists of indexed chunks of data, called resources, which are accessed by the Macintosh Resource Manager. In contrast, the data fork is an untyped sequence of numbered bytes that are accessed by the File Manager. This section discusses the data fork of a Macintosh file.

❖ *Note:* For simplicity, the term **file** is used instead of *data fork* in this chapter.

Any byte or group of bytes in the sequence composing a file can be accessed individually; that is, a program can read or write data anywhere in a file. The size of a file is limited only by the size of the volume it's on. Every volume contains descriptive information about itself, including information about the files contained on the volume.

Macintosh file systems

The original (64K ROM) version of the File Manager used a **flat file system,** with the file directory organized as a simple, unsorted list of file names. Volumes initialized by the 64K ROM have such a flat file directory. (The 128K ROM and later versions of the File Manager continue to support all operations on flat file directories.)

With the introduction of larger storage devices (several megabytes per volume) containing thousands of files each, the flat file directory became inadequate, since an exhaustive, linear search of all the files is very time-consuming. An important novelty of the 128K Macintosh Plus ROM was a new version of the File Manager that provided a **hierarchical file system (HFS),** significantly speeding up access to large volumes.

The 800K double-sided Macintosh disks always use the hierarchical file system. The single-sided 400K disks usually use the flat file system, but the hierarchical file system may also be placed on 400K disks.

The hierarchical file directory allows a volume to be divided into smaller units known as **directories.** Directories can contain files as well as other directories. Directories contained within directories are known as **subdirectories.**

The hierarchical directory structure matches the user's perceived desktop hierarchy, where **folders** contain files or additional folders. In the 64K ROM version of the File Manager, this desktop hierarchy was essentially an illusion maintained completely by the Finder, at considerable expense. The introduction of an actual hierarchical directory containing subdirectories greatly enhances the performance of the Finder by relieving it of this task. In other words, folders on the desktop are now completely equivalent to directories.

Figure 8-1 illustrates these two ways of organizing the files on a volume.

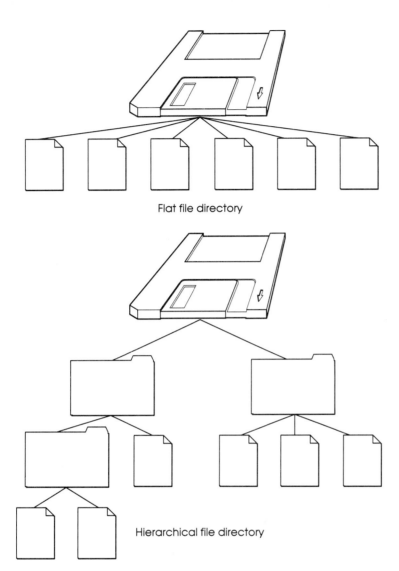

Flat file directory

Hierarchical file directory

Figure 8-1
Flat and hierarchical directories

The Standard File interface

The **Standard File Package** provides applications with the standard user interface for specifying a file to be opened or saved.

Standard Macintosh applications have a File menu from which the user can save and open documents via the Save, Save As, and Open commands. In response to these commands, the application can call the Standard File Package to find out the document name and let the user switch disks if desired. As described below, a dialog box is presented for this purpose (see Figure 8-2).

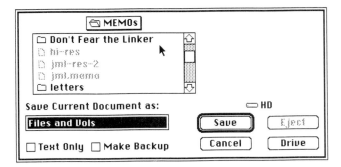

Figure 8-2
A Standard File dialog box

The disk name displayed in the dialog box is the name of the current disk, initially the disk from which the application was started. The user can switch disks by clicking the Drive button, or eject the current disk and insert another, which then becomes the current disk. The Drive button is inactive whenever there's only one disk inserted. Clicking the Drive button (or pressing the Tab key) causes Standard File to cycle through all volumes in drives currently connected to the Macintosh.

When the user selects an application's Open command, the Standard File dialog displays all files of a specified type or types (see "File Types" in Chapter 6.)

If an uninitialized or otherwise unreadable disk is inserted, the Standard File Package calls the Disk Initialization Package to provide the standard user interface for initializing and naming a disk.

The Standard File Package resides in the system resource file. The Standard File Package and the resources it uses are automatically read into memory when one of its routines is called. If a disk is ejected, the Standard File Package loads the Disk Initialization Package into memory, just in case an uninitialized disk is inserted next.

Filenames and pathnames

Volumes, directories, and files all have names. A **volume name** such as a disk name consists of any sequence of 1 to 27 printing characters, excluding colons (:). Filenames and directory names consist of 31 printing characters other than colons. A pathname is a concatenated series of names beginning with a volume name and ending with a directory name or filename. Pathnames are never typed by users except in programming systems such as the Macintosh Programmer's Workshop, but are indicated via a Standard File dialog. You can use uppercase and lowercase letters in names, but the File Manager ignores case when comparing names. It doesn't ignore diacritical marks such as an apostrophe (') or diaeresis (").

Internally, volume names and directory names are followed by a colon (:), to distinguish them from filenames. The colon after a volume name is used only by a program calling File Manager routines and is never seen by the user (except in systems such as MPW).

❖ *Note:* In the 64K ROM version of the File Manager, filenames had a practical limit of 64 characters. For compatibility with newer versions of the File Manager, filenames should never be longer than 31 characters.

Each file is further identified by a **file type** (such as 'TEXT' or 'PICT') and a **creator** (such as 'WORD'). File types and creators are explained in "Launching an Application" in Chapter 6.

Accessing files and volumes

A file can be **open** or **closed.** An application can perform certain operations, such as reading and writing, only on open files. Other operations, such as file deletion, can be performed only on closed files. When a file is opened, the File Manager creates an **access path,** a description of the route to be followed when accessing the file. The access path specifies the volume on which the file is located and the location of the file on the volume. The access path is stored in a **file control block** in memory, as described in the next section.

When an application requests that data be read from a file, the File Manager reads the data from the file and transfers it to the application's **data buffer** in memory. When an application writes data to a file, the File Manager transfers the data from the application's data buffer and writes it to the file.

A volume can be mounted or unmounted. A volume becomes **mounted** when it's inserted in a disk drive and the File Manager reads descriptive information about the volume (the **volume information,** described below) into memory. Only mounted volumes are known to the File Manager, and an application can only access information on mounted volumes. A volume becomes **unmounted** when the File Manager releases the memory used to store the descriptive information.

The number of volumes that can be mounted at one time is limited only by the number of drives attached and available memory. Disk drives connected to the Macintosh are opened when the system starts up, and information describing each is placed in the **drive queue,** a standard Operating System queue. On-line volumes in disk drives can be referred to via the **drive number** of the drive on which the volume is mounted. The internal drive is number 1, the external drive is number 2, and any additional drives connected to the Macintosh will have larger numbers. On a Macintosh SE with two internal drives, the lower internal drive is drive 1 and the upper internal drive is drive 2.

Note that a mounted volume can be **on-line** or **off-line.** That is, a disk may be ejected from a drive without being unmounted: the File Manager still has knowledge of it. (This is necessary for copying disks in a system with only one disk drive.) A mounted volume is on-line as long as the volume buffer and all the descriptive information read from the volume when it was mounted remain in memory (about 1K to 1.5K bytes); it becomes **off-line** when all but a few bytes of descriptive information is released. (The off-line volume will appear as a "ghost" icon on the Macintosh desktop.)

When an application ejects a volume from a drive, the File Manager automatically places the volume off-line. You can access information on on-line volumes immediately, but off-line volumes must be placed on-line (that is, inserted in a drive) before their information can be accessed. Whenever the File Manager needs to access a mounted volume that's been ejected from its drive, the alert box shown in Figure 8-3 is displayed, and the File Manager waits for the user to insert the disk named *volName* into a drive.

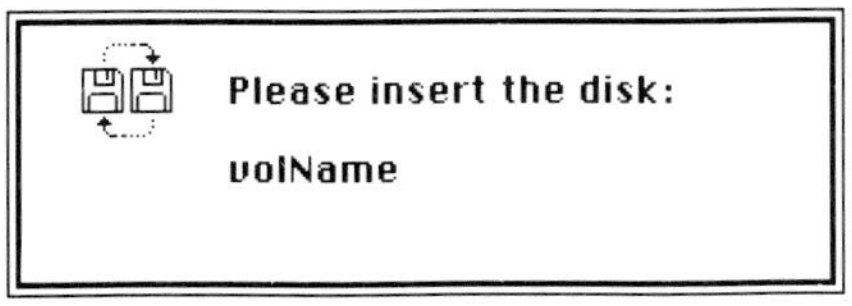

Figure 8-3
Disk-Switch alert box

To prevent spurious disk requests in a two-drive system, it's generally better for the user to unmount off-line volumes. The user can do this by dragging the disk icon to the Trash. Note that an application may itself place a volume off-line.

Volumes and files can be **locked** to prevent them from being written to. Locking a volume involves either setting a software flag on the volume or physically changing some part of the volume (for example, sliding a tab from one position to another on a 3.5-inch disk). This ensures that none of the data on the volume can be changed.

An application can also lock a file to prevent unauthorized writing to it; this ensures that none of the data in it can be changed. This lock is distinct from the user-accessible lock maintained by the Finder's Get Info command, which won't let you rename or delete a locked file but will let you change the data contained in the file.

Data organization on volumes

The information on all block-formatted volumes is organized in **logical blocks,** which contain 512 bytes of standard information (on Macintosh volumes) and some additional information specific to the Disk Driver. (See "The Disk Driver" section at the end of this chapter for more information.)

A Macintosh-initialized volume contains **system startup information** in logical blocks 0 and 1, also known as the volume's **boot blocks** (see Figure 8-4). This information is read in at system startup and consists of certain configurable system parameters, such as the capacity of the event queue, the initial size of the system heap, and the number of open files allowed. Utility programs such as Fedit can be used to modify the system startup blocks on a volume.

Figure 8-4 shows the organization of an 800K (hierarchical) volume; the rest of this section discusses some of the information on a volume that is used by the File Manager. Note that not all of this information applies to flat (nonhierarchical) volumes, which have a simpler organization.

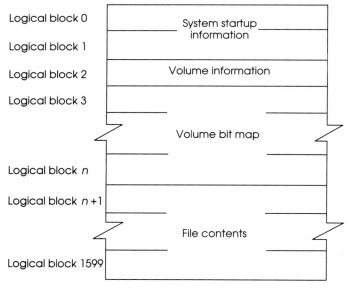

Logical block 0 — System startup information
Logical block 1

Logical block 2 — Volume information
Logical block 3

Volume bit map

Logical block n
Logical block n +1

File contents

Logical block 1599

Figure 8-4
Organization of an 800K volume

Logical block 2 of a volume contains the **volume information** (see Figure 8-4). The volume information includes a number of fields used by the File Manager, such as the volume name and the number of files on the volume. Logical block 3 of a volume begins the **volume bit map,** which records whether each block on the volume is used or unused. The rest of the logical blocks on a volume contain files or garbage, such as parts of deleted files.

The volume information is written on the volume when it's initialized and modified thereafter by the File Manager. Each time a volume is mounted, its volume information is read from it and is used to build a new **volume control block** in the system heap (unless an off-line volume is being remounted). A volume control block is a nonrelocatable block that contains information about the volume, including whether the volume has unsaved changes, the date and time of initialization, date and time of last backup, volume attributes, information describing the file directory, and so forth. The system heap contains a volume control block for each mounted volume. When a volume is unmounted, its volume control block is removed from the volume-control-block queue.

The **volume bit map** has one bit for each allocation block on the volume; if a particular block is in use, its bit is set. On hierarchical volumes, the volume bit map replaces the **volume allocation block map** that was used on flat (non-HFS) volumes. A copy of the volume bit map is also read from each on-line volume and placed in the system heap, and a volume buffer is created in the system heap. When a volume is placed off-line, its buffer and bit map are released.

A **file extent** is a series of contiguous allocation blocks. Ideally, a file would be stored in a single extent. However, except for preallocated or small files, the contents of a file are usually stored in more than one extent on different parts of a volume. With the hierarchical file system, a separate file known as the **extents tree file** contains the locations of files on the volume. The extents tree file records the location and size of the varous extents that comprise a file. Another file, the **catalog tree file,** is responsible for maintaining the hierarchical directory structure; it corresponds in function to the file directory found on non-HFS volumes.

The exact format of the volume information, volume bit map, and the associated files is explained in the File Manager chapter of *Inside Macintosh,* Volume 4.

Each time a file is opened, the file's directory entry is used to build a **file control block** in the **file-control-block buffer** in the system heap, which contains information about all access paths. Each open fork of a file requires one access path. Two additional access paths are used for the system resource file and the application resource file, whose resource forks are always open. On the Macintosh Plus, the normal capacity is 40 file control blocks. The size of the file-control-block buffer is determined by the system startup information stored on a volume.

❖ *Note:* Some of the file information is used by the Finder. File information used by the Finder includes the file's type, creator, location, and information about the file's icon. (See "Finder-related Resources" in Chapter 6.)

Disks and drivers

The File Manager communicates with device drivers that read and write data to devices containing Macintosh-initialized volumes. (Macintosh-initialized volumes are volumes initialized by the Disk Initialization Package.) The actual type of volume and device is unimportant to the File Manager; the only requirements are that the volume was initialized by the Disk Initialization Package and that the device driver is able to communicate via block-level requests.

❖ *Note:* To access files on non-Macintosh volumes, an application must provide its own external file system and volume-initializing program. A properly written external file system can be used with the Macintosh File Manager.

Disk initialization

The Disk Initialization Package initializes disks by way of the Finder's Erase Disk menu item, formatting the disk medium and writing the appropriate file directory structure on the disk. The Disk Initialization Package can format a 3.5-inch disk on either one or both sides, creating a 400K or an 800K volume. It will format other devices, such as hard disks, as well.

❖ *Note:* Original versions of the Disk Initialization Package did not support 800K disks.

The Disk Initialization Package is found in the system resource file. The package and its resources together occupy about 5.3K bytes.

When the HFS version of the File Manager is present, all volumes except the 400K, single-sided disks are automatically given hierarchical file directories. (Even the 400K disks can be given a hierarchical directory if the user holds down the Option key while selecting the Format command.) If the HFS version of the File Manager is not present, all volumes are given flat file directories.

❖ *Note:* With older versions of the Disk Initialization Package, if the user places a double-sided disk into a single-sided drive, an error is returned and the message "This disk is unreadable" is displayed; if the user tries to erase or format a disk that's write-protected, the message "Initialization failed!" is displayed.

With other types of devices, the user can choose to eject the volume or format it with a size determined by the driver.

The Macintosh Disk Driver

The **Disk Driver** is a Macintosh device driver used for storing and retrieving information on Macintosh 3.5-inch disks and on the Apple Hard Disk 20. The Disk Driver does not format disks—that task is accomplished by the Disk Initialization Package.

Information on disks is stored in 512-byte **sectors,** which correspond to the logical blocks known to the File Manager. There are 1600 sectors on a double-sided 800K Macintosh disk, and 800 sectors on a single-sided (400K) disk. Consecutive sectors on a disk are grouped into **tracks.** There are 80 tracks on one 400K Macintosh disk. Track 0 is the outermost and track 79 is the innermost. On 800K double-sided disks, there are also 80 tracks (or *cylinders* as they are sometimes called when information is distributed vertically as well as laterally). However, there are twice as many sectors per track on 800K disks, since sectors for a given track are stored on both sides of the disk.

Macintosh disks are formatted in a manner that allows a more efficient use of disk space than most microcomputer formatting schemes. The tracks on each side are divided into 5 groups of 16 tracks each, and each group of tracks is accessed at a different rotational speed from the other groups. Those at the edge of the disk are accessed at slower rotational speeds than those toward the center, so the linear speed of the media as it passes under the drive head remains constant.

The Disk Driver can read or write data in whole sectors only. When the application specifies the data to be read or written, the Disk Driver automatically calculates which sector to access.

As Figure 8-5 indicates, the 3.5-inch floppy drives on the Macintosh (both internal and external) are accessed via the Disk Driver. Other Macintosh-initialized volumes on Small Computer System Interface (SCSI) devices and other types of devices require their own device drivers. (Although typically used for hard disks, the SCSI bus can be used for a variety of I/O devices. For this reason, the SCSI Manager is discussed separately in the next chapter.)

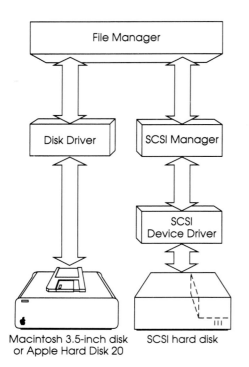

Figure 8-5
Relationship of the File Manager to disk devices

This chapter completes the overview of how data is stored on the Macintosh, both in volatile memory and on a disk. We've also seen an outline of how the File Manager relates to device drivers in order to communicate with various types of disk drives. The next chapter steps back and looks at the use of device drivers in more general terms, discussing the interactions of the Operating System as a whole.

Chapter 9

The Macintosh Operating System

This chapter surveys the components of the Macintosh Operating System, the set of routines that form the bridge between an application and the computer's hardware. Unlike some conventional operating systems, the Macintosh Operating System is not an executable program or set of programs. Rather, it is a decentralized set of routines and data structures, most of which reside in ROM, and many of which rely on other Operating System routines.

Several of the most important Operating System topics—printing, memory management, and file I/O—have already been introduced in previous chapters and are only discussed in passing in this chapter. This chapter begins with a discussion of the remaining I/O topics: device drivers, sound, SCSI, serial, and AppleTalk communication. It wraps up by touching on some other important Operating System topics: numerics support, system startup and shutdown, the timing of system operations, and the treatment of system errors.

Overview of the Operating System

Conventionally, a computer's operating system has been a low-level program that is always resident in memory and includes an interactive monitor mode and various utility routines for handling files, disks, and other I/O functions. In the Macintosh system, the responsibility for keeping things moving has been shifted to the application, which has at its disposal the many routines in the Macintosh ROM.

The Macintosh never runs without an application. On the Macintosh, there is no such thing as an operating-system mode, no sphinx-like system prompt to mutely challenge the user. The modeless design of the Macintosh means that the user is always at the highest level. Although the Finder handles many of the traditional functions of an operating system, it is just another application, and is no longer present when other applications are run. (The MultiFinder, however, does remain active while other applications are running. Like the Switcher, it intercepts some Operating System calls; nevertheless, it is an application and not part of the Operating System.)

As stated above, the Macintosh Operating System is a decentralized set of routines. Because the Operating System is composed of a multitude of ROM routines, there is no simple hierarchy of programs: almost any routine can call any other. Figure 9-1 is one possible view of the rough hierarchy of the parts of the Operating System that are related to I/O functions. At the core is the application, whose contact with the outside world (the user and hardware devices) is mediated through the various software managers, device drivers, and I/O ports.

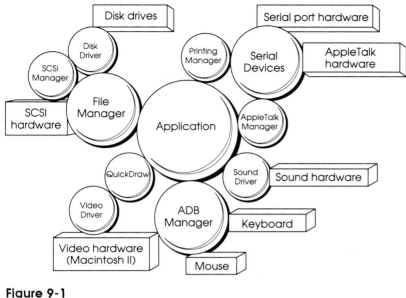

Figure 9-1
Layers of the Operating System

Devices and device drivers

A **device** is a part of the Macintosh or a piece of external equipment that can transfer information into or out of the computer. Macintosh devices include disk drives, I/O ports, and printers.

❖ *Note:* On the Macintosh Plus and Macintosh SE, the display screen is *not* a device in the usual sense: drawing on the screen is handled directly by QuickDraw without the mediation of a device driver. On the Macintosh II, the display screen is a device, because some QuickDraw calls are translated through a video driver.

There are two kinds of devices: **character devices** and **block devices.**

□ A character device is a device such as a serial port or printer that reads or writes a stream of characters, or bytes, one at a time. It can neither skip bytes nor go back to a previous byte. Character devices are used to communicate with the world outside the computer's operating system and memory. A character device can be an input device, an output device, or an input/output device.

□ Block devices, such as disk drives, read and write entire blocks of bytes at a time. A block device can read or write any accessible block on demand. Block devices are usually used to store and retrieve information.

Applications communicate with devices through a set of routines called the **Device Manager.** Applications may talk to devices directly through the Device Manager or indirectly, through another part of the Operating System or Toolbox, which in turn calls the Device Manager. For example, an application can communicate with a disk drive directly by means of Device Manager calls or indirectly by calling the File Manager.

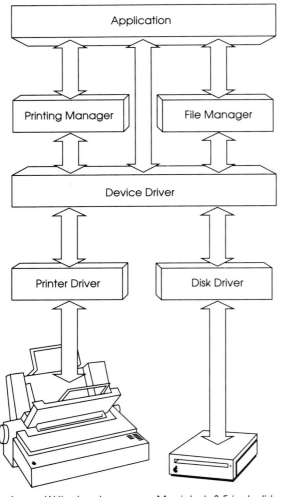

Figure 9-2
Example of communication with devices

The Device Manager doesn't manipulate devices directly; it calls **device drivers** that do (see Figure 9-2). Device drivers are programs that take data coming from the Device Manager and convert them into actions by the device, or convert device actions into data for the Device Manager to process. This arrangement provides a standard interface to higher-level parts of the software, making it possible for one general set of calls to drive a variety of hardware devices.

The Operating System includes the following standard device drivers in ROM:

☐ the Disk Driver, for reading and writing to Macintosh disks

☐ the Sound Driver, for generating sound on the Macintosh Plus and Macintosh SE

☐ the Serial Driver, for controlling serial I/O through the Modem and Printer ports

There are also a number of standard RAM drivers, including

☐ the printer drivers

☐ the AppleTalk drivers

☐ desk accessories

RAM drivers are resources and are read from the system resource file as needed. The resource type for drivers is 'DRVR'. The resource name is the driver name. (By convention, driver names always begin with a period.) Desk accessories are a special type of device driver and are manipulated via the routines of the Desk Manager.

A programmer can add other drivers independently or build on the existing drivers. For example, the Printer Driver is built on the Serial Driver. (Note that drivers are usually written in assembly language.)

A device driver can be either **open** or **closed.** The Sound Driver and Disk Driver are opened when the system starts up; other drivers are opened at the specific request of an application. After a driver has been opened, an application can read data from and write data to it. The application can close device drivers that aren't in use and recover the memory they were using.

Upcoming sections of this chapter discuss input and output via the Sound Driver and Sound Manager, the Serial Driver, the SCSI Manager, and the AppleTalk Manager. (Some device drivers have already been discussed in previous chapters. Printer drivers and Macintosh II video drivers were discussed in Chapter 5, and the Disk Driver was discussed in Chapter 8.)

Sound

Prior to the introduction of the Macintosh II, sound generation on the Macintosh was controlled by the Macintosh **Sound Driver.** A new **Sound Manager** on the Macintosh II replaces the Sound Driver, providing additional functionality.

The Macintosh Sound Driver

The Sound Driver is a device driver in the ROM of the Macintosh Plus and the Macintosh SE that is used to synthesize sound and music in a Macintosh application. The sound driver contains three different **sound synthesizers** that enable it to generate sounds characterized by any kind of waveform:

- The **four-tone synthesizer** is used to make simple musical tones, with up to four voices producing sound simultaneously. It requires about 50 percent of the microprocessor's attention during the time the sound is being produced.

- The **square-wave synthesizer** is used to produce less musical sounds, such as beeps. It requires about 2 percent of the processor's time.

- The **free-form synthesizer** is used to make complex music and speech. It requires about 20 percent of the processor's time.

Figure 9-3 depicts the waveform of a typical sound wave and the terms used to describe it.

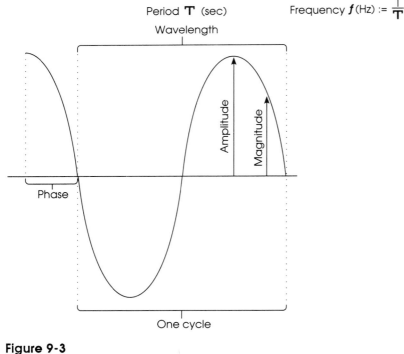

Figure 9-3
Waveform

The **magnitude** is the vertical distance between any given point on the wave and the horizontal line about which the wave oscillates; you can think of the magnitude as the volume level. The **amplitude** is the maximum magnitude of a periodic wave. The **wavelength** is the horizontal extent of one complete cycle of the wave. Magnitude and wavelength can be measured in any unit of distance. The **period** is the time elapsed during one complete cycle of a wave. The **frequency** is the reciprocal of the period, or the number of cycles per second, which is also called *hertz (Hz)*. The **phase** is some fraction of a wave cycle (measured from a fixed point on the wave).

There are many different types of waveforms, three of which are depicted in Figure 9-4. *Sine waves* are generated by objects that oscillate at a single frequency (such as a tuning fork). *Square waves* are generated by objects that toggle instantly between two states at a single frequency (such as an electronic beep). *Free-form waves,* the most common of all, are generated by objects that vibrate at rapidly changing frequencies with rapidly changing magnitudes (such as your vocal cords).

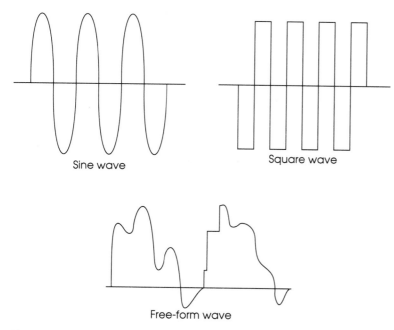

Sine wave

Square wave

Free-form wave

Figure 9-4
Types of waveforms

The Sound Driver represents waveforms digitally, so all waveforms must be converted from their analog representation to a digital representation. A digital representation of a waveform is simply a sequence of wave magnitudes measured at fixed intervals. This sequence of magnitudes is stored in the Sound Driver as a sequence of bytes, each one of which specifies an instantaneous voltage to be sent to the speaker. The bytes are stored in a **waveform description,** contained in a data structure called a **synthesizer buffer.** A synthesizer buffer contains the duration, pitch, phase, and waveform of the sound the synthesizer will generate. The exact structure of a synthesizer buffer differs for each type of synthesizer being used.

The four-tone synthesizer is used to produce harmonic sounds such as music. It can simultaneously generate four different sounds, each with its own frequency, phase, and waveform.

The free-form synthesizer is used to synthesize complex music and speech. The sound to be produced is represented as a single waveform whose complexity and length are limited only by available memory.

The Macintosh II Sound Manager

On the Macintosh II, the Sound Manager replaces the original Sound Driver. While supporting the old Sound Driver routines and synthesizers, the Sound Manager offers more flexibility and new features, and requires less programming effort.

A major advantage of the Sound Manager is that sounds and music can be created independent of the particular hardware used to play them. In addition, the Sound Manager synthesizers, utilizing the power of the new Apple Sound Chip, use much less of the MC68020's processing time.

Another innovation is the introduction of resource types for sounds and synthesizers, providing simple, portable solutions for incorporating sound into any application. The Sound Manager supports two new resource types: 'snth' and 'snd ':

□ A 'snd ' resource can describe a sound to be played, an instrument, or both, making it possible to produce sounds, music, and even speech by calling a single procedure. Creating sound resources requires some understanding of sound theory; using these resources, however, requires no more than passing the resource ID.

□ The 'snth' resources contain the executable code for synthesizers and, in some cases, modifiers (described in the next section).

The MIDI synthesizer provides all the functionality of the current MIDI specification. The Musical Instrument Data Interface is a worldwide standard for controlling music synthesizers. It allows synthesizers to be played remotely (from a computer or another synthesizer). In addition, many parameters of a synthesizer can be altered and controlled in real time. Each Sound Manager channel that uses the MIDI synthesizer corresponds to 1 of the 16 MIDI channels.

Sound Manager synthesizers

With the Sound Manager, sound is produced by sending commands to synthesizers via channels. A Sound Manager synthesizer is like a device driver. A **channel** is a queue that's used to pass commands to a particular synthesizer. To produce complex sounds like music and speech, an application must generate multiple sounds at the same time; for this reason, multiple channels can be created. Commands are placed one after another into the channel. At the other end, they're taken from the channel one at a time, processed by the synthesizer, and played on the hardware associated with that synthesizer. If three channels are open, the synthesizer will receive three commands at a time, process them, and produce the three sounds simultaneously.

There are four standard synthesizers available with the Sound Manager; each is capable of producing its own type of sound and providing different degrees of expressive control:

- □ The **note synthesizer** lets you generate simple melodies and informative sounds such as error warnings. (The note synthesizer is functionally equivalent to the old square-wave synthesizer.) The melody must be monophonic; that is, only one note can play at a time. Each note has the attributes of frequency, amplitude, and duration. At any time in a melody, the timbre can be changed to one of several different sounds.

- □ The **wave-table synthesizer** produces more complex sounds and multipart music. (Using the old four-tone synthesizer results in four channels of wave-table synthesis.) The wave-table synthesizer plays out monophonic or polyphonic sounds using wave-table lookup synthesis. Polyphony can be achieved with several monophonic channels or one polyphonic channel.

- □ The **MIDI synthesizer** provides a way to play out music on an external synthesizer via a Musical Instrument Data Interface (MIDI) adapter connected to one of the serial ports. This synthesizer can be polyphonic if the external synthesizer allows it.

- □ The **sampled-sound synthesizer** plays out prerecorded or precomputed sounds. The sounds are passed to the synthesizer in buffers containing samples of the sound to be played. (The sampled-sound synthesizer is functionally equivalent to the old free-form synthesizer.) The buffers can be played out at either the original sampling rate or at higher or lower rates, effecting the same pitch, a higher pitch, or a lower pitch, respectively. The rate can be changed over time.

A basic set of commands is understood by all four synthesizers; these commands produce similar results within the limits of the particular synthesizers. All four synthesizers ignore commands that they don't understand.

An enormous range of sounds is possible with this synthesizer. The results depend largely on the external equipment and its current state. This also means that it's possible that the sound will be incomprehensible or that no sound will result at all if the equipment is set to an unexpected state.

A synthesizer is a complex piece of software that's not easily modified. For this reason, the Sound Manager provides hooks for smaller routines, called **modifiers,** which can process commands as they pass through a channel. Figure 9-5 shows the entire path a command might take from an application to the Sound Manager.

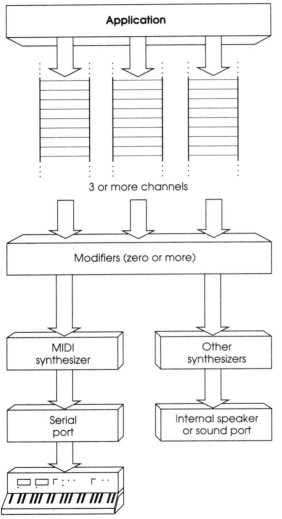

Figure 9-5
Path of a Sound Manager command

The SCSI bus

The **Small Computer System Interface** (SCSI, or "scuzzy" in daily parlance) is an industry-standard specification, based on the ANSI X3T9.2/82-2 draft proposal, of a set of mechanical, electrical, and functional standards for connecting small computers with intelligent peripherals, such as hard disks, tape drives, high-speed line printers, and optical disks. The **SCSI Manager** provides routines and data structures for controlling the exchange of information between a Macintosh and peripheral devices connected to a SCSI bus.

In addition to the Macintosh itself, up to seven devices can be connected in a daisy-chain configuration to a SCSI bus.

When two SCSI devices communicate with each other, one acts as the **initiator** and the other as the **target.** The initiator asks the target to perform a certain operation, such as reading a block of data. A SCSI device typically has a fixed role as an initiator or target; for instance, the Macintosh always acts as initiator to one or more peripherals, such as hard disks, that act as targets. There may also be intelligent peripherals capable of acting as initiators. Multiple initiators and multiple targets are allowed on a SCSI bus, but only one Macintosh computer can be connected to a SCSI bus at a time.

Each device on the bus has a unique ID, which is an integer from 0 to 7. The Macintosh always has an ID of 7; an internal SCSI hard disk on the Macintosh SE or Macintosh II is given ID 0; peripheral devices should use other numbers.

At any given time, the Apple SCSI bus is in one of seven phases:

- **Bus-free phase.** When no SCSI device is actively using the bus, the bus is in the bus-free phase.

- **Arbitration phase.** Since there may be multiple initiators on the bus, an initiator must first gain control of the bus; this process is called the *arbitration phase.* If more than one initiator arbitrates for use of the bus at the same time, the initiator with the higher ID gains control first. Once an initiator, regardless of ID, gains control of the bus, no other device can interrupt that session.

- **Selection phase.** Once the initiator has gained control of the bus, it selects the target device that will be asked to perform a certain operation. This phase, known as the *selection phase,* includes an acknowledgment from the target that it has been selected. (In the event that the target suspends the communication, an optional reselection phase lets the target reconnect to the initiator.)

- **Command phase.** In the command phase, the initiator tells the target what operation to perform.

- **Data phase.** This is when the actual transfer of data between initiator and target takes place.

- **Status and message phases.** When the data transfer is completed, the target sends two completion bytes. The first byte contains status information and the second contains a message.

A typical communication might involve a Macintosh requesting a block of data to be read from a hard disk connected to a SCSI bus. The Macintosh waits for a bus-free phase to occur and then arbitrates for use of the bus. It selects the hard disk as target and sends the command for the read operation. The hard disk transfers the requested data back to the Macintosh and completes the session by sending the status and message bytes.

At system startup time, the Macintosh loads the driver for each SCSI device. The system startup procedure first tries to select the target device on the bus having the highest ID, beginning with the device having an ID of 6. After finding the driver and reading it into the system heap, it calls the driver and checks the device having the next lower ID on the bus. As of System file version 4.1, the user can use the Control Panel to choose which SCSI device is the default startup device.

Each SCSI device must have certain data structures in the first two physical blocks to identify its device driver (or drivers) and to describe the allocation of blocks on the device for different partitions or operating systems. The drivers themselves can be located anywhere else on the device and can be as large as necessary.

On the Macintosh SE and Macintosh II, the SCSI Manager supports hardware handshaking for much faster access times.

Serial communication

The Macintosh **Serial Driver** is a device driver in ROM for handling serial communication. The Serial Driver allows Macintosh applications to communicate with serial devices via the two serial ports on the back of the Macintosh. The Serial Driver supports other device drivers such as the Printer Driver and the AppleTalk drivers.

❖ *64K ROM note:* Previous to the 128K ROM, there were two serial drivers: one in ROM and one in RAM. If the 128K (or 256K) ROM is present, the new driver is automatically substituted for the old ones.

The Serial Driver supports full-duplex asynchronous serial communication. **Serial data** is transmitted over a single-path communication line, one bit at a time (as opposed to parallel data, which is transmitted over a multiple-path communication line, multiple bits at a time). **Full-duplex communication** means that the Macintosh and another serial device connected to it can transmit data simultaneously (as opposed to half-duplex operation, in which data can be transmitted by only one device at a time). **Asynchronous communication** means that the Macintosh and other serial devices communicating with it don't share a common timer, and no timing data is transmitted. The time interval between characters transmitted asynchronously can be of any length.

When a transmitting serial device is not sending data, it maintains the transmission line in the idle state, as shown in Figure 9-6. The transmitting device may begin sending a character at any time by sending a **start bit.** The start bit tells the receiving device to prepare to receive a character. The transmitting device then transmits 5, 6, 7, or 8 **data bits,** optionally followed by a **parity bit** for error checking. The value of the parity bit is chosen such that the number of 1's among the data and parity bits is even or odd, depending on whether the parity is even or odd. Finally, the transmitting device sends 1, 1.5, or 2 **stop bits,** indicating the end of the character. The measure of the total number of bits sent over the transmission line per second is called the **bit rate** and measured in **baud.** The time elapsed from the start bit to the last stop bit is called a **frame.** Figure 9-6 illustrates the format of asynchronous serial data used by the Serial Driver.

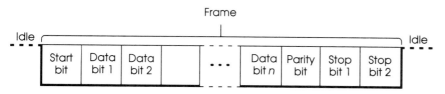

Figure 9-6
Format of data used in serial communication

If a parity bit is set incorrectly, the receiving device will note a **parity error.** After the stop bits, the transmitting device may send another character or maintain the line in the idle state.

The Serial Driver actually consists of four drivers: one input driver and one output driver for the modem port, and one input driver and one output driver for the printer port (see Figure 9-7). Each **input driver** receives data via a serial port and transfers it to the application. Each **output driver** takes data from the application and sends it out through a serial port. The input and output drivers for a port are closely related and share some of the same routines. An individual port can both transmit and receive data at the same time. The serial ports are controlled by the Macintosh's **Serial Communications Controller (SCC):** channel A of the SCC controls the modem port, and channel B controls the printer port.

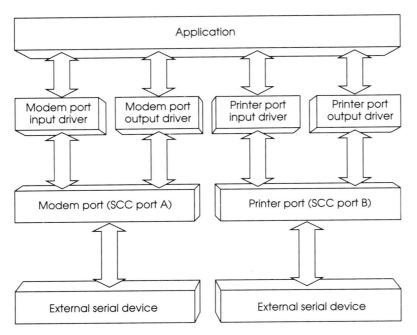

Figure 9-7
Serial input and output drivers

Data received via a serial port passes through a three-character buffer in the SCC and then into a buffer in the input driver for the port. Characters are removed from the input driver's buffer each time an application issues a read call to the driver. Each input driver's buffer can initially hold up to 64 characters, but an application can specify a larger buffer if necessary. If the SCC buffer ever overflows because the input driver doesn't read it often enough, a **hardware overrun error** occurs. If an input driver's buffer ever overflows because the application doesn't issue read calls to the driver often enough, a **software overrun error** occurs.

Both ports can be operated up to about 256K baud using the internal baud-rate generator, or up to about 1 megabaud using an externally supplied clock. The only difference between the two ports is that the modem port has a slightly higher priority in the SCC chip. For example, AppleTalk runs at 256K baud using the printer port to provide the LaserWriter connection. On the Macintosh SE and Macintosh II, the modem port only can use a new incoming handshake line as a second external clock source to support synchronous modems requiring separate receive and transmit clocks. (For information about the serial communications hardware, see "Serial Communication" in this chapter and the *Macintosh Family Hardware Reference* manual.)

All four drivers default to 9600 baud, eight data bits per character, no parity bit, and two stop bits. You can change any of these options. The Serial Driver supports Clear To Send (CTS) hardware handshake and XOn/XOff software flow control.

The AppleTalk network

AppleTalk is Apple's local-area network for connecting Apple and other manufacturers' computers with each other and with shared resources, such as printers, file servers, and the many facilities available on wide-area networks.

AppleTalk is a simple, easily installed, and very low-cost local-area network system that delivers all the benefits of multiuser communication and shared resources at a fraction of the cost usually associated with these features.

A single AppleTalk network, as shown in Figure 9-8, connects up to 32 workstations, or nodes. A **node** is a device that is attached to and communicates over an AppleTalk network. Nodes are easily added and removed from an AppleTalk network; if an AppleTalk connector box is already in place, this can be done without disrupting service to other nodes. A node can even fail without disturbing network communications. You can connect Macintosh computers to AppleTalk by plugging an AppleTalk connector into the printer port (serial port B) of the Macintosh; other devices such as a LaserWriter are just as easily connected.

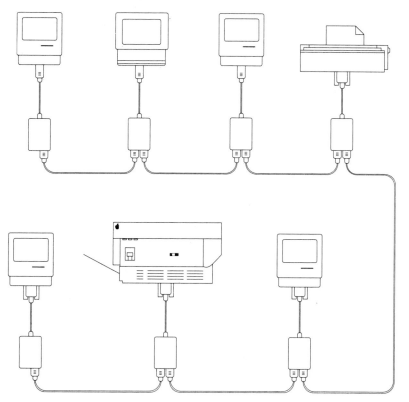

Figure 9-8
An AppleTalk network

In designing AppleTalk, careful attention has been paid to small workgroups, where small cluster networks feed into large backbone networks, resulting in a mixture of networks and technologies. AppleTalk supports larger networks, both local- and wide-area, through the use of bridging devices and gateways.

AppleTalk communicates via channel B of the Serial Communications Controller (SCC). When the Macintosh is started up, the status of serial port B (the printer port) is checked. If port B isn't being used by another device driver and is available for use by AppleTalk, the AppleTalk drivers are loaded into the system heap, as described in the next section.

Important

For software reasons, it's imperative that the Macintosh be connected to the AppleTalk network through serial port B (the printer port) before being switched on.

Networking applications

Apple provides a number of networking products that support the AppleTalk network; many more are available from other manufacturers. The Apple products include

☐ The AppleShare® File Server, which allows several users to share the same files and applications. AppleShare is a software package that allows you to set up any Macintosh with a hard disk as a dedicated file server.

☐ The LaserShare™ Print Spooler, a program that offloads LaserWriter printing tasks to a server, thereby freeing the Macintosh for other work.

☐ The EtherTalk™ card, an expansion card for the Macintosh II, which enables the Macintosh II to communicate over an EtherNet network or to run AppleTalk over the EtherNet hardware.

☐ The AppleTalk PC card, a half-sized expansion card for MS-DOS-based personal computers. This card enables MS-DOS machines to share information on an AppleTalk network and access shared resources, such as a LaserWriter. This card supports the conversion of several file formats, including ASCII, Lotus 1-2-3, Microsoft Word, and PostScript.

☐ The Apple DCA filter, a utility that translates documents in the IBM DCA (Document Content Architecture) RFT file format to and from the Macintosh format.

☐ The AppleLine™ 3270 File Transfer program, a utility program for transferring files between the IBM 3270 mainframe environment and the Macintosh environment.

AppleTalk network architecture

Sockets are software entities within the nodes of a network. On a single AppleTalk network, a socket is uniquely identified by its **AppleTalk address**—that is, its socket number together with its node ID.

Two or more AppleTalk networks can form an **internet.** Internets are formed by interconnecting AppleTalk networks via intelligent nodes called **bridges.** A network number uniquely identifies a network in an internet. A socket's AppleTalk address together with its network number provide a unique internet-wide identifier called an **internet address.**

Sockets are owned by **socket clients,** which are typically software processes in the node. Socket clients are also known as **network-visible entities,** because they're the primary accessible entities on an internet.

The **AppleTalk Manager** is an interface to a set of device drivers that allow Macintosh programs to send and receive information over an AppleTalk network. There are two AppleTalk device drivers in ROM, one named .MPP and one named .ATP. The AppleTalk Manager and all of the AppleTalk drivers are included in the 256K ROM.

On startup, the .MPP driver installs its own interrupt handlers, installs a task into the vertical retrace queue, and prepares the Serial Communications Controller (SCC) chip for use. It then chooses a node ID for the Macintosh and confirms that the node ID isn't already being used by another node on the network.

The AppleTalk Manager provides a variety of services that allow Macintosh programs to interact with programs in devices connected to an AppleTalk network. This interaction, achieved through the exchange of variable-length blocks of data (known as *packets*), follows well-defined sets of rules known as **protocols.**

As shown in Figure 9-9, the AppleTalk system architecture consists of a number of protocols arranged in layers. Each protocol in a specific layer provides services to higher-level layers by building on the services provided by lower-level layers. A Macintosh program can use services provided by any of the layers in order to construct more sophisticated or specialized services.

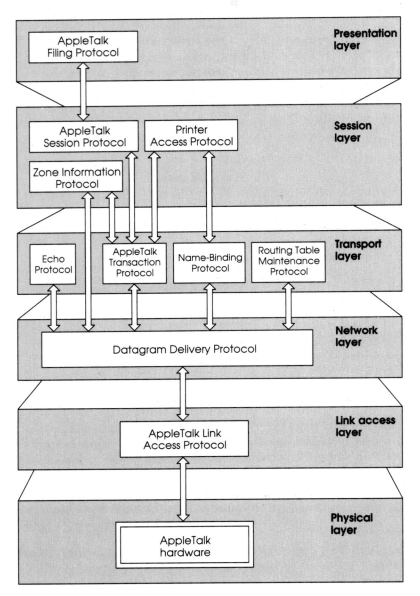

Figure 9-9
AppleTalk Manager protocols

These protocols serve a number of functions:

- The AppleTalk Link Access Protocol (ALAP) provides the lowest-level AppleTalk services, providing its clients with node-to-node delivery of **data frames** on a *single* AppleTalk network. (A data frame is a variable-length packet of data preceded and followed by control information referred to as the frame header and frame trailer. An ALAP frame can contain up to 600 bytes of client data.)

  This protocol's main function is to control access to the AppleTalk network among various competing devices. ALAP can have multiple clients in a single node.

- The Datagram Delivery Protocol (DDP) provides the next higher-level protocol in the AppleTalk architecture, managing socket-to-socket delivery of datagrams over AppleTalk internets. DDP uses the node-to-node delivery service provided by ALAP to send and receive datagrams. **Datagrams** are packets of data transmitted by DDP. A DDP datagram can contain up to 586 bytes of client data.

- Bridges on AppleTalk internets use the Routing Table Maintenance Protocol (RTMP). This protocol is used internally to maintain tables for routing datagrams through the internet.

- The Name-Binding Protocol (NBP) converts entity names to their internet socket addresses. NBP maintains a name table in each node that contains the name and internet address of each entity in that node.

- The AppleTalk Transaction Protocol (ATP) uses the services provided by DDP to transmit requests and responses with guaranteed delivery. ALAP and DDP provide best-effort delivery services with no recovery mechanism when packets are lost or discarded because of errors. Although such a service suffices for many situations, ATP provides a reliable loss-free transport service. ATP continues to transmit a transaction request until it receives a complete response, thus allowing for recovery from the loss of a packet.

- The Printer Access Protocol (PAP) supports the use of the Apple LaserWriter printer.

- The AppleTalk Filing Protocol (AFP) provides support for file servers such as the AppleShare file server.

Detailed information about AppleTalk protocols is available in *Inside AppleTalk* (see Appendix B).

This concludes the discussion of Macintosh I/O functions. The rest of this chapter covers the remaining parts of the Operating System: numerics support, system startup and shutdown, timing of system operations, and the handling of system errors.

Numerics

The Macintosh computers provide several levels of numerics support for applications. The options range from fast fixed-point operations for graphics, to very precise floating-point operations supported in software, to (on the Macintosh II) floating-point operations supported by a hardware floating-point unit, the Motorola MC68881.

In software, the **Floating-Point Arithmetic Package** and the **Elementary Functions Package** provide facilities for extended-precision floating-point arithmetic and advanced numerical applications programming. These two packages support the **Standard Apple Numeric Environment (SANE),** which is designed in strict accordance with IEEE Standard 754 for binary floating-point arithmetic.

On the Macintosh II, fixed-point routines and the numerics packages have been written to exploit the 68881 coprocessor. Programs using either fixed-point or the numerics packages will enjoy much improved performance even if they are unaware of the 68881. Each MPW programming language provides the option of generating either numerics package call or direct 68881 code. See the section "Macintosh II Floating-Point Coprocessor (MC68881)" in Chapter 10 for further details.

❖ *Note:* Most programmers will rarely, if ever, need to deal explicitly with either the numerics packages or the 68881. These facilities are built into MPW (and many other) programming languages; that is, the language compilers recognize SANE data types, and automatically make floating-point calls for standard arithmetic operations (+, −, *, /) as well as for data type conversion. Mathematical functions that aren't built in can be accessed through a run-time library.

For more information about SANE, refer to the *Apple Numerics Manual,* the standard reference guide to SANE.

System startup and shutdown

When power is first supplied to the Macintosh computer, a carefully orchestrated sequence of events takes place:

1. First, a series of hardware circuits get the system ready for operation. The MC68000 and the various I/O chips are initialized, and the mapping of ROM and RAM is temporarily altered by causing an image of the ROM to appear at the location where RAM normally starts (address 0), while RAM is moved to a location higher in memory. Under this mapping scheme, the Macintosh software still executes out of the normal ROM locations, but the MC68000 can obtain some critical low-memory vectors from the ROM image it finds at address 0.

2. After the system is initialized, the software maps the system RAM back where it belongs, starting at address 0.

3. Next, software performs a number of tests and determines how much RAM is present in the machine. After the system is fully tested, the disk startup process begins.

4. The first step in the disk startup process is to check the disk in the internal drive (drive 1), or on the Macintosh SE and Macintosh II, the disk indicated by the user as the startup device (via the Control Panel desk accessory). If a disk is already present, the system attempts to read it and looks for a System file. If a floppy disk with no System file is found, the disk is ejected, and the search continues. If no disk is found in the internal floppy drive, the system looks for a disk in the external drive, and then for a disk connected to the SCSI port, starting with the device that has an ID of 6 and counting down. If no startup disk is found, the question-mark disk icon is displayed until a disk is inserted. If the disk startup fails for some reason, the "sad Macintosh" icon is displayed and the Macintosh goes into an endless loop until it's turned off again.

5. Once a readable disk has been found, the system reads in the first two sectors of the disk, which contain the system startup blocks. At this point, the normal disk load begins.

Timing of system operations

For the Macintosh to run, numerous internal and external operations must be perfectly coordinated. These operations include refreshing the built-in screen (except on the Macintosh II), tracking the cursor, checking for events, and various time-dependent actions by the application. These operations are scheduled by the **Vertical Retrace Manager** and the **Time Manager.**

Vertical retrace tasks

Sixty times a second, the electron beam of the video display tube returns from the bottom of the screen to the top to display the next frame. At this time, the built-in Macintosh video circuitry generates a **vertical retrace interrupt,** also known as the **vertical blanking (VBL) interrupt.** This interrupt is used as a convenient time for performing a number of recurrent system tasks.

❖ *Note:* Because the video is not built-in on the Macintosh II, the VBL interrupt is not related to actual video. It's still generated, but by a separate timer, for compatibility with the other Macintosh machines.

The Vertical Retrace Manager schedules and performs recurrent tasks during vertical retrace interrupts. Tasks performed during the vertical retrace interrupt are known as **VBL tasks.**

The following sequence of recurrent tasks executes at regular intervals based on the VBL "heartbeat" of the Macintosh:

1. Increment the number of ticks since system startup (every interrupt).

2. Check whether the stack has expanded into the heap; if so, the task calls the System Error Handler (every interrupt).

3. Handle cursor movement (every interrupt).

4. Post a mouse event if the state of the mouse button has changed from its previous state and has then remained unchanged for four interrupts (every other interrupt). (Macintosh Plus only.)

5. Reset the keyboard if it's been reattached after having been detached (every 32 interrupts). (Macintosh Plus only.)

6. Post a disk-inserted event if the user has inserted a disk or taken any other action that requires a volume to be mounted (every 30 interrupts).

Information describing each VBL task is contained in the **vertical retrace queue,** a standard Macintosh Operating System queue. An application can add any number of its own VBL tasks for the Vertical Retrace Manager to execute. VBL tasks can be set to execute at any frequency (up to once per vertical retrace interrupt). For example, an electronic mail application might add a VBL task that checks every tenth of a second (every six interrupts) to see if it has received any messages.

❖ *Note:* When interrupts are disabled (during a disk access, for example), or when VBL tasks take longer than about a sixtieth of a second to perform, one or more vertical retrace interrupts may be missed, thereby affecting the performance of certain VBL tasks. For instance, while a disk is being accessed, the updating of the cursor movement may be irregular.

For more information about how the screen itself is refreshed, see "The Video Interface" section of Chapter 10.

The Time Manager

The Time Manager makes it possible for a program to schedule a routine to be executed after a given number of milliseconds has elapsed. The Time Manager also provides the user with an asynchronous "wakeup" service with one-millisecond accuracy; it can have any number of outstanding wakeup requests. Because the Time Manager is independent of clock speed or interrupts, it provides a hardware-independent means of timing program operations, thus ensuring compatibility with the different Macintosh machines.

System errors

When a fatal system error occurs, the **System Error Handler** (the "Bomb Manager") assumes control. Its main function is to display an alert box with an error message called a **system error alert** and to provide a mechanism for the application to resume execution, if possible. Figure 9-10 shows the ugly form of a system error alert.

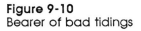

Sorry, a system error occurred.

(Restart)   (Resume)   ID = 12

Figure 9-10
Bearer of bad tidings

Such alerts notify the user of system errors. The bottom-right corner of a user alert contains a **system error ID** that identifies the error. Usually the message "Sorry, a system error occurred," a Restart button, and a Resume button are also shown. If the Finder can't be found on a disk, the message "Can't load the Finder" and a Restart button will be shown. The Macintosh will attempt to restart if the user clicks the Restart button, and the application will attempt to resume execution if the user clicks the Resume button.

❖ *Note:* The system error alerts simply identify the type of problem encountered and, in some cases, the part of the Toolbox or Operating System involved. They don't tell you where in the application code the failure occurred.

Because a system error results from a failure in a very low-level part of the system, the System Error Handler uses as little of the system as possible. To do its job, the System Error Handler requires only the following conditions:

☐ The trap dispatcher is operative.

☐ The Font Manager has been initialized (this occurs when the system starts up).

☐ Register A7 (the stack pointer) points to a reasonable place in memory (for example, not to the main screen buffer).

☐ A few important system data structures aren't too badly damaged.

Note that the System Error Handler doesn't require the Memory Manager to be operative.

If a program writes to video RAM or the sound buffer, there may be nothing the System Error Handler can do. In this case, the screen may go haywire as the computer's software dies, making horrible "machine gun" noises. If this happens, just press the Reset switch or turn off the computer's power.

The content of the alert box displayed is determined by a **system error alert table,** a resource stored in the system resource file. There are two different system error alert tables: a system startup alert table used when the system starts up and a user alert table for informing the user of system errors.

The system startup alerts are used to display messages at system startup, such as the "Welcome to Macintosh" message (see Figure 9-11). They're displayed by the System Error Handler instead of the Dialog Manager because the System Error Handler needs very little of the system to operate.

Figure 9-11
System startup alert

The "Please insert the disk" and power-off messages are also user alerts.

Table 9-1 in the section "System Error Messages" lists the system error IDs for the various user alerts and explains the meanings of these errors. The table also lists the system startup alert messages.

Recovering from system errors

An application recovers from a system error by means of a **resume procedure.** When the user clicks the Resume button in a system error alert, the System Error Handler attempts to restore the state of the system and then calls the resume procedure designated by the application. (This is typically extremely difficult for an application to do.)

If there isn't a resume procedure, the Resume button in the system error alert will be dimmed.

System error messages

Table 9-1 lists the system error alerts on the Macintosh. The explanations for some of these errors list assembly-language instructions that may have caused the error. None of this information will help you to recover from a system error at the time it occurs; it only gives you some idea where your program may have gone wrong.

Table 9-1
System error messages and startup alert messages

ID	Explanation or message
1	Bus error: Invalid memory reference (Macintosh II and Macintosh XL only).
2	Address error. A word or long-word reference has been made to an odd address.
3	Illegal instruction. The MC68000 received an instruction it didn't recognize.
4	Zero divide. A divide instruction (DIVS or DIVU) with a divisor of 0 was executed.
5	Check exception. A Check Register Against Bounds (CHK) instruction was executed and failed. Pascal "value out of range" errors are usually reported in this way.
6	TrapV exception. A Trap On Overflow (TRAPV) instruction was executed and failed.
7	Privilege violation. The Macintosh Plus and Macintosh SE always run in supervisor mode; perhaps an erroneous Return From Execution (RTE) instruction was executed.
8	Trace exception. The trace bit in the 68000's status register is set.
9	Line 1010 exception. The 1010 trap dispatcher has failed.
10	Line 1111 exception. Unimplemented 68000 instruction.
11	Miscellaneous exception. All other 68000 exceptions.
12	Unimplemented core routine. An unimplemented trap number was encountered.
13	Spurious interrupt. The interrupt vector table entry for a particular level of interrupt is NIL. This usually occurs with level 4, 5, 6, or 7 interrupts.
14	I/O system error. The File Manager or Device Manager encountered an error.

(continued)

Table 9-1 (continued)
System error messages and startup alert messages

ID	Explanation or message
15	Segment Loader error. A call to read a segment into memory failed.
16	Floating-point error. The halt bit in the floating-point environment word was set.
17–24	Can't load package. A call to read a package into memory failed.
25	Can't allocate requested memory block in the heap.
26	Segment Loader error. A call to read 'CODE' resource 0 into memory failed; usually indicates a nonexecutable file.
27	File map destroyed. A logical block number was found that is greater than the number of the last logical block on the volume or less than the logical block number of the first allocation block on the volume.
28	Stack overflow error. The stack has expanded into the heap.
30	"Please insert the disk." File Manager alert.
41	The file named "Finder" can't be found on the disk.
100	Can't mount system startup volume. The system couldn't read the system resource file into memory.
32767	"Sorry, a system error occurred." Default alert message.

System startup alert messages

"Welcome to Macintosh"
"Disassembler installed"
"MacsBug installed"
"Warning—this startup disk is not usable"

In surveying the Macintosh software over the last eight chapters, we've seen that the Macintosh Operating System and Toolbox are essentially the same for all Macintosh computers. In fact, a major achievement of the Macintosh Operating System is the provision of a unified software interface to a variety of Macintosh machines.

On Macintosh computers that provide for hardware expansion (the Macintosh SE and the Macintosh II) there is the possibility of running another operating system as an alternative to the Macintosh Operating System. Currently, Apple provides one such alternative operating system for the Macintosh II: **A/UX,** an enhanced implementation of the standard AT&T UNIX Operating System, which includes support for the Macintosh Toolbox. But before outlining the features of the A/UX Operating System, we'll explain the Macintosh hardware itself, describing in some detail the specific differences between each of the Macintosh machines.

Chapter 10

The Macintosh Family Hardware

This chapter describes the hardware features of the Macintosh Plus, Macintosh SE, and Macintosh II computers. Much of the discussion is common to all Macintosh computers, but the particulars of each machine are also described.

Every subject touched on here is explained in greater detail in the *Macintosh Family Hardware Reference,* which describes the hardware for the Macintosh, Macintosh Plus, Macintosh SE, and Macintosh II. Specifications for each of the Macintosh machines can be found in Appendix A.

Overview of the Macintosh hardware

The hardware architectures of all Macintosh machines share many similarities. In particular, the integral Macintosh machines—the original Macintosh, Macintosh Plus, and Macintosh SE—follow the same general line of evolution: they are all compact machines with built-in video. However, the Macintosh SE is distinguished by several important innovations, including an expansion slot, as we'll describe in a moment.

Each of the Macintosh computers is built around a Motorola 68000-family microprocessor, together with random-access memory (RAM), read-only memory (ROM), and several chips that enable the computer to communicate with external devices.

The Macintosh II hardware, while based on many of the same components used in the other machines, marks a significant departure from previous Macintosh models, above all in its use of expansion slots and a separate video card. The Macintosh II still uses the same processor family, the same Operating System software, and the same disks, serial ports, device drivers, and bit-mapped graphics, which remain black-and-white by default.

Macintosh programs communicate with devices by using memory-mapped I/O, which means that a program accesses each device in the system by reading or writing to specific locations in the **address space** of the computer. (For a discussion, see the section "Address Space" later in this chapter.) The following chips handle external I/O functions on the Macintosh computers:

☐ A **Versatile Interface Adapter (VIA)** chip for the mouse, keyboard, and miscellaneous other functions. (The Macintosh II includes a second VIA chip for handling interrupts from NuBus slots.)

☐ A **Serial Communications Controller (SCC)** chip for serial communication

☐ An Apple custom chip, called the **IWM (Integrated Woz Machine),** for floppy disk control

□ A **Small Computer System Interface (SCSI)** chip for high-speed parallel communication with devices such as hard disks. (This chip is not found on the Macintosh 128K and Macintosh 512K or 512K enhanced.)

□ The **Apple Sound Chip (ASC)** on the Macintosh II. (On the Macintosh Plus and Macintosh SE, the Sony sound chip is not an addressable I/O device, as explained in a later section, "The Sound Generator.")

The video display is built-in on the Macintosh Plus and Macintosh SE. On the Macintosh II, an external video monitor is controlled by a NuBus video card.

A separate section of this chapter is dedicated to each of the devices listed above.

The classic Macintosh hardware

As explained in Chapter 1, the Macintosh Plus hardware differs in only a few particulars from the earlier Macintosh hardware: the new 128K ROM, more RAM, the 800K floppy disk drive, the SCSI port, and a new type of connector for the serial ports.

The microprocessor, RAM, ROM, and the various I/O chips and connectors are located on the Macintosh **digital board** (also called the **main logic board**). The upright **analog board** contains the power supply and video circuitry for the built-in monitor. Figure 10-1 illustrates these components.

As in the preceding chapters, the rest of this Chapter describes the classic Macintosh hardware from the standpoint of the Macintosh Plus. In cases where earlier models differ, this fact is called out in a separate note.

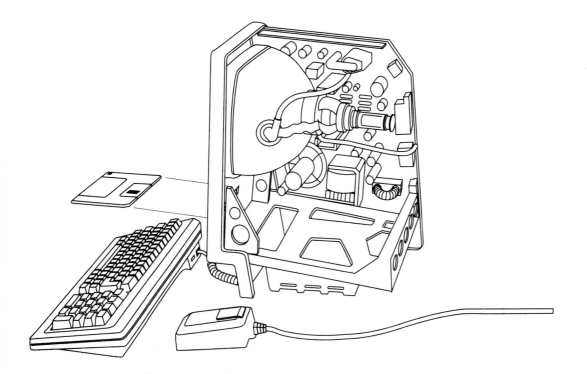

Figure 10-1
Inside the Macintosh Plus

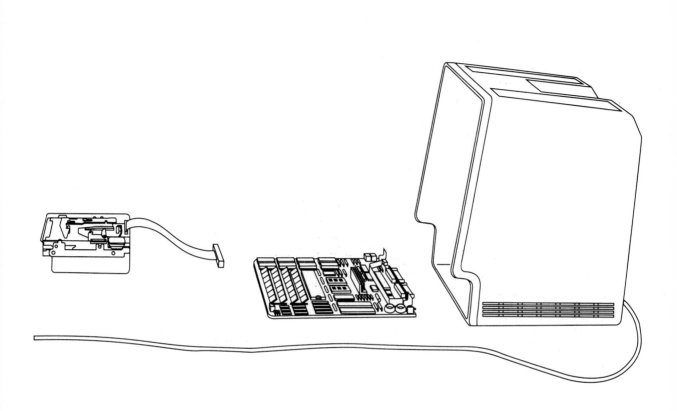

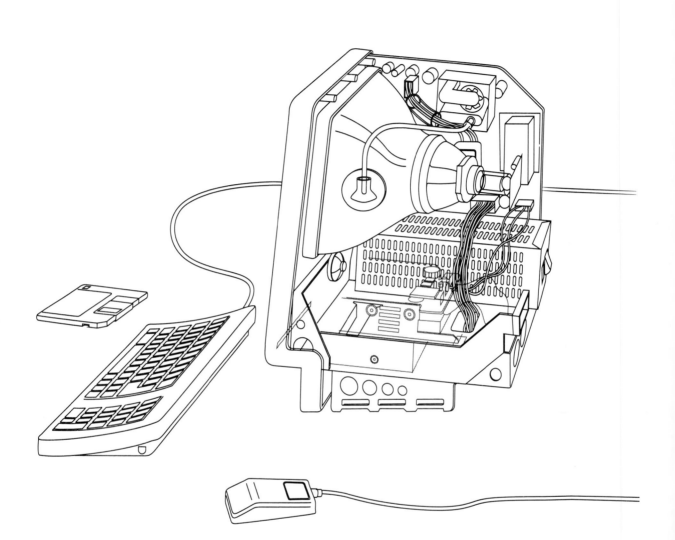

Figure 10-2
Inside the Macintosh SE

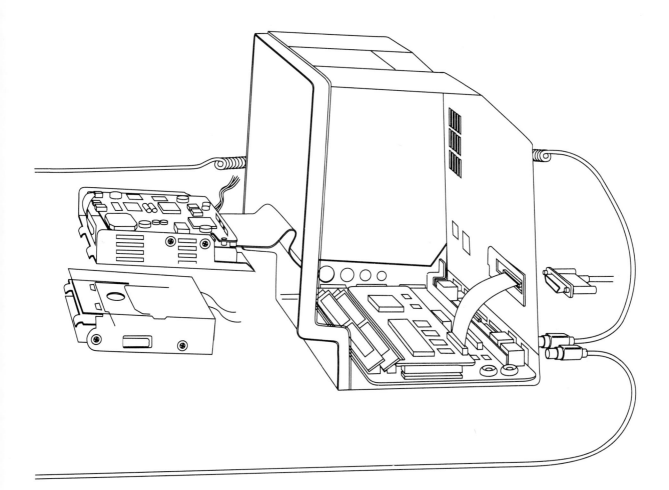

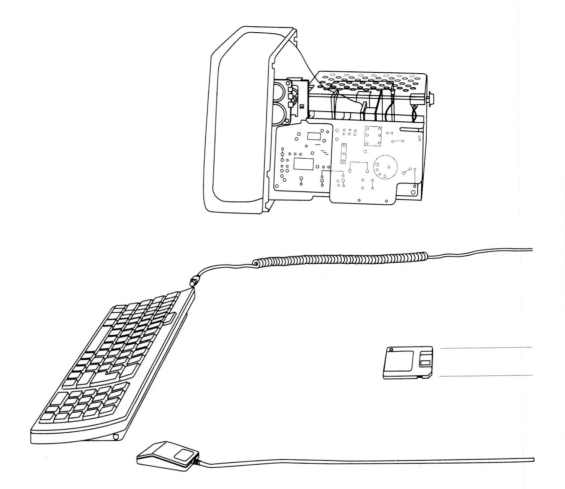

Figure 10-3
Inside the Macintosh II

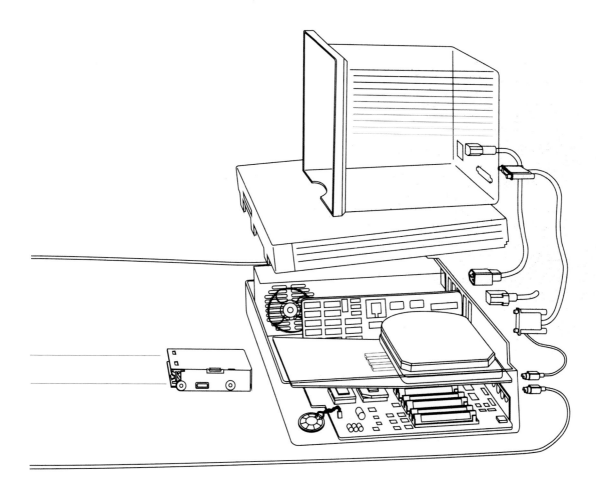

The Macintosh SE hardware

The basic layout of the Macintosh SE is similar to that of the Macintosh Plus, but aside from the built-in monitor and I/O chips, most of the components are new. The most noTable new features of the Macintosh SE are

- □ new 256K ROM
- □ change in the processor/video display interleave, resulting in faster RAM access
- □ improved hardware interface with the SCSI chip, resulting in faster hard-disk access
- □ use of the **Apple Desktop Bus™ (ADB)** for keyboard and mouse support
- □ second internal disk drive: either an internal 20 MB SCSI hard disk or a second built-in floppy drive
- □ provision for an internal expansion card to communicate directly with the 68000 bus
- □ a removable accessory access port to allow access to custom connectors on an expansion card

To handle the needs of an internal hard disk and expansion card, an upgraded power supply and a cooling fan have been added. Figure 10-2 shows how the pieces fit together.

Numerous other new features not listed here are described in later sections of this chapter.

The Macintosh II hardware

The Macintosh II is a big, open-architecture Macintosh based on the MC68020 microprocessor. The main logic board of the Macintosh II contains the 68020 microprocessor, RAM, ROM, and various I/O chips and connectors. There is also a built-in 3.5-inch floppy disk drive and an optional second floppy drive, as well as an optional internal SCSI hard disk. Six NuBus slots and the enclosed power supply complete the picture (Figure 10-3).

As you can see, the video monitor is no longer built into the Macintosh II. A variety of monochrome or color monitors can be used with the system.

Figure 10-4 illustrates how I/O devices connect to the Macintosh II system. As shown in the figure, the Macintosh II has six built-in I/O ports: the sound connector (output only), two low-speed serial ports for the Apple Desktop Bus (ADB), two high-speed serial ports for AppleTalk, printers, modems, and so on, and a SCSI parallel port. Additional I/O devices may be present on expansion cards in the NuBus slots. (At least one of these slots ordinarily contains a video card; the other five slots may contain other sorts of I/O devices, coprocessors, or memory.)

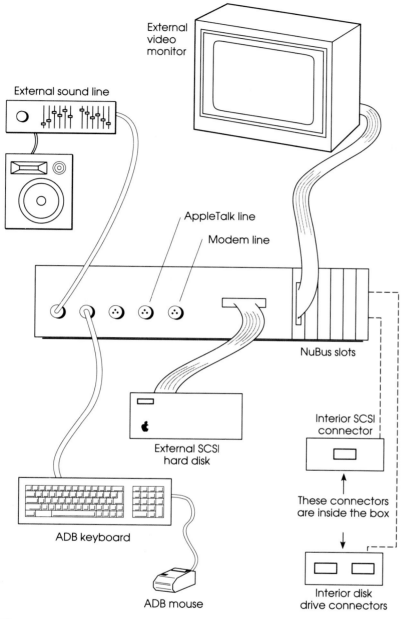

Figure 10-4
Macintosh II I/O

The next four major sections of this Chapter discuss the core of the Macintosh hardware design: the microprocessors, the expansion slots, built-in memory, and the Macintosh I/O devices in general. Subsequent sections will treat each of the Macintosh I/O subsystems in turn: video, sound, floppy disk I/O, SCSI I/O, serial I/O, the keyboard, and the mouse.

The microprocessor

The Macintosh computers are built around the 68000 family of microprocessors, known among assembly-language programmers for their elegant instruction set and high performance.

The heart of the Macintosh Plus and Macintosh SE is a Motorola MC68000 microprocessor clocked at 7.8336 megahertz (MHz). The 68000 chip has a 16-bit external data bus and a 24-bit external address bus. Internal address and data registers are all 32 bits wide. The 24-bit addressing means that the 68000 can directly access up to 16 megabytes (MB) of **address space** (that is, memory or I/O devices, as explained in the next section).

The Macintosh II uses the more powerful MC68020 processor, clocked at 15.6672 MHz, which is twice the speed of the microprocessor on the other Macintoshes. The 68020 instruction set is a superset of the 68000 instructions, which means that programs written for the 68000 will also run on the 68020. The 68020 chip provides a full 32-bit architecture, and thus can address up to 4 gigabytes (or 4096 MB) of address space. The 68020 provides the following advantages:

□ A true 32-bit microprocessor. Address bus, data bus, and internal registers are all 32 bits wide. This means that applications specially written for 32-bit mode will go very fast. Other features, such as the internal code cache, make the system go even faster.

□ Virtual paging of memory (with the MC68851 PMMU). This is required for multitasking systems such as UNIX. (See the section "Hardware Memory Management on the Macintosh II" in this Chapter for more details.)

□ Downward compatibility with the 68000 chip used in the other Macintosh computers. Even in 24-bit mode, software runs faster.

□ Extended instruction set. New instructions can do more in less time compared to the instructions used on the 68000. (Of course, new 68020 instructions won't work on the 68000.)

It's important to note, however, that certain 68000 instructions don't work the same way on the 68020. For information, see the chapter on compatibility guidelines of *Inside Macintosh,* Volume 5.

A full description of the two processors can be found in the Motorola *MC68000 16/32-Bit Microprocessor Programmer's Reference Manual* and the *MC68020 Programmer's Reference Manual.*

One of the major design advantages of the 68000 family is the provision for **traps.** Calls to the Macintosh Toolbox and Operating System are implemented as unimplemented 68000 instructions and work with either version of the microprocessor. (See the section "The Trap Mechanism" in Chapter 2.)

Address space

As we've mentioned, the Macintosh uses memory-mapped I/O, which means that software communicates with each device in the system by reading or writing to specific locations in the address space of the computer.

The address space reserved for the I/O devices contains blocks devoted to each of the devices within the computer: the SCSI chip, the Serial Communications Controller (SCC) chip, the disk controller chip (IWM), the VIA chip(s), and, on the Macintosh II, devices in NuBus slots.

68000 address space

The MC68000 can directly access 2^{24} addresses, or 16 megabytes (MB) of address space. In the Macintosh Plus and Macintosh SE computers, the 16 MB of addressable space is divided into four equal sections, as shown in Figure 10-5. The first 4 MB megabytes of address space are for addressing RAM, the second 4 MB are for ROM and the SCSI interface, the third are for the SCC, and the last 4 MB are for the IWM and the VIA.

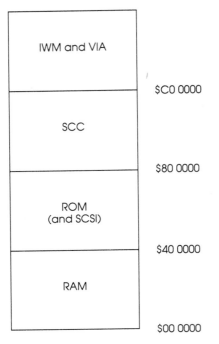

Figure 10-5
68000 address space

Since the devices within each block may actually have far fewer than 4 MB of individually addressable locations or registers, the addressing for a device may be repeated within its block, as described further in the *Macintosh Family Hardware Reference* manual.

Recall that in the Macintosh system, programs can remain compatible with all machines by avoiding the use of "hard" addresses. Programs normally access hardware locations by using a set of predefined assembly-language constants, defined as offsets from locations pointed to by global variables.

68020 address space

The MC68020 processor can directly access 2^{32} addresses, or 4 gigabytes (GB) of address space. Address space is used for RAM, ROM, NuBus, the SCSI chip, the SCC, the IWM, the VIAs, and the Apple Sound Chip (ASC), a custom sound chip on the Macintosh II. The division of address space is shown in Figure 10-6.

❖ *Note:* The MC68881 floating-point coprocessor and the MC68851 Paged Memory Management Unit (described in the next two sections) are also address mapped, but not in the same map with the RAM, ROM, I/O devices, and NuBus. See the *Macintosh Family Hardware Reference* for details.

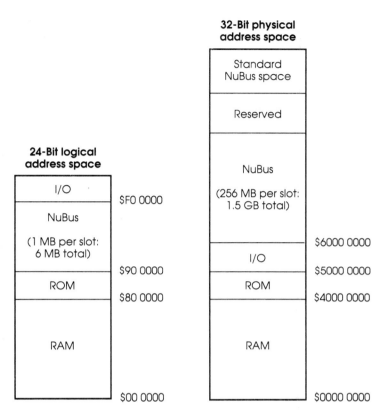

**24-Bit logical
address space**

I/O	$FO 0000
NuBus (1 MB per slot: 6 MB total)	
	$90 0000
ROM	$80 0000
RAM	
	$00 0000

**32-Bit physical
address space**

Standard NuBus space	
Reserved	
NuBus (256 MB per slot: 1.5 GB total)	
	$6000 0000
I/O	$5000 0000
ROM	$4000 0000
RAM	
	$0000 0000

Figure 10-6
68020 address space (24- to 32-bit mapping)

Some programs written for the 68000-based Macintosh machines make use of the high-order 8 bits of the 32-bit internal address registers, knowing that only the lower 24 bits will appear on the external address bus. To provide compatibility with those programs, the Macintosh II has provided a 24-bit external addressing mode that ignores the 8 upper bits. It is usually possible to run Macintosh software on the Macintosh II in the 24-bit mode. A set of Operating System Utilities calls provide for switching between the 24-bit mode (16 MB address space) and the 32-bit mode (4 GB address space).

Hardware memory management on the Macintosh II

On the Macintosh II, a built-in 24- to 32-bit **Address Mapping Unit (AMU)** handles the job of switching from 24-bit mode to 32-bit mode. As we mentioned in the previous section, the high-order 8 bits are ignored in 24-bit mode, and all bits are used in the 32-bit mode. This 24- to 32-bit address translation allows for running existing Macintosh software on the Macintosh II.

However, multitasking operating systems such as UNIX rely on virtual memory and require a logical-to-physical translation of an address from the processor. To handle that need, the Macintosh II supports an optional **Paged Memory Management Unit (PMMU),** the Motorola MC68851. The PMMU supports the usual 24- to 32-bit switching, as well as providing hardware memory management and virtual memory support. The PMMU can be installed in a socket on the main logic board of the Macintosh II, replacing the existing 24- to 32-bit address mapping unit.

The 68851 PMMU is designed to support a demand-paged virtual memory environment with the MC68020, as explained in the next section. It also provides some protection so that an application can't write to places that it shouldn't, such as to memory belonging to another task that is currently running. The PMMU is a coprocessor to the 68020; the interface is transparent to the programmer so that the PMMU registers and instructions are an extension of the 68020's. For more information, see the Motorola *MC68851 User's Manual.*

Virtual memory

Compared to the microprocessor's addressing range, only a relatively limited amount of RAM (physical memory) is available; however, a far larger **virtual memory** can be maintained on disk. Virtual memory is a technique that evolved on mainframe and minicomputers and has now been implemented on 32-bit microcomputers. Virtual memory means that a program can behave as if the 68020's entire logical addressing range were available to it.

The 68020 and PMMU together provide support for virtual paging of memory, required for multitasking by systems such as UNIX. A **page** is a fixed-size chunk of memory that is swapped in and out from the disk; the PMMU keeps track of 64 pages in memory. When the 68020 tries to access a memory location that's not in RAM (that is, data not in one of the 64 pages), a **page fault** is generated, and the page containing the data is swapped in from the disk to RAM.

For more information about Apple's implementation of UNIX for the Macintosh II, see Chapter 11.

Macintosh II floating-point coprocessor (MC68881)

The Motorola MC68881 floating-point coprocessor (also called a *Floating-Point Unit* or *FPU*) is built-in on the Macintosh II. The floating-point coprocessor greatly benefits calculation-intensive applications such as accounting, 3-D modeling, CAD/CAM, and scientific programs.

The 68881 coprocessor is a high-performance floating-point device designed to have a high degree of compatibility with the 68000 and 68020. The 68881 uses the 68020's coprocessor interface to operate in parallel with 68020 program execution. When the 68020 encounters a 68881 floating-point instruction, it passes it directly to the coprocessor.

A version of the **Standard Apple Numerics Environment (SANE)** works with the 68881 coprocessor. (SANE was introduced in the "Numerics" section of Chapter 9.) Figure 10-7 shows the relationship between SANE and the floating-point chip. Many of the operations performed by SANE are taken over by the 68881, although some operations continue to be performed in software.

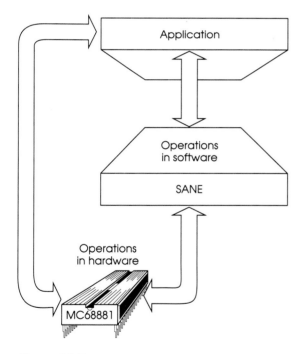

Figure 10-7
Relationship of SANE to the 68881 coprocessor

On the Macintosh II, all floating-point operations and even some fixed-point operations are assisted by the 68881. Programs that have used the standard SANE interface can expect an automatic speed improvement of 5 to 50 times for floating-point operations (with an average speed gain of about 10 times over the Macintosh Plus). Programs using the SANE interface will run on all Macintosh computers and will deliver results that are bit-for-bit identical on any machine.

If developers use the 68881 directly, the improvement can be anywhere from 40 to 700 times (with an average speed gain of about 100 over the Macintosh Plus). Macintosh II developers can make their programs access the 68881 by using assembly-language calls or by requesting the MC68881 option from any MPW programming language. Note however that such programs will not run on Macintosh computers without a 68881, nor will they deliver results that are bit-for-bit identical with other Macintosh computers. For more information, see the *Macintosh Programmer's Workshop Pascal 2.0 Reference*, *Macintosh Programmer's Workshop C 2.0 Reference*, or *Macintosh Programmer's Workshop Assembler Reference (Revision 2.0)*.

Macintosh SE expansion connector

The Macintosh SE is the first member of the Macintosh family to provide the capability for internal hardware expansion. The Macintosh SE expansion connector makes it possible to connect an expansion card with dimensions of approximately 4 inches by 8 inches directly to the 68000 microprocessor bus. Such an expansion card can also be connected to devices external to the computer through a snap-out accessory access port in the rear of the case. The design of the Macintosh SE also provides for the physical requirements of expansion cards through the addition of an upgraded power supply and a cooling fan.

❖ *Note:* Third-party products that adhere to the recommended expansion guidelines, use the Apple-supplied expansion features, and do not require physical alteration of the Macintosh SE will not void the Apple Limited Warranty. See *Designing Cards and Drivers for Macintosh II and Macintosh SE* for guidelines.

The expansion connector is a 96-pin connector that provides power, timing, and direct access to the 68000 bus. Figure 10-8 shows an illustration of this connector.

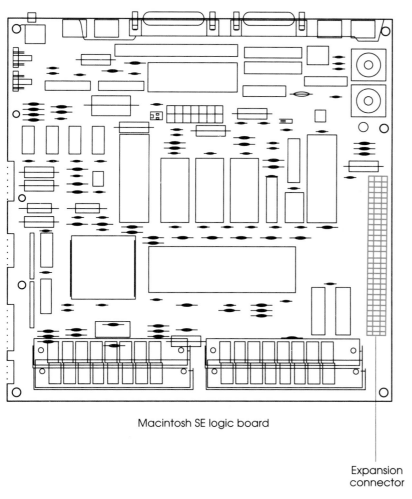

Macintosh SE logic board

Expansion
connector

Figure 10-8
Macintosh SE expansion connector

Macintosh II expansion slots

The Macintosh II has six expansion slots; each slot consists of a 96-pin DIN connector and uses the **NuBus** interface. NuBus is a 32-bit wide address and data bus based on a Texas Instruments specification. The Apple implementation of NuBus is supported in software by the Macintosh **Slot Manager.**

Figure 10-9 shows the layout of NuBus slots on the Macintosh II.

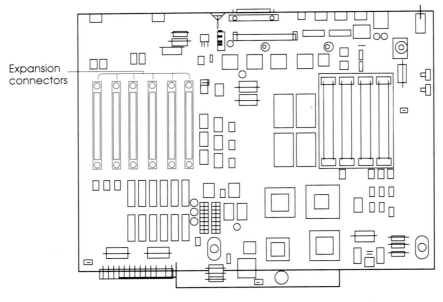

Expansion connectors

Macintosh II logic board

Figure 10-9
Macintosh II expansion slots

Cards that can go in the NuBus slots include (but are not limited to):

☐ video cards

☐ processor cards

☐ extra memory cards

☐ network interface and other I/O cards

NuBus cards are self-configuring: the slots are mapped into different address ranges, and the ROM on each card provides the operating system with information about its parameters and drivers. The Control Panel desk accessory displays the hardware configuration and allows you to configure the peripheral cards in the slots and to set their parameters, as provided by the software that supports the cards. At startup time, the system automatically configures the cards according to the parameters specified in the Control Panel.

In the Macintosh II ROM, the Slot Manager software consists of several system routines that communicate with the **configuration ROM** contained on each NuBus card.

For more information on NuBus, see *Designing Cards and Drivers for Macintosh II and Macintosh SE.*

Like other Macintosh I/O devices, devices in NuBus slots are addressed by writing to locations in the computer's address space. They can also send interrupts to the microprocessor, as explained in the section "I/O Devices" later in this chapter.

Memory

Built-in memory in the Macintosh consists of RAM and ROM. Certain devices within the computer, such as the Apple Sound Chip and the video card on the Macintosh II, also have their own RAM and ROM.

Macintosh RAM

RAM is the working memory of the system. Up to 4 megabytes (MB) of RAM can be installed on the Macintosh Plus and the Macintosh SE. (The standard configuration is 1 MB.) As of this writing, up to 8 MB can be accommodated on the Macintosh II main logic board; the theoretical limit is 128 MB, as higher-density RAMs become available. More than two gigabytes can be accommodated on expansion cards.

Each time you turn on the computer, the system software does a memory test and determines how much RAM is present in the machine. (This Figure is available to programs via a global variable.)

The RAM is divided into the **application space** and the space used by the system for information such as the system globals and for the screen buffer (on the Macintosh models with built-in video). The organization of the Macintosh RAM is discussed in Chapter 7, and a memory map is given in Figure 7-1.

RAM access time

On the Macintosh Plus, the microprocessor's accesses to RAM are interleaved (alternated) with the video display's accesses during the active portion of a screen scan line. (Video scanning is described in the next section.) The sound generator and disk speed controller are given the first access after each scan line. At all other times, the MC68000 has uninterrupted access to RAM, yielding an average RAM access rate of about 2.56 MB per second.

RAM access has been speeded up by some 25 percent on the Macintosh SE. This is done by allowing the 68000 three accesses during the active portion of the screen scan line, and then allocating one long-word access to the video display, for an average RAM access rate of 3.22 MB per second.

The Macintosh II uses faster RAM ICs that are not interchangeable with the type of RAM normally used in the Macintosh Plus and Macintosh SE. (The access time for the Macintosh II RAM ICs is 120 nanoseconds; the Macintosh Plus and Macintosh SE normally use slower 150-nanosecond memory ICs, although 120-nanosecond ICs can also be used.) The RAM access rate on the Macintosh II is further speeded up because the 68020's accesses to RAM are not interleaved with the video display's accesses, yielding an average RAM access rate of 12.53 MB per second. (Macintosh II video RAM is located on the video card in one of the expansion slots.)

Adding RAM

On the Macintosh Plus, Macintosh SE, and Macintosh II, RAM is provided in packages known as **Single In-line Memory Modules (SIMMs)**. The Macintosh Plus and Macintosh SE contain two or four SIMMs; the Macintosh II contains four or eight. Each SIMM contains eight surface-mounted RAM ICs on a small printed circuit board with electrical "finger" contacts along one edge, as shown in Figure 10-10.

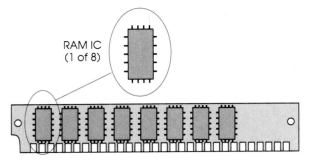

RAM IC
(1 of 8)

Figure 10-10
SIMMS and RAMs

Various RAM configurations are possible depending on how many SIMMs are used and on the density of the RAM ICs that are mounted on the SIMMs. On the Macintosh Plus and Macintosh SE, the standard configuration provides 1 megabyte (MB) of RAM (four SIMMs containing 256 kilobit RAM chips). Using 1 megabit RAM ICs will provide up to 4 MB of RAM on the Macintosh Plus or Macintosh SE.

On the Macintosh II, RAM is divided into two banks of four SIMM sockets each. The standard configuration, 1 MB of RAM, consists of four SIMMs containing 256 kilobit RAM ICs. Using 1 megabit RAM ICs will provide up to 8 MB of RAM. In the future, even denser RAM ICs will allow up to 128 MB of RAM in the SIMM sockets. Even more RAM (up to a theoretical maximum of 2 GB) may be added via expansion cards in NuBus slots.

The SIMMs can be changed by simply releasing one and snapping in another. However, there are also two resistors on the logic board in the Macintosh Plus and Macintosh SE that must be installed or removed to tell the electronics how much RAM is installed.

❖ *Note:* Opening the case of the classic Macintosh or Macintosh SE requires special tools; it also voids your warranty.

Some configurations, such as a single SIMM or mixing different-density RAM ICs in a pair of SIMMs, are not allowed. If different-density RAM ICs are used, their placement in the SIMM sockets is critical. Also recall that the SIMMs used in the Macintosh Plus or Macintosh SE can only be used in a Macintosh II if the SIMMs contain 120 nanosecond or faster RAM. (Macintosh II SIMMs can always be used in a Macintosh Plus or Macintosh SE.) For exact instructions about installing more memory in your computer, refer to the *Macintosh Family Hardware Reference.*

Warning

Because the video monitor is built-in, there are dangerous voltages inside the case of the original Macintosh, Macintosh Plus, and Macintosh SE computers. In particular, the video tube and video circuitry may hold dangerous charges long after the computer's power is turned off. Only qualified service personnel should reconfigure the computer's RAM.

The Macintosh ROM

ROM is the system's permanent read-only memory. Two ROM chips on the Macintosh Plus contain 128K of carefully hand-crafted system code. This code, which consists of over 700 routines written in assembly language, comprises the core of the Macintosh computer's Operating System and Toolbox, and the various system traps. Unlike RAM, the ROM is used exclusively by the microprocessor and is always accessed at the maximum rate of 3.92 MB per second.

The Macintosh Plus has 128K bytes of ROM, contained in two 512-kilobit ROM chips. The Macintosh Plus ROM sockets, however, can accept ROM chips of up to 1 megabit in size. A configuration of two 1 megabit ROM chips would provide 256K bytes of ROM. (For instance, the Japanese kanji version of the Macintosh Plus uses the 1 megabit ROMs to provide kanji and kana fonts in ROM.)

❖ *Note:* 128K is the largest size of ROM that can be installed in a Macintosh 128K, 512K, or 512K enhanced.

The Macintosh SE and Macintosh II computers each have a 256K of ROM, containing many new routines as well as improved versions of older ones. Many parts of the system software that were RAM-based on the Macintosh Plus have been put into the 256K ROM. The Macintosh SE and Macintosh II ROMs are not identical, however—the Macintosh II ROM includes color, sound, and NuBus support not found in the Macintosh SE ROM, which is only partially full.

The Macintosh II ROM consists of four 512-kilobit ROM chips. The four Macintosh II ROM sockets can also accommodate 1 megabit ROM chips; a configuration of four 1 megabit ROM chips would provide 512K bytes of ROM.

An optional configuration for the Macintosh II ROM is the installation of a 64-pin Single In-line Memory Module (SIMM) in the SIMM socket on the Macintosh II main logic board. The ROM SIMM option provides another way to upgrade your ROM.

The video interface

As described in Chapter 5, the Macintosh video display is driven in software by QuickDraw, which presents substantially the same program interface on a color Macintosh II as on the original monochrome models with built-in video. In video hardware, however, the Macintosh II is completely different from the Macintosh Plus and Macintosh SE, as the following sections explain.

Integral Macintosh video

The Macintosh video display is created by a moving electron beam that scans across the screen; as it scans, it turns on and off in order to create black-and-white pixels. Each pixel is a square, approximately 1/74 of an inch on a side. (This comes close to the points used in typography, which measure 1/72 of an inch.)

To create a screen image, the electron beam starts at the top-left corner of the screen. The beam scans horizontally across the screen from left to right, creating a line of graphics. Each time the scanning beam reaches the right edge of the picture, it flicks invisibly back to the left edge and down a pixel to the beginning of the next line, much as you move your eyes when you read a line of print. This technique is called **raster scanning.** (*Raster* is Latin for *rake* and means a group of equally spaced lines.)

When the scanning beam reaches the bottom of the picture, it flicks back to the beginning of the top line and repeats the entire process. The time between the last pixel on the bottom line and the first one on the top line is called the **vertical blanking interval.** At the beginning of the vertical blanking interval, the VIA chip generates a **vertical blanking interrupt.**

The electron beam's video scanning pattern is shown in Figure 10-11.

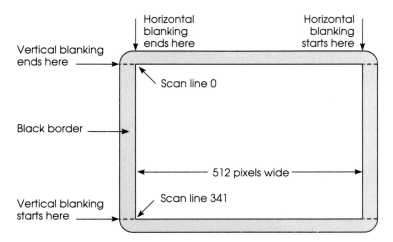

Vertical blanking ends here

Horizontal blanking ends here

Horizontal blanking starts here

Scan line 0

Black border

512 pixels wide

Vertical blanking starts here

Scan line 341

Figure 10-11
Video scanning pattern

Each full scan line takes 44.93 microseconds, which means the horizontal scan rate is 22.25 kilohertz (KHz). An entire screen scan, including the vertical blanking interval, takes 16.6 milliseconds, for a frame rate of 60.1 hertz (Hz).

On the Macintosh Plus and Macintosh SE, the video generator uses 21K of RAM (called the **screen buffer**) to compose a bit-mapped video image 512 pixels wide by 342 pixels tall. Each bit in this range controls a single pixel in the image: a 0 bit is white and a 1 bit is black.

Each scan line of the screen displays the contents of 32 consecutive words of memory (64 bytes), each word controlling 16 horizontally adjacent pixels; 64 bytes times 342 scan lines yields 21888, or 21K bytes, the size of the screen buffer. Recall that a program may use a much larger area of memory for graphic operations, using QuickDraw to create off-screen images so that they can be displayed more rapidly. QuickDraw takes care of associating areas in graphics space with the screen buffer: by default, a grafPort's bit map points to the screen buffer in memory, and drawing to the grafPort writes to the screen. A program can change this to write to another area in memory (for later moving onto the screen, for instance.)

On the Macintosh Plus and Macintosh SE, there are actually two screen buffers: the main buffer and the alternate buffer. The hardware displays the contents of one or the other, depending on how software sets a bit in the VIA. This lets a program create an image in the buffer not being displayed, and then instantly flash it on the screen, which is useful for animation.

Macintosh II video

On the Macintosh II, video is no longer an integral part of the computer as it was on all previous machines. The Macintosh II system supports a wide variety of color or monochrome video devices, which are connected to the system through interface cards plugged into NuBus expansion slots. The screen buffer is located on the video card. Each device must also have its own specialized device driver for communication with the rest of the system.

Like all slot-based expansion cards, a video card must include information in its ROM about its capabilities and possible configurations. Video cards also have their own parameter RAM. For instance, you can use the Control Panel desk accessory to set the pixel depth; this information is stored in the card's paramenter RAM.

At this writing, Apple is providing two video monitors for the Macintosh II:

- [ ] 12" 640-pixel by 480-pixel black-and-white monitor
- [ ] 13" 640-by-480 color monitor

As on previous Macintosh computers, graphics on the Macintosh II is supported by QuickDraw, which has been extended to provide sophisticated color support, as we outlined in Chapter 5. While providing full color support, Color QuickDraw remains compatible with existing applications.

I/O devices

In the Macintosh system, external peripheral devices communicate with the computer via one of the following I/O chips:

- [ ] a Versatile Interface Adapter (VIA) for miscellaneous, including the mouse, keyboard, and real-time clock. On the classic Macintosh, the mouse and keyboard are handled directly through the VIA; on the Macintosh SE and Macintosh II, they are controlled by an Apple Desktop Bus chip, which is addressed through the VIA.
- [ ] a second VIA on the Macintosh II for handling interrupts from NuBus slots
- [ ] a Serial Communications Controller (SCC) for serial communication
- [ ] an Apple custom chip, the IWM (Integrated Woz Machine), for floppy disk control

□ a Small Computer System Interface (SCSI) chip for high-speed parallel communication with up to seven devices

□ the custom Apple Sound Chip on the Macintosh II

The Macintosh communicates with I/O devices by writing to locations in the computer's address space, as we outlined earlier. Devices can initiate communication with the Macintosh by sending **interrupts** to the microprocessor.

Interrupts

An interrupt is an exception that is signaled to the processor by a hardware device (as opposed to a **trap,** which arises directly from the execution of an unimplemented instruction). An **exception** is an error or abnormal condition detected by the processor in the course of program execution.

On the Macintosh Plus, three devices can initiate interrupts: the Versatile Interface Adapter (VIA), the Serial Communications Controller (SCC), and the programmer's interrupt switch. On the Macintosh SE, the SCSI controller can also generate an interrupt, as can devices connected through the expansion connector. On the Macintosh II, slot devices can also initiate interrupts, which are transmitted through a second VIA chip. All of these devices use interrupts to notify the processor of a change in the device's condition, such as the completion of an I/O request.

An interrupt causes the processor to suspend normal execution, save the address of the next instruction and the processor's internal status on the stack, and execute a routine called an **interrupt handler.** Each device indicates to the processor which device is interrupting, and which interrupt handler should be executed. On completion of a particular task, the handler restores the internal status of the processor from the stack and resumes normal execution from the point at which processing was suspended.

The block diagrams given in the following sections illustrate how all these elements fit together on the various machines. The VIA, which figures in much of the computer's I/O activity, is discussed following the block diagrams.

Macintosh Plus block diagram

Figure 10-12 shows a functional block diagram of the Macintosh Plus computer.

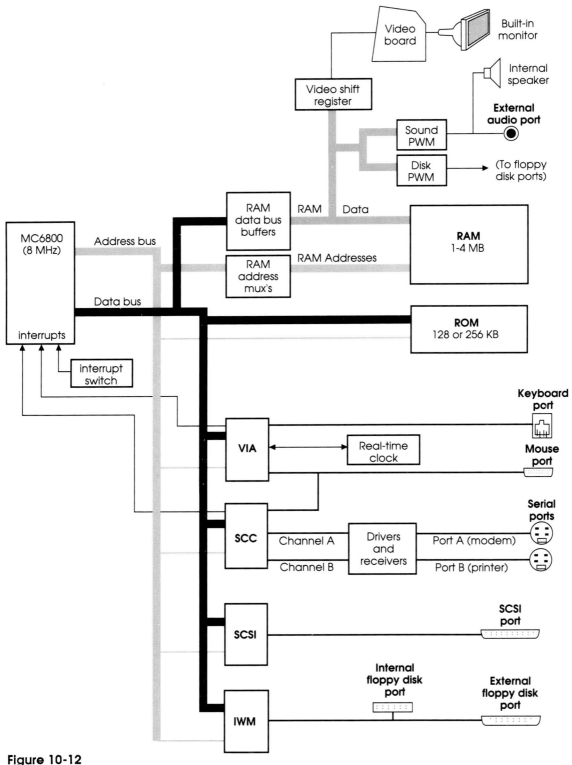

Figure 10-12
Macintosh Plus block diagram

The only real difference between the layout shown in Figure 10-13 and the corresponding figure for a Macintosh 128K or 512K is a different-sized RAM and ROM, the use of a new type of serial port on the Macintosh Plus, and the addition of the SCSI port on the Macintosh Plus.

Macintosh SE block diagram

A functional block diagram of the Macintosh SE is presented in Figure 10-13.

A comparison of this figure with the block diagram of the Macintosh Plus in Figure 10-12 will reveal some differences. The chief differences are a pair of new devices:

□ A custom gate-array chip, called the **BBU,** that handles RAM, video, sound, and that selects devices and performs other functions.

□ An Apple Desktop Bus (ADB) controller chip, handled through the VIA. ADB is a low-speed serial bus for the keyboard, mouse, and other input devices.

The system has also been modified to handle additional disk drives. An internal SCSI connector is provided, and the IWM chip can now handle up to three 3.5-inch floppy disk drives.

Macintosh II block diagram

A functional block diagram of the Macintosh II is presented in Figure 10-14.

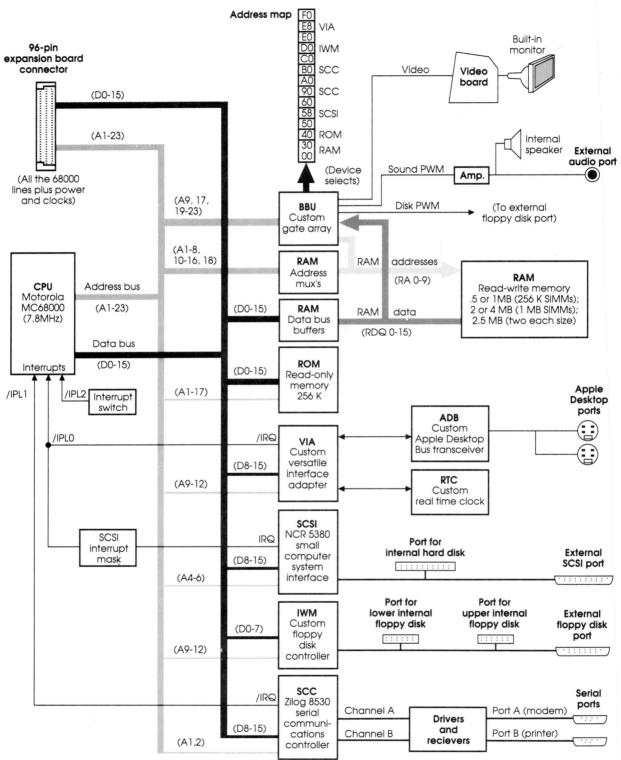

Figure 10-13
Macintosh SE block diagram

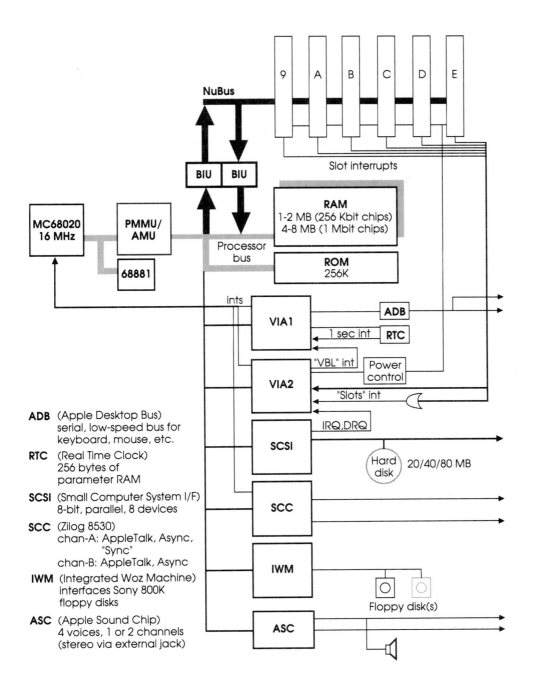

NuBus 9 A B C D E

Slot interrupts

BIU BIU

MC68020 16 MHz

PMMU/ AMU

68881

Processor bus

RAM
1-2 MB (256 Kbit chips)
4-8 MB (1 Mbit chips)

ROM
256K

ints

VIA1

ADB

1 sec int RTC

"VBL" int

Power control

VIA2

"Slots" int

SCSI

IRQ,DRQ

Hard disk 20/40/80 MB

SCC

IWM

Floppy disk(s)

ASC

ADB (Apple Desktop Bus)
serial, low-speed bus for
keyboard, mouse, etc.

RTC (Real Time Clock)
256 bytes of
parameter RAM

SCSI (Small Computer System I/F)
8-bit, parallel, 8 devices

SCC (Zilog 8530)
chan-A: AppleTalk, Async,
"Sync"
chan-B: AppleTalk, Async

IWM (Integrated Woz Machine)
interfaces Sony 800K
floppy disks

ASC (Apple Sound Chip)
4 voices, 1 or 2 channels
(stereo via external jack)

Figure 10-14
Macintosh II block diagram

The most notable change with the Macintosh II is the addition of the six NuBus slots and the removal of the video interface to a device in one of the slots. Two new I/O chips have been added: a second VIA chip to handle interrupts from slot devices, and the custom Apple Sound Chip (ASC) for enhanced sound production.

The VIA

The **Versatile Interface Adapter (VIA),** as its name suggests, controls a variety of functions on the various Macintoshes.

On the classic Macintosh, a single VIA chip controls the keyboard, internal real-time clock, parts of the disk, sound, and mouse interfaces, and various internal Macintosh signals. The Macintosh SE also uses a single VIA chip, although a few of its signals have changed due to the addition of the Apple Desktop Bus and other new features.

The many new features of the Macintosh II required the addition of a second VIA chip. The VIA1 chip provides most of the signals from the original Macintosh configuration, ensuring maximum compatibility with existing Macintosh software. The VIA1 chip also provides access to new features, including the Apple Desktop Bus and a signal for synchronous modem support. The VIA2 chip provides control of the 24- to 32-bit address mapping unit (the AMU), decoding for the NuBus slot interrupts, a SCSI interrupt, and other new features.

The real-time clock

The Macintosh real-time clock is a custom chip whose interface lines are controlled by the VIA. The clock contains a four-byte counter that is incremented once each second, as well as a line that can be used by the VIA to generate an interrupt once each second.

The clock chip also contains 256 bytes of battery-powered RAM. These RAM bytes, called **parameter RAM,** contain important data that needs to be preserved even when the Macintosh is turned off. The clock chip is powered by a battery when the system is off, thereby preserving all the settings stored in it. You can change most of the values in parameter RAM via the Control Panel desk accessory. (The values contained in the parameter RAM are discussed in "The Control Panel" section of Chapter 6.)

The date and time setting is also copied at system startup from the clock chip into a low-memory location. This setting is stored as the number of seconds since "antiquity"—midnight January 1, 1904—and is updated every second.

The clock chip on the Macintosh SE and Macintosh II is powered by a long-life (seven- to ten-year) lithium battery mounted on the main circuit board, so its parameter RAM remains valid even if you do not turn your computer on for extended periods of time.

The sound generator

As with video, the sound capabilities of the Macintosh II represent a major departure from the sound provided by the Macintosh Plus and Macintosh SE. As indicated in "The Sound Manager" section of Chapter 9, the Macintosh II continues to support software written for the original Sound Driver used on the Macintosh Plus and Macintosh SE.

Macintosh Plus and Macintosh SE sound

On the integral Macintoshes, the sound circuitry and the disk speed controller circuitry share a special 740-byte buffer in memory, of which the sound circuitry uses the 370 even-numbered bytes to generate sound. Every horizontal blanking interval (every 44.93 microseconds—when the beam of the display tube moves from the right edge of the screen to the left), the MC68000 automatically fetches two bytes from this buffer and sends the high-order byte to the sound circuitry.

❖ *Note:* The period of any four-tone or free-form sound generated by the Sound Driver is a multiple of this 44.93-microsecond interval. The highest frequency is 11128 hertz (Hz), which corresponds to twice this interval.

By storing a range of values in the sound buffer, a program can create the corresponding waveform in the output sound channel. This signal drives a small speaker inside the Macintosh and is connected to the external sound jack on the back of the computer. The external sound line can drive a load of 600 or more ohms—that is, the input of almost any audio amplifier, but not a directly connected external speaker. You can disable the internal speaker by inserting a plug into the external sound jack.

Every vertical blanking interval (every 16.6 milliseconds—when the beam of the display tube moves from the bottom of the screen to the top), the Sound Driver fills its half of the buffer with the next set of 370 values, each specifying the sound amplitude for one 44.93-microsecond interval. For **square-wave** sound, the buffer is filled with a constant value; for more complex sound, it's filled with many values.

The sound generator uses a form of **pulse-width encoding** to create sounds. The pulses come at fixed 44.93 microsecond intervals; the *width* of each pulse conveys the *amplitude* of the sound wave. The Sony Sound Chip integrates the pulse train to make a smoothly varying amplitude for the sound output. Figure 10-15 shows the relationship between the pulse width and the amplitude of the sound wave.

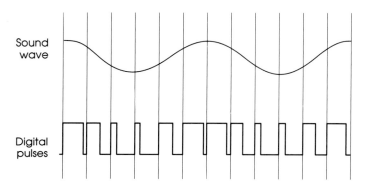

Figure 10-15
Sound signals

The sound circuitry reads one word in the sound buffer during each horizontal blanking interval, including the virtual intervals during vertical blanking, and uses the high-order byte of the word to generate a pulse of electricity whose duration, or width, is proportional to the value of the byte.

The Sony Sound Chip converts this pulse into a voltage that is attenuated or reduced by a value from the VIA. This reduction corresponds to the current setting of the volume level. After attenuation, the pulses are integrated, or smoothed, and the resulting sound signal is passed to the audio output line.

❖ *Note:* The low-order byte of each word in the sound buffer is used to control the speed of the motor for the original single-sided floppy disk drives. Any sound information stored there will interfere with the single-sided disk I/O.

On the Macintosh Plus, there are two sound buffers in RAM, just as there are two screen buffers. The alternate sound buffer is not supported in the Macintosh SE and Macintosh II. On Macintosh II, the sound buffer is located on the Apple Sound Chip (ASC).

The Macintosh II sound chip

The Macintosh II sound circuit uses the Apple Sound Chip (ASC) and two Sony sound chips to drive the internal speaker or external stereo mini-phono jack. The Apple Sound Chip generates a stereo/audio signal. This signal pair is then filtered and buffered by the Sony sound chips, and output via the speaker or stereo mini-phono jack.

The Apple Sound Chip allows superior sound generation that is compatible with existing Macintosh software. In addition to the previous Macintosh sound capabilities, the Apple Sound Chip offers

□ four-voice hardware synthesis (this mode is a hardware implementation of the four-voice driver in the Macintosh ROMs)

□ stereo free-form sound

□ increased fidelity

A new set of ROM tools (the Sound Manager) provides new options and features; however, ASC sound generation will work with existing Macintosh software.

In place of a single RAM address space, the ASC adds two 1024-byte first-in, first-out memories to accept the sound values. This removes much of the time-critical nature of sound generation and gives stereo sound.

The sound generator produces sound in two ways: through the on-board speaker, and through the external headphone jack. The internal speaker is a 2-1/4-inch speaker, driven by a power amplifier.

The headphone jack is a stereo mini-jack, compatible with headphones for portable cassette recorders. It will not drive a speaker directly. As on other Macintosh models, the speaker is disconnected if a plug is inserted in the external sound connector. If no plug is inserted in the jack, the default sound mode will be switched to monaural to allow both channels of the stereo sound to play through the Macintosh II internal speaker. The jack is capable of driving headphones of 8 to 600 ohms and is short-circuit protected.

The sample rate is 22.25454 KHz, for a useful bandwidth of approximately 7 KHz. Volume is controlled in eight increments of 8.75 decibels each, for a total output dynamic range of 70 decibels.

The disk interface

The Macintosh disk interface uses a design similar to that used on the Apple II and Apple III computers, employing the Apple custom IWM chip. On the classic Macintosh, another custom chip called the *Analog Signal Generator (ASG)* reads the disk speed buffer in RAM and generates voltages that control the disk speed for single-sided disk drives. (On the Macintosh SE, this function has been integrated into the custom gate array chip, the SELU.)

Together with the VIA, these chips generate all the signals necessary to read, write, format, and eject the 3.5-inch disks used by all Macintoshes. On the Macintosh Plus and Macintosh SE, the disk interface can also support an external Apple Hard Disk 20.

❖ *Note:* The external double-sided drive can be attached to a Macintosh 512K through the back of an Apple Hard Disk 20. The software on the Hard Disk 20 Startup disk contains a device driver for this drive as well as the HFS (128K ROM) version of the File Manager.

On the Macintosh SE, the IWM can handle up to three floppy disk drives and operates at 16 MHz. On the Macintosh II, it handles two floppy disk drives and operates at 16 MHz.

In software, disk I/O is supported by the Macintosh Disk Driver. The Macintosh File Manager supports higher-level file access.

800K floppy disk drive

The Macintosh Plus, Macintosh SE, and Macintosh II each contain a built-in double-sided 3.5-inch disk drive. The double-sided drive can format, read, and write both 800K double-sided disks and 400K single-sided disks. A single mechanism positions two read/write heads—one above the disk and one below—so that the drive can access two tracks simultaneously. (For 400K disks, the double-sided drive restricts its operation to one side of the disk.)

On the Macintosh Plus and Macintosh SE, you can also attach an external double-sided drive or one of the older single-sided drives. On the Macintosh SE and Macintosh II, a second internal floppy drive can be added. On the Macintosh II, however, there is no external disk drive port: the task of handling external disk I/O is taken over fully by the SCSI port.

❖ *Note:* By default, single-sided disks do not use the hierarchical file system (HFS). You can place the HFS on a single-sided disk by holding down the Option key when you select the format command.

❖ *Note:* On the older 400K disk drives, a buffer in RAM (actually the low-order bytes of words in the sound buffer) is read by the Analog Signal Generator (ASG) to generate a pulse-width modulated signal, like the sound signal, that controls the speed of the disk motor. This speed variation is responsible for the characteristic humming of the disk drive. The Macintosh Operating System uses this speed control to store more sectors of information in the tracks closer to the edge of the disk by running the disk motor at slower speeds. On the 800K drives, the variable disk speed is automatically controlled by the disk drive hardware.

The SCSI interface

The Macintosh Plus, Macintosh SE, and Macintosh II computers each have a built-in SCSI port for high-speed parallel communications. **Small Computer System Interface (SCSI)** is an industry-standard interface, defined by the American National Standards Institute (ANSI). The SCSI interface can communicate with up to seven SCSI devices, such as hard disks, streaming tapes, and high-speed line printers. The external SCSI port is a DB-25 connector on the back of the computer.

The SCSI port on the Macintosh SE and Macintosh II is identical to the SCSI port on the Macintosh Plus, except that faster transfer rates are supported by special hardware.

The SCSI port is controlled by an NCR 5380 SCSI chip. The SCSI controller chip is connected to an internal SCSI-standard 50-pin ribbon connector and the external DB-25 connector. The SCSI port can be used to implement the full SCSI interface as defined by the ANSI X3T9.2 committee. The Macintosh Plus's SCSI port differs from the ANSI committee's standard in two ways:

□ First, it uses a DB-25 connector instead of the standard 50-pin ribbon connector. You can convert the DB-25 connector to the standard 50-pin connector with an Apple adapter cable.

□ Second, power for termination resistors is not provided at the SCSI connector nor are termination resistors provided in the Macintosh Plus SCSI circuitry. This means the SCSI bus must have a termnation pack somewhere outside the Macintosh Plus. The termination pack must be powered by the external SCSI device, which must be turned on *before* turning on the computer.

Warning

Never connect an RS-232 device to the SCSI port. Even though the connector looks like an RS-232 port, it is not a serial port or a parallel printer interface. Don't plug anything but a SCSI device into that connector. The SCSI interface is designed to use standard TTL logic levels of 0 and +5 volts, but RS-232 devices may impose levels of –25 and +25 volts on some lines, thereby frying the SCSI chip.

The Macintosh Plus SCSI port supports approximate transfer rates of 142K bytes per second for **nonblind transfers** and 312K bytes per second for **blind transfers.** (With nonblind transfers, the SCSI chip is is polled, or checked for the successful transfer of each byte.) The Macintosh SE and Macintosh II, where blind transfers have been made more secure, support maximum rates of approximately 600 kilobytes per second and 1.2 megabytes per second, respectively.

The SCSI bus is supported in software by the SCSI Manager, introduced in Chapter 9.

Serial I/O

All Macintosh computers have two RS-422 serial I/O ports for printers, modems, and other standard I/O devices. The Macintosh Plus, Macintosh SE, and Macintosh II use two Mini-8 connectors for the two serial ports.

❖ *Note:* The Macintosh 128K, 512K, and 512K enhanced used the larger DB-9 connectors for the two serial ports. An Apple adapter is available for connecting the two types of connectors.

The two serial ports are controlled by a **Serial Communications Controller (SCC)** chip. The port known as SCC port A is the one with the modem icon on the back of the Macintosh; SCC port B is the one with the printer icon.

The two serial ports are identical except that the modem port (port A) has a higher interrupt priority, making it more suitable for high-speed communication. The user can select which port to use by means of the Chooser desk accessory. (Recall that, for software reasons, devices connected over AppleTalk must use port B, the printer port.)

Macintosh serial ports conform to the EIA (Electronics Industry Association) standard RS-422, which differs from the more common RS-232C standard. While RS-232C modulates a signal with respect to a common ground (called *single-ended transmission*), RS-422 modulates two signals against each other (called *differential transmission*). The RS-232C receiver senses whether the received signal is sufficiently negative with respect to ground to be a logic "1," whereas the RS-422 receiver simply senses which line is more negative than the other. This makes RS-422 more immune to noise and interference, and more versatile over longer distances.

If you ground the positive side of each RS-422 receiver and leave the positive side of each transmitter unconnected, you've converted to EIA standard RS-423, which can be used to communicate with most RS-232C devices over distances up to 50 feet or so.

❖ *Note:* The Mini-8 connectors provide an output handshake signal, but do not provide the +5 volts and +12 volts found on the Macintosh 128K, 512K, and 512K enhanced serial ports.

See the *Macintosh Family Hardware Reference* manual for the serial port pinouts.

Macintosh SE and Macintosh II serial port differences

The Macintosh SE and the Macintosh II accept an extra input handshake signal on their serial ports. This new input allows for a number of improvements, including the ability to choose a second input clock on port A and the ability to choose different transfer protocols, allowing for faster data transfer rates and the ability to communicate with more different kinds of modems and computers. The Macintosh SE and Macintosh II can now use a **synchronous modem** on SCC channel A (the modem port).

Applications that use the Macintosh Serial Driver won't experience any problems because of these changes. (The Serial Driver is discussed in the "Serial Communication" section of the previous chapter.)

Macintosh keyboards

In surveying the topography of Macintosh keyboards, the introduction of the Apple Desktop Bus (ADB) on the Macintosh SE and Macintosh II appears as a watershed. The keyboards on the original Macintosh and Macintosh Plus are fully interchangeable with each other but are not compatible with the ADB connectors used on the Macintosh SE and Macintosh II.

In software, keyboard events are detected by the Operating System Event Manager and passed in turn to the Toolbox Event Manager, as described in Chapter 3.

The Macintosh Plus keyboard

The Macintosh Plus keyboard, which includes a built-in numeric keypad, contains an Intel 8021 microprocessor that scans the keys. The 8021 chip contains ROM and RAM and is programmed to conform to the Macintosh keyboard's interface protocol. (On older models, the detached numeric keypad also has its own 8021 chip.)

❖ *Note:* The Macintosh Plus keyboard reproduces all of the key-down transitions produced by the keyboard and optional keypad used by earlier Macintoshes. These keyboards are completely interchangeable.

The Macintosh Plus keyboard plugs into the machine through a four-wire RJ-11 telephone-style jack. If a separate numeric keypad is installed in the system, the keyboard plugs into the keypad and the keypad in turn plugs into the Macintosh.

International keyboards may have different arrangements of keys but are otherwise identical with the U.S. keyboard. Keyboard mapping is handled in software, as explained in the "Keyboard Events" section of Chapter 3.

The Apple Desktop Bus

On the Macintosh SE and Macintosh II, the keyboard and mouse are supported by a new input bus, the Apple Desktop Bus (ADB). The ADB is a serial communications bus designed to accommodate low-speed input devices. ADB has three functions in the Macintosh II and Macintosh SE:

☐ supporting the detached keyboard

☐ supporting the mouse

☐ supporting additional input devices, such as graphics tablets and light pens

The ADB is also used on the Apple IIGS computer, meaning that the Apple IIGS keyboard and mouse are completely compatible with the keyboards and mouse devices used with the Macintosh SE and Macintosh II.

ADB can theoretically support up to 16 devices, although performance will probably deteriorate if more than 3 devices are daisy-chained to an ADB bus (giving an effective total of 6 devices). Even though there are two ADB *ports,* there is only one ADB *bus:* the two ADB connectors are attached in parallel on the same bus. Figure 10-16 shows the Apple Desktop Bus.

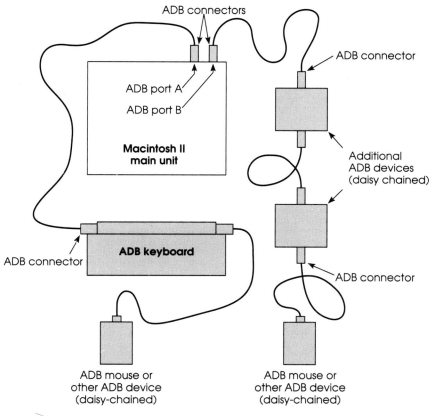

ADB connectors

ADB connector

ADB port A

ADB port B

**Macintosh II
main unit**

Additional
ADB devices
(daisy chained)

ADB connector

ADB keyboard

ADB connector

ADB connector

ADB mouse or
other ADB device
(daisy-chained)

ADB mouse or
other ADB device
(daisy-chained)

Figure 10-16
The Apple Desktop Bus

The ADB is controlled by an independent microprocessor accessed through the VIA chip, and is supported in software by mouse and keyboard drivers, which pass mouse and keyboard events to the Toolbox Event Manager.

ADB devices typically default to the same address or device number on power-up or reset. At startup time, devices are randomly assigned new, distinct addresses, and software then talks to them at those addresses.

Warning

Do not connect a device to the Apple Desktop Bus while the system is on. Connecting the device will reset all devices on the bus to their power-up addresses, which may cause the system to lose the addresses of input devices. Only the mouse and keyboard default to and keep known addresses, so they may not be affected by being plugged in or reset.

ADB keyboards

On the Macintosh SE and Macintosh II, two ADB keyboards are supported. The standard keyboard, named the Apple Keyboard, is pictured in Figure 10-17. This keyboard has a new key cap for the Command (propeller) key, which now features the Open Apple symbol as well. (This key is the equivalent of the Command key on the Macintosh Plus keyboard.)

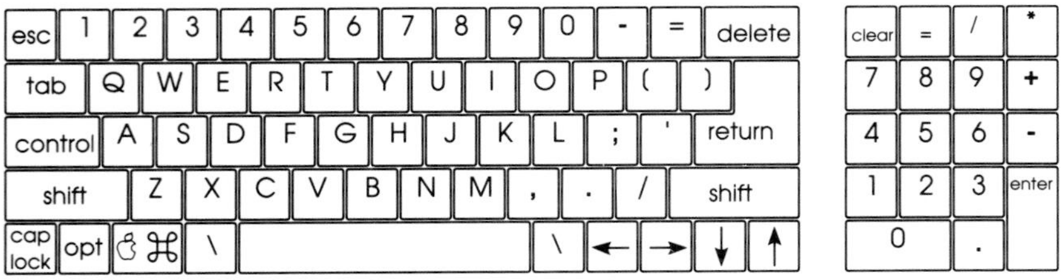

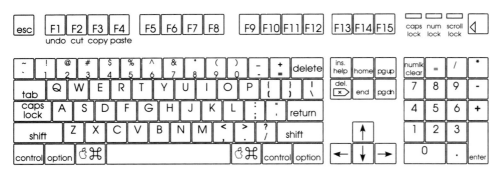

Figure 10-17
Apple (ADB) keyboard layout

Another ADB keyboard, the Apple Extended Keyboard, can also be used with the Macintosh SE and Macintosh II. This keyboard, mimicking the keyboards used on traditional computer terminals, includes 15 programmable function keys, an Alt key, and many additional keys, as shown in Figure 10-18.

Figure 10-18
Apple extended keyboard layout

The function keys generate key codes just like character keys; software can map these key codes to whatever character code is desired. (See the "Keyboard Events" section of Chapter 3.)

The mouse

On the Macintosh and Macintosh Plus, the DB-9 connector labeled with the mouse icon connects to the mouse. (Apple II, Apple III, Lisa®, and classic Macintosh mouse devices are electrically identical.) The ADB mouse used on the Macintosh SE and Macintosh II is different, as we'll explain shortly.

Classic Macintosh mouse operation

The classic Macintosh mouse generates four signals that describe the amount and direction of the mouse's travel. Interrupt-driven routines in the Macintosh ROM convert this information into the corresponding motion of the pointer on the screen.

You can change the amount of screen pointer motion that corresponds to a given mouse motion with the **mouse scaling** option in the Control Panel desk accessory. Mouse scaling may be on or off—initially it's turned on. (This setting is stored in parameter RAM, described in "The Real-Time Clock" section of this chapter.) If mouse scaling is on, the system looks every sixtieth of a second at whether the mouse has moved. If the sum of the mouse's horizontal or vertical changes in position in that time exceeds the **mouse-scaling threshold** (normally six pixels), the cursor will move twice as far horizontally and vertically as it would if mouse scaling were off.

Unlike input devices such as graphics tablets or light pens, the mouse is a relative-motion device; that is, it doesn't report where it is, only how far and in which direction it's moving.

❖ *Note:* When graphics tablets, touch screens, light pens, or other absolute-position devices are connected to the mouse port, software must either convert their coordinates into motion information or provide custom device-handling routines.

The mouse operates by sending square-wave trains of information to the Macintosh that change as the velocity and direction of motion change. The rubber-coated steel ball in the mouse contacts two capstans, each connected to an interrupter wheel. Motion along the mouse's X-axis rotates one of the wheels and motion along the Y-axis rotates the other one (Figure 10-19).

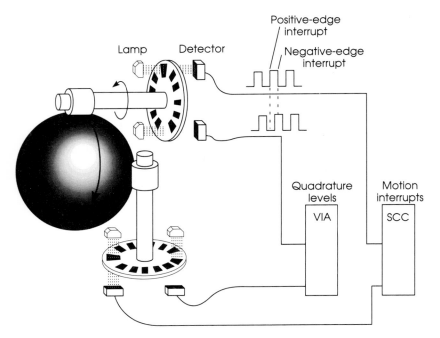

Figure 10-19
Mouse mechanism

The Macintosh uses a scheme known as *quadrature encoding* to detect which direction the mouse is moving along each axis. There is a row of slots on an interrupter wheel, and two beams of infrared light shine through the slots, each one aimed at a phototransistor detector. The detectors are offset just enough so that as the wheel turns, they produce two square-wave signals (called the *interrupt signal* and the *quadrature signal*) 90 degrees out of phase. The quadrature signal precedes the interrupt signal by 90 degrees when the wheel turns one way, and trails it when the wheel turns the other way.

The mouse's signals are interpreted by the VIA and SCC, and translated by software into the movement of the pointer on the Macintosh screen.

❖ *Note:* On the Macintosh SE and Macintosh II, motion signals are processed by the mouse itself, and translated by the ADB controller chip, as explained in the next section.

ADB mouse

The Apple Desktop Bus mouse used on the Macintosh SE and Macintosh II communicates with the system through the ADB. The mouse can be plugged directly into either of the ADB ports or into the ADB keyboard (that is, "daisy-chained"). The ADB controller chip keeps track of the mouse and provides position and status information to the system. The mouse also has its own little microprocessor on board.

This use of a peripheral processor is a departure from other Macintosh computers, which use the SCC and the VIA. The intelligent ADB mouse handles the quadrature mechanism on its own: the mouse's microprocessor sends the motion information to the ADB chip, which in turn sends it to the VIA, where the computer can read it. On the Macintosh Plus, the CPU itself must monitor the keyboard and mouse to see if anything has happened. The ADB controller on the Macintosh SE and Macintosh II takes over that function, freeing up the CPU for other work, and making it less likely that keyboard or mouse activity will be missed when the processor is busy.

An additional improvement with the ADB mouse is that mouse-scaling is multilevel (rather than on or off as on the Macintosh Plus), giving the user closer control over the relationship between mouse movement and the movement of the cursor on the screen.

ADB mouse devices do their own processing of motion signals, allowing more things to happen simultaneously in the Macintosh system. On the Macintosh II, the 68020 CPU and the optional 68851 memory management unit make possible true multitasking at the software level. This means that the Macintosh II can run a multitasking operating system such as UNIX, which is described in the next chapter.

Chapter 11

The UNIX
Operating
System

This chapter introduces A/UX, Apple's implementation of the UNIX operating system for the Macintosh II computer. For more detail, and for a guide to the UNIX documentation suite, refer to the *A/UX System Overview*.

About the UNIX operating system

A/UX is an enhanced implementation of the industry-standard UNIX operating system, designed to run on the Macintosh II computer as an alternative to the Macintosh Operating System. To accommodate UNIX's high performance demands, the PMMU chip must be added to the base Macintosh II machine; a minimum of 2 MB of RAM and an Apple HD 80SC hard disk are also required.

A/UX is based on the AT&T System V, Release 2 version of UNIX. Besides offering all of the features of the System V version of UNIX, A/UX adds important extensions from the Berkeley Software Distribution (BSD) 4.2 version of UNIX, as well as Apple's own enhancements.

Originally developed by Bell Laboratories, **UNIX** is a general-purpose time-sharing system that has become a standard in university computing environments, on high-end engineering workstations, and in government computer installations. Businesses have also applied the multiuser, multitasking capabilities of UNIX to a great variety of tasks, particularly in the fields of computer-aided design, data base management, and publishing.

UNIX provides a vast and powerful operating system for many types of hardware, and developers have ported versions of UNIX to a multitude of machines. This has been accomplished quickly because UNIX is written almost entirely in C, a high-level language that makes the system relatively easy to read, understand, and modify.

The full distribution of A/UX, including executable programs, language compilers, libraries, programming tools, and on-line documentation, amounts to more than 40 MB, and the full documentation set is nearly 6000 pages long.

Features

A/UX provides the following features:

- **Multitasking capability.** You can run multiple jobs simultaneously.

- **Multiuser capability.** A/UX supports up to 16 users working simultaneously. Users can easily share files and tools without sacrificing system security or reliability.

- **Macintosh user interface and powerful graphics capabilities.** Although the standard video mode is terminal emulation, applications developed under A/UX can incorporate the Macintosh user interface. The Macintosh User Interface Toolbox is available to applications running under A/UX through the A/UX Toolbox.

- **Hardware-independent development environment.** UNIX software is portable and can run on different manufacturers' hardware. Software developed on any type of UNIX machine can be easily ported by recompiling the source code on another UNIX machine.
- **Flexible command interpreters.** The command shell interface to A/UX can be tailored to suit your individual needs.
- **Useful applications.** A/UX includes powerful tools for such tasks as document preparation and software development. Several MPW tools including the Rez resource compiler and DeRez decompiler are also supported.
- **Hierarchical file system.** The UNIX file system permits flexible organization and facilitates file sharing for group projects.
- **Networking capabilities.** Through serial lines, modems, and Ethernet connections, you can share files, tools, and hardware resources with users across local-area and wide-area networks.
- **Simplified system administration.** By automating many of the usual UNIX administration tasks and by providing documentation aimed at nonprogrammers, A/UX reduces special system administration requirements.

UNIX has developed along two branches, and two de facto standards now exist: System V, AT&T's own UNIX specification, and the Berkeley Software Distribution (BSD), adapted from AT&T UNIX at the University of California and adding many enhancements to UNIX.

A/UX adheres fully to the System V Interface Definition, AT&T's formal specification for UNIX systems, and includes important Berkeley extensions, allowing it to maintain source code compatibility with software running under BSD 4.2 and 4.3. A/UX incorporates the following features of the BSD versions of UNIX:

- selected kernel extensions
- BSD 4.3 Transmission Control Protocol/Internet Protocol (TCP/IP) network protocols
- C shell (an alternative shell)
- BSD 4.3 sockets (a network communication mechanism implemented for TCP/IP)
- important utilities

Additionally, Apple has incorporated many of its own enhancements into A/UX:

- Macintosh User Interface Toolbox
- LaserWriter support (via TranScript, a set of programs for printing to PostScript printers)
- Network File System (NFS) support (developed and licensed by Sun Microsystems, Inc.)
- Apple Desktop Bus (ADB) support

- floating-point support (for the Macintosh II's MC68881 floating-point coprocessor)
- automatic startup and crash recovery
- automatic device configuration

Figure 11-1 illustrates some of the most important features of the A/UX system.

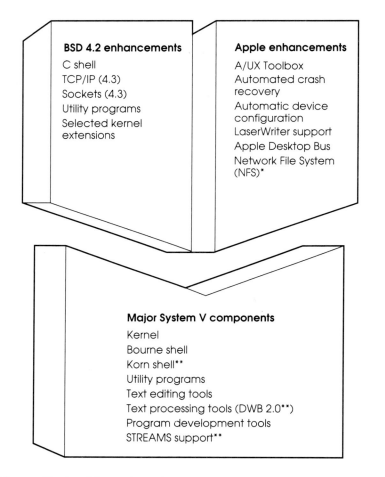

BSD 4.2 enhancements
C shell
TCP/IP (4.3)
Sockets (4.3)
Utility programs
Selected kernel
extensions

Apple enhancements
A/UX Toolbox
Automated crash
recovery
Automatic device
configuration
LaserWriter support
Apple Desktop Bus
Network File System
(NFS)*

Major System V components
Kernel
Bourne shell
Korn shell**
Utility programs
Text editing tools
Text processing tools (DWB 2.0**)
Program development tools
STREAMS support**

* Licensed by Sun Microsystems, Inc.
** Separately licensed AT&T developments are not part of System V, release 2

Figure 11-1
A/UX features

Apple peripherals are fully supported, including the LaserWriter and ImageWriter printers, the SCSI tape backup unit, SCSI hard disks, and Apple modems.

Memory requirements

UNIX is a huge system, and the A/UX implementation is even larger than most, due to the addition of the Berkeley extensions and Apple enhancements to a complete System V, Release 2 system. The full A/UX distribution, including object code and on-line documentation, amounts to more than 40 MB.

However, most actual installations will not be so large. You may, for example, delete utilities that you don't use. If your workstation is connected to other hosts across a network, you may store data or system files on other computers.

Given the versatility of A/UX and the many possible configurations, the following will give you a rough idea of the memory resources your system may require:

- kernel size, from 800K to over 1.5 MB of RAM

- swap space, at least an additional 8 MB of free disk space to accommodate page swapping (moving code between disk memory and RAM as needed)

- user space, 3 to 5 MB of free disk space for each user's individual files; 2 MB of RAM for each additional user

As you can see, a single 80-MB hard disk might be adequate for a single user system. Accommodating additional users, however, requires either extra disk storage or else a pared-back configuration of A/UX. (Additional disk storage need not necessarily be attached directly to your Macintosh II; the disk could belong to another machine connected over a network.)

Overview of the A/UX system

Figure 11-2 presents a spatial metaphor for the layout of the A/UX system.

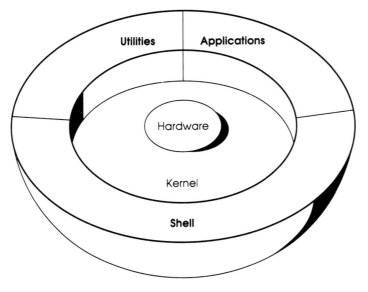

Figure 11-2
Layers of the A/UX system

The Macintosh II hardware is at the core of the system, the pearl in the oyster of A/UX. A program called the **kernel** controls this hardware. The A/UX kernel manages files, communicates with peripherals, and handles other low-level, machine-dependent details.

The kernel insulates the hardware from the utilities, so that applications software can be written independent of specific hardware. This allows you to easily transport a UNIX application from one machine to another, regardless of differences in their architectures, by recompiling the source code.

A/UX's basic utilities constitute the first layer generally available to the user. Utilities include commands for file manipulation, process management, user communication, software development and maintenance, and other housekeeping functions.

The **shell** reads and interprets the commands that users type; it forms the interface between users and the rest of the system. A/UX offers three of these command interpreters: the Bourne shell, the C shell, and the Korn shell. With its own internal commands, the shell also acts like a high-level, interpreted programming language that handles variables, case statements, subroutines, parameter passing, and interrupt handling. This programming capability allows you to easily compose and perform complex commands and procedures known as **shell scripts.**

Device I/O

The hierarchical UNIX file system treats devices like files. The output of a software process (that is, the output of an executing program) can be directed to a device, such as a printer, as easily as to a file. Likewise, the input from a device such as a modem or the console can be sent to a process as easily as data from a file. Removable mass storage media can be mounted and unmounted from the system as easily as files are added and removed.

The A/UX Toolbox

The **A/UX Toolbox** is a set of libraries and programs that bridges the gap between A/UX and the standard Macintosh environment. The A/UX Toolbox gives programs running under A/UX access to the Macintosh User Interface Toolbox and to most of the Macintosh Operating System, actually making it possible for the same Macintosh program to run in both environments.

The A/UX Toolbox performs two basic functions:

■ **Translation of Toolbox calls.** A/UX Toolbox calls are translated into Macintosh ROM calls, thereby providing full support for menus, windows, dialogs, and the rest of the Macintosh user interface.

■ **Reimplementation of the Macintosh Operating System.** Macintosh OS calls are redirected to A/UX libraries. These libraries include new implementations of the Memory Manager, the Segment Loader, the Vertical Retrace and Time Managers, and much of the File Manager. (Note, however, that several of the Operating System managers connected to input and output are not currently available; see *A/UX Toolbox: Macintosh ROM Interface* for details.)

Currently, the Finder is also unavailable and desk accessories are not supported.

Figure 11-3 shows how the Toolbox libraries fit into the A/UX system.

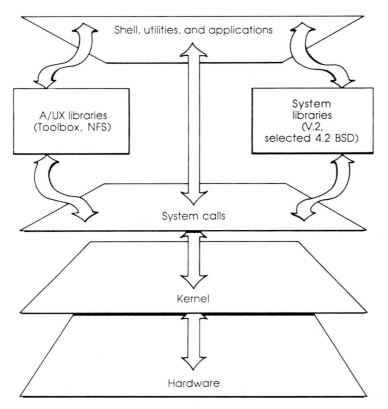

Figure 11-3
Relationship of the A/UX Toolbox to the rest of the system

With the A/UX Toolbox, you can port a binary Macintosh application to A/UX, but only if the application follows the recommendations in *Inside Macintosh,* Volumes I through V, and in *A/UX Toolbox: Macintosh ROM Interface*. Applications that bypass the Macintosh User Interface Toolbox to manipulate memory and hardware directly are not compatible with the A/UX Toolbox. With some modifications, most Macintosh applications can be made to run with A/UX.

The A/UX Toolbox includes special utilities both for porting Macintosh applications to A/UX and for developing A/UX applications that take advantage of the Macintosh User Interface Toolbox. Several MPW tools, including the resource compiler and decompiler, have been ported to A/UX.

Software development environment

One of the strengths of UNIX lies in its software development environment. Because A/UX adheres to the System V Interface Definition, it can be used to write application software that is independent of specific computer hardware. This allows you to port your UNIX programs to other UNIX machines. A/UX also offers a good environment for cross-development of programs for other personal computers, including Apple II and MS-DOS machines, and for developing Macintosh-like programs under UNIX. The Macintosh family's powerful native development environment, the Macintosh Programmer's Workshop (MPW), combines many of the elements of the UNIX development environment and the Macintosh interface. As we mentioned in the previous section, A/UX also supports several MPW tools, including the resource compiler and decompiler.

The programming tools of A/UX include C and Fortran compilers together with utility programs and subroutine libraries that simplify program creation and maintenance, including tools for configuration management, automating program builds, and debugging.

C is the main A/UX system programming tool. C is a portable, high-level language that also offers very low-level operations, making it a flexible and efficient language for both application and system programming. In fact, like other UNIX systems, almost all of A/UX—including the C compiler itself—is written in C. A/UX provides the complete set of standard C libraries, compiler preprocessor directives, and operators associated with the System V version of UNIX, as well as many BSD extensions.

A/UX's C compiler supports the 68881 floating-point hardware, user-defined data types, arbitrary-length variable names, pointer variables and address arithmetic, a full macro processor, fully recursive procedures, and the run-time library that gives access to all system facilities.

A/UX also supports the Fortran-77 programming language through its f77 compiler. Fortran-77 is a high-level language that is especially useful for scientific and mathematical applications. The efl compiler is also included with A/UX.

Document development applications

A/UX supplies a variety of text editing tools, which allow you to create and modify text files. Also provided is the Documentor's Workbench (DWB 2.0), a set of utility programs that can format text files for output to a variety of devices. A/UX's extensive printer and typesetter support includes postprocessor filters for the APS-5 phototypesetter, for the Xerox 9700 printer, as well as for the Apple LaserWriter and ImageWriter.

Communications

A/UX supports a variety of networking solutions, including serial communications, TCP/IP, and NFS (Network File System). These facilities make it possible to share computers, terminals, files, printers, modems, software, electronic mail, and other resources with other network users.

Serial communications

The standard Macintosh II configuration includes two Mini-8 RS-422 serial ports. Additional serial ports can be added via the computer's NuBus expansion slots. By connecting a serial line from one of these ports to another computer running a standard version of UNIX, you can use A/UX utilities to connect to a remote UNIX system, send files from one UNIX system to another, and enter commands from A/UX that are executed on a remote UNIX system.

TCP/IP network

The BSD 4.3 networking package is standard with every A/UX distribution. Called *B-NET* on this implementation, this network uses Ethernet coaxial cable as the physical medium that links computers and requires that an optional Apple EtherTalk card be installed in your Macintosh II. B-NET supports the widely used Transmission Control Protocol/Internet Protocol (TCP/IP) suite.

TCP/IP supports both local-area and wide-area configurations, and A/UX's B-NET implementation supports Internet domains and subnetwork address routing. TCP/IP has found its way from the university and research facilities' ARPANET network, across the Defense Data Network, and into commercial applications, office automation, and personal computer networks.

B-NET applications allow you to communicate with other TCP/IP-supported computers on your network, regardless of their operating systems. These applications include

- **telnet,** a virtual terminal program, allows you to log into and use remote computers as if your terminal were directly connected to those computers

- **ftp,** a file transfer facility, allows you to transfer ASCII and binary files between computers on your network. You do not need to know the remote host's operating system to transfer files between it and your local A/UX computer.

- **mail,** the network mail facility, gives you electronic mail service to users across the network.

B-NET also offers a set of network commands, in many ways more convenient than telnet and ftp, which can be used between computers running operating systems like A/UX that support a derivative of the BSD 4.2 or 4.3 networking package. These utilities include a log-in facility to remote computers, a remote shell facility that allows users to execute UNIX commands on remote computers, a utility for copying files between computers, a communication program that copies lines from your terminal to that of another user, and utilities that report on the status of each computer and on who is logged on to the local network.

Besides offering these standard applications, A/UX also provides the tools for you to develop your own custom network applications based on the TCP/IP protocols.

Network File System (NFS)

Besides the serial and B-NET network applications, A/UX also provides client support for the Network File System (NFS), designed and licensed by Sun Microsystems, Inc. NFS helps to solve the problem of file sharing in a network of heterogeneous machines and operating systems by making various file systems transparently accessible to users across the network.

Like A/UX's B-NET, NFS operates on an Ethernet local-area network and requires the optional Apple EtherTalk controller board.

The major benefit NFS brings to a network is file sharing. Files on a computer with large disk storage can be accessed and shared by many other users at their workstations. This consistency creates a more efficient work environment because the problems of multiple copies of a file are eliminated. The result can be substantial storage savings. For instance, ten A/UX workstations on a network can save over 200 MB of disk storage by sharing the on-line manuals, the standard utility programs, the spelling dictionary, and so on, all stored on another A/UX workstation with larger storage facilities.

NFS is especially useful in a mixed-workstation network since it prevents you from becoming tied to one particular workstation family by providing access to the files and the work environments of other types of computers.

Transparent access to file systems is achieved by mounting file systems from remote machines onto your local A/UX file system. You can then access and manipulate remote files with A/UX commands. Other computers can also access A/UX files through their own commands.

Simplified system administration

The complexities of dealing with UNIX systems have traditionally required highly trained system administrators to keep things running. But with UNIX systems proliferating on smaller workstations, not every user at every workstation can be expected to possess the training and skills of a UNIX guru.

One of Apple's goals in the development of A/UX has been the simplification of system administration. Several of the other ways in which A/UX simplifies system administration are described below.

Automatic device configuration

Since device drivers must be integrated at the kernel level, adding devices to UNIX systems normally requires considerable system knowledge. A/UX has greatly simplified this task by automatically configuring devices upon system startup.

When you attach a new device, you log into A/UX under the privileged superuser account, place the disk containing the device's installation software into the drive, and enter a command to run a shell script that automatically installs the software. You will then shutdown A/UX and power down the Macintosh II to install the device's controller board.

When you restart A/UX, routines in the Macintosh II ROM determine that the new hardware is not configured to the kernel. A/UX then begins to build a new kernel for itself, locating the new device name and the new device driver, both of which were installed with the software. It then links the device's object modules into the new kernel. When it's done configuring the system for the new device, A/UX shuts down and reboots the newly configured kernel.

Automated startup and crash recovery

Under A/UX, you have the option of bringing up the system manually or letting it automatically boot itself up to multiuser mode. While the automated boot procedure takes a little longer than manually booting the system, the automated procedure does not require a system expert to perform it and will bring up a working multiuser system if at all possible.

The automated approach is especially useful for restarting a system that has crashed, and enables Apple to provide a reliable version of the UNIX system that can be started up by almost anyone. Because redundant copies of critical files are maintained on separate areas of the disk, and because several critical UNIX utilities have been made stand-alone, upon reboot A/UX can check and repair file system corruption, fix bad blocks on the disk, and replace missing files.

Having considered the Macintosh II implementation of UNIX, we conclude the discussion of the Macintosh architecture. A/UX provides a strong alternative operating system for Macintosh II users who need access to UNIX-based software or UNIX-based computing resources available over a network. The A/UX system also provides an entry from the UNIX world to the Macintosh system, allowing UNIX applications to implement the standard Macintosh interface described earlier in this volume.

Appendix A

Macintosh Family Specifications

This appendix gives the specifications for the Macintosh Plus, Macintosh SE, and Macintosh II computers.

Macintosh Plus specifications

Processor	MC68000, 32-bit internal architecture, 16-bit external data bus, 24-bit external address bus, 7.8336 MHz clock frequency
RAM memory	1 MB RAM (expandable to 4 MB) 256 bytes of user-settable parameter memory
ROM memory	128K ROM (expandable to 256K)
Floppy disk	800K on double-sided 3.5-inch floppy disks, one built-in, optional external
Hard disk	Optional external Apple Hard Disk 20 Optional external 20 MB, 40 MB, and 80 MB SCSI hard disks
Screen	9-inch diagonal, high-resolution, 512-pixel by 342-pixel bit-mapped display (built-in)
Interfaces	Synchronous serial keyboard bus Two RS-232/RS-422 serial ports, 230.4K baud maximum (up to 0.920 megabit per second if clocked externally) Mouse interface External floppy disk interface SCSI interface Sound port for external audio amplifier
Sound generator	4-voice sound with 8-bit digital-analog conversion using 22 KHz sample rate
Keyboard	Macintosh Plus keyboard

Mouse	Mechanical tracking, optical shaft encoding 3.54 pulses per mm (90 pulses per inch) of travel
Clock/calendar	CMOS custom chip with rechargeable 4.5 volt (Eveready No. 523 or equivalent) user-replaceable battery backup
Line input	Line voltage: 200–240 volts AC, RMS Frequency: 50 or 60 Hz Power: 60 watts

Size and weight

	Weight	Height	Width	Depth
Main unit	7.5 kg (16 lbs 8 oz)	344 mm (13.5 in)	246 mm (9.7 in)	276 mm (10.9 in)
Keyboard	1.2 kg (2 lbs 10 oz)	65 mm (2.6 in)	395.4 mm (15.6 in)	146 mm (5.8 in)
Mouse	.2 kg (7 oz)	37 mm (1.45 in)	60 mm (2.4 in)	109 mm (4.3 in)

Environment

Operating temperature	10° C to 40° C (50° F to 104° F)
Storage temperature	-40° C to +50° C (-40° F to 122° F)
Relative humidity	5% to 95% (noncondensing)
Altitude	0 to 4615 m (0 to 15,000 ft)

Macintosh SE specifications

Processor	MC68000, 32-bit internal architecture, 16-bit external data bus, 24-bit external address bus, 7.8336 MHz clock frequency
RAM memory	1 MB RAM (expandable to 4 MB) 256 bytes of user-settable parameter memory
ROM memory	256K ROM
Floppy disk	800K on double-sided 3.5-inch floppy disks, one built-in, optional second internal and external drives
Hard disk	20 MB on optional internal hard disk Optional external Hard Disk 20 Optional external 20 MB, 40 MB, and 80 MB SCSI hard disks
Screen	9-inch diagonal, high-resolution, 512-pixel by 342-pixel bit-mapped display (built-in)

Interfaces	Two Apple Desktop Bus connectors for communication with keyboard, mouse, and other devices over low-speed, synchronous serial bus
	Two RS-232/RS-422 serial ports, 230.4K baud maximum (up to 0.920 megabit per second if clocked externally), synchronous modem support on one port
	External floppy disk interface
	Expansion connector (CPU bus connector)
	SCSI interface
	Sound port for external audio amplifier
Sound generator	4-voice sound with 8-bit digital-analog conversion using 22 KHz sample rate
Keyboards	Apple Keyboard or Apple Extended Keyboard (Apple Desktop Bus)
Mouse	Apple Desktop Bus mouse; mechanical tracking, optical shaft encoding 3.54 pulse per mm (90 pulse per inch) of travel
Clock/calendar	CMOS custom chip with 7-year lithium battery
Line input	Line voltage: 200-240 volts AC, RMS
	Frequency: 50 or 60 Hz
	Power: 60 watts
Fan	10 CFM cross clow

Size and weight

	Weight	Height	Width	Depth
Main unit	7.7–10 kg* (17–22 lbs.*)	344 mm (13.55 in)	246 mm (9.69 in)	276 mm (10.87 in)
Apple Keyboard	1.0 kg (2 lbs 4 oz)	44.5 mm (1.75 in)	418.3 mm (16.48 in)	140.0 mm (5.52 in)
Mouse	.96 kg (7 oz)	37 mm (1.45 in)	60 mm (2.36 in)	109 mm (4.29 in)
Apple Extended Keyboard (optional)	1.6 kg (3 lb 10 oz)	56.4 mm (2.25 in)	486 mm (19.125 in)	188 mm (7.4 in)

*Weight varies depending on installed optional hard disk or second 3.5-inch floppy disk drive.

Environment

Operating temperature	10° C to 40° C (50° F to 104° F)
Storage temperature	-40° C to +47° C (-40° F to 116.6° F)
Relative humidity	5% to 95% (noncondensing)
Altitude	0 to 4572 m (0 to 15,000 ft)

Macintosh II specifications

Processor	MC68020, 32-bit architecture, 15.6672 MHz clock frequency
RAM memory	1 MB, expandable to 8 MB on board (eventually to 128 MB); expandable to 2 GB in NuBus slots 256 bytes of user-settable parameter memory
ROM memory	256K (standard), expandable to 512K on board
Coprocessor	MC68881 floating-point unit (IEEE standard 754 and proposed standard p854)
Memory management	Optional MC68851 Paged Memory Management Unit (PMMU)
Floppy disk	800K on double-sided disk 3.5-inch floppy disks optional second internal disk drive
Hard disk	Optional internal and external 20 MB, 40 MB, and 80 MB SCSI hard disks
External monitors	Apple options include 12-inch, 640-by-480 pixel monochrome monitor and 13-inch, 640-by-480 pixel RGB monitor
Interfaces	Two Apple Desktop Bus connectors for communication with keyboard, mouse, and other devices over low-speed, synchronous serial bus. Two mini-8 serial (RS-422) ports Six NuBus internal slots supporting full 32-bit address and data lines SCSI interface (one internal port, one external port) Sound port for external audio amplifier
Sound generator	Apple custom sound chip (ASC) including 4-voice wave-table synthesis and stereo sampling generator capable of driving stereo mini-phono jack headphones or stereo equipment
Keyboards	Apple Keyboard or Apple Extended Keyboard (Apple Desktop Bus)

Mouse	Apple Desktop Bus mouse; mechanical tracking, optical shaft encoding 3.54 pulses per mm (90 pulses per inch) of travel		
Clock/calendar	CMOS custom chip with 7-year lithium battery		
Line input	Voltage: 90 to 140 VAC and 170 to 270 VAC, automatically configured Frequency: 48 to 62 Hz Max power: 230 watts, not including monitor power		

Size and weight

	Weight	Height	Width	Depth
Main unit	10.9 to 11.8 kg (24 to 26 lbs)	140 mm (5.51 in)	474 mm (18.66 in)	365 mm (14.37 in)
Apple Keyboard	1.0 kg (2 lbs 4 oz)	44.5 mm (1.75 in)	418.3 mm (16.5 in)	142 mm (5.6 in)
Mouse	.17 kg (6 oz)	27.9 mm (1.1 in)	53.3 mm (2.1 in)	96.5 mm (3.8 in)
Apple Extended Keyboard (optional)	1.6 kg (3 lbs 10 oz)	56.4 mm (2.25 in)	486 mm (19.125 in)	188 mm (7.4 in)
Apple High-Resolution Monochrome Monitor	7.7 kg (17 lbs)	255 mm (10.04 in)	310 mm (12.2 in)	373 mm (14.68 in)
Apple High-Resolution RGB Monitor	15.45 kg (34 lbs)	281 mm (11.06 in)	344 mm (13.54 in)	402 mm (15.83 in)

Environment

Operating temperature	10° C to 35° C (50° F to 95° F)
Storage temperature	−40° C to 47° C (−40° F to 116.6° F)
Relative humidity	5% to 95% (noncondensing)
Altitude	0 to 3048 m (0 to 10,000 ft)

Appendix B

For More Information

This appendix introduces some valuable information resources for Macintosh programmers: books, user groups, and developer support from Apple.

Where to write for more information

Several organizations exist to provide support for Macintosh programmers and users.

Apple Programmer's and Developer's Association (APDA)

Many of Apple's official technical manuals and developer-oriented products have only a limited audience and are not available in stores. The Apple Programmer's and Developer's Association (APDA) in Renton, Washington, is an organization that makes these books and development tools available through mail-order. Apple works closely with APDA to ensure that technical tools and information is available on a timely basis. APDA membership is open to anyone. You can get more information by contacting APDA at the following address:

APDA
290 SW 43rd Street
Renton, WA 98055
(206) 251-6548

User groups

For information about Apple user groups in your area, call this toll-free number: (800) 538-9696, and ask for extension 500.

Apple Developer Services

For information about getting started as a Macintosh developer, contact Apple Developer Services at the following address:

Apple Developer Services
Mailstop 27-S
Apple Computer, Inc.
20525 Mariani Avenue
Cupertino, CA 95014

Apple Developer Services also publishes a series of Macintosh Technical Notes containing useful information for programmers.

Apple technical documentation

To program the Macintosh, you'll need, *as a minimum,* the original *Inside Macintosh:*

☐ *Inside Macintosh,* Volumes 1–5

You may also find the following books helpful.

☐ *Programmer's Introduction to the Macintosh*

☐ *Macintosh Family Hardware Reference*

☐ *Human Interface Guidelines: The Apple Desktop Interface*

You'll also need a Macintosh development system and the supporting documentation.

The following sections describe the entire Macintosh technical library, including the books we've just listed.

Original *Inside Macintosh* (Volumes 1–5)

The original *Inside Macintosh* books consist of the following:

- **Volumes 1–3.** Definitive guide to the Macintosh Toolbox and Operating System for the original 64K ROM. Volume 3 also includes hardware information and comprehensive summaries.

- **Volume 4.** A delta guide to the Macintosh Plus, introducing the hierarchical file system (HFS), the Small Computer System Interface (SCSI), and the other new features available with the 128K Macintosh Plus ROM.

- **Volume 5.** A delta guide to the Macintosh SE and Macintosh II, introducing color, slots, new sound capabilities, the new Apple Desktop Bus (ADB), and all the other features available with the 256K versions of the ROM.

These books are published by Addison-Wesley and are available at bookstores or through APDA.

Inside Macintosh Library

These books are published by Addison-Wesley and are available in bookstores or by mail-order through APDA.

Besides the present manual, the *Inside Macintosh Library* consists of the following books:

- ***Programmer's Introduction to the Macintosh Family.*** A short guide replete with examples, illustrating the ins and outs of Macintosh programming.

- ***Macintosh Family Hardware Reference.*** Describes the hardware of the various Macintosh machines. It provides the information you'll need to connect non-Apple devices to the computer and to write device drivers or other low-level programs. The book consists of three parts, which comprehensively describe the classic Macintosh (Macintosh and Macintosh Plus), the Macintosh SE, and the Macintosh II.

- ***Designing Cards and Drivers for Macintosh II and Macintosh SE.*** A guide to developers who are creating hardware products that will plug into the expansion slots of the Macintosh II and Macintosh SE. In the Macintosh II, the interfacing is to NuBus; in the Macintosh SE, to the MC68000 bus. Parts of this book are also important to application software developers who need to understand slot devices.

General documentation

These manuals describe features that are now supported by all Apple computers:

- **_Human Interface Guidelines._** A description of the Apple user interface for the benefit of people who want to develop applications.

- **_Apple Numerics Manual._** A guide to the Standard Apple Numerics Environment (SANE), a full implementation of the IEEE floating-point standard, for developers who need high-precision floating-point support.

Development system documentation

Apple's Macintosh development system, the Macintosh Programmer's Workshop (MPW), is documented in the following manuals:

- **_Macintosh Programmer's Workshop 2.0 Reference._** A heart-pounding ride through the MPW shell and utilities, including the resource editor (ResEdit), resource compiler (Rez), linker, Make facility, and debugger.

- **_Macintosh Programmer's Workshop Assembler Reference (Revision 2.0)._** A guide to the MPW macro assembler for the MC68000 family. (You'll also need the appropriate microprocessor documentation from Motorola.)

- **_Macintosh Programmer's Workshop C 2.0 Reference._** A guide to the MPW C compiler. (For a guide to the C language itself, you'll need _The C Programming Language_ by B. Kernighan & D. Ritchie, or a similar C manual.)

- **_Macintosh Programmer's Workshop Pascal 2.0 Reference._** A guide to the MPW Pascal compiler.

- **_MacApp Programmer's Reference._** A guide to MacApp, an expandable Macintosh application based on Object Pascal.

Further reading

In addition to the *Inside Macintosh Library,* you can benefit from reading some of the useful books listed in this section.

Macintosh programming:

☐ Scott Knaster, *How to Write Macintosh Software* (Howard W. Sams & Co., 1986)

☐ Steve Chernicoff, *Macintosh Revealed,* Volumes 1 and 2 (Hayden Book Company, 1985)

Object-oriented programming:

☐ Kurt Schmucker, *Object-Oriented Programming for the Macintosh* (Howard W. Sams & Co., 1986)

C programming:

☐ Jim Takatsuka, Fred A. Huxham, and David Burnard, *Using the Macintosh Toolbox with C* (Sybex Books, Inc., 1985)

Assembly-language programming:

☐ Dan Weston, *The Complete Book of Macintosh Assembly Language Programming,* Volumes 1 and 2 (Scott, Foresman and Co., 1986)

☐ Gerry Kane, Doug Hawkins, and Lance Leventhal, *68000 Assembly Language Programming* (Osborne/McGraw-Hill, 1981)

☐ Motorola, Inc., *M68000 16/32-Bit Microprocessor Programmer's Reference Manual* (Prentice-Hall, 1984)

AppleTalk and networking:

☐ Apple Computer, *Inside AppleTalk* (APDA, 1987)

The UNIX Operating System:

☐ Maurice J. Bach, *The Design of the UNIX Operating System* (Prentice Hall, 1986)

☐ S. R. Bourne, *The UNIX System* (Addison-Wesley, 1983)

☐ Brian W. Kernighan and Rob Pike, *The UNIX Programming Environment* (Prentice-Hall, 1984)

Glossary

access path: A description of the route that the File Manager follows to access a file; created when a file is opened.

activate event: An event generated by the Window Manager when an inactive window becomes the active window.

active window: The frontmost window on the desktop.

ADB: See **Apple Desktop Bus.**

additive color primaries: Three colors of light (red, green, and blue) that can be combined to produce a wide range of other colors; not the same as the subtractive primaries (magenta, yellow, and cyan) used with colored pigments.

address: A number that specifies a location in memory.

Address Mapping Unit (AMU): The IC in the Macintosh II that performs 24- to 32-bit address mapping. Can be replaced by the optional PMMU.

address space: The set of all addresses a computer is capable of generating. In a Macintosh, the address space includes not only all of the memory, but the address-mapped I/O devices as well.

alert: A warning or report of an error, in the form of an alert box, sound from the Macintosh's speaker, or both.

alert box: A modal dialog box that appears on the screen to convey an alert.

A-line instructions: Unimplemented 68000-family instructions, used by the Macintosh to implement Toolbox and Operating System calls.

allocate: To reserve an area of memory for use.

allocation block: Volume space composed of multiples of logical blocks.

amplitude: The amount by which a time-varying quantity, such as sound pressure, deviates from some reference point, such as zero pressure.

analog board: The circuit board in a Macintosh that contains the power supply and video circuits. See **digital board.**

Apple Desktop Bus (ADB): A low-speed serial bus that connects the keyboard, mouse, and optional input devices to the Macintosh SE and Macintosh II.

Apple Sound Chip (ASC): A custom IC with dual waveform buffers and pulse-width modulators for enhanced sound capability on the Macintosh II.

AppleTalk Manager: An interface to a pair of device drivers that enables programs to send and receive information via an AppleTalk network.

application: A Macintosh program, such as MacPaint or the Finder, that runs stand-alone. An application's file type is 'APPL'.

application font: The font your application will use unless you specify otherwise—Geneva, by default.

application heap: The portion of the heap available to the running application program and the Toolbox.

application list: A data structure, kept in the Desktop file, for launching applications from their documents in the hierarchical file system. For each application in the list, an entry is maintained that includes the name and signature of the application, as well as the directory ID of the folder containing it.

application space: The area of memory that is available for dynamic allocation by applications.

ascent: The vertical distance from a font's base line to its ascent line.

ascent line: A horizontal line that coincides with the tops of the tallest characters in a font.

asynchronous communication: A method of data transmission where the receiving and sending devices don't share a common timer, and no timing data is transmitted.

asynchronous execution: After calling a routine asynchronously, a program is free to perform other tasks until the routine is completed.

auto-key event: An event generated repeatedly when the user presses and holds down a character key on the keyboard or keypad.

auto-key rate: The rate at which a character key repeats after it has begun to do so.

auto-key threshold: The length of time a character key must be held down before it begins to repeat.

A/UX: Apple's enhanced implementation of the standard AT&T UNIX operating system.

baseline: A horizontal line that coincides with the bottom of each character in a font, excluding descenders (such as the tail of a *p*).

baud: The unit of measure of bit rate. See **bit rate.**

Binary-Decimal Conversion Package: A Macintosh package for converting integers to decimal strings and vice versa.

bit image: A collection of bits in memory that represent a two-dimensional surface. For example, the screen is a visible bit image.

bit map: A set of bits that represents the position and binary state of a corresponding set of items. (See **bit image.**) In QuickDraw, a bitMap is a special data type consisting of a pointer to a bit image, the row width of that image, and its boundary rectangle.

bit rate: The information capacity of a communications channel, measured in *baud,* or the number of bits—both data and nondata—carried by the channel per second. Bit rate is often miscalled *baud rate.* See **baud.**

blind transfer: On a SCSI device, a data transfer without polling of the receiving device to confirm the success of the transfer.

block: A group regarded as a unit; usually refers to data or memory in which data is stored.

block device: A device that reads and writes blocks of bytes at a time. It can read or write any accessible block on demand.

boot blocks: The first two logical blocks of a volume, which contain the system startup information.

bridge: An intelligent link between two or more AppleTalk networks.

buffer: A holding area in RAM where information can be stored temporarily.

bundle: A resource (of type 'BNDL') that maps local IDs of resources to their actual resource IDs; used to associate file references and icon lists for the Finder.

button: A standard Macintosh control that causes some immediate or continuous action when clicked or pressed with the mouse. See **radio button.**

catalog tree file: A file that maintains the relationships between the files and directories on a hierarchical directory volume. It corresponds to the file directory on a flat directory volume.

cell: The basic component of a list from a structural point of view; a cell is a box in which a list element is displayed.

channel: A queue that's used by an application to send commands to the Sound Manager.

character code: An integer representing the character that a key or combination of keys on the keyboard stands for.

character device: A device that reads or writes a stream of characters, one at a time. It can neither skip characters nor go back to a previous character.

character image: An arrangement of bits that defines a character in a font.

character key: A key that generates a keyboard event when pressed; that is, any key other than a modifier key.

character offset: The horizontal separation between a character rectangle and a font rectangle; that is, the position of a given character within the font's bit image.

character origin: The point on a baseline used as a reference location for drawing a character.

character position: An index into an array containing text, starting at zero for the first character.

character rectangle: A rectangle enclosing an entire character image. Its sides are determined by the image width and the font height.

character style: A set of stylistic variations, such as bold, italic, and underline.

character width: The distance to move the pen from one character's origin to the next character's origin.

check box: A standard control that displays a setting, either checked (on) or unchecked (off). Clicking inside a check box reverses its setting.

Chooser: A desk accessory that provides a standard interface so that device drivers can solicit and accept specific choices from the user.

classic Macintosh: A term encompassing the original Macintosh (128K and 512K models), the Macintosh 512K enhanced, and the Macintosh Plus.

Clipboard file: The file used by the Scrap Manager and applications for holding data that is cut and pasted.

clipping: Limiting drawing to within the bounds of a particular area.

clipping region: The region to which an application limits drawing within a graphics port.

clock chip: A special chip in which parameter RAM and the current date and time are stored. This chip is powered by a battery when the system is off, thus keeping correct time and preserving the parameter RAM information.

closed file: A file without an access path. Closed files cannot be read from or written to.

code resource: A resource that contains a program's code—most commonly a resource of type 'CODE' (for applications and MPW tools), but other resource types such as 'DRVR' and 'PDEF' also contain code.

code segment: An individual 'CODE' resource, comprising part of the code of a Macintosh application. Segments are loaded in and out of memory by the Segment Loader.

color lookup table: A table that translates color specifications into their corresponding hardware values.

Color Picker: The desk accessory that enables the user to select colors for the display.

Color QuickDraw: An expanded version of QuickDraw that performs the graphic operations on the color display of the Macintosh II.

command file: (MPW, UNIX) A file consisting of executable commands that can be run from the shell. Also called a *script*.

compaction: The process of moving allocated blocks within a heap zone in order to collect the free space into a single block.

content region: The area of a window that the application draws in.

control: An object in a window on the Macintosh screen with which the user, using the mouse, can cause instant action with visible results or change settings to modify a future action. The control is internally represented in a control record.

control character: A nonprinting character that controls or modifies the way information is printed or displayed. In the Apple II computer family, control characters have ASCII values between 0 and 31, and are typed from a keyboard by holding down the Control key while pressing some other key. In the Macintosh family, the Command key performs a similar function.

control definition function: A function called by the Control Manager when it needs to perform type-dependent operations on a particular type of control, such as drawing the control.

Control Manager: The part of the Toolbox that provides routines for creating and manipulating controls, such as buttons, check boxes, and scroll bars.

Control Panel: A desk accessory that lets you change the speaker volume, the keyboard repeat speed and delay, mouse tracking, and other features.

control template: A resource that contains information from which the Control Manager can create a control.

coordinate plane: A two-dimensional grid. In QuickDraw, the grid coordinates are integers ranging from –32767 to 32767, and all grid lines are infinitely thin.

creator: One of the fields in a file that helps to identify the file. In a document file, the creator field normally contains the signature of the application that created the document. See **signature.**

cursor: A 16-by-16 bit image that appears on the screen and is controlled by the mouse; called the "pointer" in Macintosh user manuals.

data bits: Data communications bits that encode transmitted characters.

data buffer: Heap space containing information to be written to a file or device driver from an application, or to be read from a file or device driver to an application.

data fork: The part of a file that contains data accessed via the File Manager.

data frame: A packet plus accompanying frame control information, the form in which data is handled at the lowest level of AppleTalk. See **packet.**

Datagram: A packet in AppleTalk.

data rate: The number of data bits carried by a communication channel per second. Not the same as bit rate. See **baud, bit rate.**

date/time record: An alternate representation of the date and time, which is stored on the clock chip in seconds since midnight, January 1, 1904.

dead key: A key press for which there is no corresponding event; for example, the combination of the Option key and another key that generates an accent for the next character typed. (The accented character is reported as a single key-down event.)

declaration ROM: Read-only memory on a NuBus expansion card that contains information about the card and may also contain code or other data.

default button: In an alert or modal dialog, the button whose effect will occur if the user presses Return or Enter.

deferred printing: Writing a representation of a document's printed image to disk or to memory, and then printing it (as opposed to immediate printing).

definition function: A function, stored as a resource, that determines the appearance and behavior of a particular Toolbox object such as a window.

definition procedure: A procedure, stored as a resource, that determines the appearance and behavior of a particular Toolbox object such as a menu.

delta guide: A description of something new in terms of its differences from something the reader already knows about. The name comes from the way mathematicians use the Greek letter delta (Δ) to represent a difference.

derived font: A font modified, as by scaling or slanting, before it is drawn on the screen.

descent: The vertical distance from a font's base line to its descent line.

descent line: A horizontal line that coincides with the bottoms of the characters in a font.

desk accessory: A "mini-application," implemented as a device driver, that can be run at the same time as an application. Desk accessories are files of type 'DFIL' and creator 'DMOV', and are installed by using the Font/DA Mover.

Desk Manager: The part of the Toolbox that supports the use of desk accessories from an application.

desk scrap: The place where data is stored when it is cut (or copied) and pasted among applications and desk accessories.

desktop: The screen as a surface for doing work on the Macintosh.

Desktop file: A resource file in which the Finder stores the version data, bundle, icons, and file references for each application on the volume.

device: A part of the Macintosh, or a piece of external equipment, that can transfer information into or out of the Macintosh.

device driver: A program that controls the exchange of information between an application and a device.

device driver event: An event generated by one of the Macintosh's device drivers.

Device Manager: The part of the Operating System that supports device I/O.

device resource file: An extension of the printer resource file, this file contains all the resources needed by the Chooser for operating a particular device (including the device driver code).

dial: A control with a movable indicator that displays a quantitative setting or value. Depending on the type of dial, the user may be able to change the setting by dragging the indicator with the mouse.

dialog: Same as **dialog box.**

dialog box: A box that a Macintosh application displays in order to request information, or in order to report that it is waiting for a process to complete. A dialog is internally represented in a dialog record.

Dialog Manager: The part of the Toolbox that provides routines for implementing dialogs and alerts.

dialog record: The internal representation of a dialog, where the Dialog Manager stores all the information it needs to operate on that dialog.

dialog template: A resource that contains information from which the Dialog Manager can create a dialog.

digital board: The circuit board in a Macintosh that contains the RAM, ROM, microprocessor, and other digital logic circuits. Also called the main logic board. See **analog board.**

dimmed: Drawn in gray rather than black.

directory: A subdivision of a volume that can contain files as well as other directories; equivalent to a folder.

disabled: A disabled menu item or menu is one that cannot be chosen; the menu item or menu title appears dimmed. A disabled item in a dialog or alert box has no effect when clicked.

Disk Driver: The device driver that controls data storage and retrieval on 3.5-inch floppy disks.

Disk Initialization Package: A Macintosh package for initializing and naming new disks; called by the Standard File Package.

disk-inserted event: An event generated when the user inserts a disk in a disk drive or takes any other action that requires a volume to be mounted.

document window: The standard Macintosh window for presenting a document.

double-click time: The greatest interval between a mouse-up and mouse-down event that would qualify two mouse clicks as a double-click.

draft printing: Another term for **immediate printing.**

drag region: A region in a window frame. Dragging inside this region moves the window to a new location and makes it the active window unless the Command key is down.

drive number: A number used to identify a disk drive. The internal drive is number 1, the external drive is number 2, and any additional drives have larger numbers.

drive queue: A list of disk drives connected to the Macintosh.

driver I/O queue: A queue containing the parameter blocks of all I/O requests for one device driver.

driver name: A sequence of up to 255 printing characters used to refer to an open device driver. Driver names always begin with a period (.).

edit record: A complete editing environment in TextEdit, which includes the text to be edited, the grafPort and rectangle in which to display the text, the arrangement of the text within the rectangle, and other editing and display information.

Elementary Functions Package: A Macintosh package that supports transcendental functions in extended-precision arithmetic according to the IEEE Standard 754.

empty handle: A handle that points to a NIL master pointer, signifying that the underlying relocatable block has been purged.

event: A notification to an application of some occurrence that the application may want to respond to.

event-driven: A style of programming in which program actions are based on events generated by the user, rather than on some sort of fixed script.

Event Manager: See **Toolbox Event Manager** or **Operating System Event Manager.**

event mask: A parameter passed to an Event Manager routine to specify which types of events the routine should apply to.

event queue: The Operating System Event Manager's list of pending events.

event record: The internal representation of an event, through which your program learns all pertinent information about that event.

exception: An error or abnormal condition detected by the processor in the course of program execution; includes interrupts and traps.

exception vector: One of 64 vectors in low memory that point to the routines that are to get control should an exception occur.

exclusive OR: A logical operation that produces a true result if one of its operands is true and the other false, and a false result if its operands are both true or both false.

extents tree file: Contains the locations and sizes of the extents making up a file on a volume. See **file extent.**

external reference: A reference to a routine or variable defined in a separate compilation or assembly.

file: A named, ordered sequence of bytes; a principal means by which data is stored and transmitted on the Macintosh. A file consists of a data fork and a resource fork.

file control block: A fixed-length data structure, contained in the file-control-block buffer, where information about an access path is stored.

file directory: The part of a volume that contains descriptions and locations of all the files and directories on the volume. There are two types of file directories: hierarchical file directories and flat file directories.

file extent: A series of contiguous allocation blocks.

File Manager: The part of the Operating System that supports file I/O.

filename: A sequence of up to 31 printing characters (excluding colons), which identifies a file. See **pathname.**

file object: A resource of type 'FOBJ'.

file reference: A resource (type 'FREF') that provides the Finder with file and icon information about an application.

file tags: Information associated with each logical block, designed to allow reconstruction of files on a volume whose directory or other file-access information has been destroyed.

file type: A four-character sequence, specified when a file is created, that identifies the type of file. (Examples: 'TEXT', 'APPL', 'MPST'.)

Finder: The application that maintains the Macintosh desktop and launches other programs. The Finder is also the default startup application.

Finder information: Information that the Finder provides to an application upon starting it, telling it which documents to open or print.

fixed-point number: A signed 32-bit quantity containing an integer part in the high-order word and a fractional part in the low-order word.

fixed-width font: A font whose characters all have the same width.

flat file system: The nonhierarchical file system used on 400K disks and Macintosh XL hard disks.

Floating-Point Arithmetic Package: A Macintosh package that supports extended-precision arithmetic according to IEEE Standard 754.

floating-point coprocessor (MC68881): A coprocessor chip on the Macintosh II that provides high-speed support for extended-precision arithmetic.

folder: A holder of documents and applications on the desktop. Folders, like subdirectories, allow you to organize information in any way you want.

fond: A resource of type 'FOND' containing information about a family of fonts and used by the Font Manager to provide the appropriate fonts to an application.

font: A complete set of characters of one typeface. A font may be restricted to a particular size and style, or may comprise multiple sizes or multiple sizes and styles.

font association table: The table of font resources in a fond.

font characterization table: A table of parameters in a device driver that specifies how best to adapt fonts to that device.

Font/DA Mover: An application, available on the *System Tools* disk, used for installing desk accessories in the System file.

font family: A group of fonts of one basic design but with variations in, for example, weight and slant.

font height: The vertical distance from a font's ascent line to its descent line.

Font Manager: The part of the Toolbox that supports the use of various character fonts for QuickDraw when it draws text.

font number: The number by which you identify a font to QuickDraw or the Font Manager.

font record: A data structure, derived from a font resource, that contains all the information describing a font.

font scaling: Deriving a font from a larger or smaller font by shrinking or expanding it. Scaled fonts in larger sizes are usually not as attractive as the installed font.

font size: The size of a font in points; equivalent to the distance between the ascent line of one line of text and the ascent line of the next line of single-spaced text.

fork: One of the two parts of a file; see **data fork** and **resource fork.**

four-tone record: A data structure describing the tones produced by a four-tone synthesizer.

four-tone synthesizer: The part of the Sound Driver used to make simple harmonic tones, with up to four "voices" producing sound simultaneously.

fractional character widths: A font attribute that improves the spacing of characters.

frame: The time elapsed from the start bit to the last stop bit during serial communication.

frame pointer: A pointer to the end of the local variables within a routine's stack frame.

free block: A memory block containing space available for allocation.

free-form synthesizer: The part of the Sound Driver used to make complex music and speech.

frequency: The number of cycles per second (also called *hertz*) at which a wave oscillates.

full-duplex communication: A method of data transmission in which two devices transmit data simultaneously.

full pathname: A pathname beginning from the root directory. A full pathname is a pathname that contains embedded colons but no leading colon.

global coordinate system: The coordinate system based on the top-left corner of the bit image at (0,0).

global variable: A variable that is valid for all applications.

go-away region: A region in a window frame. Clicking inside this region of the active window makes the window close or disappear.

grafPort: A data structure in QuickDraw that contains a complete drawing environment, including such elements as a bit map, a character font, and patterns.

graphics port: A complete drawing environment in QuickDraw (data type grafPort), including such elements as a bit map, a character font, patterns for drawing and erasing, and other graphics characteristics.

grow region: A window region, usually within the content region, where dragging changes the size of an active window.

handle: A pointer to a master pointer, which designates a relocatable block in the heap by double indirection.

heap: The area of memory in which space is dynamically allocated and released on demand by means of the Memory Manager.

heap zone: An area of memory initialized by the Memory Manager for heap allocation.

HFS: See **hierarchical file system.**

hierarchical file system (HFS): The file system used on hard disks and 800K floppy disks.

hierarchical menu: A menu in which an individual menu item can spawn a submenu.

highlight: To display an object on the screen in a distinctive visual way, such as inverting it.

horizontal blanking interval: The time between the display of the right-most pixel on one line and the left-most pixel on the next line.

hot spot: The point in a cursor that is aligned with the mouse location.

icon: A 32-by-32 bit image that graphically represents an object, concept, or message.

icon list: A resource (type 'ICN ') consisting of a list of icons.

icon number: A digit from 1 to 255 to which the Menu Manager adds 256 to get the resource ID of an icon associated with a menu item.

image width: The width of a character image.

immediate printing: Printing a document immediately as it is drawn in the printing grafPort.

initiator: When two SCSI devices communicate with each other, the one that issues commands is the initiator. A SCSI device typically has a fixed role as an initiator or target; for instance, the Macintosh always acts as initiator to one or more peripherals, such as hard disks, that act as targets. See **target.**

input driver: A device driver that receives serial data via a serial port and transfers it to an application.

insertion point: An empty selection range; that is, the character position where text will be inserted (marked with a blinking vertical bar).

interface routine: A routine called from Pascal whose purpose is to trap to a certain ROM or library routine.

International Utilities Package: A Macintosh package that provides country-independent routines for formatting for numbers, currency, dates, times, and so on.

internet: An interconnected group of AppleTalk networks.

internet address: The AppleTalk address and network number of a socket.

interrupt: An exception that's signaled to the processor by a device in order to notify the processor of a change in condition of the device, such as the completion of an I/O request.

interrupt handler: A routine that services interrupts.

interrupt vector: A pointer to an interrupt handler.

intrinsic font: A font displayed without modification. See **derived font.**

invert: To highlight by changing white pixels to black and vice versa.

I/O request: A request for input from or output to a file or device driver; caused by calling a File Manager or Device Manager routine asynchronously.

item: In dialog and alert boxes, a control, icon, picture, or piece of text, each displayed inside its own display rectangle. See **menu item.**

item list: A list of information about all the items in a dialog or alert box.

IWM: Acronym for Integrated Woz Machine, the custom chip that controls the 3.5-inch floppy disk drives.

journaling mechanism: A mechanism that allows a program to feed events to the Toolbox Event Manager from some source other than the user.

jump table: A table that contains one entry for every routine in an application or MPW tool and that is the means by which the loading and unloading of segments is implemented.

justification: The horizontal placement of lines of text relative to the edges of the rectangle in which the text is drawn.

kern: To draw part of a character so that it overlaps an adjacent character.

kernel: The program in A/UX that operates at the lowest level, handling machine-dependent operations such as file management and peripheral I/O.

key code: An integer representing a key on the keyboard or keypad, without reference to the character that the key stands for.

keyboard configuration: A resource that defines a particular keyboard layout by associating a character code with each key or combination of keys on the keyboard or keypad.

keyboard equivalent: The combination of the Command key and another key, used to invoke a menu item from the keyboard.

keyboard event: An event generated when the user presses a character key on the keyboard. A key-down event is generated when the user presses a character key; a key-up event is generated when the user releases a character key. *Auto-key events* are repeatedly generated when the user holds down a character key.

keyboard mapping procedure: A routine, stored as a resource, that determines the character code for each key on the keyboard.

leading: The amount of blank vertical space between the descent line of one line of text and the ascent line of the next line of single-spaced text.

library file: A code file that contains procedures and functions available to a program.

ligature: A character that combines two letters.

linker: A program that connects program segments compiled or assembled at separate times so that they can be executed together.

list definition procedure: A procedure called by the List Manager that determines the appearance and behavior of a list.

list element: The basic component of a list. From a logical point of view, a list element is simply bytes of data.

List Manager: The part of the Operating System that provides routines for creating, displaying, and manipulating lists.

list record: The internal representation of a list, where the List Manager stores all the information to operate on that list.

local coordinate system: The coordinate system local to a grafPort, imposed by the boundary rectangle defined in its bit map.

localization: The process of adapting an application to different languages, which may include conversion to a non-Roman script system.

lock: To temporarily prevent a relocatable block from being moved during heap compaction.

locked file: A file whose data cannot be changed.

locked volume: A volume whose data cannot be changed. Volumes can be locked by either a software flag or a hardware setting.

logical block: Volume space composed of 512 consecutive bytes of standard information and an additional number of bytes of information specific to the Disk Driver.

magnitude: The vertical distance between any given point on a wave and the horizontal line about which the wave oscillates.

main event loop: In a standard Macintosh application program, a loop that repeatedly calls the Toolbox Event Manager to get events and that then responds to them as appropriate.

main segment: The segment containing the main program.

manager: The term used to characterize a set of data structures and routines that perform a set of related Toolbox or Operating System functions. For instance, the Window Manager handles the display and manipulation of windows on the Macintosh screen.

master pointer: A single pointer to a relocatable block, maintained by the Memory Manager and updated whenever the block is moved, purged, or reallocated. All handles to a relocatable block refer to it by double indirection through the master pointer.

memory block: An area of contiguous memory within a heap zone.

Memory Manager: The part of the Operating System that dynamically allocates and releases memory space in the heap.

menu: A list of menu items that appears when the user points to a menu title in the menu bar and presses the mouse button. Dragging through the menu and releasing over an enabled menu item chooses that item. A menu is internally represented in a menu record.

menu bar: The horizontal strip at the top of the Macintosh screen that contains the menu titles of all menus in the menu list.

menu definition procedure: A procedure, stored as a resource, that is called by the Menu Manager and determines the appearance and behavior of a particular menu.

menu item: A choice in a menu, usually a command to the current application.

Menu Manager: The part of the Toolbox that deals with setting up menus and letting the user choose from them.

MIDI synthesizer: A Sound Manager synthesizer that interfaces with external synthesizers via a Musical Instrument Data Interface (MIDI) adapter connected to one of the serial ports.

missing symbol: A character (□) to be drawn in case of a request to draw a character that is missing from a particular font.

modal dialog: A dialog that requires the user to respond before doing any other work on the desktop.

modeless dialog: A dialog that allows the user to work elsewhere on the desktop before responding.

modifier: A program that interprets and processes Sound Manager commands as they pass through a channel.

modifier key: A key (Shift, Caps Lock, Option, or Command) that generates no keyboard events of its own but that changes the meaning of other keys or mouse actions.

mounted volume: A volume that has been inserted into a disk drive and has had descriptive information read from it by the File Manager.

mouse event: An event generated when the user presses and releases the mouse button. A mouse-down event is generated when the user presses the mouse button. A mouse-up event is generated when the user releases the mouse button.

mouse scaling: A feature that causes the cursor to move farther during a mouse stroke than it would have otherwise, provided that the change in the cursor's position exceeds the mouse-scaling threshold.

mouse-scaling threshold: A number of pixels that, if exceeded by the changes in the cursor position within one tick after the mouse is moved, causes mouse scaling to occur (if that feature is turned on). On the Macintosh Plus, this is normally six pixels.

MPW: The Macintosh Programmer's Workshop, Apple's software development system for the Macintosh family.

MPW Shell: The application that provides the environment within which the other parts of the Macintosh Programmer's Workshop operate. The Shell combines an editor, command interpreter, and built-in commands.

MPW tool: An executable program (file type 'MPST') that is integrated with the MPW Shell (contrasted with an application, which runs stand alone).

MultiFinder: A special Finder option available with Finder version 6.0 that allows more than one Macintosh application to be open simultaneously.

network event: An event generated by the AppleTalk Manager.

network-visible entity: A named socket client on an internet. See **internet** and **socket client**.

newline character: Any character, but usually Return (ASCII code $0D), that indicates the end of a sequence of bytes.

newline mode: A mode of reading data in which the end of the data is indicated by a newline character (and not by a specific byte count).

node: A device that's attached to and communicates by means of an AppleTalk network.

nonblind transfer: On a SCSI device, a data transfer followed by polling of the receiving device to confirm the success of the transfer.

nonbreaking space: The character with ASCII code $CA; drawn as a space the same width as a digit, but interpreted as a nonblank character for the purposes of word wraparound and selection.

non-HFS: The "flat" file system, used on 400K disks and Macintosh XL hard disks.

nonrelocatable block: A block whose location in the heap is fixed and can't be moved during heap compaction.

note synthesizer: Functionally equivalent to the Sound Driver's square-wave synthesizer, the note synthesizer generates simple melodies and other sounds.

NuBus: A computer bus specification created by Texas Instruments and used in the Macintosh II to support six expansion slots.

NuBus slots: Expansion slots in the Macintosh II, designed according to the NuBus standard created by Texas Instruments.

null event: An event reported when there are no other events to report.

off-line volume: A mounted volume with all but the volume control block released.

off-screen drawing: Drawing an image in an area of RAM other than the display, making it possible to prepare an image without disturbing the screen.

on-line volume: A mounted volume with its volume buffer and descriptive information contained in memory.

open driver: A driver that can be read from and written to.

open file: A file with an access path. Open files can be read from and written to.

Operating System: The lowest-level software in the Macintosh. It does basic tasks such as I/O, memory management, and interrupt handling.

Operating System Event Manager: The part of the Operating System that reports hardware-related events, such as mouse-button presses and keystrokes.

Operating System Utilities: Operating System routines that perform miscellaneous tasks, such as getting the date and time, finding out the user's preferred speaker volume and other preferences, and doing simple string comparison.

output driver: A device driver that transfers data from an application via a serial port.

overrun error: See **hardware overrun error** and **software overrun error.**

package: A set of routines and data types that forms a part of the Toolbox or Operating System and is stored as a resource. On the original Macintosh, all packages were disk-based and brought into memory only when needed; some packages are now in ROM.

Package Manager: The part of the Toolbox that lets you access Macintosh packages.

packet: A standardized, variable-length block of data sent over a network.

page: A contiguous segment of main memory.

page fault: A condition that occurs in a virtual-memory system whenever the processor tries to access a location that is not currently in RAM, and that normally causes the system to initiate a page swap from the disk.

Paged Memory Management Unit (PMMU): The Motorola 68851 Paged Memory Management Unit, an optional integrated circuit that provides full memory mapping in the Macintosh II, including 24- to 32-bit address mapping and virtual memory support. See **AMU.**

parameter RAM: Battery-powered RAM contained in the clock chip, where settings such as those made with the Control Panel desk accessory are preserved.

parity bit: A data communications bit used to verify that data bits received by a device match the data bits transmitted by another device.

parity error: The condition resulting when the parity bit received by a device isn't what was expected.

partial pathname: A pathname beginning from any directory other than the root directory. A partial pathname either contains no colons or has a leading colon.

patch: To replace a piece of ROM code with other RAM-based system code by "patching" a new entry into the trap dispatch table. Also, a resource of type 'PTCH' containing the patched code.

pathname: A series of concatenated directory and filenames that identifies a given file or directory. See also **partial pathname** and **full pathname.**

path reference number: A number that uniquely identifies an individual access path; assigned when the access path is created.

pattern: An 8-by-8 bit image used to define a repeating design (such as stripes) or tone (such as gray).

period: The time elapsed during one complete cycle of a wave.

phase: The amount by which the cycles of one wave precede or lag behind the cycles of another wave of the same frequency.

picture: A saved sequence of QuickDraw drawing commands (and, optionally, picture comments) that you can play back later with a single procedure call; also, the image resulting from these commands.

picture comments: Data stored in the definition of a picture that doesn't affect the picture's appearance but may be used to provide additional information about the picture when it's played back.

picture frame: A rectangle, defined as part of a picture, that surrounds the picture and gives a frame of reference for scaling when the picture is played back.

pixel: An individual dot on the screen. For simple monochrome, the visual representation of a single bit in the video RAM (white if the bit is 0, black if it's 1). For color or gray-scale video, each pixel on the screen may represent several bits in the RAM image.

pixel value: The definition of a color as parameter values for a particular display device.

plane: The front-to-back position of a window on the desktop.

point: The intersection of a horizontal grid line and a vertical grid line on the coordinate plane, defined by a horizontal and a vertical coordinate; also, a typographical term meaning approximately 1/72 of an inch.

pointer: An item of information consisting of the memory address of some other item.

polygon: A sequence of connected lines defined by QuickDraw line-drawing commands.

port: See **graphics port.**

post: To place an event in the event queue for later processing.

PostScript: The page-description language used with the LaserWriter.

print record: A record containing all the information needed by the Printing Manager to perform a particular printing job.

Printer Driver: The device driver for the currently installed printer.

printer font: A font designed for printing on the LaserWriter and having character shapes defined as curved outlines.

printer resource file: A file containing all the resources needed to run the Printing Manager with a particular printer.

printing grafPort: A special grafPort customized for printing instead of drawing on the screen.

Printing Manager: The routines and data types that enable applications to communicate with the Printer Driver to print on any variety of printer via the same interface.

proportional font: A font whose characters all have character widths that are proportional to their image width.

protocol: A well-defined set of communications rules.

pulse-width encoding: A method of creating sound waves by generating a stream of pulses at a constant (ultrasonic) rate while varying the widths of successive pulses. When the pulse stream is low-pass filtered, the different-width pulses create the different amplitudes of the sound wave.

purge: To remove a relocatable block from the heap, leaving its master pointer allocated but set to NIL.

purgeable block: A relocatable block that can be purged from the heap.

queue: A list of identically structured entries linked together by pointers.

QuickDraw: The part of the Toolbox that performs all graphic operations on the Macintosh screen.

radio button: A standard control, one of a set of buttons, only one of which can be on at any one time. Clicking inside a radio button automatically turns off the other buttons in the set.

RAM: The Macintosh's random-access memory, which contains exception vectors, buffers used by hardware devices, the system and application heaps, the stack, and other information used by applications.

raster: The pattern of parallel lines making up the image on a video display screen. The image is produced by controlling the brightness of successive points on the individual lines of the raster.

raster scanning: The process of generating a video image by moving an electron beam rapidly and repeatedly in a pattern of closely spaced parallel lines. See **raster.**

read/write permission: Information associated with an access path that indicates whether the file can be read from, written to, both read from and written to, or whatever the file's open permission allows.

reallocate: To allocate new space in the heap for a purged block, updating its master pointer to point to its new location.

region: An arbitrary area or set of areas on the QuickDraw coordinate plane. The outline of a region should be one or more closed loops.

relocatable block: A block that can be moved within the heap during compaction.

resource: Data or code stored in a resource file and managed by the Resource Manager.

resource attribute: One of several characteristics, specified by bits in a resource reference, that determine how the resource should be dealt with.

Resource Compiler: A program that creates resources from a textual description. The Resource Compiler in MPW is named Rez.

resource data: In a resource file, the data that comprises a resource.

resource description file: A text file that can be read by the Resource Compiler and compiled into a resource file. The Resource Decompiler disassembles a resource file, producing a resource description file as output.

resource file: Common parlance for the resource fork of a Macintosh file.

resource fork: The part of a file that contains data used by an application, such as menus, fonts, and icons. An executable file's code is also stored in the resource fork.

resource header: At the beginning of a resource file, data that gives the offsets to and lengths of the resource data and resource map.

resource ID: A number that, together with the resource type, identifies a resource in a resource file. Every resource has an ID number.

Resource Manager: The part of the Toolbox that reads and writes resources.

resource map: In a resource file, data that is read into memory when the file is opened and that, given a resource specification, leads to the corresponding resource data.

resource name: A string that, together with the resource type, identifies a resource in a resource file. A resource may or may not have a name.

resource reference: In a resource map, an entry that identifies a resource and contains either an offset to its resource data in the resource file or a handle to the data if it's already been read into memory.

resource type: The type of a resource in a resource file, designated by a sequence of four characters inside single quotation marks, such as 'MENU' for a menu resource.

resume procedure: A procedure within an application that allows the procedure to recover from system errors.

RGB color: A method of displaying color video by transmitting the three primary colors (red, green, and blue: thus, RGB) as three separate signals.

RGB space: The color space defined by coordinate axes corresponding to red, green, and blue.

RGB value: The definition of a color as the coordinates of a point in RGB space.

ROM: The Macintosh's permanent read-only memory, which contains the routines for the Toolbox and Operating System and the various system traps.

root directory: The directory at the base of a file catalog.

row width: The number of bytes in each row of a bit image.

sampled-sound synthesizer: Functionally equivalent to the Sound Driver's free-form synthesizer, the sampled-sound synthesizer can play prerecorded or application-generated sounds.

scaling factor: A value, given as a fraction, that specifies the amount a character should be stretched or shrunk before it is drawn.

SCC: See **Serial Communications Controller.**

scrap: A place such as the desk scrap where cut or copied data is stored.

scrap file: The file containing the desk scrap (usually named "Clipboard File").

Scrap Manager: The part of the Toolbox that enables cutting and pasting between applications, desk accessories, or an application and a desk accessory.

screen buffer: A block of memory from which the video display reads the information to be displayed.

screen font: A font designed for printing on the screen or on an ImageWriter and character shapes defined as bit maps.

script: A writing system, such as Chinese or Arabic. This book is printed in the Roman script.

script: (MPW and UNIX) Same as **command file.**

script interface system: A set of routines and data structures the Script Manager uses to support a particular wirting system or script.

Script Manager: A set of extensions to the Macintosh Toolbox and Operating System that enables applications to use non-Roman writing systems, such as Japanese, Chinese, Arabic, and Hebrew, as well as Latin-based alphabets, such as English, French, and German.

SCSI: See **Small Computer System Interface.**

SCSI Manager: The part of the Operating System that controls the exchange of information between a Macintosh and peripheral devices connected through the Small Computer System Interface (SCSI).

SE Logic Unit (SELU): A custom gate-array chip on the Macintosh SE that handles RAM, video, sound, and that selects devices and performs other functions.

sector: Disk space composed of 512 consecutive bytes of standard information and 12 bytes of file tags.

segment: One of several parts into which the code of an application may be divided. Not all segments need to be in memory at the same time.

Segment Loader: The part of the Operating System that loads the code of an application into memory, either as a single unit or divided into dynamically loaded segments.

selection or **selection range:** A series of characters, or a character position, at which the next editing operation will occur. Selected characters in the active window are inversely highlighted.

Serial Communications Controller (SCC): The chip that handles serial I/O through the modem and printer ports.

serial data: Data communicated over a single-path communication line, one bit at a time.

Serial Driver: A device driver that controls communication, via serial ports, between an application and serial peripheral devices.

shell: An application or development program that interprets commands from the user and provides an environment in which other programs are executed.

shell application: The application that takes control when you quit another application. See also **shell, startup application**.

shell program: A program that runs in the environment provided by a shell.

shell script: A stored sequence of commands that can be executed by a shell to carry out a complex operation such as the compiling and linking of several program segments.

signature: A four-character sequence that uniquely identifies an application to the Finder.

SIMM: see **Single In-line Memory Module**.

Single In-line Memory Module (SIMM): A memory-expansion module used in some models of Macintosh, consisting of a small printed-circuit card with eight (sometimes nine) surface-mount RAM ICs and with electrical contacts along one edge for insertion into a connector on the main logic board.

Slot Manager: On the Macintosh II, the part of the Operating System that controls the exchange of information between a Macintosh and cards installed in the expansion slots.

Small Computer System Interface (SCSI): A specification of mechanical, electrical, and functional standards for connecting small computers with intelligent peripherals such as hard disks, printers, and optical disks.

sockets: Software entities within the nodes of a network.

socket clients: A software process in a node that owns a socket; see **network-visible entity**.

sound buffer: A block of memory from which the sound generator reads the information to create an audio waveform.

Sound Driver: The device driver that controls sound generation in an application. (Superseded by the Sound Manager on the Macintosh II.)

Sound Manager: The device driver that controls sound generation on the Macintosh II. It supports all the functions of the older Sound Driver and makes it easier to produce music and speech. See **Sound Driver**.

sound procedure: A procedure associated with an alert that will emit one of four sounds from the Macintosh's speaker. Its integer parameter ranges from 0 to 3 and specifies which sound.

spooling: See **spool printing**.

spool printing: Storing a representation of a document's printed image on a disk or in memory, then printing it later.

square wave: A type of sound wave produced by switching between two constant amplitudes at an even rate. A similar wave with uneven switching such that the time at one level is different from that at the other is called a rectangular wave.

square-wave synthesizer: The part of the Sound Driver used to produce less harmonic sounds than the four-tone synthesizer, such as beeps.

stack: The area of memory in which space is allocated and released in last-in, first-out (LIFO) order.

stack-based routine: A Toolbox or Operating System routine that receives its parameters and returns its results, if any, on the stack.

stack frame: The area of the stack used by a routine for its parameters, return address, local variables, and temporary storage.

Standard Apple Numeric Environment (SANE): The set of methods that provides the basis for floating-point calculations in Apple computers. SANE meets all requirements for extended-precision, floating-point arithmetic as prescribed by IEEE Standard 754 and ensures that all floating-point operations are performed consistently and return the most accurate results possible.

Standard File Package: A Macintosh package for presenting the standard user interface when a file is to be saved or opened.

start bit: A serial data communications bit that signals that the next bits transmitted are data bits.

startup application: The application that takes control when the system is first started up.

stop bit: A serial data communications bit that signals the end of data bits.

structure region: A window, in the sense of its entire structure.

style: See **character style.**

subdirectory: Any directory other than the root directory.

switch-launch: To launch an application from a disk containing a system folder on a floppy-disk-only system, causing the Macintosh to switch folders.

Switcher: A Macintosh application that allows you to keep more than one application loaded in memory and to switch from one application to another instantly.

synchronous communication: A method of data transmission where the receiving and sending devices share a common timer.

synchronous execution: After calling a routine synchronously, an application cannot continue execution until the routine is completed.

synchronous modem: A modem that provides two clocks for synchronous communication with its host computer—one clock for sending data from the host computer to the modem, and a second clock for sending data from the modem to the host computer.

synthesizer: A program that, like a device driver, interprets Sound Manager or Sound Driver commands and produces sound.

synthesizer buffer: A description of the sound to be generated by a synthesizer.

system error alert: An alert box displayed by the System Error Handler.

system error alert table: A resource that determines the appearance and function of system error alerts.

System Error Handler: The part of the Operating System that assumes control when a fatal system error occurs.

system error ID: An ID number that appears in a system error alert to identify the error.

system event mask: A global event mask that controls which types of events get posted into the event queue.

System file: Same as **system resource file.**

System Folder: The folder that contains the System file and the Finder.

system font: The font that the system uses (in menus, for example). In Roman-based writing systems, the system font is Chicago, and the system font size is 12 points.

system heap: The portion of the heap reserved for use by the Operating System.

system resource: A resource in the system resource file.

system resource file: A resource file containing standard resources, accessed if a requested resource wasn't found in any of the other resource files that were searched. See *System file*.

system software: The term used to describe the contents of the System Folder: the RAM-based software that the Macintosh needs in order to run.

system startup information: Certain configurable system parameters that are stored in the first two logical blocks of a volume and that are read in at system startup.

system window: A window in which a desk accessory is displayed.

target: When two SCSI devices communicate with each other, the device that carries out an operation at the command of the other. A SCSI device typically has a fixed role as an initiator or target; for instance, the Macintosh always acts as initiator to one or more peripherals, such as hard disks, that act as targets. See **initiator.**

TextEdit: The part of the Toolbox that supports the basic text entry and editing capabilities of a standard Macintosh application.

TextEdit scrap: The place where certain TextEdit routines store the characters most recently cut or copied from text.

tick: A sixtieth of a second (approximately).

Time Manager: The part of the Operating System that lets you schedule a routine to be executed after a given number of milliseconds have elapsed.

Toolbox: Same as **User Interface Toolbox.**

Toolbox Event Manager: The part of the Toolbox that allows your application program to monitor the user's actions with the mouse, keyboard, and keypad.

Toolbox Utilities: The part of the Toolbox that performs generally useful operations such as fixed-point arithmetic, string manipulation, and logical operations on bits.

track: Disk space composed of 8 to 12 consecutive sectors. A track corresponds to one ring of constant radius around the disk.

Transcendental Functions Package: A Macintosh package that contains trigonometric, logarithmic, exponential, and financial functions, as well as a random number generator.

trap: A microprocessor exception caused by instruction execution.

trap dispatch table: A table in RAM containing the addresses of all Toolbox and Operating System routines in encoded form.

trap dispatcher: The part of the Operating System that examines a trap word to determine what operation it stands for, looks up the address of the corresponding routine in the trap dispatch table, and jumps to the routine.

trap macro: A macro that assembles into a trap word and that is used for calling a Toolbox or Operating System routine from assembly language.

trap number: The identifying number of a Toolbox or Operating System routine; an index into the trap dispatch table.

trap word: An unimplemented instruction representing a call to a Toolbox or Operating System routine.

unimplemented instruction: An instruction word that doesn't correspond to any valid machine-language instruction but instead causes a trap.

UNIX: The AT&T UNIX operating system, an enhanced version of which is implemented on the Macintosh II under the name A/UX.

unlock: To allow a relocatable block to be moved during heap compaction.

unmounted volume: A volume that hasn't been inserted into a disk drive and had descriptive information read from it, or a volume that previously was mounted and has since had the memory used by it released.

unpurgeable block: A relocatable block that can't be purged from the heap.

update event: An event generated by the Window Manager when a window's contents need to be redrawn.

update region: A window region consisting of all areas of the content region that have to be redrawn.

User Interface Toolbox: The software in the Macintosh ROM that helps you implement the standard Macintosh user interface in your application.

VBL task: A task to be executed during the vertical retrace interval. See **vertical retrace queue.**

vector table: A table of interrupt vectors in low memory.

Versatile Interface Adapter (VIA): The I/O chip that handles the ADB, real-time clock, and various other control signals and interrupts. On the Macintosh II, a second VIA handles control and interrupts for RAM, SCSI, and NuBus.

version data: In an application's resource file, a resource that has the application's signature as its resource type; typically a string that gives the name, version number, and date of the application.

vertical blanking (VBL): An interrupt signal generated by the video timing circuit each time it finishes a vertical scan, 60 times a second. See **vertical retrace interrupt.**

vertical blanking interval: The time between the display of the last pixel on the bottom line of the screen and the first one on the top line; see **VBL** and **vertical retrace interrupt.**

vertical retrace interrupt: An interrupt generated 60 times a second by the Macintosh video circuitry while the beam of the display tube returns from the bottom of the screen to the top; also known as the *vertical blanking interrupt.*

Vertical Retrace Manager: The part of the Operating System that schedules and executes tasks during the vertical retrace interval.

vertical retrace queue: A list of tasks to be executed during the vertical retrace interrupt.

VIA: See **Versatile Interface Adapter.**

Video Driver: The device driver that handles the interface between QuickDraw and a slot-based video device. (Macintosh II only.)

virtual memory: A technique for making a computer's memory seem larger than it actually is, by keeping programs and data on a mass storage device and automatically loading parts of them into main memory in such a way that the programs run as if all the data were in main memory all the time.

volume: A piece of storage medium formatted to contain files; usually a disk or part of a disk. A 3.5-inch Macintosh disk is one volume.

volume allocation block map: A list of entries, one for each allocation block, that indicate whether the block is currently allocated to a file or free for use, and which block is next in the file.

volume attributes: Information contained on volumes and in memory indicating whether the volume is locked, whether it's busy (in memory only), and whether the volume control block matches the volume information (in memory only).

volume bit map: Records whether blocks are used or unused.

volume control block: A nonrelocatable block that contains volume-specific information, including the volume information from the master directory block.

volume information: Volume-specific information contained on a volume, including the volume name and the number of files on the volume.

volume name: A sequence of up to 27 printing characters that identifies a volume; followed by a colon (:) in File Manager routine calls to distinguish it from a filename.

waveform: The shape of a wave (a graph of a wave's amplitude over time).

waveform description: A sequence of bytes describing a waveform.

wavelength: The extent of one complete cycle of a wave.

wave-table synthesizer: Similar to the Sound Driver's four-tone synthesizer, the wave-table synthesizer produces complex sounds and multipart music.

window: An object on the desktop that presents information, such as a document or a message. Each window is internally represented in a window record.

window definition function: A function, stored as a resource, that is called by the Window Manager and determines the appearance and behavior of a particular window.

window frame: The structure region of a window minus its content region.

Window Manager: The part of the Toolbox that provides routines for creating and manipulating windows.

Window Manager port: A grafPort that has the entire screen as its portRect and is used by the Window Manager to draw window frames.

window template: A resource (type 'WIND') that contains information from which the Window Manager can create a window.

word: A group of bits that is treated as a unit; the number of bits in a word is a characteristic of each particular computer.

word wraparound: The process of keeping words from being split between lines when drawing text on the screen.

working directory: An alternative way of referring to a directory. When opened as a working directory, a directory is given a working directory reference number that is used to refer to it in File Manager calls.

wraparound: The automatic continuation of text from the end of one line to the beginning of the next, so that you don't have to press the Return key at the end of each line as you type.

Index